The Color of ____

New Hope Falls: Book 3

By

KIMBERLY RAE
JORDAN

THREE**STRAND**
P R E S S

A CORD OF THREE STRANDS IS NOT EASILY BROKEN.

A man, a woman & their God.
Three Strand Press publishes Christian Romance stories
that intertwine love, faith and family. Always clean.
Always heartwarming. Always uplifting.

The Color of Love/ Kimberly Rae Jordan. -- 1st ed.
ISBN-13: 978-1-988409-35-1

These things I have spoken to you,
that in Me you may have peace.
In the world you will have tribulation;
but be of good cheer,
I have overcome the world.
John 16:33 (NKJV)

CHAPTER ONE

Charles Beaumont Allerton Junior tugged at the hem of his button-up shirt, hoping to work out some of the wrinkles that his rapid—and poor—packing job had created. If he'd been staying at his normal caliber of hotel, he'd have been able to get the shirt ironed. Unfortunately, that was not a service offered at his current accommodation. There was definitely no concierge waiting to help him with whatever he might need at this place.

Coming to the realization that the tug-method of wrinkle removal wasn't going to work all that well, Beau let out a sigh, resigning himself to looking slightly wrinkled for the day. He tucked the shirt into his pants then did up his belt. His less-than-stellar appearance was just one more thing that left him feeling out of sorts and ill-prepared for whatever was to come.

As Beau sat down on the loveseat positioned in front of the large windows that looked out on a forest, he glanced around the room he'd been shown to upon his arrival the previous evening. Much to his dismay, the décor hadn't changed during the hours he'd been sleeping.

The furniture, which had a decidedly rustic appeal, looked as if it had been fashioned from logs hewn from the surrounding forest by some flannel-wearing lumberjack. He didn't mind the sturdy look of the furniture so much. The walls, however... Beau shook his head as he took in the floral scheme that looked like a bouquet had exploded across them.

The only things the room had in its favor were the comfortable bed and the private bathroom with luxury fixtures. He hadn't been entirely sure about the privacy of the bathroom in the small lodge until he'd done a thorough search the night before and confirmed that there was no second entrance to the room.

Beau glanced at his watch, noting that he needed to make a decision. Was he going to make an effort to change the time, or did he want to spend the next month subtracting two hours every time he looked at the timepiece? Maybe he'd save that decision until after he saw how much aggravation the day ahead held.

Whatever thoughts had been in his father's mind when he'd packed Beau off to a small town to meet a man he'd hadn't known existed, hadn't been shared with Beau. All he'd said was that Beau needed some time away from Houston to consider his actions.

Consider *his* actions? Okay, so maybe getting into a very public, very vocal fight with his fiancée—ex-fiancée now, apparently—wasn't the best decision he'd ever made. But given that Beau wasn't the most troublesome one in the family, surely his father could have cut him some slack. The only thing Beau could think was that losing the potential connection with a powerful politician had been the ultimate faux pas in his father's eyes.

Though he hadn't said as much, Beau's banishment to the backwoods town of New Hope Falls for a month so soon after the fight, was too much to be a coincidence. Hopefully, that day would reveal the hoops he needed to jump through in order to return to his life in Houston. To his sprawling apartment with a stellar view of the city of Houston. To his car that he'd spent a fortune on to get exactly what he wanted. To his closet full of *un*wrinkled clothes.

And jump through hoops he would, because Beau had just one year left until he gained the freedom he'd had his sights set on for all of his adult life. Freedom that his father could withhold if he decided the terms of the trust fund hadn't been met.

With that thought in mind, Beau slapped his hands on his thighs and got to his feet. Though it was already seven-thirty in Houston, it was only five-thirty in New Hope Falls. He could only hope that despite the early hour, there was a pot of coffee brewing somewhere in the lodge. If not, he'd have to figure out where to get some if he wanted to have any chance of getting through the day.

As soon as Beau opened the door to the hallway, it seemed his day was taking a turn for the better. The smell of coffee greeted him, and he moved down the hallway to the wide staircase that led from the second floor of the lodge to the main level. He wasn't sure if the coffee was available to guests just yet, but he wasn't above begging for a cup.

The dining room was empty, so Beau turned toward another doorway, hoping it was the kitchen. As he stepped into the room, he spotted a woman standing with her back to him. He recognized the dark brown braid she wore and hesitated. The young woman he'd met the night before who'd sported that braid hadn't been the most welcoming, though the older woman with her certainly had been.

The kitchen was large and airy with stainless steel appliances and an island counter that had stools along one side of it. The window over the sink showed that the sun still hadn't risen, which wasn't a big surprise given how early it was. Music played softly as the woman—Leah, if he recalled her name correctly—reached into the cupboard and pulled down a glass.

Resolved to do what he needed to in order to get himself a cup or two of coffee, even speaking to the woman who hadn't exactly given him a warm welcome the night before, Beau cleared his throat.

The woman jumped then spun around, her eyes widening as she spotted him. Her surprise quickly gave way to a smile as her hand went to rest just below her throat. "You scared me."

"I'm sorry about that," he said, trying to reconcile the smiling woman before him with the frowning version of the night before. Could be she'd just had as bad a day as he'd had.

"No worries." She gave a wave of her hand then turned to pull a mug from a wrought iron tree on the counter. "Want a cup of coffee?"

"Yes, please."

When she began to hum as she poured coffee into a mug, he did wonder if perhaps the woman had some sort of mental issue. Maybe one of those multiple personality disorders he'd seen described on a documentary show a few months ago. Or maybe she was just really a morning person.

"I'm Sarah, by the way," she said as she set the mug on the counter in front of him. "Cream or sugar?"

"Black is fine, thanks." He picked the mug up and took a sip. Then figuring he should introduce himself to this personality since it was clear she didn't remember him, he said, "I'm Beau."

She gave him another beaming smile, the edges of her blue eyes crinkling with it. "Nice to meet you, Beau." Tilting her head a bit, she said, "I'm guessing, from the slightly bewildered look on your face, that you met Leah last night."

"Uh, yes. Leah." He guessed it stood to reason that she was aware of her other personality.

Sarah laughed, a delightfully light and infectious sound. "My twin."

"Twins." Of course...twins. Beau wondered what it said about him that he'd assumed she had multiple personalities instead of a twin sister. "You're very similar."

"Identical, in fact. Well, in appearance, anyway."

He wasn't so sure about identical. If he'd already seen both their default personalities, he doubted he'd ever get them mixed up. "Yes, you do seem to be...different in other ways."

"Yep. We definitely are. You'll pretty much know it's me if you're greeted with a smile. Leah saves hers for people she knows well."

"Good to know." He wasn't sure that he'd be interacting with either of them very much, but he tucked the info away for future reference.

"Would you like some breakfast?" she asked. "If you want a bagel and cream cheese, I can help you out. I can even make you some eggs, as long as you don't mind them scrambled. Otherwise, your options are to wait for my mom, who'll be up in a bit to start breakfast for the guests, or head into town to *Norma's.*"

"Norma's?" Before committing himself to anything, Beau wanted a little more information.

"Yeah, my aunt's restaurant. She serves the best food." She gave him another smile. "Next to my mom, of course."

"Of course," he murmured. His mother's food was not anything he'd ever brag about. That was mainly because he'd never tasted anything she'd cooked.

Beau knew he should probably wait for the breakfast provided by the lodge, but he'd hardly eaten anything since his dad had pronounced his judgment on Beau's life. "If it's not too much of a hassle, a bagel would be nice."

"No hassle at all," Sarah said as she headed to a wooden box on the counter. "I'm fixing one for myself as well."

He sank down on a stool at the counter and watched as she took out a bag of bagels. Working quickly, she sliced a couple and put them in a toaster that had long enough slots to hold two halves each.

"So what brings you to New Hope Falls?" she asked as she walked to the fridge and opened it.

"I'm visiting my grandfather."

"Really?" She turned to look at him, still holding onto the handle of the stainless-steel fridge. "Who is he?"

Beau stared at her for a moment, wondering if there was any chance she'd actually know him. "His name is Gregory Stevens."

"Oh, Mr. Stevens!" If it was possible, her smile grew even bigger as she turned from the fridge, a container in her hand. "He is such a dear."

"I'm afraid I wouldn't know."

For the first time, her smile disappeared as her brow furrowed. "You wouldn't?"

He shrugged, uncertain why he was sharing that info with a virtual stranger, friendly though she might be. There was just something compelling about her that he couldn't remember having encountered in another person before. "I've never met him."

"Oh." She pulled the bagels from the toaster when they popped up. "Well, then you're in for a real treat. He is such a sweet man."

He sat for a moment, wondering if he'd even know what to do with someone described as sweet. Would anyone else in his life fit that description? He didn't think so. Not even himself.

She put the plate with the toasted bagel in front of Beau then slid the container of cream cheese toward him with a knife resting on top of it. "If you want another one, just let me know."

"This is fine," he assured her, picking up the knife and using it to smear cream cheese on his bagel.

As Beau ate the bagel and drank the surprisingly good cup of coffee, he watched Sarah moving around the kitchen, taking bites of her own bagel. Her braid swung down over her shoulder as she opened the dishwasher and bent to pull dishes out of it. She was barefoot and wore a pair of black leggings and a large white T-shirt that slid off one shoulder, revealing the strap of the tank top she wore underneath it.

There were splashes of color on her clothes, and when she came over to take another bite of her bagel, he noticed more smudges of paint on her hands. It made him wonder what she'd been doing to get them.

"Are you in town for long?" Sarah asked as she brought the caddy from the dishwasher over to where he sat. She began to put the silverware into a drawer on the other side of the island.

"A month." A month that stretched out before him like a century, not just thirty days.

Sarah glanced up, her eyes widening. "I'm sure your grandfather will enjoy having you around. And there are worse places to be than New Hope Falls at this time of year."

Beau wasn't totally convinced of that, but he kept that thought to himself, choosing instead to eat the last bite of his bagel. "Is the personal care home far from here?"

"Not really. About fifteen minutes or so." Sarah closed the drawer. "Do you need directions?"

"I was just planning to use the GPS in my car."

"That should get you there," she said with a nod, flashing him a quick smile before turning back to the dishwasher. "And if you do get lost, just go into any store, and they'll point you in the right direction."

He wasn't sure why he found Sarah so interesting. It wasn't like he'd ever sat in the kitchen at his house or his parents' house and watched the staff do things like unload the dishwasher. It really shouldn't have been that fascinating, and yet, it was.

However, if the next month was made up solely of watching people go about life in New Hope Falls, he was going to be bored out of his mind. At the very least, he hoped that he'd be able to continue to work remotely because he would need the diversion if he was going to retain his sanity.

It occurred to Beau as he sat there, that perhaps he should have taken his bagel and coffee into the dining room. Though Sarah hadn't made him feel uncomfortable, he did wonder if perhaps his presence in the kitchen might be making her uncomfortable.

"Good morning, darling." Beau turned to see the older woman who had checked him in the previous evening. "Oh. And good morning to you too, Beau."

Beau got to his feet as she came further into the kitchen. "Good morning."

"You're certainly up early," she said with a smile. "But it looks like Sarah has taken care of you."

"She has, yes." He settled back on the stool as Nadine made her way to the coffee pot.

"Would you like a refill?" she asked as she poured herself a mugful.

"Do you mind if I take it up to my room? I need to do a bit of work."

"That's fine," Nadine said as she removed the carafe from the coffee maker again and came to refill his cup. "I know it takes me more than just one cup to get going in the morning."

"Thank you," he said.

"If you want more breakfast, it will be served starting at seven." She glanced over at the doorway. "Morning, Leah-love."

Well, if Beau had doubted Sarah's twin claim, that would have been quashed by the presence of the sisters in the same room at the same time. Leah gave him a frown as she made her way to the coffee pot.

"What are you doing up?" she said with a glance at Sarah.

"Haven't been to bed yet." It seemed the statement reminded Sarah that she should be tired because she reached up to cover a yawn. "But I'm on my way there soon."

"Guess you won't be helping out today then," Leah said as she leaned back against the counter, cupping her mug of coffee between her hands.

"I unloaded the dishwasher." Sarah gestured toward the appliance. "And I'll be up to help with dinner."

"Don't let your schedule stay out of whack for too many days," Nadine said as she doctored her coffee. "Remember, you're helping Norma out later this week."

"Yep. I remember."

Beau wondered what it was that had kept Sarah up through the night. He'd just assumed she was up early like him. He felt a bit like he was imposing on a family situation, and if these people were anything like his family, it was likely to become more awkward.

With mug in hand, he got to his feet. "If you'll excuse me, I need to try and get some work done."

"If you plan to be here for dinner, we eat at six," Nadine said.

"I'm not sure yet what my schedule for the day will be," he told her. "But I assume I'll be back in time."

Having said that, he made his escape from the kitchen. Up in the room, he set his mug on the desk then pulled his laptop from its bag. After the unconventional start to the day, he needed to focus on what he knew—what was most familiar to him—at least for an hour or so. And then he would be diving into the unknown.

As Beau walked out of the kitchen, Sarah took a deep breath and let it out. And for the first time since he'd scared her earlier, her heart stopped pounding against her ribcage as if trying to escape its confinement. There had been no reason for her heart rate to continue to race once she'd recovered from the surprise of Beau's presence in the kitchen, but it had.

Of course, it could have had something to do with the man himself. His imposing presence, along with the way his piercing blue-green gaze had focused in on her, had taken her breath away. His looks could have landed him on the cover of a men's magazine, and for all she knew, they had.

Not that she would ever be focused solely on looks alone, but there was no denying that Beau was an attractive man. Someone that she would really like to paint a portrait of.

"Thanks for making the coffee and helping our guest out," her mom said.

"You're welcome." She fought against another yawn. "And on that note, I think I'm going to head for bed."

Sarah gave her mom a quick hug then left the kitchen. Glancing at the stairs leading to the second floor, she made her way to the ones that led to the basement where her room was.

She'd been up through the night working on a painting that she hoped would become part of a show she was having at a small local gallery in the fall. Although she'd had pieces available there for the last couple of years—of which several had sold—this would be her first show. Sarah hoped that it would be the first of many to come.

This was hardly the first time she'd gotten so caught up in her painting that she'd ended up working through the night. The night hours were definitely her favorite when she was working on an art project, but when she wasn't caught up in that, she preferred to be awake during the day.

Of course, if she'd been keeping normal hours, she wouldn't have had that lovely interaction with the GQ model.

When she walked into her bathroom and caught a glimpse of herself in the mirror, she reconsidered the positive feelings she had about the meeting with Beau. Her clothes—while comfortable for painting—weren't exactly fit for public display. She plucked at a smear of red on her shirt, wincing as she caught sight of the paint smudges on her hands. Yeah, she was a mess. She could only imagine the thoughts that had gone through Beau's mind at her appearance.

With a sigh, she turned from the mirror and leaned into the shower to twist the faucet on. As she waited for the water to warm up, she tugged off her paint-splattered clothes then pulled on a cap to protect her hair. She didn't have the time or energy to wash and dry it before crawling into bed.

She spent most of her time beneath the water working the paint from her skin. It took a bit of effort, but it was something she was used to doing. Some girls removed makeup at the end of their day, she removed paint. Of course, she removed makeup too, but not that day. Just one more thing about her interaction with their newest guest that made her sigh.

Once she'd finished in the shower, Sarah pulled on a pair of sleep shorts and a clean tank top then closed the curtains over her windows to block the sunlight while she slept. Then she crawled into bed and tugged the comforter up to her chin.

Closing her eyes, she let out a long sigh then allowed her mind to focus on what helped her relax. She knew that Leah tended to think about music before she fell asleep, but for Sarah, her thoughts were always about art or color.

Most of the time, she imagined painting. Sometimes it was broad, calming brushstrokes of colors across a large canvas. Other times it was streaks of paint with her fingers. Rarely, she would imagine smaller, more detailed work or even sketching a portrait of someone who'd piqued her interest.

That day, it wasn't much of a surprise that a sketch of Beau began to take shape in her thoughts. She drifted off to sleep dreaming of pencil strokes outlining hooded eyes, a square chin with just the tiniest bit of a cleft, and a Roman nose.

CHAPTER TWO

A woman's voice sounded from the dashboard of his rental vehicle, telling Beau that he was to take the next right-hand turn. He wasn't sure exactly what he'd expected of the personal care home, but the building that appeared once he made the final turn wasn't it.

It was a sprawling single floor building that looked like it had been around for a few decades. The paint looked faded and dull, and there were plenty of cracks in the surface of the parking lot that had grass growing up through them. The flowers in the beds and pots around the entrance added a splash of color, but they couldn't hide the drabness of the building. Overall, the place looked like it could use a facelift. He could only hope that the interior was in better shape.

Frowning, he pulled into an empty spot close to the entrance. There weren't a lot of cars in the lot, and he guessed that the majority of those parked there belonged to the home's employees. His rental was definitely the nicest of the vehicles there.

Before getting out of the car, he checked his phone again. One of the things he'd done earlier at the lodge was to send an email to his dad about the status of the files he'd been working on before his banishment. He was relieved to see a reply and quickly tapped on the email to read what his father had to say.

You don't need to concern yourself with any of those projects. I would suggest you concentrate on figuring out how to get things back on track with Tiffany.

Say what? The relief he'd felt when Tiffany had ended their epic fight with the proclamation that she wouldn't marry him if he was the last emotionally-stunted man on earth, was sucked away at his father's words. Beau was willing to do almost anything the man asked of him in order to get his trust fund, but his father's demand that he reunite with Tiffany felt like an unreasonable request.

I'm hoping that given a bit of distance, the two of you will be able to come together again. Absence making the heart grow fonder and all that.

Clearly no one had briefed his father on the details of their fight. Because if they had, he would know that absence wasn't going to fix things between him and Tiff. In fact, she would probably interpret his departure from Houston as more *emotionally stunted* behavior on his part.

Suddenly, being in New Hope Falls didn't feel quite as much a banishment as a reprieve. He wasn't going to bother trying to figure out how to make things right with Tiffany because she'd been right to end things between them. All he could hope was that she wouldn't allow anyone to change her mind for her.

Deciding not to reply to his dad's message, Beau closed out his email program and got out of the car. He was supposed to meet his grandfather at nine, and it was a couple of minutes to the hour. The morning air held a bit of a chill, and the sky was gray, making him wonder if rain was imminent.

With that in mind, he headed for the entrance to the building where the glass doors slid open at his approach. Beau stepped inside, then paused to look around to get the lay of the land. There were a couple clusters of chairs in the small foyer area as well as a large elevated counter with a couple people behind it. After a glance at the few occupied chairs, Beau made his way to the counter.

"Hello." One of the women there greeted him with a smile. "Can I help you?"

"I'm here to see Gregory Stevens."

The woman's smile broadened, making him recall Sarah's words from earlier about his grandfather. "He told us he was expecting company today. If you come with me, I'll take you to him."

Beau followed the woman as she led him down a short hallway to a medium-sized room with big windows that looked out over a wooded area. Set around the room were various potted plants. Some stood tall in their containers while others spilled over the sides of theirs.

There were a couple of tables set out in the room as well as a game table and some furniture groupings with comfortable looking chairs. The woman headed for one of the tables near the windows where a couple of men were seated.

"Your guest has arrived, Mr. Stevens," she announced as they came to a stop at the table.

"Thank you, Marianne," one of the men said. He had a surprisingly full head of pure white hair and blue eyes that looked familiar. Beau saw them every time he looked at his mom. The man patted the wheelchair he was seated in. "You'll have to excuse me for not getting up."

His grandfather held out his hand, which Beau took and gave a firm shake. "It's nice to meet you, sir."

"You too, son. Have a seat."

Marianne left them as Beau sank down onto one of the chairs at the table. The other man there got to his feet and rested his hand on his grandfather's shoulder. "I'll catch up with you later, Greg."

He reached up and patted the man's hand. "You owe me another game of chess, so I'll be looking for you."

"Can't believe you're so desperate to lose again." The other man chuckled as he wandered away.

Alone with his grandfather, Beau wasn't sure what to say. It was one of the few times he actually wished his younger brother was there. Rhett would have already been several paragraphs into a conversation with their grandfather. The guy, who was seven years his junior, had never met a stranger.

It drove his parents nuts, especially his mom, who viewed such behavior as uncouth and beneath people of their station. Whenever she tried to rein Rhett in, he just laughed.

His hijinks should have resulted in him being banished on a regular basis, but nope. Somehow, Rhett got away with his actions while Beau got punished the one time he stepped out of line, even though it hadn't even been him who had caused the scene with Tiffany. She'd done all the yelling in that fight.

His grandfather regarded him with a steady gaze, then said, "So what did you do wrong, son?"

Beau fought the urge to bristle at the man's assumption. "How do you know I did something wrong?"

"I'm pretty sure your father wouldn't have sent you here unless they needed you out of Houston for some reason."

Rather than denying it, Beau said, "I was involved in a bit of a scene that resulted in my fiancée ending our engagement."

A thoughtful look settled over his grandfather's face. "Was any of what she said true?"

Beau frowned. It seemed that the man was a bit more well informed than he had assumed. "I suppose that she might have had a few points."

"Which were?"

What on earth was the man after?

Beau wanted to lie rather than reveal which of the many things Tiffany had shrieked at him had been true. But there was something in the man's expression that seemed to say he'd know. That, in fact, he already knew the answer to his own question.

The sound of voices drew Beau's attention from what he needed to say to his grandfather, and he turned to see two elderly women walking into the room. They waved in their direction but settled themselves on a couple of loveseats on the far side of the room.

When Beau looked back at his grandfather, he found the man watching him with that same steady look, but there was something else in his gaze. Something Beau didn't quite understand. A softness...a gentleness that he had never seen aimed in his direction before.

Beau cleared his throat. "She said I wasn't emotionally invested in the relationship." The older man nodded but didn't say anything, just regarded him with a look of expectation. "She might have mentioned that I didn't give her priority in my life. That my work was more important to me than she was."

"Do you think her points were valid?"

Sure, he'd agreed, but at the same time, he'd also felt she was being unrealistic in her expectations of their engagement. Their relationship hadn't been any different from how his parents was or even what he'd seen of her parents' marriage.

"There was no expectation for anything different," Beau stated.

Their first dates which had been arranged by their parents, were mainly to fundraisers for her father's political campaign. He'd been fine with that arrangement because it saved him from having to find his own date for the events his father expected him to attend as a representative of the family and the company.

"Maybe not by you, but clearly, she didn't feel the same."

Beau couldn't argue with him there. He just wished that Tiffany had chosen to air her objections to the state of their relationship in private. Maybe things would have still ended the same because he wouldn't have been able to give her the emotional investment she wanted, but at least they wouldn't have become the talk of the town.

Even though his name didn't normally appear on news sites devoted to business and politics, Tiffany's certainly did. As the daughter of a potential presidential candidate, interest in her family was growing. Because of that, their fight had drawn the spotlight in a way it might not have otherwise.

"My father expects me to make an attempt to patch things up," Beau found himself confessing as he thought of the email he'd read in the car. "He's hoping that time apart will help Tiffany reconsider ending our engagement."

"How do you feel about that?"

Beau stared at his grandfather. Did the man have a degree in psychology? He was certainly acting like he did. "I think Tiffany has made it clear what she wants from any relationship, and I think that it's also pretty clear that I'm unable to give that to her."

"Unable or unwilling?"

At that moment, Beau wasn't too keen to confess the absolute relief he'd felt when Tiffany had declared that things were over between them. If she wanted more from a relationship, she certainly deserved that, but she wasn't going to get it from him.

He'd only gone along with the relationship because it had seemed easy enough. But when things had become more challenging, to him, it hadn't been worth the time and energy he would have had to devote to it.

Did that make him selfish? Probably. But with his parents' relationship as an example, he hadn't anticipated ending up in a relationship that required much work. They rarely spent time around each other, and he certainly didn't see either of them reaching out to the other with affection or love.

Given that he wasn't all that keen to devote more time to a relationship, Beau had a feeling he just wasn't cut out to be in one, let alone be a husband.

"Possibly a bit of both."

At that, his grandfather nodded. "Well, it seems your father has sent you to me for a month, but he hasn't specified what is to transpire during this time."

"He wants me to consider how I can win Tiffany back," Beau told him.

His grandfather sighed and gave a shake of his head. "Well, that won't fill all your time, so it looks like I get to implement my own plan." The wrinkles in his cheeks deepened as a smile broke out on his face. "I've enlisted some of my friends here in town to help with that."

"To help fill my time?" Beau wasn't sure how he felt about that.

"Yes. I realize that you are used to a certain job and lifestyle, but perhaps it might be good for you to see how most people live and work." His grandfather lifted the mug from the table in front of him and took a sip. "What was your first job?"

Beau thought back to the days following his graduation from Harvard with degrees in finance and business. He'd been handed a portfolio of low-level clients in the investment division of his father's company. When he told his grandfather what his first position had entailed, the man nodded solemnly.

"I figured as much," he said when Beau was done. "I think I will take advantage of your time here to help you experience what you've missed out on."

"What I've missed out on?" Beau felt a bit like he was in the Twilight Zone.

"Well, let's just say that your average person gets their first job sometime in high school, and it's usually not overseeing an investment portfolio."

Beau really didn't like the sound of that, and he wondered what would happen if he refused to fall in line with whatever plan his grandfather had for him. It wasn't that he was lazy. He spent more hours at his desk than most of the people in the company.

"I've talked to a few of my friends here in town to see if you could spend some time at their businesses."

"You want me to help them out with their finances?" That didn't sound so bad. He could likely look over the books of a business and give some pointers on how to improve their bottom line.

"No, nothing like that. You've already proven to be quite adept at that. I think it's time for you to try your hand at a job you might not have quite as much experience with."

He wanted to ask what would happen if he said no, but he held his tongue. There was a gleam in his grandfather's eyes that made Beau think the man was expecting him to do just that. He'd never been one to back down from a challenge—provided it didn't require him to invest his emotions—and he wouldn't start now. It wasn't as if whatever his grandfather asked him to do would change the trajectory of his life. He had a plan, and he'd do whatever he had to in order to have it come to fruition.

"Just tell me where to go and what to do," he said, feeling a spark of gratification when his grandfather's eyes widened slightly.

"Well, I won't be the one telling you what to do, but I will tell you where to go." He paused to take another sip of coffee. "You'll report to *Norma's* tomorrow morning at six am."

"Norma's?" The name sounded familiar, and then he remembered that Sarah had mentioned it as somewhere he could get some breakfast. So, a restaurant then.

He wasn't all that excited at the prospect of working in the food-service industry, but he supposed as long as they didn't require him to cook, he should be able to do almost anything else in a restaurant even if he'd never done it before. After all, how hard could clearing tables and washing dishes be?

"Yes. The owner and her family are good friends." His grandfather pinned him with a hard look. "So don't mess up."

Beau thought perhaps it was unrealistic for the man to toss him into a totally unknown situation and then tell him to not mess up. Realistically, being in a completely new job, the chances of him messing up at least a little were fairly high, although it wouldn't be on purpose.

He wasn't one to act out of spite like his sister was prone to, or even just for the fun of it like Rhett often did. No, when he messed up, it was usually an accident—kind of like what happened with Tiffany. Or maybe, in that case, he'd just been clueless, not picking up on any of her hints, which had led to messing things up.

"I'll do my best."

His grandfather's expression softened. "That's all I can ask." He hesitated. "Well, not *all* I can ask. I want you to do a few other things for me."

Beau sat back in his chair with a stifled sigh. "Which are?"

"Well, to start with, I'd like you to go park your car on Main Street and wander the town a bit. Go into the stores. See what New Hope Falls has to offer."

"Why?" Beau asked. "I'm not moving here."

"I know that, but I'm taking advantage of your presence in New Hope to broaden your horizons. I'm certain your mother has made sure that you lived a pretty insular life, keeping you within a world of her choosing." His grandfather tilted his head. "How *did* your mother feel about you coming here?"

"She wasn't happy about it." More accurately, she'd been furious with his father for making the arrangements without consulting her. Although, from the snippets of arguing he'd heard between them, his father probably hadn't needed to consult her to know how she felt about it.

Beau still hadn't figured out why his father had felt it necessary to send him to New Hope. Was it really just to give him time to consider what had happened with Tiffany? Or was there something more to this banishment?

He gave himself a mental shake. He wasn't truly banished. Nothing was keeping him from getting on a plane and heading back to Houston. There had been no gun held to his head to get on the plane in the first place.

Nothing except for the trust fund that his father retained control of.

"She couldn't seem to wait to leave New Hope, so I'm sure that's true."

Beau just shrugged because he had no insight for his grandfather. His mother had always refused to talk about her life before marrying Beau's father. He hadn't even known either of her parents were still alive until his father had told him where he'd be going and who he'd be meeting.

He eyed the man sitting at the table with him, wondering if there was something about the man that had driven his mother away. So far, his grandfather seemed decent enough, even if he was trying to get Beau to do things he'd rather not do.

"Also, I'd love to spend some time with you each day. You can come here in the afternoon once you're done work or come for supper. Whatever you'd prefer."

"I can come here for dinner?"

"Sure. I just need to let them know I'll have a guest. They encourage family to come and spend time with us."

As his words sank in, Beau had to wonder if his grandfather had many visitors. As far as he knew, his mother was an only child, so unless there was extended family in the area, there was likely no one to visit the older man.

"I'll let you know. They said at the lodge that they provide dinner, but I suppose I could let them know that I'll eat here sometimes."

"I'm certain Nadine will be fine with that as long as you give her a head's up."

"I'll be sure to decide early enough in the day to let everyone know." When he'd lived at home, his mother had always insisted he let her know if he would be there for dinner each day. However, in her case, he was pretty sure it had less to do with making sure there was enough food and more to do with her wanting to know his plans.

"Thank you."

Conversation faltered as more people came into the room, some stopping by the table to greet his grandfather and eyeing Beau with obvious curiosity. His grandfather introduced him to each of them, but Beau wasn't sure he'd remember any of their names.

During a lull in the introductions, his grandfather said, "I'm going to have to go back to my room and lay down for a bit before lunch."

"Do you need help?"

He shook his head. "One of the aides will help me." He paused then said, "Will you do as I asked?"

Beau thought back over their conversation. "You mean me playing tourist in New Hope?"

"Yes."

"I will. It's not like I have anything else to do today." He planned to check his email again and to log into his computer so he could check on his accounts. If his father didn't like that, he could lock him out.

"So I'll see you tomorrow then?" his grandfather asked.

"You will." He got to his feet then held out his hand, waiting for his grandfather to take it before he said, "It was a pleasure to meet you."

A smile wreathed the man's face. "For me as well."

As Beau walked to his car a few minutes later, he couldn't help but shake his head as he wondered what his life had just become. But he wasn't going to allow this detour to derail his plans. This was just a little blip on the road. And as long as he did as his father had demanded—well, *most* of what he demanded—he hoped he would get the trust fund as promised when he turned thirty, and finally, his father would have no more control over his life.

If that meant he had to spend a month in this town, doing his grandfather's bidding, then so be it.

With that in mind, he headed out to start his tour of Main Street.

CHAPTER THREE

When the melodious notes of her alarm slowly pulled Sarah
from sleep, she didn't move at first, letting colors flood her mind.
Pastel shades of pinks, blues, and purples swirled around her
thoughts as she prepared to get up.

Whispering, she recited the verse from Psalm 143 that liked to
start her day with. *Let the morning bring me word of your unfailing
love, for I have put my trust in you. Show me the way I should go,
for to you I entrust my life.*

This was how she preferred to wake up. Slowly, with beautiful
colors to guide her way to full wakefulness.

When a handsome face superimposed itself over the colors, she
let out a laugh and opened her eyes, pushing her comforter back.
For a moment, she lay with her arms and legs stretched out like a
starfish. Though she would have loved to stay like that for longer,
she'd promised to help with dinner so she couldn't linger.

Of course, she didn't really want to miss dinner since, unless
plans had changed, Beau would be there. Not that his presence at
dinner should be her motivation, but he sure was nice to look at.

With a sigh, she swung her feet over the edge of the bed and got
up. She wandered into her studio and pushed open the curtains,
not too surprised to see that the sky had turned gray and was spit-
ting out drops of rain. Though her favorite days were sunny yellow
ones, she had no problem with the gray ones, especially if she
didn't have to go out.

Her favorite way to view her world and her emotions was using
colors. Sometimes people inspired colors in her too, but not in an
aura sort of way. Just that they just made her think of certain colors

because of their personalities or the way they interacted with her. If she had her way, everyone would be yellow because that was her favorite color.

Turning from the window, she headed for her closet, where she picked out a pair of mustard-colored jeans and a dark blue T-shirt. This time, she made sure her outfit had no smears of paint on it. She took a few minutes to put on a little makeup then braided her hair again. She had the urge to take more time on her appearance because she found herself wanting Beau to see that she cleaned up nicely.

Admonishing herself for that thought, Sarah made her way upstairs to the kitchen.

"Hey, darling," her mom said when she walked in. "How did you sleep?"

"Good, but I need some coffee." Sarah headed for the Keurig machine on the counter. Her mom would make coffee for the guests after the meal, but it was usually decaf. Sarah needed some caffeine. "What's for supper?"

"Spaghetti, breadsticks, and a salad."

"Hmmm." Sarah loved her mom's spaghetti. "What do you need me to do?"

"Well, once you're done with your coffee, you can help Anna make the breadsticks."

"Don't worry," Leah said. "I already made the dough."

"Thanks, Lee-yah," Sarah said, reaching out to pat her twin's cheek.

Leah batted her hand away. "Go drink your coffee."

Sarah removed her mug from the Keurig and dumped some sugar into it before carrying it to the fridge for enough cream to lighten the color a bit. She gave a contented hum after her first sip.

"How're the wedding plans coming?" she asked Anna, her brother Eli's fiancée, after a couple more sips.

"They're going great!" Anna grinned. "It helps that we're not aiming for anything too fancy."

"How did your mom react to that plan?" Leah asked.

They all knew that money wasn't an issue for Anna or her family, and Sarah had assumed that the wedding would reflect that.

"Oh, my mother was thrilled. I'm flying to New York for a couple of days to go dress shopping with her. But aside from that, she's extremely happy to not have to go through all the fussiness of planning a wedding. She and my father had a simple ceremony at the courthouse, so she's never seen the sense in spending thousands of dollars on a single event."

Sarah had often thought about the type of wedding she'd like. Depending on the day, she sometimes imagined a small intimate exchange of vows somewhere outdoors. Other times, she thought it would be nice to invite everyone they knew to the church. She supposed her groom would want to have some say in that decision, so she knew better than to set her heart on either plan.

Now, if she could just meet that man and move onto that next stage of her life. She was ready. More than ready.

After she finished helping Anna with the breadsticks, Sarah went to set the table in the dining room, using the number her mom had given of the people who had said they'd be there for dinner. Unless the lodge was fully booked, they didn't usually have a large number. On nights like that one, when they weren't expecting many guests at dinner, the family ate with them.

Their large wooden table was something Eli had designed then made himself, carving the legs with intricate patterns. It could seat up to ten people comfortably, but until summer was in full swing, it was rare they had that many guests eating there.

Sarah couldn't deny she was a little excited at the prospect of spending more time around Beau. Sure, he was nice to look at and really appealed to the artist in her, but she also found herself a little intrigued about him now that she knew he was Mr. Stevens' grandson. Like, how did someone get to adulthood without knowing their grandparent?

She and her siblings hadn't known their dad's parents too well since they'd only seen them once a year, if that. Sarah's memory of them was that they'd been rather reserved, never seeming to enjoy being around her, Leah, and Eli. It hadn't been a big surprise—or a loss really—when they'd had no contact with them once their father had left.

Harder to experience had been the deaths of her mom's parents, though she didn't have a lot of memories of her grandfather since he'd passed away when she was eight. Her grandmother had died the year before their father had left, which had just compounded their deep sense of loss.

So she couldn't help but wonder what circumstances had kept Beau from his grandfather. Even more than feeling sorry for Beau, Sarah felt for Mr. Stevens at the thought that he'd been denied the joy of knowing his grandson.

"Where's my coffee?" Sarah asked when she walked back into the kitchen once she'd finished setting the table.

"I poured it out," Leah said from where she was dumping noodles into a pot of boiling water.

"Whatever." Sarah rolled her eyes. "Seriously, though. Where is it?"

Her mom sighed. "Just make yourself a fresh cup."

Sarah turned to look at Leah. "You really dumped it?"

"It was cold, so yeah."

"You are just..." Sarah sighed and decided not to bother making another cup until after supper.

She had one more overnight painting session before she'd have to change her schedule to help at the diner for a couple of days. Her cousin, who was the main waitress at *Norma's*, had taken a couple of days off to go on a short trip with her husband to celebrate their anniversary.

Though working at the restaurant wasn't her favorite thing, Sarah was happy to help out when needed. She'd worked there through her teen years, so it wasn't too hard to slip back into the role when necessary.

"Here's the salad," her mom said as she handed her a large bowl. "Can you put it on the table."

Over the next little while, they worked together to get the meal on the table. Eli came in partway through and gave Anna a kiss before washing up. He'd been focused on a custom woodworking order for the past several weeks which meant he wasn't as available to help out at the lodge.

As she poured water in glasses at the table, Sarah heard Eli greet the guests that would be joining them for dinner, and she turned to see Beau shaking his hand. Seeing the two men side by side, she noticed the differences between them. They were both tall, though it appeared Beau had an inch or so on her brother. Eli had a bulkier build, no doubt from his very physical work. Beau was lankier, though he still had broad shoulders.

Beau wore a light blue button-down shirt and dark gray trousers, which were in sharp contrast to Eli's T-shirt and faded jeans. Eli looked like he needed a haircut, while Beau's hair was styled to perfection. They were definitely different men in their style and appearance.

Once again, her desire to capture the man on canvas spiked. When he glanced her way, their gazes met, and she gave him a quick smile before going back to her job of pouring water.

After the food had been brought to the table, her mom invited everyone to find a seat. Sarah didn't try to grab a seat close to Beau, but she wasn't disappointed when she ended up across the table from him.

Beau looked a little surprised when her mom asked Eli to say a blessing for the food. Most guests were aware from previous visits or from information on their website that they were a family of faith, but apparently, that had escaped Beau's notice. His brow was furrowed when Sarah looked up at him following the prayer, but his expression quickly smoothed out.

"So did you have a chance to see a bit of our town today?" her mom asked as they began to pass food around the table.

"I did," Beau said, using the tongs to put some noodles on his plate. "After I visited my grandfather, I spent some time visiting the businesses on Main Street."

"Did you go to *Norma's*?" Sarah asked.

Beau looked at her, his beautiful eyes capturing her attention again. "Yes. I stopped there for lunch. It was very delicious."

Though she didn't need people to tell her what she already knew, it always made Sarah feel good when someone mentioned how much they liked her aunt's food. The only thing that made her feel even better was when they complimented her mom's or Leah's cooking.

Throughout the meal, Beau spoke when a question or a comment was directed at him, but otherwise, he focused on his meal. Given his attire and demeanor, Sarah wondered if he was uncomfortable with them. Not everyone was at ease with their family-style meals, which made her wonder why he'd reserved a room in the lodge instead of a cabin where he could have taken his meals on his own. She was pretty sure that at least one cabin was available.

The other guests were people who had stayed with them before, so conversation still flowed even though Beau was on the quiet side. Sarah wished he would volunteer more information about himself. Though she was obviously drawn to his appearance, she knew there was more to the man than what met the eye. The complexities of a person's personality helped her create depth in a painting. Not that she planned to paint him, unless he agreed, and she usually didn't ask for that privilege until she knew a person better.

She didn't like to just paint a portrait without seeing a bit of a person's character, though she did do it. She didn't always have the opportunity to speak with the people she painted. Sometimes people sent her pictures to use in creating a portrait. That was not her favorite way to work, but even pictures could reveal something about a person.

When Leah jostled her elbow, Sarah looked over at her. "What?"

"She asked you a question."

Sarah glanced across the table at one of their other guests. "I'm sorry. My mind was elsewhere, and I missed what you said."

The woman gave her a friendly smile. "I was just wondering if you have new paintings available for sale."

"My most recent ones are at the gallery in town. You can also check out my website to see others I have available."

"We've gotten so many compliments on the mountain painting we bought the last time we were here."

"Oh, I'm so glad you liked it."

"And you, too, Eli." The woman smiled in his direction. "That nativity set you carved that we bought at the Christmas market has garnered a lot of attention as well." Her gaze moved to their mom. "You are blessed with some very talented children."

"Yes," her mom agreed. "And you'll experience Leah's talent for cooking and baking during your visit here."

Though her sister likely hated the attention, Sarah was glad her mom had included Leah. Most people assumed that Leah had no talent when, in fact, she was extremely talented. Beyond just cooking and baking. If only their father's departure hadn't robbed her of the desire to share her other talent with the world. Maybe that would change one day.

"Did you make this meal?" the woman asked.

"I made the breadsticks and the dessert," Leah said, her voice subdued. "Mom has a special recipe for the spaghetti sauce that she hasn't trusted me with yet."

"One day soon," her mom said with a laugh. "I have to have some reason to stick around."

Sarah glanced at Beau and found him regarding her with a curious look. Given that this was his first interaction with their family, she wasn't surprised to see the curiosity. She just couldn't let herself attach any meaning to it.

His stay was going to be longer than most of their guests—with the exception of Anna—so they would likely get to know each other better, regardless. Well, unless he kept completely to himself.

Sarah hoped that wasn't the case, as she wanted to get to know him better. As a friend, of course. A desire for anything else would be just plain foolishness.

She wanted a relationship like Anna and Eli had. Like her friend Cara had with her boyfriend, Kieran. And Sarah knew she couldn't have that with someone whose life was clearly far away from New Hope Falls. If nothing else, Beau's whole persona—from his perfect hair to the clothes that he wore to the expensive watch on his wrist—spoke to a life very different from what she had in New Hope.

Of course, Anna had also seemed to come from a different world than what they were used to, but she'd wanted to fit in. Had seemed to delight in the life they had in New Hope. She also hadn't been afraid to get her hands dirty.

Once the meal was over, Beau accepted the offer of coffee with dessert while they cleared the dishes and food from the table. Eli took care of providing coffee to their guests as Anna carried out the dessert Leah had made. It was a light and airy puff pastry with fresh strawberries and whipped cream.

Sarah didn't have the patience or the talent to make desserts like Leah did, but she sure enjoyed eating them. And judging from the appreciative murmurs of the others at the table, she wasn't the only one.

"This is absolutely delicious, Leah." The woman who had admired Sarah and Eli's talents earlier seemed to relish Leah's in that moment. "Truly heavenly."

Sarah looked over at Leah in time to catch a rare smile—small though it was—cross her face.

Once dessert was over, Beau got to his feet, and, after letting her mom know he wouldn't be there for breakfast in the morning, he said goodnight and left them.

Sarah hung around to help get everything cleaned up and prepped for the next morning, then she made her way downstairs to begin painting. As she walked into her studio space, she flicked on the bright lights that she used when painting.

Most of the time, even while painting during the day, she couldn't rely on natural light since a lot of the days were overcast. Even when they weren't, the trees outside the windows of her walk-out basement room blocked the sun.

It didn't take her long to change into the clothes she'd used the previous night for painting. She had a few different T-shirts and leggings that she rotated through that were already splattered with paint. The floor beneath her easel was covered with drop cloths, though it was rare that she dropped paint. But having them there just removed the necessity for her to be super careful when she got into *the zone*.

Tilting her head, she cast a critical eye over the work she'd done so far on the painting. Her plan for the show included paintings that captured the beauty of the area since she was featured in the gallery as a local artist. This first one had a view of the Cascade Mountains towering in the background, craggy and gray, with a foreground filled with an assortment of trees.

She'd chosen to set it in early autumn, so while a lot of the trees were still green, a few of the shade trees were beginning to turn color. The previous night, she'd focused on the mountains, so she took a couple steps back from the easel to make sure she was pleased with how they looked.

Spying a couple of areas she wanted to add a bit more contrast to, she turned to begin mixing her colors. Once everything was ready, she turned on the playlist she liked to work to and began to paint. Thoughts of Beau slipped away as she focused in on the mountains.

CHAPTER FOUR

Beau wasn't sure he'd ever been so tired and sore in his life. Not even after a session with his trainer at the gym. He'd slept horribly the night before. Worried that he'd miss his alarm if he slept too deeply, he'd spent most of the hours before it went off tossing and turning.

So he'd been off to a bad start that morning. He would have liked to have taken a shower to help him wake up, but there'd been no time for that. At least, he hadn't thought there was. Turned out, he was at the restaurant early, but thankfully, that meant he had time for a cup of coffee before being thrown into the thick of things.

Never again would he underestimate the stamina needed to bus tables at a restaurant. The first couple of hours had been a rush of trying to keep tables cleared and clean for the revolving door of breakfast customers. He'd tried his best to stay on top of things, but considering he'd never cleared a table in his life, he'd fallen behind more than a few times.

Thankfully, the women working with him had picked up his slack without complaining, swiftly clearing off a few tables when he struggled to keep up. The rush hadn't lasted forever, though, and around ten he'd had a chance for another cup of coffee and the best blueberry muffin he'd ever eaten in his life.

Then the influx had started all over again with the lunch crowd. By the time he left the restaurant just after one, all he wanted to do was sleep...for a whole day. Unfortunately, he had to do it all over again the following morning.

He was supposed to eat dinner with his grandfather, but at the end of his shift, he'd called the home to speak to his grandfather to see if he could visit right away. Once he got back to his room at the lodge, he didn't want to have to go out again until the next morning. His grandfather had seemed to sense his tiredness and told him to head on back to the lodge, and they'd catch up the next day.

He'd told Nadine—who he'd discovered was Norma's twin sister, strangely enough—that he wouldn't be at the lodge for dinner, so he wasn't altogether sure what to do about his evening meal. In the end, he ordered some food from the restaurant before he left, planning to eat it later on.

Though he'd never eaten the type of food *Norma's* served, it must have been good if the steady stream of customers was anything to judge by. His mom had always insisted on having French chefs, and when he'd moved out, she'd hired a chef for his new apartment as well. If he'd had a chef who cooked and served portions like *Norma's* did, he might have had to work out a whole lot harder.

Back in his room, he bent to put the two takeout containers filled with his food for dinner into the small fridge hidden behind a beautifully finished wooden cupboard door, groaning as the pain in his back spiked. After he closed the fridge door, he turned and fell face-first on the bed.

He was going to have to talk to his personal trainer about their workouts. Clearly, he had missed working on a whole muscle group, if the ache in his lower back was anything to go by.

The muscles of his back pulsed dully with pain as he lay there debating whether he had the energy to get up and change into something more comfortable. Finally, he decided that being uncomfortable might help to prevent him from sleeping away the remainder of the day.

As it turned out, he was right. When he next awoke, it was just after seven. With a groan, Beau rolled onto his back and stared up at the ceiling. It took him a minute to recall where he was and why his back hurt so badly.

But remember, he did, and then he let out a sigh, realizing he'd have to do it all again the next day. He wasn't sure what his grandfather hoped to achieve by having him do that kind of work, but he wasn't about to complain about it to him. Something told Beau that the man was waiting for him to do just that.

He pushed up to sit on the edge of the bed, dragging his hands through his hair. His stomach rumbled, reminding him he hadn't eaten since his early lunch at the restaurant. Though he would have liked something more substantial than the sandwich and salad he'd brought back to the lodge, at least he didn't have to worry about heating them up before he ate.

It didn't take him long to consume his food as he sat at the small table in the room. It was as good as he'd expected it to be, and all he needed now was a cup of coffee to accompany the blueberry muffin he'd also bought. He'd seen a Keurig machine in the kitchen so likely he could get a cup of coffee from that, though it would be a far cry from the coffee he usually drank from his five-hundred-dollar coffee maker.

He left his room, inhaling the aroma of whatever they'd eaten for dinner. It smelled delicious, but layering over it was the smell of coffee, and he wanted that more than anything else right then.

The dining room was empty, and all food was cleared away, but he could hear voices from the direction of the kitchen, so he headed that way.

"Hello, Beau." Nadine greeted him with a smile as he walked in. "We missed you at dinner. Did you get something to eat?"

"I did, thank you. I'm in search of a cup of coffee at the moment, however. If it wouldn't be too much trouble."

"No trouble at all," she assured him. "We have an assortment of flavors or just plain, regular or decaf. Whatever you'd prefer. Sarah? Can you get Beau a mug, please?"

"Sure." Sarah reached out and pulled one from the mug tree next to the Keurig. "Do you want something flavored?"

"Nope. I'm a plain coffee sort of guy. Decaf, please."

"I like the flavors, though the plain will do in a pinch." Sarah dropped a pod into the Keurig and set the mug in place. "And you take it black, right?"

"I do." Beau found himself impressed, though he probably shouldn't have been. After all, it had only been the day before when she'd made him a cup.

"Would you like some dessert?" Nadine asked. "We had a dark chocolate torte."

"I feel bad taking dessert when I wasn't here for dinner." Though it did sound like something he'd love to try. He could save the muffin for the morning before he started work.

"Don't worry about that. We had leftovers, so no problem," she said with a wave of her hand. "Just have a seat there, and we'll cut you a slice."

Beau settled on one of the stools at the island, once again marveling at the fact that he was hanging out in the kitchen. And it felt surprisingly normal. Sarah took the mug from the machine then handed it across the island to him, giving him a bright smile as she did so.

Leah came to her sister's side and slid a plate toward Beau. She didn't smile at him, but he didn't think she hated his guts or anything. Though he was drawn to Sarah's smile, he understood where Leah might be coming from. The two of them reminded Beau of himself and Rhett. His younger brother had an easy smile for everyone, and he constantly ragged on Beau for not smiling enough.

It wasn't that he didn't like to smile. It was more that it wasn't his automatic response in most situations. His sister seemed to fall somewhere between the two of them. When she was with her friends, her smiles came easily. With strangers, not so much, but even then, she did the polite smile better than he ever did.

"Thank you," he said as he lifted the mug to take a sip.

Though it wasn't the best cup of coffee he'd ever had, when he took his first bite of the torte, it more than made up for the mediocre coffee. He alternated sips of coffee with bites of the torte, listening as they talked about the meals for the next day.

When he heard what they were planning for dinner the following evening, he almost wished he'd be eating at the lodge instead of at the care home. However, he refused to bail on his grandfather two nights in a row. He kind of doubted that the meals at the personal care home were all that tasty, although he hoped that, for his grandfather's sake, they were.

"I hear you helped out at my sister's place today," Nadine said when they'd finished their menu discussion.

Beau couldn't help but wonder what Norma had said to Nadine. Something told him that Nadine wouldn't reveal if her sister had told her how poorly he'd performed.

"Yes. My first experience in foodservice. Can't say I excelled."

Nadine laughed. "None of us did, the first time we helped out there. Leah and Sarah have stories to tell from their time working at the restaurant."

"And who knows, I might have more after the next couple of days," Sarah said with a laugh.

"Are you working there?" Beau asked.

She nodded. "Missy and her husband are going away for a few days to celebrate their anniversary. I agreed to go in and help out."

"In the morning?"

"Yep. Gotta be there for the opening."

"Me, too." Beau found the idea of having a friendly face around comforting, though she might also be witness to his humiliation. That thought didn't sit as well with him.

Sarah lifted the mug she held. "Here's hoping we have happy customers and easy orders."

"I just hope they're not messy eaters. As far as I know, my only job is to clear tables and wipe them down. After watching the servers today, I have to say that I hope I don't get promoted anytime soon."

"Why are you working there?" Leah asked. "From the look of you, it's not because you need the money."

"Leah," Sarah said with a groan. "That's rude."

"Don't worry about it," Beau said. "She's not wrong. I don't need the money, which is why I'm not being paid. I think my grandfather arranged it because he wanted me to have a chance to see how..." He paused, trying to figure out the right way to phrase it.

"The ninety-nine percent live?" Leah volunteered.

He nodded. "I guess you could put it that way. I sit behind a desk all day, so I think he wanted me to experience something different."

"Well, you're at a good place to do that," Nadine said. "Norma prides herself on running a positive work environment. As much as is possible when dealing with the public."

When Beau had finished his dessert and coffee, Sarah took the dishes and put them in the dishwasher then punched some buttons that made it start to whir.

"Thank you so much for the coffee and dessert. It hit the spot."

"You're welcome," Nadine said. "Feel free to make yourself coffee whenever you want. In the mornings, we usually keep a pot on the go, but if it's empty, just use the Keurig."

"I'm a bit of a coffee addict, though I do try to keep my consumption down to three or four cups a day. It's just taking a little extra caffeine to get me going these days."

"I hear you on that," Sarah said with a grimace. "I'll be drinking plenty of it myself tomorrow. Early mornings aren't really my thing."

"Not unless you're seeing them before you go to bed," Leah pointed out.

"We're what you might call opposite twins," Sarah said as she looked from her sister to Beau. "I like late nights. She likes early mornings. She's good in the kitchen. I'm not. I'm friendly. She's not."

"I'm friendly," Leah stated.

"Yes. You're as friendly as a porcupine."

Leah didn't seem to take offense at her sister's words. "Just don't call me porky, and we'll be fine."

Nadine slipped her arm around Leah's shoulders. "You may be a little prickly, but we love you just the same."

"Yeah, we do," Sarah said as she went to her sister's side and sandwiched her in a hug that Leah looked decidedly uncomfortable being a part of. From the look on Sarah's face, she was well aware of that fact, and as any sibling would, she reveled in it.

Beau wasn't super close to his siblings. Part of that was because of the difference in their ages. Five years between him and Julianna. Seven between him and Rhett. Maybe if they'd been closer in age, he might have had a closer relationship with them.

Julianna and Rhett hung out together more. He usually only saw them when his mother summoned them all to the house for a meal. He hadn't heard from either of them since his banishment, and it was unlikely he would.

"Okay. Enough of that." Leah wriggled her way out from between the two women.

Beau felt a smile tugging at his lips when Sarah captured her sister in another hug.

"You can never have enough hugs," she exclaimed, rocking the two of them back and forth.

"I can have enough from you," Leah informed her.

"Am I missing out on group hugs with Leah?"

Beau turned to see that Anna had joined them. Holding her hands out, she went straight to the two women and wrapped her arms around them. Leah let out an audible sigh, and a resigned look settled over her face as Anna and Sarah held on to her.

"What on earth did I miss?" Eli's question drew Beau's attention. When Eli met his gaze, he said, "Is the world coming to an end?"

Beau couldn't help the laugh that escaped him. The more he was around this obviously close-knit family, the more they were growing on him.

"I'm being accosted with affection," Leah groused. "Like seriously?"

Eli settled on a stool next to Beau and laughed. "Just let it happen, Lee. One day you might actually come to enjoy it."

Sarah and Anna finally let Leah go, and Anna came to give Eli a kiss. "Are you ready to head out?"

"Where are you guys going?" Sarah asked.

"Pastor Evans wants to meet with us for some pre-marital counseling, so our first session is tonight."

Beau had never heard of such a thing, though in all honesty, it wasn't as if he'd had a bunch of friends who'd gotten married. The couple of guys he would have considered more than mere acquaintances were also still single. He would have been the first to get married if things hadn't gone south with Tiffany.

The other guys appeared to have no interest in settling down and had cautioned him about getting engaged. He'd gotten a *don't you wish you'd listened to me* text from both of them after his engagement had ended, but there hadn't been any communication from either of them since.

They hadn't understood that he hadn't felt like he had much of a choice. At the time, his father had pressured him with the threat of changing the terms of the trust fund yet again.

I would much rather see you settled before I turn over the trust fund to you. It's important to know that you are responsible enough before you have that sort of money.

It was ridiculous that he kept buying into these things that his father said would guarantee him access to the money he needed to carry out the plans for his future. And yet here he was, buying into it yet again.

"Ready to go, love?" Eli asked as he got up off the stool.

"Whenever you are."

Eli took her hand. "See you guys later."

Once they were gone, Beau got to his feet. "I'm going to call it a night since morning comes early on this particular shift."

"Guess I should too," Sarah said with a sigh. "Did you want to carpool? Unless you're not coming back here afterward."

He had planned to come back to the lodge since he didn't have to be at the personal care home until five or so. "Sure. Might as well. What time do you want to leave?"

"Probably five-thirty."

"Yeah. That's about when I left this morning."

"Great." Sarah's smile lit up her face. "See you in the morning."

"Goodnight." Beau gave a small nod to the women then left the kitchen.

Back in his room, he logged into his laptop—grateful the lodge had decent internet—but then frowned when he tried to log into the company's server.

Invalid entry.

Letting out an irritated sigh, Beau entered his username and password again, being careful to make sure he made no mistakes. When the same error popped up, he sat back in his chair and stared at the screen. So now his father was going to cut him off from his work? To what end?

Picking up his phone, he tapped his contacts to pull up his father's info. As he waited for him to answer, he got to his feet and wandered over to the window. The sun hadn't quite set yet, so he had a view of the forest behind the lodge as well as the mountains beyond it. The picture-perfect setting should have been calming, but it did nothing to quell the anger churning in his gut.

"Beaumont." His father's voice when he answered the phone was measured and deep. "To what do I owe the pleasure?"

"There appears to be an issue with the company server. I'm unable to log in."

"The server is fine," his father said. "Your credentials have been temporarily suspended."

"Why?" He kind of doubted his father would answer, but he needed to at least try to figure out the man's reasoning.

"Don't worry about it. You just focus on figuring out how to get Tiffany to take you back."

"That hardly takes up all my time." The truth of the matter was, it hadn't taken up *any* of his time, but he wasn't going to tell his father that. "I don't mind continuing to work while I'm here."

"You need to consider the ramifications of your actions, Beaumont. Why you risked your future like that, I'll never know, but you need to spend some time thinking about what you truly want out of your life."

The subtle threat in his father's words was almost enough to douse the anger inside him. Almost...

It still lingered there, however, joined by a desperation that he hated. Beau liked to think he was a strong man, and with most people, he could be. But without fail, his father managed to reduce him to nothing every time they had a personal conversation.

When his father ended the call without even saying goodbye, Beau clenched the phone in his hand as he lowered it from his ear. Turning from the window, he went back to his laptop, wishing he had a connection in the company IT department who would feel more loyalty to him than to his father.

Unfortunately, no one dared defy Charles Beaumont Allerton Senior. Not even Charles Beaumont Allerton Junior, apparently.

CHAPTER FIVE

Even with her usual wakeup ritual, Sarah had to drag herself out of bed the next morning, feeling much worse than she should have, considering she'd actually gone to bed at a decent hour. Of course, she hadn't fallen asleep right away, so that had cut into her available hours of sleep.

Scrubbing her hands over her face, she made her way into the bathroom. She flicked on the light, wincing a bit at the brightness. After splashing some water on her face and brushing her teeth, she settled on a stool at the vanity in the bathroom and began to unbraid her hair.

She'd taken a shower and washed her hair the night before, but even though she'd dried and braided it before bed, it looked a bit fuzzy. Once it was free, she brushed through the strands before she pulled them back into a ponytail, then she quickly braided the loose hair and coiled the braid around into a bun. She usually left the braid free, but when she was working around food, she knew that her aunt preferred her hair to be up and out of the way.

Some days she wondered why she kept it long. For some reason, both she and Leah had grown their hair out. In Leah's case, Sarah was pretty sure it was because she was too lazy to go for haircuts. In her case...well, the long hair made her feel pretty and feminine. Not that she viewed women with short hair as unfeminine, but for Sarah, it was just how she felt about herself. Maybe someday she'd cut it...maybe.

Once her hair was secure, she turned her attention to applying some makeup. Normally she didn't wear a lot, but when dealing with the public, she preferred to have on a full face.

After she was done, she pulled on a pair of black jeans and the white shirt she wore whenever she worked at the restaurant. She grabbed her purse, then headed up to the kitchen, hoping she'd have enough time to make a quick cup of coffee and eat a bagel before they left.

As soon as she walked into the hallway, Sarah realized that Beau had already beaten her to the coffee. Light spilled out of the kitchen doorway, and the scent of coffee lingered in the air. When she rounded the corner, she spotted him leaning back against the counter, his phone in one hand, a mug in the other.

"Morning," she said as she walked toward him.

His head came up, his blue-green gaze meeting hers. A smile quirked the corners of his mouth then slid away. He wasn't a smiler, that was for sure. It reminded her a bit of Leah, except his gaze remained friendly even after his smile had disappeared.

He lifted his mug. "I was in desperate need of some coffee this morning."

"So am I." She plucked a pod from the carousel and a mug from the tree and quickly got the Keurig going. "Are you hungry? I think we have time for a bagel before we leave."

"If you're going to have one," he said, straightening from the counter. "What can I do?"

Sarah pulled the bag of bagels from the bread box and took two out. "You can get the cream cheese from the fridge. There are some flavored ones in the door. I like the strawberry."

Beau made his way to the fridge and opened the door. He returned with two tubs of cream cheese and set them on the counter.

While she waited for the toaster to pop up, she doctored her coffee the way she liked it and took a sip. Humming in appreciation of that first hit of caffeine, she took another sip before setting her mug down to get a couple of plates from the cupboard. When the bagels popped up, she placed one on each plate them handed one plate to Beau.

"Are you ready for another day in hospitality?" Sarah asked as she smeared her favorite cream cheese across the bagel's toasted surface.

"As ready as I'll ever be," he said with a faint grimace, which, she couldn't help but notice, did nothing to detract from his good looks. "I appreciate that my grandfather feels that I need to be aware of other walks of life, but I really don't think I'm cut out for work in the hospitality field. At least I only have to clear tables. If your aunt had to rely on me to take orders and deliver food, I think she would have politely asked me to leave the building."

"Oh, she'd give you a chance to improve first, but yeah, too many mistakes, and you'd probably be out of a job."

Sarah shared some of her experiences from working at the restaurant as they finished their bagels and coffee. She counted it a win when she got a couple more smiles out of him.

When he offered to drive his car, there was no way she'd turn him down. From the look of things, his was way more top of the line than her ten-year-old car had ever been. She knew it was a rental, but she suspected the car he drove regularly was probably just as nice, if not nicer.

After they got to the restaurant, they spoke with Norma for a few minutes, and then Sarah went over the breakfast and lunch specials with her while Beau began prepping the napkins and silverware for the tables. It might not have been a job he had experience with, but it seemed he was a quick learner.

By the time the doors opened at six-thirty, Sarah was as ready for the day as she was likely to be. It had been a while since she'd last worked at the restaurant, but she knew that all the little details would come back to her once she got going.

The early breakfast crowd was made up of several familiar faces who greeted her cheerfully before giving her their orders. It was a nice way to ease back into the job. The next wave was made up of mainly strangers, though they were still polite as they placed their orders and even tipped decently.

Beau appeared to be keeping up with the rush fairly well. She noticed he didn't really talk to any of the diners, but then, that wasn't really his job, though Norma did encourage her staff to always be friendly.

It was one of the reasons that Leah had been moved from the front of the restaurant to the back. Her default mode was reserved, so engaging in friendly banter with strangers didn't come easily to her.

"Hey, you!"

Sarah turned toward the sound of the voice. A young man with a scowl on his face, who was seated with three other guys his age, motioned her over. "Hi. What can I do for you?"

He waved a hand at the plate in front of him. "You can take this back to the kitchen and bring me what I ordered."

She looked down at his half-eaten plate of food. "What appears to be the problem?"

"I ordered my eggs sunny-side up. *Not* scrambled."

It was interesting that the guy had managed to eat half the eggs before apparently recalling what he'd actually ordered. Or what he was saying he ordered. She knew from personal experience how particular people were about their eggs—how particular she was about *her* eggs—so she always double-checked a person's egg specifications. He had definitely ordered scrambled.

Though she wanted to argue with him, Norma had always told them not to do that. So instead, she pulled out her order pad and made a notation on it before turning it so the guy could see it. "I just want to make sure I've got it right this time. You know, so I don't bring you the wrong thing again."

She'd crossed out the word *scrambled* on the original order and written *sunny-side-up* next to it. The man's face flushed as he gave a short nod. His friends at the table were snickering and elbowing each other.

"Everything okay with your meals?" she asked them.

"Uh, yep. Mine's perfect, sweetheart," one of them said with a wink at her.

"So glad to hear it." Shifting her attention back to the other guy, she picked up his plate and said, "I'll be right back with your sunny-side up eggs."

She stopped by another table to let them know she'd be back to take their order shortly then made her way to the kitchen. Out of earshot of the people in the restaurant, Sarah approached the cook and said, "Got an *incorrect* order."

The cook glanced over at her and rolled his eyes. "Let me guess. They didn't like their eggs."

"Yep. After eating half of them."

The man muttered something under his breath, then said, "So what do I need to make?"

"Make 'em sunny side up this time."

"Will do."

Sarah returned to the dining room and took a couple more orders before going back to pick up the freshly cooked eggs along with the remainder of the customer's pancakes and bacon.

"Are these the same pancakes?" the guy asked with a scowl when she set the plate in front of him.

"I believe so. Your only complaint was about the eggs, so the cook returned the plate to the warmer while he replaced your eggs."

"Are you kidding me? I should have gotten a fresh meal for the inconvenience of your mistake."

Sarah only just managed to keep from crossing her arms, but she still lifted her eyebrows at his words and stared him down.

"Dude. Let it go," one of his friends said. "Just eat so we can leave."

"You're *so* not getting a tip after this," the guy muttered as Sarah walked away.

She didn't do the job for the tips, so she really didn't care if he didn't tip her. In fact, she really didn't want his money. Of course, the kid struck her as the sort of guy who'd be going online on his phone while he scarfed down his *not-scrambled* eggs to leave a scathing review on Yelp.

Thankfully, there were enough great reviews of her aunt's restaurant that one review by an idiot wouldn't hurt her reputation much. Unless, of course, he tried to rally support on Twitter with some doctored story about what had happened. She could only hope that his more level-headed friends could rein him in.

"Does that happen often?" Beau asked in a low voice when she made her way back to the kitchen with another order.

She gave a small shrug. "Not too often. Most people are nice."

"He was being a jerk." Beau's statement held a hard edge. "I heard him order scrambled eggs while I was clearing the table next to them."

"He did order scrambled eggs," she concurred. "But this way, he got a little extra food and tried to aggravate me in the process." She glanced up, and when she saw the expression on Beau's face, she smiled at him. "It's fine. I don't let things like that bother me too much. It's not worth letting them win."

"I wanted to say something."

Her smile grew at his statement. "It's just as well that you didn't. Norma prefers we don't make a big deal out of situations like that."

Beau scowled briefly before his expression smoothed out. "I get that."

Patting his arm, she said, "I do appreciate the sentiment, however."

That got another brief curve of his lips before he nodded back in the direction of the dining room. "Guess I'd better get back to it."

Sarah watched him go, a smile lingering on her face. It felt...good to have him indignant on her behalf. Aside from Eli, she'd never really had that before. It helped to soothe some of the irritation left by the ignorant fool and his friends.

Thankfully, the remainder of her shift went smoothly, and once the lunch rush was over, she and Beau left the restaurant. Beau had a bakery bag filled with a few of her aunt's fresh-baked muffins, while Sarah had a smaller bag with a chocolate muffin of her own and a strawberry muffin for Leah. She wouldn't eat hers on the ride home like she would have had she driven her own car because Beau's lovely car didn't need chocolate muffin crumbs all over it.

"I'm going to guess that guy hasn't worked in hospitality before," Beau said.

"Hmmm?" Sarah looked up from where she was checking her messages on her phone.

"That guy who was rude to you this morning."

"Oh, I'm sure that's true," Sarah said with a laugh, completely unable to imagine them waiting on anyone.

"I'm beginning to think it should be a requirement for every teen to work in some sort of service position as part of a class in high school."

Sarah shifted so she could face him more fully. "Really?"

"I've only had two shifts, but they have changed how I view workers in restaurants."

"Well, that's good. The problem is, it's more about a certain type of person as opposed to having a certain type of experience."

"What do you mean?"

"Let me ask you a couple of questions." Sarah waited until he nodded before continuing. "Would you have ever acted the way those guys did today?"

"Of course not." His indignant tone made her smile.

"And do you think you're a good tipper?"

He glanced at her before focusing back on the road. "I think so. I tip fifteen percent for decent service. Twenty for good service and more for exceptional."

"See! You were already doing all of that, and you wouldn't have behaved like those guys did even before you worked your first shift at the restaurant. You didn't need to work in hospitality in order to know not to behave that way. I kinda doubt they'd be any different even if they had worked a hundred shifts as servers or bussing tables." She gave a slight shudder. "They'd probably be the sort of person who would spit in your drink or your food."

Beau shot her a horrified look. "People *do* that?"

Sarah lifted her brows. "A certain type of person might."

"I'm not sure I ever want to eat in a restaurant again."

She had to wonder just how sheltered a life he'd led. Did he not read the internet at all? Had he not had some idiot friends as a teen? Even if the guys in her high school hadn't done anything like that, they'd sure talked about it.

"I think you can trust that most reputable restaurants won't have that problem. And if you treat your server well, even if you do get someone who *might* consider doing something gross, they likely won't."

"Likely..." Beau scoffed. "Your assurances are not quite so...reassuring."

Sarah shrugged with a laugh. "Oh well, I tried."

"I think I've learned the lesson I needed to during this short conversation today. I wonder what my grandfather will think when I report this to him."

"Are you required to report to him what you've learned?" Sarah asked, her curiosity getting the better of her.

Beau shrugged but didn't look her way. "I have no idea what he wants, honestly."

"You're a puzzle, Beau," Sarah said, then wondered if perhaps she shouldn't have.

"I've never been accused of that before. It's better than some things I've been accused of lately," he muttered.

Sarah suspected there was a story there and wondered if she dared ask what it was. Unfortunately—or maybe, fortunately—she didn't have the chance since he was pulling into a spot in front of the lodge.

"Thanks for the ride," Sarah said as they walked up the steps to the front door.

"You're welcome." He held the door for her, then followed her inside. "We can do it again tomorrow if you want."

"I'd like that. Thank you."

"I'll talk to you later," he said, then headed for the stairs.

Sarah watched him go then turned to find Leah leaning against the doorjamb leading into the kitchen, her arms crossed. "What?"

Leah stared at her for a moment before straightening up. "You crushing on him?"

As she brushed past her to go into the kitchen, Sarah rolled her eyes. "No. He was just nice enough to give me a ride."

Sarah dropped the bakery bag on the counter and moved toward the Keurig, feeling the need for another hit of caffeine with her muffin.

Snagging the bag, Leah settled on a stool at the counter where a mug of coffee already sat. She opened the bag and pulled out the strawberry muffin. "You two are not in each other's league. Just sayin'."

Frowning, Sarah turned to look at her sister. "What on earth does that even mean?"

CHAPTER SIX

Leah carefully peeled the wrapper from her muffin, spreading it out flat on the counter, like a plate. "Clearly, he's way out of our financial sphere."

"So is Anna," Sarah said as she focused back on her coffee. "And she and Eli are doing just fine."

"Yep, but Beau is on a whole other level. Like he's even above Anna and her parents, if Google is to be believed. He doesn't belong here."

Turning from her coffee once again, Sarah glared at her sister. "You googled Beau?"

"Sure," Leah said with a shrug. "We could have figured out about Anna, too, if we'd just done a little googling."

"We didn't need to know about Anna until she was ready to let us know."

Leah looked up, piercing Sarah with an all-too-familiar look. "This is different. Eli could take care of himself. You're my sister. My twin. I'm going to look into any guy who even has a passing chance of becoming important to you."

When she put it like that... Sarah tried to let her irritation go and pulled her own muffin from the bag. "Still, I don't think you should have looked into him like that. Plus, how could you know that he has a passing chance of becoming important to me?"

Leah gave her an exasperated look. "I have eyes."

"What's that supposed to mean?"

"It means," Leah began. "That every time he's in the room, you're looking at him."

"Well, of course I am. Have you looked at him yourself?" Sarah arched her brows. "He's gorgeous, and I'd love to paint him. But that *doesn't* mean I'm looking at him as anything more than that."

"You just keep telling yourself that," Leah murmured.

"Oh, I will," Sarah assured her. And she would because she knew falling for a guest whose life was far away from New Hope Falls was the height of foolishness.

"Do you want to know what else I found out about him?" Leah asked as she broke off a piece of her muffin then popped it into her mouth.

Sarah considered Leah's question for a split second then shook her head. "You're not actually telling me anything new when it comes to not being in his league. That's very apparent. And though I *am* curious about him, I know he's only here for a month. His life clearly isn't here, and I don't think he wants it to be. Not the way Anna did. So yeah, I might appreciate how he looks, but it's not going to lead to anything."

"For the record, he's not in your league either. When it comes to loving and sharing, you've got the biggest heart, and he's not anywhere near that. Not many of us are. Including me."

"You're wrong about that, Leelee. You have a big heart. You just choose to keep it hidden from most of the world." She paused then said, "And I don't think you can say that definitively about Beau. Google doesn't tell you stuff like that."

Leah just shrugged and continued to eat her muffin. Sarah was insanely curious now, but she wasn't going to follow her twin's actions and search about Beau on the internet. Anything she needed to know about him, she hoped she'd come to learn organically. As a...friend.

Plus, she had learned that a lot of what was on the internet was fake. So unless what Leah found had been posted directly by Beau, it was possible that it wasn't even true. And even then, not everything a person posted about themselves—especially on social media—was necessarily one hundred percent an accurate reflection of themselves or their lives.

So, all things considered, it would just be a waste of her time to read things about Beau that might not even be true.

"What are you two eating?" Their mom's question had them exchanging a guilty look. Normally she was at the church on Thursday afternoons. "Are those Norma's muffins?"

"Yes," they said in unison. Sarah gazed down at the small portion left of her muffin with regret.

"And you didn't bring me one?" her mom asked as she reached and took the remainders of each of their muffins and proceeded to eat them herself. "That will teach you."

"Wasn't my fault," Leah muttered. "Sarah was the one who bought them."

"Way to throw me under the bus."

"It wasn't like she couldn't figure that out for herself. You having gone to work there today and all."

"Enough fighting, girls," their mom said. "I came back because I forgot the books I'd promised to take for Ellie."

"We fell victim to your aging mind," Leah said with a smirk.

The three of them shared a laugh before her mom took a sip of Leah's coffee—she didn't like the way Sarah doctored hers—then picked up the books she'd forgotten on the counter and left again.

"What time do you need me here for dinner prep?" Sarah asked. "I think I need a little nap."

"We're having tortillas and taco salad, so there's not much to do. Just cutting up stuff. I guess four-thirty or so?"

"I'll be back," Sarah told her as she gathered up the trash and put it in the garbage can. She took a final sip of her coffee, then dumped out the rest and put the mug in the dishwasher.

As Sarah passed Leah on her way out of the kitchen, her sister grabbed her arm. "Guard your heart, sis. I know you say you're not thinking seriously about anything with Beau, but things can change quickly. Just know that Beau isn't in a position to be the person you might want him to be."

The intensity of Leah's expression matched her words and gave Sarah pause. Leah's admonition just reflected another way in which they were different. Leah knew of Sarah's propensity to lead with her heart. She'd had a lot of crushes over the years, while Leah, to her knowledge, hadn't.

Leah was very much not that way. Where Sarah wore her emotions on her sleeve, Leah kept hers tucked away, only letting them out for people that she knew beyond a shadow of a doubt she could trust. For years, that had only included their family. It was only recently that she extended that trust to Anna, who would also become part of the family in a few short months.

In high school, Sarah would fall so quickly for guys, only to be left heartbroken because they liked someone else or just wanted to be friends. She knew it was a weakness of hers, and for the most part, she'd outgrown it as she'd gotten older. There had been guys recently that she'd met that she hadn't crushed on.

Leah had cautioned her enough times in the past—often being proven right—that Sarah would never dismiss her words out of hand. There was never jealousy between them, so Leah's comments didn't stem from that. Leah had to have read something about Beau that was really bothering her.

"I'm not going to disregard what you're telling me," Sarah said. "But I'm not going to avoid him either. He seems like maybe he could use a friend or two."

"That's probably true," Leah said with a nod. "Just...you know...guard your heart."

"I will, sis." Sarah gave her a hug, not dragging it out too long because, even from her, hugs were something Leah barely tolerated.

Leah's words lingered in her mind as she made her way down to her room. And even as she curled up on her bed, they warred with the person she was beginning to get glimpses of during her interactions with Beau. Of course, Leah hadn't said he was a bad person, just that they came from very different places and that he couldn't be the person she might want him to be.

But he was Gregory Stevens' grandson, and Mr. Stevens was a kind Christian man. How bad could his grandson be?

~*~

Beau spent some time going through his email, responding to some of his clients who were wondering why he hadn't been the one contacting them in the past couple of days. As he replied to them, he was a bit surprised that his dad hadn't blocked his email as well as his access to the server. And if he'd sent any sort of email to Beau's clients explaining his absence, they didn't appear to have been satisfied with the explanation his father had given them.

Though Beau wished he could continue to work with his clients, it just wasn't possible without access to the server and his accounts. Instead, he tried to reassure them that they were in good hands with his team during his absence and that they could contact him with any concerns, and he'd address them.

Just before five, he left the lodge and headed for the personal care home. He wasn't sure what to expect of the evening, but he'd promised his grandfather he'd be there, so he would follow through on that commitment.

When he walked into the building a short time later, a woman at the desk gave him directions to the dining room. He found the room without any trouble and was pleasantly surprised by the setup. It was bigger than the room he'd previously met his grandfather in, and large windows along one wall gave it an even more spacious feel.

There were quite a few large round tables, each sporting white tablecloths and a small floral centerpiece. There were eight place settings at each table, so he'd have more than just his grandfather for company during the meal.

Glancing around the room, Beau spotted his grandfather sitting at a table next to the man he'd been with the first time they met. Also with them were three women, one in a wheelchair like his grandfather.

"Beau!" The older man greeted him with a smile. "So glad you made it."

Beau shook the man's hand as well as the others at the table as his grandfather introduced them. There was a note of pride in his voice that Beau wasn't sure he'd earned, but it was such a rare thing to hear directed at him, that it warmed him.

"This is your seat," his grandfather said, patting the chair beside him. "Hope you're ready for a nice pot roast dinner. It's what's on the menu for tonight."

Beau couldn't remember the last time he'd had the dish. "Sounds good."

After he'd settled into his seat, conversation resumed around the table. More people were coming into the room and finding seats at the tables around them.

"How has your time at *Norma's* been?" his grandfather asked.

"Interesting." Beau wasn't going to lie and say it had been good. Parts of it had been, but other parts...not so much. He figured they averaged out to *interesting.*

His grandfather chuckled. "I'm sure that's true."

"It has been eye-opening."

"Really? Like how?" The man's curious expression told Beau that this was what he wanted to hear about the most.

"Today, there was a table of guys, one of whom was being especially demanding of Sarah."

"Sarah McNamara?"

"Yes. She was covering for one of the servers who was away for a couple of days."

"I see." His grandfather tilted his head. "What happened?"

Beau recounted the details of what had transpired, frowning at the memory. "And I'm pretty sure he stiffed her on the tip too."

"Yeah, there are people like that in the world," his grandfather said with a nod. "How did Sarah handle it?"

"Better than I would have," Beau remarked. "She somehow managed to convey that she knew what the guy was up to without actually calling him out on it like I would have."

"Sarah's a real sweetheart. Leah is too, but I have a feeling she would have happily called the guy out."

A smile tugged at his lips as he thought of the twins. "Yep, and I wouldn't have blamed her. I guess in the end, Sarah's way was better for the restaurant and the other guests there."

He noticed several servers coming out from swinging doors, their hands full of trays holding plates of food. No one at their table started eating even after their plate was set in front of them.

"Shall we pray?" his grandfather asked. Then, after the people around the table had bowed their heads, he began to pray, much like Eli had done at the lodge.

That was something Beau was still trying to get used to since praying before meals—or at any time, if he were honest—wasn't something his family had ever done. He had to wonder if his grandfather had been this way when his mom had lived at home, and if so, why hadn't she prayed before meals with her family?

He knew with one hundred percent certainty that if he were ever to ask his mom what had happened to make her leave New Hope Falls and her family, she'd give him a look and ignore the question. Maybe his grandfather would be more willing to divulge that information to him.

As he ate the delicious food on his plate, Beau waited for his grandfather to ask him more questions about his time at the restaurant, but he never returned to the subject. Instead, he asked a bit about Rhett and Julianna.

"Do you have any other grandchildren?" Beau asked, wondering if he had cousins he'd never met.

"No. It's just the three of you."

The sadness on the man's face stabbed at Beau's heart. "So my mom was an only child?"

The man's sadness deepened even further. "I guess she never told you about her brother?"

Beau lowered his fork and stared at his grandfather. "She has a brother?"

"She did. He died just before she left town."

Words failed him beyond, "I'm sorry to hear that."

His grandfather nodded. "Maybe I'll share that story with you another time."

Beau was very curious now, but he wasn't about to push for information on a clearly emotional subject while they were surrounded by people. "Whenever you're ready."

The older man reached over and patted his arm. "Thank you, son."

Once they'd finished eating, their plates were cleared away, and dessert was brought out. Though the apple pie was good, it didn't come close to the desserts he'd had so far at the lodge. Still, it was a nice ending to their dinner.

Beau wasn't sure if his grandfather wanted him to hang around for long after the meal, but he was beginning to feel the effects of his early morning, plus he had another early one the next day. Thankfully, his grandfather let him know that he was free to go, clearly seeing the tiredness on his face.

"Thank you for spending time with me," his grandfather said as he guided his wheelchair toward the exit of the dining room. "Do you think you'll make it back tomorrow evening?"

"If you'd like me too, I will."

His grandfather smiled. "I would like that. Very much."

Beau felt an unfamiliar warmth spiral through him once again at the obvious joy the idea of time together brought his grandfather. His parents never made it seem like they were happy to spend time with him, Julianna, and Rhett. His mom insisted that they attend a family meal once or twice a month, but he had never felt that it had been because she actually wanted to spend time with them.

Although, maybe it had been. Beau had never *asked* her if she enjoyed spending time with him and his siblings, but her face never lit up the way his grandfather's had when he'd seen him. However, it could just have been the plastic surgery and the Botox that held her face in a calm expression all the time.

He hadn't thought much about it one way or the other until that moment. It obviously hadn't been a lack he'd felt over the years. How could you miss something you'd never had?

As he said goodbye and left the care home, however, Beau couldn't stop thinking about it. How different might things have been growing up if his parents had been more like his grandfather? Or even if they'd had their grandfather in their lives back then. It might explain a few things about his perceptions about relation-ships—both romantic and otherwise. However, Beau refused to make excuses for how he was now.

If there were areas he could better in his life as a result of meet-ing his grandfather, then he'd make the effort. Certainly his experiences at the restaurant were giving him plenty to think about, not to mention his conversations with Sarah—though he could have done without her revelation about what some servers might do to his food.

He knew these weren't the things his father had wanted him to contemplate during his banishment, but something told him these were more important things to think about.

Back at the lodge, Beau found the McNamaras gathered in the kitchen once again. He'd read articles in magazines that talked about how kitchens were the hub of a home. How improving them could help sell a home. He'd never thought about how true it might be because it certainly hadn't been the case in any of the houses he'd lived in.

However, seeing how people—himself included—tended to congregate in the kitchen at the lodge, he was beginning to understand the truth of that idea. Just one more revelation.

"Evening, Beau," Nadine said with a welcoming smile. "Would you like some dessert or coffee?"

"As much as I'd like dessert, I did have some apple pie at the home. I wouldn't turn down a cup of coffee, however."

"We had decaf with supper, and there's still some left, but if you'd prefer regular, we can do you a cup in the Keurig."

"Decaf is fine," Beau said.

Nadine set a mug on the counter in front of an empty stool. "Here you go. Cream or sugar?"

"Black is fine." After he sat down on the stool, Beau lifted the mug and took a sip.

Glancing around, he realized Sarah wasn't in the room with the others. He opened his mouth to ask where she was, but then snapped it closed, realizing that it was none of his business.

"Did you enjoy your dinner with Greg?" Nadine asked as she helped Anna and Leah put away food from their meal.

"I did. It's been interesting learning a bit more about my mom's side of the family."

"Your mom doesn't talk about her life here?"

"Not at all. I had no clue about my grandfather until last week. I'd always assumed her parents were dead just like my dad's. The few times I did ask about my grandparents, she refused to talk about them. It was like her life before my dad never even existed."

"I'm sure that's what she wishes," Nadine murmured with a nod.

"Did you know my mom?" Beau asked.

CHAPTER SEVEN

Nadine hesitated for a moment, glancing at Beau before turning her attention back to the food she was putting away. "Yes. We went to school together."

It dawned on Beau then that she might know more about his family's history. He considered asking about what had happened to his uncle, and if she knew what had driven his mom away from New Hope Falls and her family, but he decided he'd rather hear that story from his grandfather.

Movement near the kitchen door drew Beau's gaze. He thought it might be Sarah, but it was Eli with a large black dog at his side.

"Hey there, Beau," he said with a quick smile. "How're you doing?"

"I'm good. You?"

"Can't complain. Just going to head out for a walk with Anna before the sun sets."

"Who's your shadow?" Beau asked as he watched the dog approach Anna and nudge at her hand.

Anna and Nadine laughed while Eli grinned. "Well, that would be Shadow. As in, that's his name."

"Well, it's an apt name."

"He used to be strictly *my* shadow, but since Anna appeared on the scene, he's more likely to be wherever she is. Some nights he even stays in her cabin instead of at my place."

"You don't live together?" Beau asked. He'd assumed they did since they often arrived and left together.

"No," Eli said. "Anna lives in one of the cabins while I have a place further up the road. That's where we'll live once we're married."

Beau understood needing one's private space, although they seemed to actually enjoy being around each other in a way he and Tiffany never had. Or maybe it was just him that hadn't enjoyed being around her very much. Either way, he hadn't been able to fathom how he'd deal with her having the right to make demands on his time and energy whenever she wanted after they were married.

"How long until the wedding?" Beau asked.

"We've set a date for late September," Anna said. "I wanted an autumn wedding."

"Are you going to have enough time to get a dress?" Leah asked. "Don't they say it takes months to get a dress delivered once you've ordered it?"

Anna gave a sheepish smile. "I guess that's where having money and a bit of fame comes in handy. I've been in contact with a couple of smaller designers whose styles I liked on Instagram. They're meeting with me in New York when I go. I'm not looking for anything too fancy, so I think we'll be okay. I do plan to take you and Sarah shopping for bridesmaid dresses when I get back though."

Leah wrinkled her nose. "Please don't make us wear identical dresses. It's hard enough when we already look alike, but we stopped dressing the same when we were eight."

"I kept trying, to no avail," Nadine said with a shake of her head. "I think Sarah would have happily continued to dress alike, but you... Nope. I remember too many times when Sarah would turn up at breakfast in something too similar to what you'd chosen for the day. You'd make everyone late for school because you insisted on changing into something completely different."

"I'd say that you don't know what it's like, but you do, actually, which is why I could never figure out why you kept trying to dress us alike."

"I guess I didn't have a problem when my mom would dress Norma and me the same. We got lots of attention whenever she did that, and unlike you, both of us liked that."

"Yeah. I've never been one for attention. Sarah got enough of that gene for the both of us."

"Well, just so you know," Anna began, "You won't need to wear the same design or color. You'll have to agree on a dress length with Rebecca, but other than that, you can choose from different styles and the autumnal shades I've picked out."

"I'll just have to let Sarah pick hers first," Leah said. "Then I can make sure mine is as different as possible."

"Are you trying to not look like twins again, Leelee?"

This time when Beau turned, his gaze landed on Sarah. She was wearing an outfit similar to the one she'd worn that first morning. When her gaze met his, she gave him a warm smile.

"Not sure we're ever not going to look like twins, but at least we won't look so much alike."

"If you'd just chop all your hair off, no one would ever think we were twins," Sarah said as she tugged on Leah's braid.

"Not gonna happen."

"Well, if the wedding portion of this discussion is over, we'd better head out," Eli said as he held out his hand to Anna.

She quickly took it and allowed Eli to pull her close. "We'll see you guys tomorrow."

With that, they headed out of the kitchen with Shadow on their heels.

"Sorry I missed supper," Sarah said as she looped her arm around Nadine's waist and rested her head against her mom's shoulder.

"It's okay, sweetie. I know you got caught up in things." Nadine planted a kiss on her head. "I set aside some food for you."

"Thanks, Mama." Sarah straightened and walked to the fridge. She returned a minute later with a plate and a bowl in her hands. As she set them on the counter, she said, "Ready for another fun day at work tomorrow?"

Beau arched a brow at her. "I'm going to assume there's a bit of sarcasm in there somewhere."

Sarah's smile grew. "Just a bit. If those jerks are back for the second day in a row, I'm going to make Alex take their order."

"Alex? The cook?"

"Yep. I'll bet they won't pull that stunt with him."

Thinking of the burly man who ruled over the kitchen, Beau had to agree. "I think that's an excellent idea. I hope you plan to follow through with it."

"Not sure Aunt Norma would appreciate or approve of that plan." Sarah put the bowl into the microwave then removed the clear wrap from the plate.

Beau watched with some fascination a couple of minutes later as she dumped spoonfuls of meat—ground beef, by the look of it—from the bowl over the salad on the plate, then added some cheese before crunching up some tortilla chips on top of it. He couldn't decide if it looked delicious or not.

"Never had a taco salad before?" Sarah asked as she finished crunching up the chips.

"Can't say that I have," Beau confessed.

Sarah's eyes widened briefly. "Well, depending on what you ate instead of taco salads, I can't tell if you've missed out or not."

"Probably something French."

"Like French fries?"

A laugh escaped Beau before he could stop it. "Unfortunately not. French as in *escargot.*"

"Ew." Sarah slapped a hand over her mouth. "Oh, sorry, if they're your favorite food."

"They're not," Beau assured her.

"They're not that bad," Nadine said.

Sarah turned to look at her mom. "You've had them?"

"Sure." She shrugged. "Norma went through an experimental phase with her cooking. I was often her guinea pig."

"I can only imagine how well that dish would have gone over at the restaurant," Leah said.

Nadine shook her head. "Not well, if I recall."

"She actually served them?" Sarah asked.

"Back in the day, yep. But she quickly decided that sticking to food people around her actually wanted to eat would be the better way to go."

Leah snagged a chip from the bag on the counter before folding the top over and putting it in the cupboard. "I have no business or cooking degree, but I think I could have told her that before she'd actually put them on the menu."

Sarah brought her plate around to sit on the stool beside Beau's. "Well, I'll stick to my taco salad. Thank you very much."

"What did you have at the home tonight?" Nadine asked.

Beau tried to remember what his grandfather had called it. "Pot roast. It was very good. Apple pie for dessert."

"It took them awhile, but they've finally hired a good chef and competent kitchen staff. A few years ago, the food was dreadful. It was just not fair for the people living there to have to eat it."

As Nadine talked about the home, Sarah ate her meal. Beau half-expected her to pick at it, but she ate like she was hungry. The only other woman he'd seen eat that way was his sister Julianna, and that was only when his mom wasn't around to remind her to "eat like a lady." Julianna would always respond to her by saying she was "eating like a person." Tiffany, on the other hand, appeared to have listened to her mother because she never ate very heartily.

Sarah made her way through her meal, laughing and talking in between bites. Beau had shifted on his seat, angling himself more so he could see her. She reminded him a bit of Julianna, and at first, he wasn't sure why.

He hadn't spent a lot of time with his sister in recent years, but something about the way Sarah would smile and laugh reminded him of the rare moments when Julianna would show her delight in what was going on around her. As Beau thought about it, though, that was usually during the times their parents weren't around.

It was weird that he hadn't recognized those qualities in Julianna before. Maybe he just hadn't known what to look for. Or he hadn't cared enough to look for them.

Regret swirled through him at the thought.

He saw how Eli interacted with his sisters. How Sarah and Leah interacted with each other and their mom. There was a closeness there he wouldn't previously have even considered as something that was important, but he was starting to feel differently now.

Every day, it felt like his eyes were being opened. Things were being revealed to him that he'd never taken the time to think about in the past. His father had drilled into him from a very young age that he was the future leader of the company. He'd dangled it like a carrot, something for Beau to keep working toward. However, the man wasn't giving him any opportunities to lead during the learning process.

Beau knew that the lodge and the cabins—as well as the restaurant—were family businesses, and even though they were smaller than his family's company, he saw the pride and joy they all had in working there. Working together. Supporting each other. Like the way Sarah had stepped in when there was a need at the restaurant. Each of them was valued, regardless of their role.

"Thank you, Mama," Sarah said when Nadine whisked away her plate once she had finished eating.

"You're welcome, and now you need to get yourself off to bed."

"Yep. I'm exhausted. I was supposed to nap this afternoon, but I got distracted."

Nadine shook her head. "Well, just one more day at the restaurant, and then you'll be free to focus on your painting once more."

"Do you want a ride again tomorrow?" Beau asked, a bit surprised to find out how much he hoped she'd say yes.

Sarah smiled at him, and he found himself captured by it once again. "Sure. That would be nice. Then I can concentrate on waking up."

After they agreed to meet at the same time as that morning, Beau left the kitchen. He itched to log into the work server, but with no way to do that, he settled for checking his email. As each day went by that he couldn't access his accounts, he became more and more agitated. No doubt his father had known that was how it would be for Beau. It was becoming clear that his dad's plan was to aggravate Beau into submission.

There weren't any business emails in his inbox, which should have made him feel good—his team was obviously handling the issues he'd forwarded to them the night before—but now he wondered if his father was somehow diverting his email. With a sigh, he sat back and stared at his laptop screen.

Though he trusted his team, he was their leader. Working without his supervision for a day or two was okay, maybe even a week. But a month? A lot could go wrong in a month. Or had his father transferred his accounts to other team leaders?

Maybe in addition to a change in the trust fund release, his punishment was going to be that he lost all his accounts and had to start at the bottom again if he didn't fall in line and get things back on track with Tiffany. Beau had clearly underestimated his father's desire to be well-connected to a prominent politician. It made him wonder what lengths the man would go to in order to make sure Beau did what he wanted.

Beau reached out and slowly closed the lid of his laptop. Maybe the real question was...what was he willing to do to gain the future he had been planning for so long?

CHAPTER EIGHT

Even though she was running a little late, Sarah still beat Beau to the kitchen the next morning and had two cups of coffee ready when he finally walked in. He stopped when he saw her, his brows rising slightly when she lifted one of the mugs. "Coffee?"

"Yes. Please." He walked over and took it from her then sat down at the island. "Thank you."

"Bagel?" She wasn't sure when she'd decided that the morning was all about single word communication. But thanks to the tiredness she hadn't been able to shake in the hour since her alarm went, it felt like all she could manage.

He glanced at his watch, his brows drawing together. "Do we have time for that?"

"Not really." Yay. Two words. Already her day was improving. Probably the caffeine was finally kicking in.

"Then I guess there are no bagels for us this morning."

It kind of sounded like that was a horrible thing, and Sarah wasn't about to disagree with him. She kind of felt the same way. "Might have to hold out for muffins on our coffee break."

Yay. More words. Things were definitely looking up.

"At least the muffins are something to look forward to," Beau murmured before he took a sip of his coffee.

Sarah focused on him, noticing that he had more pronounced circles beneath his eyes, and there was a tightness around his mouth. She wasn't feeling great because she was just tired. It looked like Beau had other things weighing on him.

They were quiet as they finished their coffee, Beau letting out a sigh as he checked his watch again. He hadn't shown himself to be a chatty person so far, but usually, he at least felt present. With Leah's warning still circling around in her mind, she gave him the space he seemed to need, not pushing for conversation.

She didn't know anything about him and even less about what might be weighing on his mind. Plus, it wasn't her place to ask him about it. They were acquaintances. Nothing more.

Once in the car, Beau turned on an easy listening radio station, so at least there wasn't just dead air as he drove them into town. She spent the time checking to see what—if anything—had transpired in the world while they slept, humming along to the music as she did.

He finally spoke as they walked toward the restaurant. "Here's hoping you have no frat boy jerks at any of your tables."

"Yeah. It'll be busy today, most likely, but hopefully, all my customers will be friendly. Is today your last day working at the restaurant?"

"Yes." He reached out and opened the employee entrance door, holding it for her. "That's what Norma told me when I showed up the other day."

"Well, I'm sure she's grateful for your help."

"Not sure how much help I've really been, but I appreciate the experience," Beau said as he followed her into the staff room.

The day ended up being as busy as Sarah had assumed it would be. There was a steady stream of diners from the time the doors opened until early afternoon, without the usual lull between breakfast and lunch, though they still did get a break to grab a muffin and another coffee.

"Hi, Sarah."

Sarah looked up from her notepad to see a familiar face. "Jillian? Oh my word! It's so great to see you." She quickly embraced the woman then pulled back. "Are you just back for a visit?"

Jillian gave her a small smile. "Not really. My grandmother left me her house when she died."

"I didn't realize she'd passed away," Sarah said with a frown. "Was that recently?"

"Yeah. She came to live with me in Portland last year, but then she got sick. She died in February."

"I'm so sorry to hear that."

As she looked at the woman who had been the captain of their cheerleading squad in high school, Sarah found it hard to believe that she was the same person. As a teen, Jillian had been energetic and boisterous, always hyping people up. She'd been a natural for the position of captain on their team.

It wasn't just the personality change that surprised Sarah. Jillian had always been very fit, but now her figure had definitely filled out. She'd always been a big fan of exercise and had definitely been focused on her appearance. Even though she'd always been a sweetheart, Jillian's obsession with her appearance had, at times, been annoying to Sarah as a teen.

"How are you doing with her passing?" Sarah asked, remembering how difficult it had been when she'd lost her own grandmother.

A sad smile momentarily lifted the corners of her lips. "I'm alright. I had the time to say goodbye, and she helped me prepare for the moment. Not that it made her death any easier, but I'm at peace with it."

"So are you back to pack up her house?" Sarah asked.

"No. Actually, I've decided to move back. I have a job at the elementary school starting in the fall."

"That's wonderful. We'll have to get together."

Jillian smiled again, not so sad this time. "I'd like that."

"Give me your phone number, so I can call you and arrange something." She rattled off her number, and Sarah jotted it down on her notepad. "Thank you. I'll give you a call."

"I look forward to it."

"Were you coming in for a meal or to get takeout?"

"Just takeout," Jillian said.

"Did you give your order yet?" When she shook her head, Sarah said, "I can take it for you if you'd like."

"You still working here?" Jillian asked.

"Nah. I'm just filling in for Missy while she and her husband are off celebrating their anniversary. I help out at the lodge—still live there too—and I also do some art stuff."

"Nice. You were always so talented with the artsy stuff."

Sarah handed Jillian a menu. "I enjoy it, so I'm glad I can make some money at it now."

"What do you recommend?" Jillian asked as she looked over the menu.

"My personal favorite is today's soup of the day, which is a creamy cheddar bacon, and I usually get it with a sandwich or a salad, depending on my mood. If you want something a bit more substantial, the roast beef dinner is also a fav."

"Hmmm." Jillian looked up from the menu. "I think I'll go with the soup and a grilled cheese sandwich. And an order of fries."

"Oh, that sounds yummy. I love the fries here."

"I remember. They were delicious."

Sarah wasn't sure how she remembered that since she never ordered any for herself. She'd always just snagged a couple from whoever in their group had gotten an order. Still, Sarah hadn't judged her for her choices then, and she wouldn't now, either.

"I'll get your order in."

"Is it okay if I just sit here at the counter?"

"Yep. Shouldn't be too long."

"Thanks, Sarah."

"You're very welcome." Sarah gave her a smile. "I'm just so glad to see you again."

As she walked into the kitchen to hand over the order, Sarah mulled over the changes in her friend. She knew people changed, but it seemed that the changes she was observing in Jillian were significant. Was it all on account of grief over her grandmother's death? It was possible, since she knew that Jillian's grandmother had basically raised her after her mom had taken off. She'd never talked about her dad, so Sarah wasn't sure where he was or if he was even in her life.

She delivered a couple of trays of food to tables, then came back to the kitchen with another order. When Jillian's food was done and packaged, she took it back out to her. On her way, she passed Beau pushing a cart of dirty dishes.

"Ready to go in about fifteen?" she asked.

At his nod, she smiled and slipped behind the counter. She sat the bag containing the food in front of Jillian. "Here you go. Want some treats to go with it?"

Jillian's gaze slid to the cabinet that contained all the sweets the restaurant sold. "Maybe a couple muffins and some cookies."

"Do I get to choose my favorites, or do you want to pick?"

"I'll let you pick the muffins, but I'd like six chocolate chip cookies."

"Perfect." Sarah moved to the case and quickly picked out a couple muffins and a half dozen chocolate chip cookies. "Here you go."

"Thanks so much, Sarah." Jillian got up from her seat and picked up both the food bag and the small bakery bag.

After promising to call her, Sarah said goodbye and turned her attention to finishing up her orders for the day. When the server taking over for the afternoon and evening shift arrived, Sarah had a quick conversation with her, then said goodbye to her aunt before going to find Beau.

"I just want to have a word with Norma," he said. "I'll be right back."

Sarah nodded then dropped down on the small couch in the staff room. She leaned her head back and stretched her legs out, rotating her ankles. The classes she'd attended at Cara's had definitely helped with her flexibility and core strength, but being on her feet for a whole shift was murder. She didn't know how Missy did it five days a week.

Though her painting also required her to be on her feet, she could sit down whenever she wanted. Plus, she was usually so engrossed in her work that she didn't notice how her feet felt.

"You fall asleep?"

Sarah lifted her head and stared at Beau. "Not quite."

With a sigh, she got to her feet and followed him from the restaurant. As she slid into the passenger seat of his car, he handed her a bag. "Your aunt said you forgot these."

When he slid behind the wheel of the car after closing her door, she said, "Oh, boy. I would have had to drive back in if I'd shown up at home empty-handed. My brain has officially checked out."

"She gave me a bag too. I assume it's muffins."

"I don't know what she gave you, but she definitely gave *me* muffins. Strawberry for Leah. Chocolate for me. Blueberry for Mama."

"Nothing for Eli and Anna?"

"No. Not sure why. Maybe she assumes that they're dieting for the wedding." Sarah laughed as soon as she said the words. "Not that that's very likely."

"Oh? Why's that?"

"They each seem to feel that the other is perfect the way they are," Sarah said. "And Anna is gorgeous regardless. It's us bridesmaids who should probably be dieting. Or at least me."

"Are you planning to?"

Sarah turned to look at him, wondering if he was really curious about her eating habits. "No. Probably not. I don't see the sense in starving myself to fit into a certain dress size. For the most part—barring muffins and ice cream—I eat pretty well, and I try to exercise regularly. Okay, maybe semi-regularly. But depriving myself of foods I enjoy just makes me angry, and nobody likes a cranky Sarah."

"After having tasted some of your mom and Leah's cooking, it would take iron-clad willpower for me to be able to resist their food."

"Right? I just don't have it, and I don't really care." Sarah sighed, thinking again of Jillian.

She was going to have to say something to Cece, one of her good friends, to warn her ahead of any meetup that Jillian had gained weight. The last thing she wanted was for Cece to blurt out something about it. Tact wasn't Cecelia's strongest suit, and sad to say, Cece would probably be happy to see that Jillian had put on quite a few pounds. They'd had a rivalry of sorts in high school, both of them far too caught up in how they looked and what the boys thought of them.

She couldn't say for sure that Jillian didn't seem as caught up with that now, but Cece certainly still was. Her friend would probably view Jillian as competition once again, but then CeCe sort of viewed every woman around her age as competition, convinced that the reason guys liked someone else instead of her was because of how she looked.

It hadn't helped when Eli had chosen—after years of not dating at all—to date someone who looked the way Anna did. Cece couldn't seem to understand that some people just connected, and others didn't. Those connections didn't always come down to appearance.

She glanced over at Beau, wondering if he had a girlfriend, and if so, what she was like. Leah hadn't come out and said that he did, but that could be one of the reasons she was warning her off him. But if that was the case, why hadn't she just come out and said that?

"Are you glad to be done at the restaurant?" Sarah asked.

"I suppose. Like I said this morning, I've appreciated the experience, but I'm relieved to not have to work there long-term. I'm not sure I was very good at it, which hurts my pride to admit, since it was essentially clearing and cleaning tables. You'd think anyone could do that. But considering it's probably the first time in my life I've ever cleared a table, I struggled to do it quickly and well."

"You've...what?" Sarah shook her head. "You've never cleared a table before?"

"I've never had to. That French chef we had? He came with a full complement of kitchen staff whose job it was to serve and clean. My mom believed that if we could hire someone to do tasks like those, it freed us up to do what we were supposed to be doing."

"Huh." Sarah considered his words. She supposed that made a certain amount of sense. If she had the money, she'd certainly pay someone to cook and clean for her if it meant she had more time for painting. Not everyone had that luxury, unfortunately.

"Yes, I am becoming more aware of the fact that not everyone lives like that."

"You seriously thought everyone lived like that?" Sarah wondered just what kind of bubble he'd been living in.

"Well, no, I suppose not." He hesitated then said, "I didn't think much about it at all, to be honest."

Sarah wanted to judge him for that, but she also knew that it wasn't that unusual for people to not think beyond their own circumstances to how others might be living. She was probably guilty of that to some extent too. She wouldn't have a clue how a single mom or someone struggling to make ends meet might live in a way that was different from her.

At least Beau seemed to feel bad for having lived in ignorance. She wouldn't hold his ignorance against him since he seemed to be willing to learn.

"Are you working somewhere else next week?" Sarah asked.

"No clue. I've been kind of scared to ask my grandfather what's next. I didn't expect this, so who knows what he might have lined up for me."

"There isn't too much stuff that's scary here in New Hope, but then again, I don't know all the jobs that are available."

"Part of me thinks he's trying to give me the youth experience I apparently missed out on."

"He did start you off with something I did in my teens," Sarah observed.

"Where else did you work? Just to give me a head's up."

"Just the restaurant and the lodge. I did some babysitting too."

"Well, I certainly hope my grandfather doesn't expect me to do that. I refuse to be responsible for the lives of little ones."

Sarah laughed at the slightly panicked tone in Beau's voice, grateful that whatever had him quiet earlier that morning had eased its grip on him. "I doubt you'll be called on to babysit."

"That's a relief."

"Maybe your grandfather will tell you tonight."

"Or he might keep me in suspense," Beau grumbled.

"The wait won't kill you."

Beau looked her way briefly, a brow arched. "Are you sure?"

"If children around the world haven't dropped dead by Christmas morning from the suspense of waiting to open their presents, I think you'll be fine."

"I suppose you're right," he conceded with a nod. "But I still hope he tells me sooner rather than later, so I have time to prepare myself."

When he came to a stop in front of the lodge, Sarah gathered up her things then walked inside with him. "Thanks for the ride once again."

"Anytime."

That single word did something to Sarah. Maybe it was just an automatic response, but a part of her hoped it wasn't. Another part—whose voice sounded suspiciously like Leah's—told her she needed to let go of that hope stuff.

Beau headed for the stairs while Sarah went to check and see if anyone was in the kitchen. The smell of food told her dinner prep was underway, but the kitchen was empty. She put her mom's muffin in the large cookie jar then headed downstairs.

She went to Leah's door and knocked.

"Come in."

"I come bearing gifts," Sarah said as she walked into Leah's room.

Unlike her, Leah was neat, so her room was tidy with the bed made and all her clothes put away. Knowing how much it would bug her, Sarah crossed the room and dropped down on the bed, giving a couple of good bounces to mess up the bedspread before she lifted her feet to cross her legs.

Leah got up from the bench in front of her digital keyboard and turned to face her. "If you didn't bring me a muffin, you can just take yourself off my nicely made bed."

Sarah lifted the bag and wiggled it at her. "I have it."

Leah took the bag and pulled out her strawberry muffin then sat on the bed beside Sarah. "How was work?"

As they ate, she shared about seeing Jillian again and what she'd said about sticking around. "Wanna come with when I set something up with her?"

"I don't know," Leah said with a shrug. "She was never my favorite person."

"No one in high school was ever your favorite person," Sarah said with a laugh.

"Except for you."

"Sometimes not even me," she reminded her. "I'm not sure you ever forgave me for trying out and then making the cheerleading squad."

"True." Leah sighed. "If you think Jillian is different now, I might hang out with you, though you know that Cecelia gets on my last nerve."

"I know." Sarah ate the last bite of her muffin then got up. "I'm going to go take a nap."

"For real this time?" Leah asked, a skeptical look on her face.

"For real. I won't even go into my studio. I'm pooped."

When she got to her room, she kept her word, and as soon as she changed out of her work clothes into something more comfortable, she climbed into bed. She could paint after dinner. She'd told Cece she wouldn't be available to meet up with her like they sometimes did on Friday nights since she'd lost a chunk of painting time helping out at the restaurant.

She set her alarm to make sure she didn't sleep through supper, then tugged her comforter up over her shoulders. And if thoughts of her time with Beau played against the backdrop of her usual painting colors and made her smile, she was too tired to rebuke herself for it.

CHAPTER NINE

Beau kept his gaze on the front of the room, but his ears were tuned to the conversations going on around him. When was the last time he'd been inside a church? It had to have been for a wedding at some point. For sure, it had never been for an actual service that wasn't related to either Christmas or Easter.

He shifted on the chair next to his grandfather, feeling more than a little uncomfortable. He didn't belong there, that much he knew. All around them, people were greeting each other with a familiarity that spoke of more than just casual acquaintances. There were inquiries into people's health and situations. Words of encouragement. Assurances of prayer. Phrases and terms that were foreign to him.

Several people approached them and asked his grandfather how he was doing. Beau smiled and shook hands as he was introduced to each one. Each smile given to him was warm and friendly, though edged in curiosity. Sarah and her family were there, seated near the front, so it wasn't as if he didn't know anyone there, but it still wasn't enough to dispel the discomfort.

The feeling of not belonging didn't disappear when the service started, even though the person standing at the front welcomed everyone to the service. Again, it was a welcome that appeared genuine and friendly, but it didn't put Beau at ease. He was struggling enough as it was with the unexpected situations his grandfather was putting him in, having to deal with yet another one almost felt like too much.

He felt like everyone was looking at him, well aware that this wasn't a place he should be. Not to mention being so unaware of what he should be doing throughout the service. He stood when the others did, though his grandfather remained seated in his wheelchair. The songs were unfamiliar to him, and even though the words were projected onto a screen, he didn't make any attempt to sing along.

By the time an older gentleman got up and took his place behind the podium, Beau had decided he'd rather bus tables at the restaurant for another week or even babysit than to stay in that place another minute longer. Nothing about the progression of the service had put him at ease, and he doubted that would change with whatever came next.

"Good morning," the man said, a smile creasing his face. The audience responded with a *good morning* of their own. "For those of you visiting today, I'm Pastor Evans, and you're very welcome here."

There it was again...the welcome that did nothing to alleviate Beau's unease about being in the church. He let out a quick breath, then did his best to sit perfectly still. He tried to tune out the pastor, but for some reason, his thoughts kept focusing in on what the man was saying.

Though he'd always had a moral code for himself, he didn't tend to label things sin or not sin. Sure, there were things that were legal and illegal, but sin? He waited for the pastor to start lecturing about *us vs. them.* That those within the church were free of sin—even when they weren't—while those outside the church were sinners.

Strangely enough, however, the man seemed to be focusing on those within the church as he spoke on sin. That intrigued Beau more than just a little, and by the time the pastor drew his sermon to a close, he'd given up any attempt to tune the man out. And the man's words lingered with him as he and his grandfather went for lunch at *Norma's.*

He didn't say anything about the service, and his grandfather didn't bring it up either. Instead, he asked again about Beau's week.

"So tell me honestly. How was it working here?"

"Once I got used to it, it wasn't so bad. I broke a few dishes, but when I offered to pay to replace them, Norma just waved me off."

His grandfather laughed. "I'm sure she's had more than a few broken plates over the years. She probably works that into her budget."

"That would be a wise decision if she gets too many bussers like me."

"Well, I have another job lined up for you for next week."

Beau gave him a wary look as he lifted his mug to take another sip of his coffee. They'd each gotten a piece of Norma's berry pie for dessert, which had been amazing.

"Stanley Overmeier is an old friend of mine, and he owns the local grocery store. He's agreed to let you come work alongside a couple of his employees for the week."

"What will I be doing?"

"I would imagine he'll have you stocking shelves. Maybe bagging some groceries."

Beau had never bought groceries, let alone bagged them. His chef was very particular about the ingredients he used, so there was no way he'd trust Beau with his list. If Beau had wanted something specific to eat, he just asked his chef to make it, and he bought the ingredients and made it.

The revelations he'd had lately about not having done some of the things his grandfather wanted him to do made him feel as if he was lazy. But realistically, he knew that wasn't true. While in high school, he might not have had a job, but he'd certainly worked hard to get the best grades he could, and the same had been true for university.

He hadn't been one to go out and party, getting drunk and sleeping with a bunch of different girls. His father had had certain expectations of him, ones that didn't fall in line with a partying lifestyle.

"I think I saw the grocery store when I was wandering Main Street last week."

"Yep, most likely. He's got the only grocery store in town. There are others not too far away in the larger cities, but I like to support local businesses." He hesitated, his brows drawing together in a frown. "Not that I'm buying groceries these days."

"It's still a good sentiment," Beau said.

"Yes." His grandfather nodded. "It's one your grandmother and I subscribed to from the time we moved here just after we got married."

Beau wanted to know what had happened to his wife, the grandmother he'd never have the opportunity to meet, but he didn't ask.

"How are you finding it at the lodge?" he asked, clearly ready to move on from memories of the woman he'd loved.

"It's been good," Beau said.

When he'd first gotten there, he had never imagined he'd be so involved in the owners' lives. And it wasn't just Sarah. He'd had a good talk with Eli the day before about his business, and he'd even offered to give him some financial tips on how to best utilize his income, balancing it between current needs and planning for the future.

"The McNamaras are great people."

"Nadine said she knew Mom in high school."

A thoughtful look passed over his grandfather's face. "I suppose that's true." Then sadness once again took hold of his expression. "It's been so long since I last saw your mom that in my mind, she's still a teenager. I can't imagine her the age Nadine is now."

"Well, if it's any conciliation, Mom has fought hard against the aging process. I dare say she doesn't look the age that some of her peers might." Beau pulled out his phone then scanned through his photos, pausing when he got to one that was about six months old. "Mom has us do a family photo every Christmas. This was last year's."

He handed the phone to his grandfather then watched as the man bent his head to peer more closely at it. When he looked up, he said, "Julianna looks very much like how I remember your mom when she was younger."

"She and my mom have a bit of a contentious relationship," Beau confessed. "While my dad had high standards for me, my mom has similar ones for Julianna, except they didn't revolve around business like my dad's. No, she wants Juli to be the perfect society princess, doing all she can to capture the man who can afford to keep her in the style in which she's been raised...or better."

"And your sister doesn't want that?"

"I'm not entirely sure what she *does* want, but from the arguments I've heard between her and our mom, I know it's not *that*."

His grandfather sighed. "It's hard for parents not to put the weight of their expectations and even their hopes and dreams on their children. I don't pretend to understand a lot of the choices your mom has made, but I've learned the hard way that sometimes all you can do is love your child and pray that they'll make the right choices in life."

"And if they don't?" Beau asked.

"You love them anyway, and still pray for them, that God will guide them through the consequences that might come because of their decisions."

"You still love my mom? Even after the way she's treated you?"

A soft smile deepened the creases in his grandfather's face. "Yes. Until the day I die, I will love her. Just like I will love you and your siblings."

Beau felt his heart expand at his words. Love wasn't something that was mentioned in their family. He wasn't even convinced his parents loved each other. There was certainly no affection between them that Beau had ever seen, which was probably why his dad was so eager for him to make an advantageous match rather than one based on love.

And maybe Tiffany had wanted a love match rather than an arranged one, but even if she had, it wasn't something he'd been able to give her. He just hadn't felt that way about her, and he wasn't sure he ever would have.

They didn't linger too long over lunch as his grandfather needed to be back at a certain time for his medications, plus he said he was ready for his Sunday afternoon nap. After dropping him off, Beau headed back to the lodge.

He wasn't sure what to do with his afternoon, but he didn't think he'd be taking a nap. For the most part, he wasn't used to downtime. Any time he wasn't at the office, he was usually at home working or at the gym with his trainer.

The lodge was quiet when he walked inside a short time later. When he found himself glancing into the living room, dining room, and kitchen, Beau realized that he was looking to see if Sarah was around. That realization brought him up short, and he immediately turned toward the stairs and climbed to the second floor.

Once in his room, he pulled out his phone and sank down onto the small couch near the window. He turned his phone over and over in his hands, wishing, for the first time in his adult life, that he had a best friend he could talk to. Someone who already knew him so well that he wouldn't have to explain the things that were weighing on his mind since his banishment from Houston.

But he didn't have that. He hadn't ever made time for that. So he was without his work and his home, feeling adrift and unplugged in a way he never had before. What was he supposed to do with himself?

A knock on the door had him lifting his head. With a sigh, he pushed to his feet and went to open it. He was a bit surprised to see Sarah standing in the hallway. A smile lit her face when she saw him.

"Hey!" she said with an enthusiasm he was beginning to expect from her. "You busy?"

"Not particularly, no. Why?"

"A group of us are planning to go for a hike, and I wondered if you'd like to join us."

"A hike?"

"Yeah, there are some trails that run behind Eli's cabin, and we like to head out on Sunday afternoons when the weather's nice."

Given the way the afternoon and evening had been stretching out with nothing to distract him, Beau figured a hike might be a good way to fill some of that time, plus get some exercise. "What do I need to wear? I didn't exactly bring hiking gear."

"We're not going on an intensive hike—I leave those to Eli—so you'd be okay with runners, as long as you don't mind them getting a little dirty. And then just some jeans and a T-shirt. Eli can loan you a windbreaker if you don't have one. Sometimes it gets a bit cool in the shade of the trees, plus you never know when we'll get a little rain."

Beau arched a brow at her. "Are you trying to dissuade me from joining you?"

"Oh, come on," she said with a cheeky little grin. "You're not made of sugar—sweet as you might be—so a little rain won't hurt you."

She thought he was sweet? "Well, when you put it that way..."

"Excellent! We're going to meet up at Eli's place in about thirty minutes, so if you want to be downstairs in twenty minutes, we'll have plenty of time to get up there. Is that enough time?"

"Yep, that should be plenty."

"See you in a few." She gave a little wave then disappeared down the hallway.

He shut the door then went to the dresser to pull out a pair of jeans and a T-shirt. He was glad he'd packed some casual clothes and stuck in a couple pairs of runners. They weren't exactly cheap, but he didn't care a whole lot about that. They were comfortable, and that was probably a big plus when hiking.

When he got downstairs, Sarah was there along with another young woman, but there was no sign of Leah. Sarah had a backpack on and turned with a smile as he approached them.

"Beau, this is my friend, Cecelia. Cece, this is Beau. He's staying here at the lodge for the month."

The gleam of interest in Cecelia's eyes was something he'd gotten used to seeing over the years, but like with Tiffany, this woman didn't draw him in. She also looked vaguely familiar, and he realized he'd seen her in the diner a time or two. He hadn't known, of course, that she was a friend of Sarah's.

"It's nice to meet you." Beau held out his hand and gave hers a quick shake before letting it go.

"It's very nice to meet you too," Cecelia said with a smile that could only be described as coy.

"Let's head up to Eli's," Sarah said. "The others are meeting us up there."

"Let me take that for you," Beau said, touching the strap of the backpack.

"I'm okay," she assured him.

"I know you are, but let me carry it for you," he said again. "Please."

"Well, when you ask so nicely." She gave a laugh and slid the straps off and handed it to him.

Their fingers brushed as he took it, then she helped him arrange it on his shoulders. Once it was secure, Sarah led the way out of the lodge. Cecelia fell into step on one side while Sarah was on his other. Beau hadn't ventured beyond the lodge in his time there yet, so he looked around curiously as they headed to the right of the lodge.

"That's Anna's cabin," Sarah said as they passed one that had an expensive car parked in front of it. "She's staying there until after the wedding, then moving into Eli's cabin."

"How did she and Eli meet?" Beau asked. "I'm assuming she's not from around here."

"No, she's not," Sarah said. "She came here last year to get away from LA for awhile, and then she fell in love with Eli and New Hope and decided to stay."

Since Cecelia was on that side of him, Beau saw the scowl she directed at the cabin.

"She's fit in amazingly well here at the lodge," Sarah added. "She's jumped right in to help out, which has been great."

They continued on past the last of the cabins, following a curve in the narrow road that gained a bit of an incline the further they walked. When they turned another slight bend, a medium-size cabin came into view. It was two-stories with a log exterior. There were three vehicles parked in front of it, and several people stood on the wide porch talking.

"Hey there, Beau," Eli said with a smile. "Glad you could make it."

"Thanks for the invite."

"Anytime." He gestured to the group of people. "Let me introduce you. I'll do first names only, so it's not too confusing."

"I appreciate that," Beau said.

"This is Andy. He works at the bookstore in town."

Beau shook his hand. "I think I met you when I was in there earlier this week."

Andy nodded. "Yep. That was me."

Eli slapped the man standing next to him—a tall, muscled guy—on the shoulder. "This is Carter. He's a firefighter, and he's the strong silent type, so don't worry if he doesn't talk much to you."

The guy shook his hand, but aside from a slight smile and a nod, he didn't say anything.

"And this is Cara. She owns the dance studio," he said, motioning to the slender woman standing next to Anna. "Her guy is the chief of police, but he's tied up with something this afternoon so he couldn't be here. And it looks like you've met Cece."

Beau shook Cara's hand then said, "Yes. We met at the lodge."

"So, are we all ready to head out?" Eli asked.

When everyone agreed, he handed Beau a light jacket. "Sarah mentioned you might not have one."

"No. I didn't think to bring one when I left Houston." Beau tucked it under the strap of the backpack.

As they headed around the cabin, Shadow came bounding out of the trees without any prompting to fall into step beside Anna. As they approached the trail, their group thinned out into pairs to fit on the path.

Eli and Carter went first, followed by Anna, Shadow, and Andy. Beau followed them, expecting—hoping—that Sarah would walk with him, but he wasn't too surprised that it was Cecelia who took the spot. Sarah fell into step behind him with Cara.

"So, where are you from?" Cecelia asked as they walked along the path.

In all honesty, Beau had no interest in talking about all that. It was a beautiful day, the leaves rustling above them, casting dappled shadows on them as they walked. Still, he wasn't rude, so he said, "I live in Houston."

"Really? I've heard it's a lovely city. Do you like it there?"

"Sure. It's where I've lived except for my college years."

"Where did you go to college?"

Beau hesitated, feeling as if he was being forced to share parts of himself that he didn't want to. Even Sarah had respected his privacy and hadn't bombarded him with countless questions about himself. And right at that moment, he wished he was sharing these pieces of himself with Sarah instead of with Cece.

"Harvard."

"Wow. That's impressive."

Beau heard the admiration in Cecelia's voice, but it didn't stroke his ego. He didn't want to have her admire things about him that had nothing to do with who he really was. What she couldn't know about all that Beau shared with her, was that very little of it had been because of his own decisions. Going to Harvard. Staying in Houston. Working at his father's company. None of it had really been his choice. He'd just acquiesced to his father's wishes because he'd hoped that would be the fastest route to his trust fund.

"It must be quite an adjustment coming here to New Hope," she said.

"It is different, but not in a bad way. I've enjoyed being here."

"You probably wouldn't feel that way if you'd been born and raised here. Never able to escape from it."

Frustration was clear in her voice, and he had to wonder if she saw him as someone she wanted to date, or a potential ticket out of small-town USA to the bright lights of the big city. Beau found he wasn't interested in being either, so even though it felt mildly rude, he didn't respond with questions about her.

Apparently, that didn't matter because Cecelia began to share about herself, clearly ignorant of his disinterest. If he couldn't have walked with Sarah, he would have rather been paired with Andy or even Mr. Silent—Carter. Maybe on the way back, he could make sure he was with someone who wasn't determined to share their life history with him. Or if they did, it wouldn't be because they had an eye on him being boyfriend potential.

CHAPTER TEN

Sarah felt a surge of irritation as she listened to Cecelia chatter on and on to Beau. They had been best friends for a lot of years—the only person she was closer to was Leah—and for the most part, Cecelia was fine. A little snarky at times, but usually nothing worse than Leah could sometimes be as well. However, as soon as a man was introduced to her, something in Cece changed.

Even though it was already several months since Eli and Anna had gotten together, Cecelia still hadn't warmed up to Anna. Eli had been Cecelia's crush for awhile, but he'd never expressed any interest in her. Still, she'd been so angry when Eli had started dating Anna.

And now she was going after Beau.

It wasn't that Sarah had set her sights on him and was jealous that Cece was spending time with him. It just meant that Cece would lay claim to Beau, and any time Sarah spent with him or if she mentioned him in a friendly way while Cece was around would anger Cece, who would be convinced that Sarah was trying to steal him for herself.

If Beau and Cece ended up together, Sarah would never do anything to get between them. Unfortunately, Cece would never believe that to be true.

Sarah was a firm believer in two people being drawn together. Like Anna and Eli. Like Cara and Kieran. She didn't want to have to obsessively chase a man in order for him to notice her. She wanted there to be a natural draw between them, a connection that no one could break.

That was why she didn't usually discount a guy based on anything aside from availability. The main reason she was trying not to think about any sort of connection with Beau was because he was only there for a month. And, of course, there was Leah's warning.

Still, even when she found a guy interesting, she didn't inflict an inquisition on him.

"Does she not realize that she's more likely to scare a guy off talking like that?" Cara had lifted her hand to cover her mouth and lowered her voice to a whisper.

Sarah just shook her head and rolled her eyes, watching as Beau moved a branch out of the way, which allowed Cece to pass by unscathed. When she and Cara reached that spot, they just ducked.

"How is your painting going?" Cara asked.

"I'm almost done the current one. I need to get started on the next one soon. I want to get them done sooner rather than later since we're heading into our busiest time at the lodge."

"You are so amazing," Cara said. "That painting you did of me was stunning, and it wasn't because of anything I did."

"You're wrong there, hun." Sarah gave her an exasperated look. "Your picture exuded such life and emotion that it was a pleasure to be able to capture it. I hoped you'd like it since the painting wasn't an exact replica of the picture."

"It was perfect. Kieran agreed."

Sarah smiled at that. Of course, he did. The man absolutely adored Cara. She had an idea that her friend was going to be getting engaged sometime soon. Maybe not right away. But after Cara and Kieran had broken up and then gotten back together again, Sarah was pretty sure this was it for them. It would only be a matter of time before Kieran made it official. And when he did, she hoped to be able to paint an engagement portrait and, eventually, one of Cara in her wedding dress.

"How's life been for you other than your painting?" Cara asked.

"Pretty good. We're gearing up for the busyness of summer. Already we're filling up more on the weekends. Then we have the wedding plans ongoing as well. Anna leaves soon for a couple of days in New York to get her wedding dress, then we're going for fittings for bridesmaid dresses when she gets back."

"Have you been a bridesmaid before?" Cara asked.

"No. This is my first time. I just hope it's not the first of many. You know, always the bridesmaid, never the bride."

"You know, I never expected that I'd date anyone, let alone fall in love the way I did with Kieran. Love sneaks up on you sometimes. Grows out of the most unlikely of situations. And I'm glad I didn't try and push for something earlier, just for the sake of being in a relationship. Kieran was definitely worth waiting for."

"And I'm sure he feels the same way about you."

Cara laughed. "I sure hope so."

"I wish he could have joined us here today."

"Yeah, me too, but it's probably best he couldn't. The detective has been at the station again, asking Kieran about different aspects of the early investigation into Sheila's disappearance. Not sure why, because it's not like Kieran was part of that investigation. But one of the questions he's asked Kieran was if he'd seen much of Eli lately. Kieran's hoping that the detective will disappear back to whatever office he's been working out of and stay away."

Sarah felt indignation boil up within her every time she thought about what her brother had endured since his high school girlfriend had gone missing. Thankfully, those who knew Eli believed he'd had nothing to do with her disappearance. Unfortunately, Sheila's mom had insisted on the cold case being reopened ten years later, so for the last several months, Eli had been forced to relive that time and the suspicions that had come with it.

Kieran was the police chief in New Hope, but the investigation was being directed out of an office near Everett. So while Kieran also believed in Eli's innocence, the detective in charge of the case was far more skeptical.

Thankfully, Anna had stood by Eli even when the suspicions on him might have negatively impacted her career. Her love for him was solid and strong, and Sarah couldn't help but hope that one day, she could love and be loved like that in return.

"I pray that all of this will be over soon," Sarah said. "I'm just glad that, for the most part, Anna and Eli don't let it hang over them. I've never seen Eli so happy. At least not since our dad left."

Sarah watched as Cece and Beau disappeared around a turn in the path. She knew that what lay just ahead was a natural stopping spot since there was a bench there that their grandfather had crafted. Plus, there were plenty of fallen logs around to sit on.

When she and Cara joined the group, Beau approached her with the backpack in his hand. "Did you need this?"

"Are you thirsty?" she asked, taking it from him. "I brought some water bottles."

"That would be great. Thanks." He took the bottle she held out to him then opened it to take a drink. "This is absolutely beautiful."

"It is, isn't it?" Sarah agreed. "And there are lots of other beautiful spots around here."

"I haven't really thought much about sightseeing while I'm here, but I'm starting to think I should do something about that."

"You really should," Sarah agreed. "It would be a shame to leave the area without exploring more of it."

"Would you have time to play tour guide?" he asked.

Sarah ignored the flutter in her stomach at his words. "Sure. I need to go out to get some pictures for a project I'm working on. We might as well go together."

"That sounds great."

Before they could make any definite plans, Cecelia came to stand at Beau's side. "I heard you needed a tour guide. I'd be more than happy to show you around."

"Thanks for the offer," Beau said. "But it sounds like Sarah was already planning to go out, so I'll just tag along with her."

When Cecelia shot her a nasty look, Sarah just sighed. When would her friend realize that people weren't inclined to want to be with someone who showed an attitude like she did? It wasn't a competition. If Beau showed an interest in Cece, Sarah wouldn't turn on her because of it, even if she *was* interested in him in that way. Which she wasn't.

There were times she just couldn't comprehend the woman's actions at all. Even after all these years of friendship, she still didn't understand the way Cece reacted, especially when it came to men. She'd tried to talk to her about it, but her friend had just told her that she wouldn't understand.

Well, she might not understand Cecelia's issues, but she sure understood that being nasty toward women she perceived as competition was no way to gain or keep friends. Leah had no patience for Cecelia and didn't understand why Sarah remained friends with her when they both knew she'd turn on Sarah the moment she felt that a man she was interested in, was more interested in Sarah.

Even though she was certain Beau wasn't interested in her as anything but an acquaintance, Cece wouldn't see it that way. Would this be the straw that finally broke their friendship? Sarah hoped not because it would be such a stupid thing to cause a friendship to break down. It wasn't like he had moved to town. The man had said he was only there for a month.

Sarah sighed again as she watched Cecelia turn and stomp back down the trail they'd just come up. This was getting ridiculous. It was like Cecelia's desperation for a relationship was ramping up, and that worried Sarah.

"Is she going to be okay?" Beau asked. "Should someone go after her?"

"She'll be fine," Sarah said. Or at least she hoped she would be. "I love her, but sometimes she can be a little challenging."

"I hope you don't think I was leading her on," Beau said, worry creasing his brow.

"Not at all," she assured him. "She manages to lead herself on."

"What does that mean?"

"It means that she often perceives interest where there is only politeness offered. You could have a chat with Eli if you need more clarification. She still won't have anything to do with Anna because she feels that Anna stole Eli from her."

Beau's brows drew together. "Is she mentally stable? Like, do I have to worry about her stalking me?"

"No, I think you'll be fine."

"Well, you could pass on the information that I'm not available," Beau said. "If you think it would help."

Sarah's heart sank just a tiny bit at his words, and when she found herself wanting to ask if it was true or rather just a way to shut Cece down, she quickly disposed of that line of thinking. "I'll let her know."

"Thank you. I appreciate that." He put the cap back on his water bottle. "How far do you usually go on these hikes?"

"We'll go a bit further, I think," Sarah said. "We like to take advantage of the nice day."

"You've had more nice weather than I had anticipated you would," Beau said. "All I'd ever heard was how much it rained in the Pacific Northwest."

"Just like most things, some months we fit the stereotype more than others. But as far as I know, we've yet to have a year where it rained every single day."

"Why don't we continue on up?" Eli called out then headed over to where Sarah stood. "What happened to Cece?"

Sarah let out a sigh. "Two guesses."

Eli's brows rose, his gaze going briefly to Beau. "Really?"

"Yep."

"Why am I not surprised?" Eli muttered. "I guess we should have considered that before inviting her."

Sarah shrugged. "I keep trying to give her opportunities to behave differently, but she never changes."

"Not to be mean, but it's her loss," Eli remarked. "Let's keep going."

This time, Shadow fell into step with Eli and Carter while Cara walked with Anna and Andy when the path was wide enough for the three of them. Beau and Sarah brought up the rear.

"Have you known these people all your life?" Beau asked.

"No, actually, the only ones I've known for that long are Eli, of course, and Andy. Cara moved here about four or five years ago. I think Carter moved here around the same time. And Anna moved here just last year."

"For a small town, New Hope certainly seems to attract people. I thought people wanted to leave small towns."

"Oh, plenty have left," Sarah said. "But we've gained people as well. It helps that we're not too far from some bigger cities. If people want, they could commute. Even to Seattle, although that commute would be longer than I'd want to spend in a car on any given day."

"It does appear you do like to have a commute of mere minutes," Beau said with a laugh.

Sarah shot him a surprised look. It was the first time she'd heard him laugh like that, and it made her smile to think it was because of a conversation he was having with her. From what she'd seen of him so far, laughter didn't appear to be something that came to him easily.

"Yep," she agreed. "Depending on the day, it's only steps to either my studio or a few extra steps to the kitchen or the cabins. Going to the restaurant is probably my longest commute."

"I must say, it's kind of nice to be able to get to wherever I'm going within minutes," Beau admitted as he reached to move a branch out of their way. "In Houston, I spend more time than I like to, driving places."

Beau paused as they reached a spot where there was a break in the trees that allowed them to see the mountains in the distance. "That's breathtaking."

Sarah smiled because she agreed. The beauty of the area was one of the things that kept her from ever considering moving away. That and her family, of course.

Beau pulled his phone out and took a couple of pictures. Even after all these years, Sarah still took lots of pictures of the area. Her phone didn't have a lot of space available, so she constantly had to download the pictures. Her computer was now full of photos she'd taken as she sought to capture the beauty around New Hope Falls.

Last Christmas, Eli and Anna had given her a new DSLR camera that had been such a thrill for her. She was able to capture more pictures in even better quality than her phone, which was a few models below what was currently available on the market. When she went out with Beau to show him the sights, she planned to take that camera along.

Their hands brushed as the path narrowed a bit, and though she knew better, for a moment, she allowed herself to wonder what it would be like to hold Beau's hand. But she pushed that thought aside. He'd stated he wasn't available, and though she wasn't sure if that was the truth or just something to ward Cece off, Sarah needed to keep his words in mind. Regardless, she had to remember that, above all else, New Hope was not his home.

They were lagging a bit behind the rest of the group, but Sarah wasn't about to hurry Beau along when he was enjoying taking pictures. He didn't seem to want to stop now that he'd begun.

She pointed out things to him as they walked, enjoying the opportunity to share her love for the area with him, even if it was just pointing out the different types of plants and trees. At one point, when the sun disappeared behind some clouds, they stopped to pull on their windbreakers before continuing on.

Though Sarah wasn't the sportiest person and rarely went on the hardcore hikes that Eli enjoyed, these meandering walks fed her need for beauty, and if she got a bit of exercise in the process, all the better.

They eventually rejoined the rest of the group at a point higher along the trail, and after a bit of discussion, they decided to make their way back down to Eli's. This time, Beau ended up walking with Eli while Carter fell into step behind them. Sarah walked with Andy, and Cara and Anna brought up the rear.

Sarah watched Carter, wondering about the man and why he'd never, to her knowledge, dated anyone. Cecelia hadn't even bothered to crush on him, for some reason, although Sarah had to admit he did give off some serious *don't flirt with me* vibes. Apparently, those were strong enough that even Cece had picked up on them and steered clear.

"It's not often Cece gets mad at you," Andy said.

Sarah gave a snort of laughter. "And it wasn't even over something real."

"She can be so nice, though."

She gave him a glance, noticing the pensive look on his face. Sarah couldn't remember a time in her life when she hadn't known Andy. Because they had been close to the same age, they'd been in a lot of classes together at school and at the church's Sunday school.

He'd been a late bloomer, and he'd never grown much past a height of five-nine or so. He had a lean build and had never been much into sports. In some ways, she viewed him as another brother, and though it appeared that he also viewed Sarah in that light, he didn't see Cece that way.

"Do you like her, Andy?"

A blush swept up into his cheeks, and he ducked his head. "Sometimes."

That statement made all kinds of sense to Sarah because she felt the same way about her friend. She didn't want to hurt Andy because sometimes the heart had a mind of its own, but it seemed unlikely that Cece would ever look at him the way he wanted her to.

And though it pained Sarah to even think it, she didn't trust Cece to not hurt Andy if she ever got wind of how he felt.

Sarah slipped her arm around his waist and gave him a quick hug. "I don't really know what to say except be careful."

He dropped his arm on her shoulders and squeezed her back. "I am."

"You deserve someone sweet and loving all the time," Sarah said, looking up at him.

"You mean like you?" Andy asked with a lift of his eyebrows.

"Uh..."

Andy started laughing then, and Sarah quickly joined in. Apparently, they were loud enough that those ahead of them on the trail glanced back. With their laughter, the lingering yuckiness from the encounter with Cece slipped away.

When they got down to Eli's, he invited them all to stick around for some burgers. It wasn't unusual for them to do that after a hike, and since Beau was the only guest in the lodge that night, there was no rush to get back there.

Sarah was a bit surprised when Kieran showed up just as Eli was putting the burgers on the grill. Still, she was glad he came, and after greeting Cara with a lingering kiss and murmured words, he went out to join the men on the deck. Though there wasn't much to prepare since the food was pretty simple, Sarah helped Anna and Cara with the preparation. Just before it was time to eat, Leah showed up with a large bowl of potato salad.

The group members were a bit different at each hike, but whoever was there always felt like they belonged, and that didn't change at all with Beau's presence. Sarah noticed he was talking with Kieran and Carter—okay, he and Kieran were talking, and Carter was listening—and it made her happy to see that.

Being surrounded by people she cared about, filled her with contentment. Sarah just wished that Cecelia had been able to feel the same way. She'd robbed herself of good fellowship and fun with people who—for better or worse—did care about her...to varying degrees.

CHAPTER ELEVEN

Beau gazed at the people gathered around the large table in Eli's house. There was plenty of talking and laughter, but he didn't feel out of place. Everyone there had been friendly, including him in the conversation or explaining things to him that he might not understand. Most of the time, it was Sarah, but every once in awhile, Eli caught him up.

When it was time to leave, it was just him and Sarah heading back to the lodge since Leah had been among the first to leave, while the others had their vehicles at Eli's. Twilight was setting over the area as they walked along the road. He couldn't remember the last time he'd been out walking at that time of day.

"I hope that wasn't too boring for you," Sarah said.

"It wasn't boring at all." Boring was sitting through one of his mother's dinners with people whose goal in life appeared to be outdressing and outshining everyone else with their charity work. "I found it quite interesting."

"That's good. If we're comfortable enough with someone new, we often forget they haven't been around forever."

Beau decided to take that as a compliment. He appreciated that they were willing to have him join them even though he was only going to be there for a month. Well, three more weeks now.

It was hard to believe he'd been there a week already. The anger and frustration over his initial banishment from Houston had faded, and though he still harbored some resentment toward his father over taking away access to his clients, he was coming to accept that there was nothing he could do about that.

Constantly asking his dad to reinstate his computer privileges would only serve to tick him off and make him change the terms of the trust fund for certain. And Beau was trying to avoid that if at all possible.

"Do you know what you'll be doing next week?" Sarah asked.

"Yes. My grandfather said I'm to go to the grocery store in town."

"Huh. Do you know what you'll be doing?"

"Nothing too complicated, I'm sure."

"You really *are* doing all the teenage jobs," Sarah said with a laugh. "I don't know if I should feel sorry for you or admire you for doing it all without complaining."

"My guess is that you could do both."

She laughed again. "Well, then, with your permission, I shall."

"To be honest, I don't see sense in protesting doing things that won't actually kill me." Except marrying a woman he didn't love. "If teenagers can do it, I should be able to."

"You'd be surprised at the number of people who would be complaining about having to do what you've been asked to do."

"For some reason, it seems important to my grandfather, and like I said, I have no good reason to argue with him over it." And plenty of reasons not to.

They walked in silence for a short distance, then Sarah said, "I apologize again for Cece's behavior earlier."

"You don't need to apologize for that," Beau assured her.

"I kinda feel like I do because I invited her knowing full well how she can sometimes be. I just hoped..." Sarah sighed. "To be honest, I didn't really think it through like I should have."

"I'm fine, Sarah. I was more concerned with upsetting you by rebuffing her obvious interest."

"I'm used to her being that way. It was the worst when she set her sights on Eli. I'm positive that it's no girl's dream to hear how cute their brother is over and over again. It certainly wasn't mine.

Not to mention having to deal with her asking me repeatedly what she could do to make Eli like her."

Beau chuckled. "I can imagine that that was rather awkward."

"And then it came to the point where she requested rather strongly that I tell Eli all her good qualities so that he'd fall in love with her. Unfortunately, by that point, Eli knew all her bad ones because Leah isn't a fan of Cece, and she doesn't hide that from the rest of us in the family."

"Ouch. Though I have to say, I don't feel like Leah is a fan of mine either." Her unreadable look, whenever he found her gaze on him, made him uneasy. It was like she knew things about him that he didn't even know himself. Truly unnerving.

"Leah doesn't trust easily. She waits to see people's true colors before deciding whether or not to like them. I tend to be the opposite of that. I give my trust too easily, according to Leah."

Beau preferred interacting with Sarah, but he could understand Leah's reluctance to trust. As they walked into the lodge a short time later, he could hear muffled voices coming from the direction of the kitchen.

"I think I'm going to head up to my room," Beau said. "Thank you again for the invite. I really enjoyed myself."

Sarah beamed up at him. "I'm glad. It was great having you along."

Beau couldn't help but smile in return, and it wasn't the smile he gave most people. No, this was a smile he couldn't have held back even if he'd wanted to. "See you tomorrow."

When Beau got to his room a few minutes later, he found himself thinking back over the day, trying to remember when he'd had such diverse experiences in such a short time. From church to lunch with his grandfather to the hike and finally the dinner at Eli's...he wasn't sure he'd ever had a day like it before.

He sat down on the loveseat, his phone in hand as his thoughts zeroed in on the conversation he'd had with his grandfather.

Without thinking it through, he tapped his phone to find his sister's contact info and called her.

"Beaumont," she said with an exaggerated drawl. "What are you doin' callin' me so late at night? Have you lost your mind from boredom?"

"Actually, not at all."

"Really? I thought you were calling to ask me to plead your case to Dad."

"If I thought that might actually work, I would, but I'm pretty sure it won't."

Julianna sighed. "You're probably right. Mom has been on a rampage since you left, demanding that Dad let you come home."

"It's not like I can't come home on my own," Beau said. "I just need Dad to not change the terms of the trust yet again. I'm not going to do anything that might make him do that."

"Sorry to tell you, brother, but I have a feeling he's going to do just that if you don't at least try and get back together with Tiffany. In fact, I wouldn't be surprised if he changed the terms so each of us would have to be married before we'd get our trust fund."

That possibility had crossed his mind, but he was trying not to think about it until he absolutely had to. He still had three weeks to figure things out. Unless his dad demanded he return to Houston sooner.

"In between their fights, he and Mom are doing their best to placate Tiffany's parents and reassure them that you just need a little time away from work to focus on your feelings for her."

"Is that even working?" Beau asked. He didn't get the feeling that Tiffany's parents were dumb. But just as his dad wanted the political clout Tiffany's dad could bring to the table, Tiffany's dad wanted the money Beau's dad could bring to an expensive campaign. It was a match made...somewhere, but for Beau and Tiffany, it certainly wasn't in heaven.

"I don't know. I'm not privy to the conversations between them, just the convo between Mom and Dad." Julianna paused then said, "Are you going to do what Dad wants you to when you get back here?"

"I don't want to," Beau said. "If Tiffany wants more from a relationship, then she should have that opportunity, but it's not going to be with me. I don't know if Tiffany's folks have something to hold over her the way Dad does over me."

"I wish I had some advice for you, but honestly, I've got nothing. I'm sorry."

"You don't have to be sorry. This isn't your issue."

"You don't think Dad isn't already trying to match me up too? The hints may be more subtle at this point, but they're there. I figure once he's got you settled, he'll turn his sights fully on me. And Mom will be right there with him, encouraging me to accept whatever man she deems worthy."

Beau rubbed his fingers against his forehead. He knew there were cultures where marriages were still arranged, but that was not *his* culture. He'd kind of allowed it to happen with Tiffany, but now he didn't want to have to consider it again. And he doubted Julianna or Rhett wanted to consider an arranged marriage either.

"Let me know if you hear anything that might be helpful for me, and if you need to escape, let's just say that New Hope Falls isn't the worst place on earth. Plus, I think Grandfather would like to meet you and Rhett."

"Are you *trying* to put Mom into an early grave? If all three of us end up there, she'll definitely lose it."

"Just keep the thought in mind."

"For what it's worth, I kinda miss you," Julianna said.

"I kinda miss you too." And he really did. Rhett, too. Though maybe not as much.

Julianna laughed. "This is weird."

Beau couldn't argue with her there. Maybe absence was making his heart grow fonder when it came to affection for his sister. Unfortunately, that wasn't his father's goal.

After the call ended, Beau went to his laptop and pulled up the file he had been preparing for years now, changing it as things came to mind. It was what he'd been working toward, just waiting until he had his trust fund to finally strike out on his own. He knew his father planned for him to take over the family business someday, but Beau wasn't sure he could endure the years between now and then.

Working for his father gave the man too much control of his life. He wanted...needed...the freedom to live his own life. To make his own decisions without the threat of losing his trust fund hanging over his head.

But what was he willing to do to make that freedom become a reality?

That was the question of the hour. The fact that he had accepted his banishment and being cut off from his clients without argument showed he was willing to go that far at least. What he wasn't willing to do, he was coming to realize, was drag someone else along in his desperation to gain his trust fund.

He could contact Tiffany and beg her to give him a second chance. Do his best to treat her well and hope it would be enough.

But she'd made it clear during their fight that she wanted—she needed—more from him. And having watched Eli and Anna for the past week, and Cara and Kieran during that afternoon, Beau knew it wasn't fair to rob her of the opportunity to have a relationship like that. It just wouldn't be with him because he knew he didn't feel for her what Eli felt for Anna or Kieran felt for Cara.

So what was he to do?

He'd have to serve out his banishment, then return to Houston with the knowledge that the trust fund wouldn't be enough to entice him back into a relationship with Tiffany. Then he'd have to bear his father's displeasure and accept that what was to have been his within a year would now more than likely take at least five more years, and possibly a marriage, to attain.

With a sigh, Beau stared at his laptop, the words on the screen blurring as his gaze lost focus. He thought about the people he'd spent the afternoon and evening with. They seemed to have a contentment and a joy that he'd never really felt before. Though Anna appeared to be rich, the rest didn't seem to be, and yet, from the sound of it, they were content, doing things they loved. They had people in their lives they loved.

What did he have besides a job that he was good at, though it wasn't one he loved since it was performed under his father's thumb? He had a lavish apartment and an expensive car. He earned a great salary that afforded him the luxury of buying pretty much anything he wanted, but nothing touched him. Nothing about his life moved him to excitement. To laughter. To contentment.

He thought back to the hike and the beauty of the area. Of the smile and laughter on Sarah's face as they'd talked and as she'd interacted with her friends. Joy radiated from her in a way he'd never seen from anyone in his life before.

Reaching out, he closed the lid of the laptop, shutting away his dream that seemed even further out of reach than ever.

"So, how was your first day at the grocery store?" Sarah asked when Beau found his way into the kitchen after getting back to the lodge.

Nadine had offered to keep supper for him since he was at the store until six-thirty, and she began to warm it up as he sat down at the counter. He appreciated them being willing to work around his schedule. He hadn't seen his grandfather that day, but he'd be going to have coffee with him in the morning before his next shift at the store.

"It was fine. I didn't drop anything, and I've now learned the proper way to pack groceries into a bag."

Nadine chuckled. "Yes, Stan is quite particular about things in his store. He trains all his employees well."

"A teen trained me," Beau said, recalling the lanky young man with loose dark curls, and soft gray eyes that contrasted strikingly with his light brown skin.

"That was probably Julian," Sarah said. "He's such a sweetheart."

"Yes, that was his name. He was tremendously patient with me, which I really appreciated."

"He is a very patient boy and gentle too. Which is a bit surprising, considering his life."

Beau frowned. "What's wrong with his life?"

"His mother died some years back, leaving them with a very angry, and, I would venture to guess, verbally abusive, father," Nadine said. "Julian has had to raise himself and his sister, for the most part."

Beau thought of the young man who had responded to every request by a customer with patience and kindness, even when the person wasn't necessarily polite with him. "Does he work at the store all the time?"

"I think he takes all the hours he can get," Nadine said. "He is, by far, Stan's best employee. I'm always happy to interact with him when I go there."

Julian's shift hadn't started until three-thirty, and the person who'd been helping him before that hadn't been half as knowledgeable as the teen. Beau had left the store hoping that he'd work more with Julian than the other employee in his remaining days there.

It was interesting to see how intertwined the lives of the people in this town were.

Beau was a bit ashamed to admit—even to himself—that he didn't know much about the lives of the people he worked with on a daily basis. His assistant was married with kids, but he didn't know any of their names. And that was on him. He could have asked more questions about her personal life, but his parents had always impressed on him the importance of keeping his distance from employees.

Now as he thought about it, that just seemed like such a stupid way to operate. As he'd watched Julian interact with the people at the store, there were some he obviously knew quite well. He'd ask after their kids or their pets, and the people would light up as they responded.

And then there had been the elderly woman who had come through Julian's line at the register. Julian had complimented her on her hair and told her she looked beautiful. His comments seemed to be frowned on in this day and age, but the woman had absolutely beamed at Julian's words. She'd patted his cheek and told him he was such a good boy and to never change.

And while some might have questioned the sincerity of Julian's compliment, Beau had gotten the feeling that the young teen truly had seen beauty in the woman that others might have missed or been unwilling to even look for.

"Here you go," Nadine said as she set a plate of food in front of him. "What would you like to drink?"

"Just water is fine."

Sarah got a glass from the cupboard and filled it from the water cooler next to the fridge. The food on his plate looked like it was mashed potatoes on top of a mixture of ground beef, small chopped veggies, and corn. Though he didn't have high expectations of the taste of it, when he took a small bite, the flavor of the ground beef exploded in his mouth and mixed well with the creaminess of the mashed potatoes to create an immediate desire for more.

"This is very good," Beau said after he'd taken a couple more bites.

"That's my mother's recipe for shepherd's pie," Nadine said. "It's one of the few dishes that Sarah has actually managed to master."

"So, you made this?" Beau asked Sarah.

"Yep. Leah wasn't feeling well, and Mom had plans for the afternoon, so I got put to work."

"You did a great job."

Sarah gave him a beaming smile. That was the only way he could think of to describe the way she smiled. "Thank you. I'm just glad I didn't burn the potatoes. I did that a lot when I was first learning the recipe."

Beau continued to chat with Sarah after Nadine excused herself to go check on Leah. As he continued to eat, she told him about her day, which had included taking some sort of class at Cara's studio.

"Are you still up for a bit of sightseeing on the weekend?" Sarah asked as she took away his empty plate and replaced it with one containing a piece of chocolate cake.

"Yes. I would really like to see more of the area."

"I was planning to go out Saturday morning for a few hours. However, I'm flexible if you need a different time because of the schedule with your grandfather or work at the store."

"I'm only working there until Friday, and I can make arrangements with my grandfather to see him later in the day if need be."

"I'm looking forward to it. It's not often that I get a chance to show people around."

Beau found that he was looking forward to it as well, but he realized that it wasn't just about seeing the beauty of the area. He was looking forward to seeing it through Sarah's eyes. He had no doubt her joy over what she would show him would be infectious. Having never been around someone like that, he could hardly wait.

CHAPTER TWELVE

"This is a bad idea," Leah said as she sat cross-legged on Sarah's bed on Saturday morning.

"So you've said." Sarah tugged her jeans up and buttoned them before pulling a T-shirt over her head. "I've also told you that this is not a date. I know that he's not available." Though she still didn't know if that was truly the case or just an excuse to ward Cece off. "He basically said as much last Sunday, and even if he was available, I know that he's not from here. Don't. Worry."

Leah frowned. "Of course, I worry. You can tell yourself all those things, but spending time together, just the two of you, is not wise."

Sarah sighed. She sort of understood where Leah was coming from. Perhaps the fact that she enjoyed spending time with Beau *was* a red flag, but as long as she kept reminding herself that nothing could come of it...that nothing *should* come of it...she would be fine.

"Just don't come crying to me when your heart gets broken," Leah muttered as she slid off the bed and left the room.

Her statement was ridiculous because they both knew that Sarah would *definitely* go to Leah any time her heart got broken. And though a lot of people would assume that Leah would just tell Sarah that she'd told her so, she would never do that.

Sarah finished getting ready then picked up her camera bag from the chair where she'd set it earlier after checking to make sure everything she wanted was inside. There was a forecast of rain for later in the day, but the morning was supposed to still be nice. She figured they'd spend the morning seeing the sights then grab lunch before heading back to the lodge.

Upstairs, on the main floor, she found Beau chatting with Eli. From the look her brother gave her as she joined them, she knew he'd had at least one conversation with Leah. She felt a frisson of annoyance rush through her at both of her siblings.

Even though she *wanted* to be in love, that didn't mean she was going to go around falling in love with every guy she came in contact with, especially ones that had no plans to stick around New Hope. She'd like to think that Beau might become another friend, and in her mind, one could never have too many friends.

"Ready to go?"

"Yep. I'm looking forward to seeing a bit more of the area. Might even post some pictures on the social media accounts my sister insisted I set up."

"Where do you plan to go?" Eli asked.

Sarah gave him a quick run-down of the route she planned to take. She thought where she'd chosen to go would cover the two goals she had for that day. The first was to find a place to take some additional photos, hopefully including the one that would inspire her next painting. The second was to show Beau more of the beautiful Pacific Northwest.

"Sounds good. There are some gorgeous views along that route. I hope it doesn't rain."

Sarah grabbed the small backpack she'd filled with some water and snacks. There were picnic spots along the way, so they'd have something to eat and drink if they wanted to stop for some refreshment.

It was only as they walked out of the lodge that she realized that Beau might not exactly want to ride in her somewhat beat-up car. But then she gave a mental shrug. This was what she had, and maybe it would give Beau yet another experience that he needed to have.

She led him to where her car was parked, and when he eyed it dubiously, she said, "Don't worry. If it breaks down, Eli will come rescue us."

"We could take mine," he offered, a hopeful lilt in his voice.

"Nope. Mine runs just fine." She opened the passenger door, then went around to the driver's side and placed her bag on the back seat before sliding behind the wheel.

Beau's hesitation was barely noticeable, but it was there. It didn't take him too long to fold his body into the passenger seat of her car. She hadn't thought about how her smaller car might not be very comfortable for him since he was taller than even Eli.

He didn't say anything, however. Just bent his legs, spreading them to keep his knees from bumping the dashboard. His arm bumped against hers as he worked to get his seatbelt buckled.

Once they were situated, Sarah pulled out of her parking spot and drove to the entrance to the lodge property. Beau's broad form in her small car meant their arms brushed as she steered around the curves of the road.

Wondering if perhaps it would have been smarter to take Beau's larger car, Sarah still didn't turn back to the lodge. Instead of heading west toward town, she turned left and headed east along the road that would take them further into the rural area that lay in the direction of the mountains.

Almost immediately, they were surrounded on either side by towering trees. They weren't going super fast since the narrow road didn't lend itself to safe driving at higher speeds. Because of that, she rolled down her window and told Beau he could do the same. She loved the fresh air that poured in through the open windows, bringing with it the tantalizing scents of nature.

"I'm not sure when I last drove with the windows down," Beau commented.

Sarah glanced over at him with a smile. "Well, I prefer to leave the windows up when driving fast or when I'm in the city. But out this way? It seems wrong to be trapped behind glass when I could be experiencing nature blowing in my face."

"You have an interesting and unique way of looking at things."

"Thank you." Sarah wasn't sure exactly how he'd meant the comment, but she was definitely going to take it as a compliment. She'd take *interesting* over being boring, any day of the week.

Beau chuckled then said, "You're welcome."

As she drove, Sarah told him about what she was hoping to find that day, and when, about thirty minutes into their drive, they came to a spot where they could stop, she pulled over. Beau unfolded himself from the car while Sarah climbed out and grabbed her camera from the bag on the back seat.

For the next few minutes, Sarah focused on taking pictures, peering through the viewfinder of the camera. The viewfinder enabled her to focus right in on the photo she wanted to capture rather than seeing the whole view, like when she looked at the display on the back of a camera or on a phone.

Beau stood staring off at the mountains, his phone in his hand but not taking any pictures at that moment. Sarah paused in her picture taking, then lifted her camera to quickly grab a couple photos of him. His back was to her, but he was nicely framed by trees and mountains in the distance.

Sarah let out a quick breath as she turned to look back at the creek that ran near where they'd stopped. She had to push thoughts of him to the side so she could concentrate on what she'd intended to accomplish during their time out.

For a few minutes, she was able to do that, but then she turned around to look at the view behind her and found him watching her. "Sorry. I kind of get caught up in what I'm doing."

"I understand that," Beau said with a warm smile. "I will often be working away, not even realizing that hours have passed until I look at a clock."

"Sounds like you enjoy your work."

"Enjoy might be a strong word." His gaze shifted away from her. "I'm good at what I do, but I have other plans I'd like to focus on in the future. Unfortunately, it's taking longer than I would like to get those off the ground."

Sarah contemplated asking him for more details but decided it was better if she didn't. Asking him about his time in New Hope was one thing because it intersected with her life. But asking about his life back in Houston was definitely a *no go.*

"It's nice to have goals, though, especially if the job you're currently in isn't exactly what you want long-term."

"What do you see for your future?" Beau asked, apparently having no issues with crossing the line she refused to cross.

"I want to continue painting, for sure. I would love to have a gallery showing outside of New Hope someday." She lifted her camera and pointed it toward the mountains in the distance. "Of course, I hope to have a family at some point too."

Beau was silent for a moment before he said, "Will you continue to work at the lodge?"

"Oh, I think I'll always help out there." She took a picture of the snow-topped mountains then lowered her camera. "It has been in the family for a few generations, so I hope my kids will one day help to run it."

"Does Norma help with the lodge?"

"No. She wanted to start her own restaurant, so my mom and dad bought her out. They later bought out the other siblings too when they wanted to leave New Hope, so the lodge became our family's business."

"How will you, Eli, and Leah split it?"

"I don't know," Sarah said. "I haven't really thought too much about that. Right now, Leah and Eli put the most effort into maintaining it, but I love the lodge and would always want to help out when I could. Leah and I each have a piece of the land for when, or if, we'd would want to build our own places."

"Like Eli's?"

Sarah nodded. "He built first because he wanted to be on his own. Leah and I are still okay living at the lodge."

"I wasn't sure what to expect when I was told that the lodge was where I should check-in." Beau shifted his weight, his hands going into his pockets. "But it's been really nice."

Sarah beamed at his words because that was what she always hoped to hear about the lodge. Her mom—with their help—had worked hard to maintain its reputation, especially since, given the nature of his job, their dad hadn't really been all that helpful. She knew that her grandparents would be proud of how they'd continued to build on the family legacy.

"So you have your painting, and Eli has his woodworking. Does Leah have something she also does in addition to helping at the lodge?"

Sarah hesitated, then said, "She does have something, but it's not for me to share. Leah is a fairly private person, so she doesn't talk about it much. You could always try asking her."

Beau gave a huff of laughter. "I don't think she'd want to share with me."

"Sadly, I think you're probably correct, but you're in good company. Most people are unaware of her side job, if you will. Most assume her total focus is on the lodge." Sarah took a final turn. "Why don't we continue on? Did you get some pictures, or do you want to take more?"

"I'm good."

They got back in the car and continued on their tour. Even though the windows were open, it felt a bit like they were cocooned in a world of their own. It was then she realized that Beau was the first man she'd had in her car who wasn't related to her.

Well, that certainly wasn't something she could allow herself to dwell on, so she tried her best not to, as they meandered along the road.

The route she'd chosen would only have taken a couple of hours if she'd driven it straight, but since they'd stopped along the way, by the time they reached *Norma's*, three hours had passed. Sarah had them sit at the counter instead of in a booth or at a table, so it didn't feel quite so date-ish.

They didn't take too long to eat, since she knew that Beau had plans to see his grandfather that afternoon, and she was anxious to be back at her room in the lodge, reviewing the pictures on her computer. All in all, it had been a good morning, and she'd enjoyed Beau's company...but not too much.

"Thank you so much for the tour," Beau said when they got back to the lodge. "It was more beautiful than I could ever have imagined. Very different from what I see in Houston."

"I'm glad you enjoyed it."

When Eli appeared and struck up a conversation with Beau about his morning excursion, Sarah made her way to the stairs that led to her basement room. She figured it wouldn't be long before Leah came to have a chat with her. Sarah usually liked hanging out with Leah, but lately, her one and only topic of conversation had been Beau, and Sarah was beginning to find it rather wearisome.

Beau sat with his grandfather in the room where he'd first met him almost two weeks earlier. The sun was pouring in through the large windows, and Beau felt a sense of contentment he'd never experienced before.

"Did you take lots of pictures?" the older man asked as he re-garded Beau with a curious expression.

"I did." He reached for his phone and pulled up his photo app. He'd already transferred the ones he'd taken of Sarah as she'd been caught up taking pictures of her own, into another folder on his phone. He wasn't sure why he'd taken them. There had just been something about her focus and intensity while being surrounded by such beauty that had drawn him in. "Here. These are the ones I took today."

With a slightly trembling hand, his grandfather swiped through the pictures, commenting on several of them. "It's been a while since I last saw those sights."

The longing in his grandfather's voice tugged at Beau. "Would you be up for a bit of a drive? I could take you."

Excitement stirred in his eyes. "It might have to be rather short notice, depending on how I feel."

"I can work with that. Depending on what you have planned for me for next week, that is."

"Oh, yes. Next week." His grandfather handed him back his phone. "You'll be helping out at a landscape company. They also have a flower shop, and they often bring bouquets here for us to enjoy."

"I hope they don't expect me to make flower arrangements," Beau said. "I'm pretty sure that's well beyond my scope of abilities."

His grandfather patted his arm. "No worries there, son. You'll be helping out with the landscaping. One of the owners is a guy about your age, so you two should get along well."

"Surprisingly enough, last week, I got along well with a kid a decade or more my junior," Beau said.

His grandfather nodded. "I assume you're talking about Julian."

"I am. He's remarkable for someone so young."

"He had to grow up quickly when his mother died and left him with a worthless father. His mother would be so proud of him."

"I offered to help him," Beau said.

His grandfather gave him a searching look. "In what way?"

"I told him I'd invest the money he's trying to save for college, and that I'd guarantee he wouldn't lose it."

"That would probably be helpful for him."

"He was worried, though, because he needs to be able to access the money if something unexpected comes up. Apparently, he'd had to use a bunch of the money he'd saved already to pay for braces for his sister."

His grandfather muttered something under his breath as he shook his head. "Like I said, he's had to grow up and be responsible in a way no teen boy should have had to. I'm glad you're helping him. You're a good man."

Beau shifted in his seat, dipping his head. His grandfather's words of praise made him feel uncomfortable. Just three weeks ago, he would have considered himself a basically good man. Having been exposed to some of the people in New Hope Falls had him rethinking that. He would have to confess to being a lot more selfish than he should be, considering all the benefits he had. Instead of being grateful for all that he had in his life, he was discontent, wanting more.

"How did you manage to line up so many jobs for me on such short notice?" Beau asked, eager for a change in subject. "I assume this hadn't been planned before my engagement ended."

"No, it hadn't. When your dad called me, he said you needed to go somewhere to think over your actions and to consider your future."

In other words, think about where he could end up without his trust fund if he didn't get his act together where Tiffany was concerned. Unfortunately for his father, this trip had only reinforced for Beau that the two of them didn't belong together.

"Your mother would probably be horrified to know what you've been doing here."

"Oh, most definitely," Beau agreed without hesitation. "And I have no intention of telling her."

"That's probably for the best," his grandfather said. "It would just give her one more reason to hate New Hope Falls."

Beau wanted to ask what her other reasons were, but once again, he held off. Maybe if they took a drive, he could ask more about it when other people weren't around.

He stayed for a while longer, getting the information he needed for the next week, then they chatted a bit more about Beau's life in Houston. When he finally left later that afternoon, it was with the promise that he'd return in the morning to pick his grandfather up for church.

Going to church two Sundays in a row...imagine that. He was quite sure his siblings wouldn't be able to, let alone his parents.

As he drove back to the lodge, he wondered if there would be a hike again the next afternoon, and if so, would he be invited? He hoped so, but at the same time, he wasn't sure they'd put him and Cecelia together again after what had happened the previous week. By rights, she deserved to be there more than he did, so he wouldn't fault them at all for not including him.

He'd seen Sarah each evening when he'd returned from his time at the grocery store. Nadine had heated up his dinner while Sarah and Leah had cleaned up from the meal. He had enjoyed chatting with them, but most of all, he'd really enjoyed that morning's drive around the area.

Beau wasn't sure how to come to terms with the fact that while he'd usually dreaded times spent with Tiffany, he enjoyed being around Sarah. He *wanted* to be around her.

The idea left him uneasy half the time, while the rest of the time, he just let himself enjoy the feeling. It was so foreign to him to feel that way, and he really liked it.

When he returned to the lodge in time for dinner that night, however, Sarah wasn't anywhere to be found, and she still hadn't appeared by the time dinner was served.

Leah must have picked up on the fact that he was looking for her because she said, "Sarah's out for dinner."

Beau just gave her a smile and settled into his meal, intending to spend more time listening than conversing. There were several new faces at the table that night. Sarah had mentioned that guests would be arriving that day. A couple had also arrived the day before, but Beau hadn't met them.

After the dinner had finished, Beau excused himself and went up to his room. A thought had taken root as he'd eaten, and it had only continued to grow.

It was entirely possible that Sarah was out on a date. And why shouldn't she be? She was a beautiful woman whose friendly smile and loving nature drew people to her. They had surely drawn him in.

With that in mind, the idea of her being on a date with some man made him unaccountably jealous. At least he assumed the swirling pit of emotion in his stomach that made him half angry and half sick was jealousy. He didn't like the feeling, particularly when he realized there was nothing he could do about it.

How was he supposed to deal with this? Part of him actually hoped that she was on a date, with a guy she'd introduce him to soon. That would help to squash these feelings that he was dealing with where she was concerned. But then there was another part of him that didn't want to lose those feelings.

That part of him was highly irrational. His life was in Houston, and only that morning, she'd spoken about how she saw her future in New Hope Falls and with the lodge. Their lives couldn't be more different. So the sane thing to do would be to smother those feelings of jealousy until they died, leaving him only with the warm thoughts of being a friend to Sarah.

He needed to do that regardless of whether she was actually out on a date or not. It wouldn't do either of them any good to allow those sorts of feelings to grow between them, even if she was interested. To date, their time together had consisted of what he knew was her normal friendly interactions. She wasn't flirtatious with him any more than she'd been with Carter when she greeted him, or with Andy when she'd spoken with him.

If this inner turmoil continued to be a problem, he would need to find a gym or someplace he could go to work off what would undoubtedly grow into a lot of frustration over the hopelessness of the situation.

CHAPTER THIRTEEN

Sarah sighed, sadness filling her as she finally admitted that perhaps it was time to end her friendship with Cece. It pained her beyond belief to even consider doing that, but this latest outing with her had made things crystal clear for Sarah.

She realized that one of their friends felt the same way when she heard Janice say, "Cecelia. That. Is. Enough."

Cece's eyes went wide as she pressed a hand to her chest. "What are you talking about?"

Janice narrowed her eyes. "Are you being serious right now? Surely you're not really as ignorant as you're acting."

"It's okay," Jillian said, reaching out to lay her hand on Janice's arm.

Sarah knew she needed to weigh in on the situation, to show how upset she was by Cecelia's constant jabs at Jillian all evening. "No, it's really not."

This time Cecelia's gaze narrowed as she looked at Sarah. "I should have known you'd take her side. You're just mad that Beau spent more time with me last Sunday than he did with you."

Sarah had to bite her tongue to keep from spilling all the details of her time with him that morning. Instead, she just said, "I'm taking the side of compassion and friendship. You've been nothing but mean to Jillian since the moment she arrived."

"Pointing out that perhaps she didn't need to order fries instead of a salad isn't being mean. It's being a good friend since her choice puts her health at risk."

"Says the woman who works in a bakery where all you sell is stuff that puts people's health at risk," Janice scoffed. "No. You're just being mean."

Jillian sat in her chair, her shoulders hunched forward. Sarah reached out and rubbed her shoulder, waiting until Jillian looked up to give her a smile. "You're just fine the way you are, and I'm glad you're back."

The smile Jillian gave her wavered slightly, and her eyes shone with unshed tears. "Thank you."

"Well, I can see where your loyalties lie," Cecelia huffed as she pushed back from the table and got to her feet.

"My loyalties are with friends who treat other friends with care," Sarah said, sadness filling her as she observed the anger on Cece's face. She just failed to see how she was hurting those around her, and Sarah was done letting that kind of behavior continue.

If someone had attacked Cece, Sarah would have come to her defense. In fact, she *had* come to her defense over the years, with people like Leah and others who wanted to write Cece off. But there was only so much Sarah could do. Jillian needed compassion, not judgment. Well, no one needed harsh judgment from friends, but Jillian seemed...fragile in a way she never had before.

"She left without paying," Iris said, her tone incredulous.

Why she was surprised, Sarah didn't know. That was exactly something that a ticked-off Cece would do. "Don't worry about it. I'll make sure it's taken care of."

"You shouldn't have to," Janice said with a frown.

"I will, though. After all, I should have known better than to include her. She's been in a mood for awhile now."

"Ever since Eli decided to date Anna and not her?" Janice suggested.

Sarah sighed. "Yeah. It probably started around then, but it got worse when they got engaged."

And then, even worse when Beau had brushed her aside, though Sarah had later explained to CeCe that he'd said he was unavailable. Cece, of course, hadn't believed that was the truth. And if she'd challenged Sarah on it, Sarah wouldn't have been able to say she was a hundred percent sure that Beau had a girlfriend.

The meal dropped to a lower energy level with Cece's departure, and Sarah couldn't say that she minded. It hurt to realize how relieved she was to have finally reached this point in her relationship with Cecelia. She had put up with a lot from her over the years, always believing that she'd had her reasons for how she acted.

Though Leah had objected to Cecelia, Sarah had often thought that something hurtful must have happened to her at some point in her life, which was why Sarah had stuck by her the way she did. She'd heard it once said that *hurting people hurt people*, and she'd truly believed that was the case with Cecelia.

Unfortunately, Jillian was also hurting, and the fact that Cecelia couldn't see that, or that she'd seen it and not cared, pushed Sarah to her tolerance limit of Cecelia's bad behavior. It was time to move on from their friendship even though it saddened her to do so.

She wasn't someone who randomly cut people out of their life, and even when everyone else was ready to let Cecelia go, Sarah had stuck with her. She'd encouraged Cece to look at how she was treating others, and she'd definitely prayed for her because she'd been able to see that her friend had no peace in her life.

Though Sarah had peace about her role in what had just happened with Cecelia, it didn't make her feel good. All she wanted was for people to be happy—to have joy in their lives—but at the end of the day, she couldn't force that on people. They had to want it for themselves and choose to embrace those things that would bring joy and happiness into their lives.

When the dinner ended—far sooner than it might have if things had gone differently—Sarah hugged each of the women who'd joined them, then headed back to the lodge.

By the time she got there, twilight had settled over the area. Rather than go right inside, Sarah sank down onto one of the porch swings Eli had installed there. She tucked one ankle under her thigh and used the other foot to set the swing in motion. Part of her wanted to paint. To escape the emotions of the evening. But she knew that if she started, she'd get so caught up in it she wouldn't stop until far too late.

If the situation at the restaurant had developed with anyone but Cece, she might have sought out Leah to talk about it. However, she knew Leah would struggle to be sympathetic to how Sarah was feeling, and Sarah understood why. Leah had born the brunt of a few of Cece's underhanded insults. Comments like *You'd think they were identical, but Sarah is nice.*

Comments like those had brought on some of Sarah's most strongly worded rebukes, and Cece, apparently realizing that that wasn't a fight she could win, had backed off from attacking Leah. So, while Cecelia hadn't made any hurtful comments recently, Leah hadn't forgotten the ones she'd made in the past.

Sarah found herself wanting to confide in Beau about what had happened, knowing from their time together earlier that day that he was easy to talk to. He'd listened without interjecting too many opinions, and he asked questions that she'd actually enjoyed answering. She had a feeling that even though he'd had his own experiences with Cecelia, he would be a sympathetic ear.

But it was precisely those thoughts that kept her from seeking him out. She hoped that some day there would be a man she felt comfortable confiding in, but Beau was not that man.

She heard the door open, and she glanced over, half hoping she'd see Beau walk out. Disappointment warred with relief when she saw Anna instead.

"Sarah?" Anna came over toward the swing. "You okay?"

"Eh."

Anna sat down on the swing beside her. "Want to talk about it?"

Sarah supposed that of all the people at the lodge—aside from Beau—Anna would be the most willing to hear her out and to even offer some sympathy, despite her own experiences with Cece. After a few moments of hesitation, during which Anna sat patiently, Sarah shared the details of what had happened earlier.

"I admire you for sticking with her as long as you have," Anna said. "Not many others would have."

"And maybe that's why I did."

"Do you know much about her family? Although that might be a dumb question given that everyone around here knows everyone, it seems."

Sarah gave a huff of laughter. "We're not *that* small. Even so, I don't really know her parents. She's an only child. But back when the rest of us would have our friend group over to our houses, she never invited us to hers. No one pushed her on it, though a few of us wondered why she never had us over."

"Has no one else kept up their friendship with her?" Anna asked.

"Most of the other girls in our friend group moved away once we graduated high school. The ones that were with us tonight had moved to Seattle. Others went even further away. It was easier for those that left to let their friendships with Cece fade. Jillian has moved back, though, so I kind of wanted to see about rekindling old friendships. Apparently, it was a big mistake to include Cece."

"I'm sorry, sweetie," Anna said as she looped an arm around Sarah's shoulders. "She might still come around. We'll pray for that."

Sarah leaned into Anna for a moment, appreciating her support. She was so grateful for Anna's presence in their lives. She might be marrying Eli, but their whole family was gaining more than just a sister-in-law and daughter-in-law.

"Thanks for listening," Sarah said as she moved back from Anna.

"Anytime. You know that." She got to her feet. "I'd better get home. I have a couple more things to do tonight before I head to bed."

Sarah watched her walk down the steps then disappear into the darkness beyond the porch lights. There were lights further on down the road to the cabins, so she wasn't walking in complete darkness.

After a few more minutes on the swing, Sarah got to her feet and went inside. Her gaze lingered for a few moments on the stairs leading to the second floor, but she avoided them and the kitchen and went straight to the basement. It was still tempting to paint the night—and her emotions—away, but instead, she settled for getting ready for bed, then crawling between the sheets with her sketchbook.

She let her thoughts roam as her pencil moved across the paper. Her movements paused when her thoughts focused in on what she was drawing. There was only the barest of outlines on the paper, but it captured Beau's firm jawline and square chin as well as his hooded eyes.

As she stared down at the paper, she felt a twinge of longing. Though she knew Beau wasn't the man for her, there were things about him that she really appreciated.

Sure, he was an attractive man, but it was more than that. She sensed a steadiness in him that she appreciated. That she wanted in the man she hoped to someday marry.

Though she didn't often think about her dad, he lingered in her thoughts that night. He'd always had a restlessness about him. His job had seemed a good match for that aspect of his personality, the travel allowing him to be on the go in a way he seemed to need. Until it was the thing that took him away from his family permanently.

She knew she could never be with a man who had that same restlessness, so it wasn't any wonder that Beau's steady personality was a draw. And strangely enough, she also really liked his intensity. He focused on whatever was being said or done, never giving the impression that he was bored or disinterested. It had been a somewhat heady experience to have that intensity focused on her earlier that day as they'd driven around the area taking pictures.

But he wasn't for her. She knew that. She accepted that. But it still felt like a loss, and after what had happened with Cece, her sense of loss was now deeply compounded.

She let her fingertips drift over the lines she'd drawn on the paper. Her usual upbeat outlook on life was slipping. It wasn't often that it did, but it was a slippery slope for her once the slide started. She took a deep breath then let it out, trying to loosen the band that was slowly tightening around her chest.

Setting the notepad and pencil on her nightstand, she then turned off the lamp. Darkness settled around her. Settled into her, pushing into her mind. Every thought in her mind was focusing on loss. On the bad instead of the good. None of it allowing her to use her colors to relax enough to sleep.

She squeezed her eyes shut and murmured, "*These things I have spoken to you, that in Me you may have peace. In the world you will have tribulation; but be of good cheer, I have overcome the world.*"

It was a Bible verse her mom had encouraged her to memorize when she'd first begun to deal with dark moments as a teen. She struggled to understand why she could be fine so much of the time but then, *boom*...darkness.

Tears leaked from beneath her eyelids, dampening the pillow beneath her cheek. Frustration added to the tightness in her chest, causing an ache to build, growing and threatening to consume her whole body.

With a gasp, Sarah pushed up from the bed and sat on the edge of it. Her hands gripped the sheets on either side of her legs, twisting the fabric as her head dipped forward. Part of her wanted to go crawl into bed with her mom or with Leah, but she didn't want to bother them.

Please, God, take these feelings away. Take away these dark thoughts. Please. I don't want any of these things in my head. I only want joy. Peace. Please.

A headache began to build behind her eyes. As if she needed one more thing to deal with. Sighing, she got up and pulled on a pair of pajama pants and a zip-up hoodie. Making her way through the darkened rooms, she headed for the stairs.

Thankfully, the lodge was soundproof enough that she didn't have to worry about waking people as she set about making herself some tea in the kitchen. She only turned on the light over the stove since more light wouldn't do her headache any favors.

After putting water in the kettle, she found the tea her mom kept on hand to help with her headaches and put one of the bags into her favorite mug. Leaning a hip against the counter, she pulled the edges of the hoodie across her body and stared blearily at the kettle, waiting for it to boil.

Her thoughts continued to spin as she hunched against the counter. It was at moments like this, she wished she was more like Leah. Sure, her twin didn't come across as super happy or friendly, but like Beau, she was steady. She'd been Sarah's rock more times than she could count. They might argue and bicker at times, but when push came to shove, they had each other's back.

And she knew that if she went to Leah right then, she would listen if she wanted to talk, or just let her sleep in her bed if she needed the company. Unfortunately, Sarah didn't know what she wanted right then. Well, she did know...she wanted her headache gone. She wanted her dark thoughts banished. She just wanted to feel the peace she usually enjoyed.

"Sarah?"

Hearing her name, Sarah looked up from the kettle to see Beau standing on the other side of the island. Even in the dull light, she could see he wore a T-shirt that fit his arms and chest more tightly than anything she'd seen him wear yet. His hair looked like he'd been running his hands through it.

"You're wearing glasses," she said as she stared at him.

Beau lifted his hand and touched them. "Yeah. Normally I wear contacts, but I took them out already."

She'd never seen him like this before. Of course, their meetings in the kitchen had been early in the morning when Beau had been ready for his day. For all she knew, he made regular trips down to the kitchen in the middle of the night. "Want some tea?"

"Tea?"

"Yeah. I'm making myself some tea. Got a bit of a headache." She pushed the basket of assorted herbal teas toward him. "Unless you were looking for coffee?"

"I was going to get some water, but I wonder if there might be some decaf around."

"There definitely is." Sarah turned toward the carousel of pods and plucked one out. She was putting it in the Keurig machine when she heard the kettle start to whistle. Turning, she stared at it for a moment, then shook her head and shifted back to put a mug under the spout and start the coffee for Beau.

"You okay?" he asked, his voice soft with concern.

"Hmmm?" Sarah reached out to lift the kettle and pour the water over her teabag.

"You seem..."

When he didn't finish his sentence, she looked at him. "Tired?"

"Maybe? At first, I thought you were Leah."

Sarah couldn't help but smile a little at that. He wasn't the first one to mention that she seemed more like Leah when she sank into one of these dark moods. Even Leah would tell her that there was room for only one muted twin in their family.

"Perhaps the word you're looking for is muted."

"Muted." Beau picked up the mug when she set it down in front of him. "I hate to say that that sounds accurate, but it kind of does."

"It's okay. I'm not insulted by it." Sarah lifted her mug and inhaled the familiar scent before she blew on the hot liquid then took a sip. Beau's presence was a distraction that pushed back the darkness a bit, but she knew better than to think it was gone. "Leah is the one who calls me that when I get like this."

Beau didn't answer right away, and when she looked up from her mug, he was regarding her intently from behind those black-rimmed glasses. "Like what, exactly?"

She waited for him to walk back his question, but when he didn't, she shrugged. "No one can be happy all the time."

"That's true," Beau said with a nod. "It's just that you've always seemed to be happy whenever I've seen you."

"And I have been, but every once in a while, stuff kind of piles up, you know."

"I hope going on that sightseeing trip this morning didn't add to your pile of stuff."

Sarah shook her head. "Not at all."

She took another sip, wondering how much she should share with him. In the end, she decided it was better for her not to confide in him. Doing so would bring too much intimacy into the friendship that had developed between them. "I needed to do that. Plus, I really did enjoy it."

He seemed to be waiting for her to say more, but when she didn't, he just said, "I enjoyed it as well."

"So, do you have a new work assignment for next week?" Sarah asked, eager to be distracted from her own thoughts, even if for just a little while.

"Actually, I do. My grandfather said I'm going to be working at a landscape company."

"Oh. Maybe that's Michael Reed's."

"He did mention that one of the owners' names was Michael."

"Yep. That's him."

"So, you know them?"

"Not very well. But I think Eli does. It's a brother and sister who own the company, I think. They just moved here in the past two or three years."

Sarah thought about the pair. Michael Reed was a fairly regular attendee at church, but his sister didn't come as often. Though she worked in the floral shop that was part of their business, Sarah rarely saw her out and about in town.

"It will be yet another change of pace," Beau said as he settled down on one of the stools at the island.

That was something else she appreciated about him. His willingness to do whatever his grandfather had asked of him. Eli was like that as well, but Sarah knew plenty of guys who weren't. And given that it was apparent that Beau came from money, his compliant attitude became even more admirable.

She'd like to think it was strictly his good nature that kept him in New Hope Falls with his grandfather, doing menial jobs, but there was a part of her that wondered how true that was. No doubt, her current mood contributed to that thought. She wasn't as motivated to see only the good when the darkness had seeped into her mind.

Tiredness began to settle over her as she sipped at her tea. Beau was silent, too, as he continued to drink his coffee. Normally, Sarah would have tried to fill the silence, but she wasn't inclined to do so that night, and it appeared that Beau wasn't either. The silence wasn't completely uncomfortable, but it wasn't exactly comfortable either. Or maybe that's just how she felt, because Beau didn't give any indication that he was bothered by the quiet.

After she finished the last of her tea, Sarah turned to the sink and washed her mug. As she bent to put it in the dishwasher, Beau said, "I'm sure you have a lot of people to talk to already, but if you need someone removed from the situation, I'd be happy to listen."

She turned to him and smiled, though she was sure that the smile looked like a shadow of her normal one. "Thank you. I appreciate the offer."

The smile he gave her in return was soft, understanding. "But you won't take advantage of it."

"It's nothing personal," she said, hoping to reassure him. "Though I know it looks like I have a lot of people to confide in—and I suppose I do—I choose to confide in very few of my friends. I can count on one hand the number of people I talk to about important things."

"Let me guess..." Beau tilted his head, a thoughtful look on his face. "Leah. Your mom. Anna. Eli. Hmmm... And Cara?"

"I'm impressed."

"Maybe I'm just observant."

It didn't escape Sarah's notice that he hadn't included Cece in that list. Apparently, he was *very* observant. She, on the other hand, couldn't help but also be observant of Beau as he tipped his head back to drain his mug. He then got up off the stool and came around to the sink.

"I can do that for you."

"I feel I need to redeem myself," Beau said. "To prove that I am, indeed, capable of learning new things."

"I think you've already proved that," Sarah assured him, but she let him take care of it.

When she headed back downstairs, she made a quick stop in the bathroom then crawled into bed again. She didn't feel any better, necessarily, but hopefully, her tiredness would finally calm her mind enough so that she could sleep.

CHAPTER FOURTEEN

"You okay, son?"

Beau glanced at his grandfather before turning his attention back to the road that seemed so much narrower now that he was driving it instead of Sarah. "I'm fine. Why?"

"You seem a little distracted today. Did something happen with your parents?"

Of all the things on his mind, his parents definitely weren't one of them for a change. Unfortunately, most of what he was mulling over were things he wasn't comfortable talking about with his grandfather.

"No, as far as I know, they're still doing fine. Although I haven't talked to them in several days."

"If you need to talk about anything, you know I'd be happy to listen."

His grandfather's offer was similar to the one he'd made to Sarah the night before, but unlike her, he didn't have many people to confide in. In fact, he didn't really have any. Though he wasn't interested in talking to his grandfather about the thoughts he'd been having increasingly about Sarah, other things had been on his mind too.

"Would you share with me about what happened with my mom?"

His grandfather sighed. "Yes. I've wanted to tell you, but I wanted you to want to know enough to ask me about the details."

"I wanted to know, but it just seemed like when we were together, it was never the right place to ask you."

"To be honest, I'm not sure there is a right place, but this is probably better than most."

"If you'd rather wait..." Though he was very curious, Beau certainly wasn't going to pressure his grandfather into sharing.

"No." He cleared his throat. "No, I'd rather do it now."

Beau didn't say anything more, just waited for him to speak whenever he was ready.

"Though your grandmother and I had hoped to have a lot of kids, it didn't quite work out that way. It took us several years to have your mother, then eight more before we had Ritchie. Your mom was so good with him. She was eight when he was born, and she treated him like her own baby, absolutely doting on him. We couldn't have asked for a better big sister for him."

Beau frowned, trying to match that version of his mom with the one he had experience with. Though he didn't doubt that she, in some way, probably loved him and his siblings, she'd always been rather aloof in her interactions with them. To hear that she had doted on her brother in that way was mystifying.

"When she was a teen, she was still really good with him, though admittedly, her focus had shifted a bit. She had friends she liked to hang out with. School activities that kept her busy. Eventually, she had a job."

That description was a little more familiar. His mom was a good one for keeping busy with social activities and the people in their social circle.

"One day, your grandmother wasn't feeling well, so she asked your mom to pick Ritchie up from school and bring him home. She wasn't happy with the request. Not at all. She had plans with her friends, and she didn't want to have to delay them in order to deal with Ritchie."

Beau's stomach started to knot. Maybe he could wait to hear this story.

"The police chief came to tell us." His grandfather's voice wavered. "But by the time we got to the hospital, it was too late."

"What happened?" Beau could barely get the words out, but he felt it was important to know. Important because this was part of his mother's history, and it had clearly played a role in the woman she'd become.

"Witnesses said that she ran a stop sign. The thru traffic didn't have to stop, and a truck hit them on the passenger side. Ritchie didn't have a chance."

Beau blew out a long breath as nausea churned in his gut. "Was Mom hurt?"

"She had a bump on her head from where she hit the window, but otherwise, just some aches and pains from being in an accident like that."

He had more questions, but Beau sensed the story wasn't over, so he just waited for his grandfather to finish it when he was able.

"In the weeks that followed, blame and guilt laid waste to our family. My wife blamed herself for being sick and your mom for not paying attention. And of course, your mom blamed herself as well. I tried to help them move forward, but it seemed an impossible task." He paused, and the brief silence hung heavy in the air. "Your grandmother changed after that. She would lash out at us, then she'd crawl into bed and not get up for days. I asked her to speak with someone who could help her, but she refused. I think she felt like it was wrong to try to get better. Sadly, as long as she wasn't getting help, your mom refused any help as well."

The older man fell silent again, and Beau chanced a glance at him. His heart began to ache when he saw the tears trickling down his wrinkled face.

"Then came the day when the rest of my world came toppling down. My wife decided she couldn't take the pain anymore. The day after her funeral, your mom left New Hope Falls. My last clear memory of her was of her standing in the door to her bedroom that night. I told her that I loved her, but all she did was nod then close the door."

How many years had it been since that day? If his quick math was correct, it had to have been at least thirty-five. Such a long time to allow guilt and pain to ruin lives.

"For the longest time, I had no idea where she was or if she was even still alive. It was hard to keep going myself, but I did because I hoped one day, I'd be able to see her again." A hand patted his arm. "Though I still haven't seen her, God brought you to me, and I'm very grateful."

Beau had to wonder how a man who had experienced so much grief in his life could still believe in God. There was no doubt he did, though. They'd attended church again that morning, and though Beau still wasn't completely comfortable there, it had been marginally better than the week before. He'd had a better idea of what to expect, and the pastor's sermon had once again held his interest.

He wanted to ask his grandfather how he'd kept his faith in a God who had allowed so many tragedies to befall him and his family, but he didn't.

"I still haven't given up hope that your mom will want to reunite with me one day."

"How did my dad know to contact you?" Beau asked.

"This wasn't the first conversation I have had with your father."

"Really?" Beau chanced another glance at the man.

"As you are very well aware, your father is a man of significant wealth, and he was that way when he met your mom. When he'd asked her about her family, she'd said she wasn't in contact with me anymore and hadn't been for several years. Naturally, he wanted to know more, so he did a background check on her, which gave him all the details he needed to know about what had happened."

"That sounds like something he'd do," Beau said.

"I don't know your father personally, of course, and I'm not sure how much I'd really like him if I did, but I am forever grateful to him for several things. First, he phoned me after that background check to let me know that your mother was okay. Every year after that, I'd get a brief letter, letting me know she was still okay, and eventually, those letters contained bits of info about you kids too."

"Really? Now that *doesn't* sound like something he'd do." A memory of a few years earlier flickered in his mind. Perhaps he did have a bit of an understanding of what had motivated his father.

"I'm not sure why he did it, but I definitely appreciated it. I think he must have someone keeping close tabs on me because a few years ago, when my health began to decline, a man showed up and he said he was there at your father's instruction. The result of that visit was that your father covers the cost of my stay in the personal care home."

"Wow. I had no idea."

"When he called me to ask about you coming here, there was no way I'd say no, not just because I felt obliged to help, but mainly because it would give me the chance to finally meet at least one of you."

"My father has controlling tendencies." Though honestly, that was a bit of an understatement.

When his grandfather chuckled, Beau realized that maybe the man understood that. "He probably thinks he can dictate what I do with you."

"Somehow, I doubt that he'd want me to be doing the jobs you have assigned me. It probably wouldn't have even entered his mind. I have a feeling he was hoping I'd end up bored out of my mind, so I'd be willing to kowtow to what he wants." That and the threat of a loss of his trust fund might have done it, but he wasn't bored. He was far from that.

"I'm just grateful that you have proved to be willing to humor an old man."

"The first week might have been humoring you, but by the second week, I could see some merit to what you were asking me to do."

"I'm glad to hear that."

His grandfather gave him some directions that allowed him to loop around back to the town. Their trip was shorter than the one he'd taken with Sarah, but it seemed his grandfather had enjoyed it, despite the heavy turn the conversation had taken. To say the story had taken him aback was an understatement, and his heart hurt for his mom and his grandfather.

"Thank you for a wonderful afternoon," he said as Beau pulled to a stop under the portico leading to the entrance of the personal care home.

"I'm sorry that I asked about the past."

His grandfather patted his arm. "I'm not. I wanted to tell you and being able to do it between just the two of us while we toured the beauty of the area was perfect."

Beau helped him from the car into his wheelchair, then pushed him inside. Once in his room, he stopped the wheelchair by the window.

"I'll see you tomorrow," Beau said, resting his hand on the man's frail shoulder.

"I look forward to it."

Once he was back in his car, Beau sat for a moment, staring out the windshield, but not seeing what was in front of him. It was hard to believe that his family's history held so much tragedy. His mom had hidden it well, which made him a little sad and kind of mad. His grandmother and his uncle deserved to be remembered, regardless of the circumstances of their deaths. That his mom hadn't honored their lives by sharing about them made him angry.

But what was he going to do with this information? Part of him wanted to reveal it all to Julianna and Rhett, but there was a part of him that wanted his mom to be the one to tell them. It was her story, after all. It was only the knowledge that his mom would probably never share it that helped him accept that the role would fall to him.

With a sigh, he started the car and pulled out of the parking lot. Also on his mind was his interaction with Sarah the previous night. He hadn't been lying when he'd told her that he'd initially thought she was Leah. The way she'd been standing in the subdued light with slumped shoulders just staring at the kettle hadn't been reflective of the Sarah he'd come to know.

It made sense, in a way, her being more low-key. He doubted that an upbeat person could be upbeat *all* the time. They'd likely need to have mellower moments to recharge.

However, it had been alternatively concerning and yet also revealing to see Sarah that way. He wished she'd felt comfortable enough to confide in him, but he understood why she didn't. That didn't stop him, however, from wondering if something in particular had caused her down mood. Or if it was just how she got at certain times.

Tiffany had been moody at sometimes, and he was ashamed to admit—even just to himself—that he'd had little patience for her moodiness. Especially since he didn't feel that same way about Sarah. With her, he wanted to understand what might have made her feel down.

Beau couldn't discount the fact that the stress he'd been under in Houston was much more than what he was currently dealing with in New Hope Falls. He knew that that pressure made his tolerance of things like moodiness much lower. That was probably why he was more understanding of Sarah's present emotional struggles than he had been of Tiffany's.

At least that's what he told himself because he didn't want to really admit that he had been that much of a jerk to Tiffany. Maybe he would have to give her a call soon. At the very least, he owed her an apology. He didn't want to give her any false hope, but she deserved to know that she had been right about him, and she did deserve better than what he'd been able to give her.

He wanted to encourage her to hold out for what she wanted from a man. There was no need for her to have to settle for less.

When he got back to the lodge, he heard voices in the large living room. It was one of the rooms in the lodge where he hadn't spent much time. He glanced inside but didn't recognize anyone, so he assumed they were some of the guests that had come in for the weekend.

With a smile and a nod at the one person who noticed him, Beau continued on to the kitchen. There he found several of the family members, but not Sarah. Disappointment curled in his stomach.

"Hey there, Beau," Eli said with a smile. "How's it going?"

"Good. I just took my grandfather for a drive. After I told him about seeing the sights yesterday with Sarah, he mentioned how much he missed seeing the area. I thought it would be nice to take him out for a bit."

"That was sweet of you," Nadine said. "I know that a lot of the older folks miss being able to get out."

Beau nodded. "He also told me about what happened with my mom, her brother, and my grandmother."

Nadine's expression turned sad. "It was a horrible time for them, and to a lesser extent, for those of us who watched it all unfold with no idea of how to help."

"My mom never talked about it. I had no clue about any of what happened back then."

"She didn't talk to any of us about it either, and then she just disappeared." Nadine frowned. "We were really worried about her."

"I can imagine." Beau crossed his arms. "I want to talk to my mom about all of it, but I'm not sure how she'll react. She was absolutely livid that my dad had me come here."

"I would love to see her again." Nadine gave him a hopeful smile. "Maybe one day she'll come back. I know your grandfather would love to see her again too."

"I wouldn't hold my breath for that to happen, but you never know."

"That's certainly something to pray about," Nadine said.

Beau wasn't sure what to say in response to that. He couldn't say he'd ever thought too much about prayer, though from listening to the pastor's sermon that day, he'd learned it was something that Christians put great stock in.

"Hey, we're having dinner and a Bible study at my place tonight," Eli said. "You're welcome to join us."

There was a part of Beau that was interested in going just because he appreciated the social aspect. Studying the Bible, however, he wasn't so sure about.

"It's basically the same group of people that were at the hike last week—give or take a few," Anna said.

"And there's no need for you to participate," Eli assured him. "We'd just enjoy having you there with us."

Beau wasn't sure what to do. What could it hurt, though? These people actually seemed to want him there. And he kind of wanted to be there too.

"You don't need to answer now," Eli said. "If you want to come, we'll be eating at five-thirty, and the study starts around seven."

"Can I bring anything?"

"Just yourself." Anna smiled. "We'll have plenty of food, trust me. Leah always attempts to provide all the food by herself if we let her."

"Just want to make sure there's enough," Leah said. "It goes against my religion to run out of food."

"Leah," Nadine said with a shake of her head and a laugh.

"I think I'm going to head upstairs, but I'll probably see you later."

Eli smiled at his statement. "Great."

Beau managed to get himself up to his room without turning around to ask where Sarah was, even though he quite desperately wanted to know. He hoped that she would be at the study, but even if she wasn't, he figured he'd still enjoy the time outside his room. Otherwise, he'd just be sitting around doing nothing but thinking about the awful events in his family's history.

CHAPTER FIFTEEN

"He's planning to go to the Bible study, I think."

"Hmmm?" Sarah glanced over to where Leah sat leaning back against the large windows.

She'd appeared a few minutes earlier and made herself comfortable on the floor of the studio.

"Beau," Leah said. "Eli invited him to the study tonight, and he said he'd try and make it. I thought you'd want to know."

Sarah wasn't sure what to make of Leah's disclosure. She'd woken still in a funk, uncertain that she even wanted to go to church. In the end, she'd gone because she knew that one of the best ways to force the bleakness from her mind was to fill it with uplifting things. Unfortunately, it hadn't worked as well as she'd hoped, so as soon as she'd had something to eat after the service and helped clean up, she'd come down to her studio to paint.

As she stepped back to look at the painting, it didn't surprise her to see that what had flowed from her mind most easily for her that day was a stormy sky hanging low over trees, nearly obscuring the mountains in the distance. Eventually, there would be a cabin set in amongst the trees.

While she'd felt black the night before, her mood had lifted to gray after the church service that morning. It still sort of resembled the stormy sky, but painting had helped to draw her attention to one thing, rather than her having to deal with the scattered array of thoughts she'd had the night before.

"Are you planning to come?" Leah asked.

"Maybe." Sarah laid her brush down, then turned to look more fully at Leah. "I think my friendship with Cece is over."

Leah's brows rose at that, but she didn't say anything. With a sigh, Sarah sank to the floor in front of her and proceeded to spill the details of what had happened the night before. Though Leah hadn't been a fan of any of the cheerleaders, per se, she certainly wasn't a fan of anyone who kicked someone while they were down. Her expression darkened as Sarah told her about Cece's comments to Jillian.

"I know you always hoped to bring out the good in Cece, but I'm glad you stood up for Jillian. It sounds like she needs—and will probably appreciate—your friendship more than Cece ever has."

Sarah couldn't deny that the idea of being there for Jillian appealed to her because she liked to be supportive and to offer a safe place for people to share when they needed it. Cece had really never leaned on Sarah that way. She'd been more interested in having Sarah around to back her up. It was a dynamic that Sarah had allowed to go on for far too long.

"Is that why you're in this mood?" Leah asked. "You're upset over things with Cece?"

"That's part of it, for sure." Sarah shrugged. "But, you know I get this way sometimes."

"Yeah, but it's been awhile, and I'd kind of hoped you weren't having to deal with it anymore."

"I think it's partly that whole situation with Cece, but also, just feeling a bit under pressure with this upcoming show. I'm enjoying preparing for it, but I know there's a lot on the line."

"Is Beau part of it?" Leah asked.

"Not in the way you're thinking." Sarah rubbed her hands against her thighs, her palms sliding on the fabric of the paint-splattered leggings she'd changed into earlier. "I know that Beau isn't right for me, but that doesn't mean there aren't things about him that I admire. I just wonder how long it will be until I find those qualities in a man that is right for me."

"He *is* nice," Leah conceded. "But yeah, it's not a good idea to hope for something more than friendship."

"That's why I'm *not* hoping for something more." Though she couldn't say that she wished something more were possible.

Leah was silent for a moment before she said, "You know, I do understand about wanting something like that."

Sarah looked at her in surprise. To her memory, Leah had never expressed an interest in a relationship. "Really?"

This time it was Leah's turn to shrug. "When I see Eli and Anna together, I think about how nice it would be to have a connection like that with someone. But then I think of Mom and Dad..."

"Yeah." Sarah knew what she was saying, and she had to admit that the idea of trusting someone the way her mom had trusted their dad could be a little daunting. Even discouraging.

Eli hadn't had that problem, most likely because he had resolved to not be like their dad, and their mom had been a great role model in a way their dad hadn't been. An absolute rock, so steady for them even while her own world fell apart. So where did that leave her and Leah? Wanting something that, in the end, they'd be too scared to reach for?

And then what?

Somehow she knew that Leah had no answers for her either, but it was somewhat reassuring that there was someone who understood the push and pull of wanting a relationship but being fearful of one too.

Sarah laid back on the floor, looking upside down at the painting on the easel. She knew going to the Bible study would be good for her. Being around people she cared for always lifted her spirits, plus it was always good to be reminded of where her focus should be when her heart and mind became weighed down.

And if Beau was there, she just had to remind herself that he could be a good friend, even if he couldn't be a boyfriend.

"I guess I'll go tonight."

"Perfect." Leah moved to lie next to her and hooked her pinky with Sarah's.

It was something they'd done ever since they were little. It had started as a way to reassure the other one that they weren't alone, and even now, it was their way of claiming solidarity against whatever else was going on in their world.

They stayed there for a bit, then Leah sat back up. "You need to take a shower. You've got paint on you."

"What would I do without you?" Sarah asked, reaching out to jerk on Leah's braid.

Leah gave her a smirk before she got up. "See you in a bit."

Sarah pushed up to her feet and headed for her bathroom. The shower made her feel better, taking her mood from stormy to more of a soft dove gray. She wasn't feeling her usual self just yet, but things were evening out a bit in her mind.

Once ready, Sarah went up to the kitchen, where she found Leah putting together the food she'd made for the meal.

"Are we driving or taking the wagon?" Sarah asked as she eyed all the containers on the counter.

"Just the wagon, I think."

They worked together to put everything into the large wagon they used to cart things like clean towels and sheets to the various cabins. The lodge was quiet as the rest of the guests had checked out that afternoon, and they didn't have any other guests checking in until the next afternoon.

The following morning would be all hands on deck to get the lodge rooms and the cabins ready for the week. One of the young moms from church came and helped them with the cleaning each Monday and Friday as those were generally their busiest days when it came to prepping rooms and cabins.

"I forgot the whipped cream," Leah said. "I'll be right back."

Sarah tilted her head back and stared at the sky. The days were getting longer, so she was able to enjoy the blue sky with clouds streaked across it. Unlike how it had been earlier in the year when the sun would have already set by that time of day. She appreciated both the longer and the shorter days, but when her mood was the way it had been for the past day, more sunlight was definitely a welcome bonus.

"Are you heading to Eli's?"

Sarah lowered her head and turned to see Beau coming down the steps. He wore a pair of dark blue jeans and a lemon-yellow long-sleeve Henley with the sleeves pushed up to his elbows. Yellow? Really? She didn't often see guys in yellow shirts, so to see him headed her way wearing a shirt of her favorite color... How was that even fair?

His hair was in a more relaxed style than usual, a chunk of it falling low across his forehead. It seemed that the longer he was in New Hope Falls, the less he resembled the polished businessman who had arrived there two weeks earlier.

"Yep. We're apparently expecting a huge turnout if the food Leah prepared is anything to go by."

Beau's gaze went to the wagon, and he grinned. "It does look like we'll be eating well tonight."

"We always do when Leah's in charge of the food."

"Is it okay if I walk with you two?" Beau asked, his gaze shifting back to her.

"Yep." Sarah reached for the humor that had faded in her melancholy, hoping to keep Beau from seeing her in that way again. "We'll protect you from any wild animals."

Beau's smile widened. "I sure appreciate that." He hesitated then said, "You seem like you're feeling a bit better today."

She'd forgotten, for a moment, his observative nature. "I am. A bit. My downtimes don't usually last too long."

Before he could respond, Leah appeared with another bowl in her hand. She hesitated for a moment when she saw Beau, but then she gave him a nod as she approached the wagon and placed the bowl carefully among the other food items.

"May I pull that for you?" Beau asked Leah as she reached for the handle of the wagon.

She hesitated again, then stepped back. "Sure. That hill up to Eli's isn't a lot of fun with a full load."

Beau took the handle and began to pull it. Sarah fell into step beside him, while Leah moved to walk on her other side. It was no surprise that Leah remained quiet for the walk, but Beau more than held up his end of the conversation, asking about the cottages and the business as a whole.

Though she didn't have a degree in business or anything like that, Sarah was still fully aware of the ins and outs of running the lodge, so she could answer his questions fairly easily. The lodge wasn't her passion the way it was Eli's and, to some extent, Leah's, but she still knew how to keep it running if she ever had to step in. Her mom had made sure of that.

It was clear that Beau had a mind for business, though, because the questions he asked were informed. Not that he was asking for specifics, just general stuff like how they handled reservations and when they had their busy periods.

As they reached the bottom of the hill that led to Eli's, Sarah thought about offering to help him pull the wagon but decided not to. When it was just her and Leah, they would share the wide handle and pull together, but she didn't think that was a wise move with Beau. It would be too much like holding hands, plus, she didn't know if he'd be insulted if he thought she was inferring that he couldn't handle it by himself.

She didn't think he would feel that way, actually, but she left well enough alone. If he needed help, he could ask for it. Their pace did slow as the incline steepened a bit, but soon, they rounded the corner, and Eli's cabin came into view.

Sarah loved his place, and she'd painted it a few times in the years since he'd finished it. Two of those paintings hung on Eli's walls. One was a winter scene, and the other was fall. Those were the times when it looked the prettiest as far as Sarah was concerned.

The door opened as they approached the cabin, and Eli came out onto the porch to greet them. Anna followed him, and soon several people were out there, helping to carry the food into Eli's kitchen.

Sarah glanced at the people milling around, half expecting to see Cece. Though Cece hadn't always been a fan of the Bible studies, she usually came for the socializing. It was one of the reasons she'd been hesitant to invite Jillian to the study. The last thing she'd wanted was another confrontation between the two. Not that Jillian would have initiated anything, but Cece...who knew what she might have done.

An arm came around her shoulders, and Sarah looked over to see Anna beside her. "How're you doing?"

"Better," Sarah said, giving Anna a smile.

"That's good." Anna squeezed her shoulders then moved away to help Leah set out the food while the others moved back to the living room area. "Do you think Cece is coming tonight?"

"I hope not." Sarah felt a moment's guilt from her words, but at the same time, she wasn't sure she was ready to deal with her.

Sooner or later, she'd be required to interact with her, but she hoped it was later, if at all possible. She hoped it was later for Jillian as well.

Once the food was all set out, Eli prayed, then invited people to fill their plates. Most of the same people were there, although Carter was missing, which probably meant he had a shift at the firehouse. The group was made up primarily of singles from the church, but there were a few people who'd stayed in the group after they'd gotten married.

"You should introduce Beau to Michael Reed," Sarah said to Eli. "He's supposed to be working with him next week."

"Really?" Eli glanced over to where Michael stood talking to Andy. "I'll do that."

Sarah knew that her mood over the past day, plus her conversation with Leah, had led her to the realization that if she was to truly guard her heart when it came to Beau, she needed to have fewer interactions with him, especially when it was just the two of them. Allowing her hopes to focus in on something that, from the start, had been an impossibility was the height of stupidity and was a slippery slide into heartache.

So that was why, once the study was over, Sarah joined Leah when she headed home while Beau stood talking with Eli and Michael. She felt a pang of regret over leaving him to fend for himself, but it felt like an absolute necessity that she not hang around and then walk home alone with him.

The study that night had focused on facing the difficult situations in life, and it had made Sarah realize that there were enough of those that arose of their own accord that she didn't need to add any of her own making. So she was taking a step back, letting Beau return to his original status as a lodge guest who was only there for a limited time. Whose life was far removed from hers.

CHAPTER SIXTEEN

Beau stared down at his plate of food, wondering if he could somehow eat without having to lift his arms. Even if that was a possibility, however, he'd be too worried he'd just lay his head down and take a nap in his dinner.

He'd been working at Reed Landscaping for a couple of days now, and the work was physically demanding. And like he'd discovered from bussing tables, his gym workouts hadn't prepared him for that kind of work. Apparently, springtime meant endless yard work, but also, he'd chopped and stacked a lot of wood since people still burned wood in their fireplaces due to the coolness of the nights even though the days could be warm.

He glanced around the table, wishing that Sarah was there. How it had happened, he didn't know, but going for more than a few hours without seeing her made him antsy. Somehow, seeing her had become the best part of his day, but he hadn't seen her since Sunday night at Eli's, so Beau had found his mood slipping over the past couple of days.

Part of him wondered if she was avoiding him and if so...why? He'd enjoyed getting to know her, as well as the rest of the family—except for maybe Leah, but that was only because she hadn't shown any indication that she wanted to get to know him.

Eli and Nadine were still interacting with him, so it didn't seem as if it was something he'd done. And Leah hadn't been looking at him with any more suspicion than usual. He hated to admit how much it bothered him to think Sarah might actually be avoiding him.

He lingered for a bit, in case she made an appearance, but if he stayed any longer, he'd be sitting by himself at an empty table. With a sigh, he pushed his chair back and got up, just managing to stifle of groan of pain as his muscles protested the change in position. After saying goodnight to the others there, he headed up to his room, determined to take a shower hot enough to ease the ache in his muscles.

Once he'd stood under the water as hot as he could stand it for a few minutes, Beau finished his shower and dressed in a pair of pajama pants and a T-shirt. He settled on his bed with his laptop, but there were pitifully few emails in his inbox to hold his attention, and he found his thoughts constantly wandering to Sarah.

Maybe it was a good thing he hadn't crossed paths with her in the past couple of days. There was no denying she appealed to him. She was so different from Tiffany. While Tiffany was stunningly beautiful, Sarah was more on the cute side. Tiffany drew people's attention because of her looks, but people would rarely approach her unless they already knew her. Sarah, on the other hand, only had to smile, and people were drawn to her. The joy and warmth in Sarah's smile called to people like moths to a flame.

Even he'd responded to that joy and warmth. Though he didn't think he was anywhere near as captivating as she was, he had to wonder if she felt a similar draw to him. And if so, was that why she was avoiding him?

The idea that they might both be feeling similar things for each other did funny things to his stomach. But no, he couldn't allow himself to even consider anything like that. He had a plan for his life, and it didn't include leaving Houston for at least a year, probably more, if things panned out the way he hoped they would.

When Beau discovered Sarah in the kitchen the next morning before he left for his day with Michael, he let out a sigh of relief.

His heart settled, and that bright warmth he'd been missing flared to life within him at the sight of her.

"Good morning," he said as he walked into the kitchen. Though Nadine didn't serve breakfast that early, she'd told him to help himself to muffins and bagels, plus he always needed a cup of coffee to start his day.

Sarah gave him a quick smile as she moved to the fridge. Dressed like she'd been the first morning they'd met, she wore black leggings and a large paint-splattered T-shirt that she'd knotted over her hip. "Good morning."

"Are you up early or up late?" he asked as he headed for the Keurig.

"Up late," she said. "I was in the home stretch of a painting I've been working on."

"I'm amazed at how you manage to work through the night. I'd probably fall asleep before midnight."

Beau knew that when he looked back on his time in New Hope Falls, these mornings with Sarah—in fact, any of his times with her—would hold a special place in his memory.

He was coming to realize that, as a whole, his time in New Hope Falls was turning out to be a real highlight for him. There had been times their family had gone on fun vacations. They'd even gone to Disneyland a couple of times. Though, as he recalled, it had been their nannies who had actually taken them to the rides in the park while his mom had lounged by the hotel pool, and his dad had spent time on the phone with the office.

But no trip, no vacation, that he'd ever gone on had held the impact that this time in New Hope Falls had. It made him want to share it with Julianna and Rhett. He could even imagine how them being in New Hope might help bring them all closer together. And on top of that, he knew his grandfather would love to get to know the two of them.

"Did you want me to put in a bagel for you?" Sarah asked. "Or did you want a muffin?"

"I was kind of thinking about a muffin," Beau said. "Your mom mentioned there would be some fresh ones this morning."

Sarah motioned to a container sitting on the counter. "The muffins are in there."

Her bagel popped up, and she pulled down a couple of plates and gave one to him before she removed the bagel and smeared it with cream cheese. Though she seemed relaxed and at ease with him there, things seemed a bit...off between them. Reserved in a way that things had never been. Even when they'd been strangers that first morning.

Beau found he desperately needed to understand what was going on. To make sure that he hadn't done something that had upset her. He didn't think he had, but the whole situation with Tiffany had made it clear that he was a bit clueless when it came to his interactions with women.

"Have I done something?" Beau asked, deciding that subtlety probably wasn't the best way to tackle this specific issue. He suspected that if he tried to be more subtle, Sarah would just brush him off.

Sarah glanced at him as she cut her bagel into pieces. "Done something?"

"I just feel like maybe you're avoiding me." Beau paused then said, "Though as I say that, I realize it makes me sound a bit conceited. Like if you aren't spending every free minute with me, you must be avoiding me."

Her brows rose slightly, and a smile tugged at the corners of her lips. "I *have* been busy with this latest project."

"See. A perfectly logical explanation." Beau picked up a piece of muffin and crammed it into his mouth. If for no other reason than to shut himself up.

In her presence once again, he could fully admit just how much he'd missed her. Even though her behavior was a bit more reserved—still seeming a bit muted—being near her felt like finally seeing the sun after way too many cloudy days.

Her expression sobered, making his stomach clench. "That being said, I feel like I need to be honest because the project truly isn't the only reason I haven't been around."

"Oh?" Beau leaned a hip against the counter and took a sip of his coffee.

For the first time since he'd met her, Sarah looked uncomfortable, and Beau hated that because it probably meant he wasn't going to like what she said.

"The thing is, as I'm sure you're already well aware, you're a very attractive man. I noticed that first about you since, as an artist, I appreciate beauty." She picked up a piece of her bagel but didn't eat it. "And I'm always on board for more friends."

"Now that I've gotten to know you, that doesn't surprise me a bit, and I think that's a good quality to have."

"Yeah, see, I've gotten to know you a bit these last few weeks," Sarah said, her attention still on her bagel. "And it seems that in addition to your good looks, there are qualities about you that I really appreciate."

"Are you saying...that you...uh...like..." Beau allowed the sentence to trail off since he didn't know exactly how to finish it.

Her gaze lifted at that. "I don't know. But maybe? All I know for certain is that I can see it happening, and I don't need that complication in my life, to be completely honest."

Beau wasn't sure how he felt about being a complication, and yet, he completely understood what she was saying. Allowing anything to grow between them was irresponsible when they both knew that their lives were tied to two very different places.

Still, he felt the loss, not just of a possible relationship, but also of a friendship that, so far, had brought him more joy than any other friendship he'd ever had. That being said, he would never want to hurt Sarah, so if being around him caused that, he would allow her to put distance between them.

"I can respect that," Beau said softly. He respected *her*, and if this was what she needed from him, he would give it to her.

"Thank you." She kept her head bent, not allowing him to see her beautiful face, though it was what he wanted more than anything at that moment.

When Tiffany had ended things between them, he'd felt nothing but relief. Sarah's ending of their friendship—not even a relationship—brought an aching emptiness as he thought of a future without her bright cheerfulness. It pained him to think he'd been responsible for dimming that even a little.

Though Beau would have liked to hang around and chat more, he just couldn't do that when she'd made it clear that wasn't what she wanted. Plus, he did have to get to work.

"I guess maybe I'll see you later," he said. "Gotta head to work."

She looked up at him and gave him a small smile. "I hope you have a good day."

"Thanks." He wasn't so sure that was possible as he walked away from Sarah and out of the lodge into the damp morning air. There was a light drizzle that made the day somewhat less appealing, but it definitely suited his mood.

His stomach was in knots as he left the lodge and drove toward the landscape company. It wasn't something he felt often, but then, he hadn't felt like this about anyone else before either. Why couldn't he have found someone like Sarah in Houston?

Sarah finished the last of her bagel and drained her tea before putting their dishes in the dishwasher. She was tired and suddenly feeling uncharacteristically weepy. She wasn't one to cry very often, but Beau's easy acceptance of her desire to put distance between them, hurt.

She'd known she had to be honest with him when he'd asked her outright if she was avoiding him. Still, while he apparently understood what she was saying, it seemed to her that he didn't feel a similar way. The fact that that thought made her want to cry was revealing.

Clearly, she hadn't pulled back in time to avoid pain.

With a sigh, she headed back down to her room and took a quick shower before falling into bed. As she lay there, eyes wide open, Sarah was forced to acknowledge that she hadn't guarded her heart well enough. Or at all, really. She'd thought she could handle hanging out with Beau, and only view him as a friend, but she had over-estimated her ability to not be drawn in by the man.

Two days of not seeing him had only made the moment when she'd laid eyes on him in the kitchen earlier, that much sweeter. She had a feeling she wouldn't be able to truly get over him until he left New Hope Falls for good. In the meantime, she'd just have to try her best to mitigate the damage.

That, it turned out, was easier said than done.

After sleeping away a good chunk of the day, Sarah was in the kitchen helping with supper preparation when Beau walked in the door with a large bouquet of flowers in his hands. For a moment, her breath caught in her lungs, but then recalling their conversation from that morning, she pushed down the hope that had started to rise like a hot air balloon within her.

"Is Eli around?" Beau asked.

"He's out on the deck," her mom said, nodding her head toward the back door.

"Okay. Thanks." He set the vase with the beautiful flowers on the counter then stepped out of the kitchen onto the deck.

When he returned a minute later, Eli was with him. "Oh, those look really nice. Thank you for bringing them."

"No problem. I was happy to save you a trip since I was coming this way anyway."

Sarah felt a little foolish that she'd allowed herself to think—for even a second—that Beau had brought the flowers for her. Turning her attention back to the salad she was preparing, she only half-listened as Eli explained why he'd wanted the flowers for Anna.

Though she might be experiencing a little bit of jealousy, Sarah was still happy to see Eli doing such sweet things for Anna. That he had managed to do so well with his relationship with Anna when he hadn't had a good example in their dad, was no doubt an answer to their mom's prayers.

Sarah was definitely looking for a guy who more closely resembled Eli in behavior than their dad, that was for sure. And one who lived close enough to New Hope Falls that neither of them would have to move in order to be together.

"Smells good," Beau said. "I wish I was hanging around, but I promised my grandfather I'd have supper with him at the home. I just need to get cleaned up first."

"You look like you've put in a hard day's work," her mom said, and Sarah focused even more intently on the cucumber she was cutting up.

She felt a squeeze just above her elbow and glanced over to see Leah as she set a couple of large tomatoes on the counter. Sarah gave her a week smile then went back to work.

"It was an interesting day," Beau said. "The rain made work a bit of a challenge."

"Welcome to the Pacific Northwest, where learning to live with the rain is the number one lesson," her mom said with a laugh.

"It certainly is different from what we get in Houston. Mind you, I don't work outside there, so rain doesn't really impact my life very much."

Sarah listened as they chatted for a bit before Beau excused himself to get ready for dinner with his grandfather. She finished up the salad then moved on to the next task assigned by her mom. It was too bad that while the jobs kept her hands busy, they did nothing for her mind.

"You need to stop moping," Leah hissed at her. "Your down moods never last this long. Mom's going to know something more is up. You really don't want to have to explain to her why you're still feeling out of sorts."

Leah was very right about that, so Sarah tried to perk up and focus on what they were doing. But then Beau came back into the kitchen before he left, distracting her again.

"Nadine, I was wondering what your vacancy situation is like for this weekend."

"Oh. Well, let me check," her mom said. She wiped her hands on a towel then motioned for Beau to follow her.

"Wonder who's coming to visit?" Leah said. "Maybe his girl-friend?"

Sarah turned to stare at Leah, her heart thudding painfully in her chest. Keeping her voice low, she said, "He has a girlfriend?"

"Well, he actually had a fiancée, but apparently they broke up not long before he came here."

Sarah wasn't sure how to process that information. The revelation was no doubt what had fueled Leah's earlier warning about guarding her heart. Beau hadn't seemed heartbroken. Certainly not like she'd imagine someone who'd just had a serious relationship end, might act. It looked like the *unavailable* excuse he'd given her to pass on to Cece, hadn't been entirely an excuse after all.

While that information should have made her feel more determined to get over Beau, all it did was deepen the hurt she felt. What he'd awakened in her was more than just an attraction to him. Her longing for a relationship like the ones Anna and Eli and Cara and Kieran had, had intensified in his presence.

She wanted to be angry at Beau for not telling her about his past, but really, he didn't owe her any sort of explanation. And while him telling her about it might have headed off any thoughts of a relationship, it likely wouldn't have diminished the admiration she felt for him.

And if he and his fiancée really had broken up, that knowledge might not have kept her from developing feelings for him since that would have meant he was available. At least, in the sense that it meant he wasn't tied to anyone physically. The revelation also explained why it seemed she was the only one struggling with feelings. He was likely still getting over his fiancée and wasn't open to falling for anyone else just yet.

"Well, it looks like we'll have a full house this weekend," her mom said when she returned to the kitchen. "I filled one of the studio cabins and the last room here in the lodge."

"Did he say who was coming?" Leah asked.

"He's hoping his brother and sister will come. But regardless, he said he'd cover the cost of the bookings even if they didn't show."

While Sarah felt a sense of relief that it wasn't a girlfriend coming, it didn't change anything else. While Leah and her mom began to discuss menu changes for the weekend in light of extra people being present, Sarah went to set the table. She tried to focus her thoughts on her painting project and not on Beau, but it was a challenge.

She found herself wondering what Beau would think of her paintings. The ones she was currently painting were her favorite style.

Though she didn't share her inspiration with many, she really wanted to paint pictures like Thomas Kinkade had. Not necessarily the exact same style since that was unique to him. What she loved was the escape he created in his works. An idyllic world, full of light.

Though she wasn't seeking the same success he'd had, Sarah wanted to paint pictures that didn't require people to think too deeply when they looked at them. What she wanted most was for them to feel a sense of peace and tranquillity when they looked at the scenes she painted. An appreciation for God's creation.

She might never garner accolades from the elite art world, but that wasn't her goal. Sarah wanted her paintings to be loved and appreciated by the average person. Maybe someday she'd be able to have a gallery of her own that was comfortable and welcoming to all, not just those who felt that art had to look a certain way in order to be appreciated and considered worthwhile.

"Thanks for doing that, sweetheart," her mom said when she came into the dining room.

"You're welcome."

"Those flowers Eli ordered for Anna were quite lovely."

Sarah glanced at her mom, trying to figure out what had prompted the change of subject. "Yes. They were very nice. I know Anna will love them."

"I think I'd like to have some fresh flowers for the weekend," she said. "Could you get me a couple bouquets tomorrow?"

"Sure. I'll head into town in the morning and order them. Do you trust me to choose the designs?"

"Definitely." Her mom gave her a one-arm hug. "Thanks, love."

Maybe she'd stop in at the small art gallery in town while she was there. It would be good to touch base with the owner and let her know how things were progressing with the paintings she hoped to have ready for the show.

That meant she couldn't work through the night, which was fine. She needed a bit of a break before she dove into another painting, which she hadn't decided on yet.

The next morning, Sarah was up and out of the lodge by ten. She'd decided to make a day of it. Order the flowers, go by the gallery, lunch at *Norma's*, maybe visit the bookstore, then pick up the flowers. At one time, she might have gone by the bakery, but she still wasn't in the mood to deal with Cece, so she'd have to forego that stop for the time being.

Leah had gone with her mom to pick up groceries for the weekend, while Eli and Anna had gone into Seattle for something wedding related. Soon she and Leah would be going with Anna to meet up with Anna's assistant to pick out their bridesmaid dresses.

As she drove to town, Sarah thought about where to go for the flowers. Since the bouquet Eli had ordered for Anna the day before had been so beautiful, she had just assumed she'd go to Reeds' Florals, but as she got closer to town, she decided to go to the florist shop that had been in town for as long as she could remember.

Originally run by a woman her mom's age, it was now operated by the woman's daughter after the woman had been tragically killed in a car accident the previous fall. Her husband had been badly injured in the same accident but was still alive—last Sarah had heard. She figured it would be a good chance to check up on the daughter and give them some business.

The shop was operated out of a small two-story building on a side street. The florist business was on the bottom floor while there was an apartment on the upper one. The building looked a little rundown, but the lights were on inside, so Sarah made her way up the steps and pulled open the door, a bell jangling overhead as she stepped into the shop.

Sarah looked around the space, seeing far fewer flowers than she'd remembered from previous visits. There was no one behind the counter, but she heard a noise in the back, and then Leilani Alexander appeared in the doorway. Sarah's heart clenched as she took in the gauntness of the woman and the dark circles under her eyes.

"Hi, Lani," she said as she approached the counter. "How are you doing?"

Sarah realized what a dumb question that was when the woman said, "I'm fine. How are you?"

"I'm good." She gave her a smile then said, "I'd like to order a couple of bouquets."

"Oh, sure." Lani glanced around the room. "What did you have in mind?"

"Just an assortment of flowers. Mom wants some for the lodge this weekend."

"I don't have a lot on hand, but if you want to pick them up tomorrow, I'll have more available."

"Sure, that would be fine."

They spent some time discussing the flowers Lani would have available the next day, and Sarah was happy with the nice bright spring bouquets they decided on.

"Thank you so much for the order," Lani said. "I'll make sure they're ready for you by noon."

"That's wonderful. I can't wait to see them."

Lani looked a little happier when Sarah said goodbye and left the shop. As she got in her car, Sarah wondered how Lani was *really* doing. Sarah couldn't imagine losing her mom. That would utterly destroy her, she was sure. The very idea made her heart ache for Lani.

They'd been in the same grade at school, but Lani had been super studious, never getting involved in any extra-curricular activities. She'd also worked a lot at the flower shop with her mom. So while they hadn't been close, as with most people, Sarah still considered Lani a friend.

Once she got to Main Street, Sarah parked in front of the gallery then made her way inside. Irene, the gallery owner, greeted her with a smile and a hug. They discussed the paintings of hers that were currently available in the gallery, and when Sarah left, it was with a better idea of how many more paintings she could do for the show.

Feeling encouraged, Sarah headed over to *Norma's* for some lunch. Rather than waiting for a table, she gave her aunt a quick wave and made her way to the counter seats.

As she waited for Missy to come take her order, Sarah opened her social media and began to flip through her different timelines. She'd noticed a couple of days earlier that Cece had unfriended or unfollowed her on all the social media platforms. That made her sad. It seemed to make it all the more real that their friendship was truly over. Despite their previous ups and downs, she'd never gone that far before.

"Is this seat taken?"

CHAPTER SEVENTEEN

Sarah looked up from her phone to see Beau standing behind the seat next to her. "Uh. Nope."

"Fancy meeting you here," he said with a smile as he sat down beside her.

At his smile, she had to remind herself that while she could appreciate it, she couldn't attach any significance to it. "Yep. I'm running errands today, so I decided to stop in."

"I've been on lunch-fetching duty all week. I think Michael or Taylor phoned in the order a few minutes ago."

"Hey, you two," Missy said as she came to stand behind the counter. "What can I get for you?"

Beau motioned for Sarah to go ahead. "I'm just here to pick up an order for the Reeds."

"Okay. They're working on getting it together." Missy turned to Sarah. "What about for you, hun?"

"Chicken strips and fries."

"Milkshake?"

Sarah sighed. "Sure. Why not."

"I'll get that right out for you." Missy gave them another smile then headed for the kitchen.

"How's the work going with Michael?" Sarah asked, for the first time feeling a bit lost over what to talk about with Beau.

She'd allowed herself to be lulled into a feeling of familiarity that clearly wasn't shared. Not that they'd owed each other their life histories or anything.

"It's gone well. The physical work has been something to get used to, but I've also been able to offer the Reeds some advice on the business, which I've enjoyed." He shifted on the seat. "I don't mind the hard labor, but I have missed using my brain more."

Sarah wanted to ask about his job, but she didn't. Instead, she just hummed like she understood. And while she didn't necessarily understand about using his brain for business, she did know what it was like to go back to what she most enjoyed doing after having to do non-energizing stuff. Like going back to painting after having done a bunch of cleaning or cooking at the lodge.

His phone rang, and after he glanced at the display, he said, "Excuse me. I need to take this."

She'd thought he'd get up from the counter to take the call, but he answered it right there.

"How are you doing?" he asked after greeting the person.

Missy returned with her milkshake, and Sarah took a sip as she focused on her phone once again. She'd sent requests to Jillian for any social media she'd been able to find her on, but so far, her requests hadn't been accepted. Sometimes she forgot that there were people who spent way less time on social media than she did.

It had taken her awhile to figure out a way to not be bombarded by negative stuff on her accounts. Not that she avoided the sad posts or anything like that, but she certainly tried to keep from reading the negative posts and argumentative comments. By far, her favorite accounts to follow were the aesthetically pleasing ones on Instagram. They didn't just lift her spirits, they also created inspiration for her own art.

And she had a whole private board on Pinterest with pins of what she wanted for her own home someday.

"Can you come with Julianna?" Beau asked whoever he was speaking too. "I think you'd both really like it here."

Sarah didn't like to eavesdrop, but if he'd been concerned about that, he could have moved away. Short of putting her fingers in her ears, she couldn't avoid hearing his side of the conversation.

"I've booked rooms for you for the weekend, but if you want to come for longer, I could see if they have space available."

She was pretty sure they would. At that time, they were busiest on the weekends, but even then, they weren't full all the time. Once late-June rolled around, they began to get a lot busier. That was when they'd begin to be busy all the time. But since it was still mid-month, their vacancy levels fluctuated a bit more, especially during the week.

"I'm really not joking," Beau said. "I think you'd enjoy it. I mean, there's no party life here, so you might have to forgo that for one weekend, but that wouldn't kill you."

She wondered if Beau was used to a party life and if he was missing that while he was in New Hope. While she enjoyed a fun night with the girls, it was usually held at a restaurant or someone's place and consisted of food, music, games, and lots of laughter.

"Seriously. Talk to Julianna. You're best to fly into Everett, and I'll pick you up." Beau sighed. "We're all adults, so she'll just have to get over it. Besides, since when do you care if she's going to be upset. You do plenty that ticks her off."

It was highly irritating to only be hearing one side of a conversation. Sarah couldn't help but make assumptions. Like that part of the conversation sounded as if it was about their mom, but she couldn't say for sure. And she wasn't about to ask.

"Okay. Let me know what you decide."

Missy reappeared and set a bag down in front of Beau and a plate in front of Sarah. "Enjoy!"

Like there was any doubt. Sarah bowed her head and said a prayer before picking up a fry. Beau ended the call then lowered his phone with a sigh.

"Guess I'd better get this food back to the hungry masses. I'll see you later."

"Have a good afternoon."

"You too."

For all the pleasantries between them, there was no denying that there was an awkwardness that hadn't been there before. Or maybe that was just on her part. He'd seemed comfortable enough.

She hadn't made much of a dent in her food when Andy settled onto the chair Beau had vacated. "Hey. How's life in the land of the written word?"

"Good. Met with a couple of people who want us to stock some of their books. More local stuff."

"Anna still raves about the books she bought from you when she first arrived. They're on her coffee table now."

Andy chuckled. "I remember the stack of books she bought that day. Drake actually called me to check that the numbers were accurate."

"You've always impressed Anna with your book suggestions."

Andy's smile turned shy. "She indulges me when I ramble on. Not everyone does."

Missy came to take Andy's order, and their conversation as they ate was exactly what Sarah needed. When he finished eating and went back to work, Sarah also paid for her meal and left the restaurant. She glanced across the street at the bakery, wondering if Cece was working.

Thankfully, since she'd had a milkshake with her meal, she wasn't too interested in another sweet drink or treat. But in the past, even if she hadn't gotten something from the bakery, she would have stopped in just to say hi.

Instead, she went to her car and drove back to the lodge.

Once there, she checked if her mom and Leah needed help. When they didn't, she headed for her studio. She needed the distraction of painting, but first she had to figure out what to work on next.

She settled down in front of her computer to review the pictures she'd been considering. By the time she headed back upstairs to help with supper, she'd made a decision and had already begun to prepare the canvas.

It wasn't any surprise that she'd settled on one of the pictures she'd taken of Beau facing the mountains as the inspiration for her next painting.

For some reason, she'd assumed that Beau would be with his grandfather for dinner again, but he showed up a few minutes before they were ready to eat and joined them. There was only one other couple at the table with them that evening, but thankfully Anna and Eli were there too, so they helped to keep the conversation flowing.

Usually, Sarah participated in the talk around the table with guests, but she honestly felt like she'd reached maximum saturation when it came to what was on her mind. *Beau. Cece. Jillian. The paintings.*

It had been hard enough to decide keep Beau at arm's length while she'd thought she was doing that just because of the distance between where they lived. Finding out he either currently had, or had recently had, a fiancée, just cast everything she'd been thinking and feeling in a whole new light.

"I'm the quiet one." Leah's whispered words pulled Sarah from her thoughts. "I can't take up the slack when you stop talking. Snap out of it."

"I'd let you talk if you wanted," Sarah muttered under her breath. "I wouldn't tell you to be quiet."

Leah let out a huff of laughter. "Like that would ever happen."

Sarah felt her heart lift a bit as she smiled at her twin. It was a source of confidence to know that no matter what happened in the rest of her life, Leah would always be there for her. And Sarah would always be there for Leah. That assurance didn't do anything to remove the ache in her heart, but it made it easier to bear.

The other couple at the table didn't linger long once dessert was finished, and when they'd left, Beau said, "I just want to confirm that my brother and sister will be arriving tomorrow afternoon. And they'll stay until Monday morning. I hope that is okay."

Most of the time, their weekend guests tended to leave Sunday afternoon, but Sarah had a feeling that her mom wouldn't care. She seemed to quite like Beau, and no doubt would make whatever allowances were necessary to accommodate him and his family.

"That's perfectly fine," her mom said. "Just let me know about the meals you'll need. I assume you'll want to spend time with your grandfather?"

"Yes. I plan to take them to the home on Saturday. I think we'll have dinner here tomorrow night for sure, and I'll let you know about other meals once I've had a chance to talk more with them."

"If you need any sightseeing ideas, let us know. I'm sure we can help you out."

"Julianna might be interested, but I doubt Rhett would be."

"Are you the oldest?" Eli asked.

Beau arched a brow. "Is it obvious?"

"I do recognize a few traits, being the oldest child myself." He grinned in Sarah and Leah's direction. "And some of the frustrations of having younger siblings."

"From what I've seen, you have it easy with Sarah and Leah. Julianna is fine, if a bit of a rebel at times. At least in my mother's eyes. Rhett, on the other hand, is apparently determined to put my parents in an early grave. His antics drive them crazy."

"How old is he?" her mom asked.

"Twenty-two. Julianna is twenty-four."

"Well, we look forward to meeting them," her mom said.

"I'm actually surprised that they agreed to come, to be honest, but I'm glad they did."

Sarah still wasn't sure if Beau was close to his siblings the way she was close to Eli and Leah. She thought probably not because he hadn't talked about them much at all. Eli and Leah were so important to her that she couldn't imagine having a conversation with someone new in her life and not talking about them.

"I guess, from what you've said, there's not much chance your mom and dad would come to visit as well," her mom said.

"That is highly unlikely." Beau shook his head and frowned. "My mom only travels to places like New York and Paris. She doesn't do small towns in general, to my knowledge, and definitely not this town in particular."

Her mom nodded, a sad look on her face. "I can't say I blame her, really, but I know it would mean the world to her father if she'd come for a visit."

"I'm not sure that anything will change her mind, but you never know."

"I know that Gregory prays for her every day, and he's asked for prayer from others as well, so maybe her heart will soften enough to allow her to return home for a visit."

"It would definitely take a miracle," Beau replied.

Though Sarah had seen Beau at church and noticed that he hadn't objected to the prayer before meals at the lodge, she wasn't certain about his spiritual status. The more he talked about his family, however, the more she began to think that likely he had attended church in New Hope at his grandfather's request, not because church was his habit or because he had wanted to be there.

It was one more thing that seemed to reinforce that a relationship couldn't work for them. One more thing that widened the chasm between them. Sadness swelled within her once more, and she knew she needed to remove herself from the conversation.

She just had to survive one more week. He was only supposed to be there for a month, and three weeks had passed already. Seeing him every day wasn't making her feel any better. Maybe she wouldn't be able to truly get past this dark funk until he left.

And yet the idea of never seeing him again only made her heart hurt worse.

The situation was horrible. Why had she ever wanted this? Why had she thought that falling in love would be a good thing? Not that she wanted to believe that she was in love with Beau after knowing him just three weeks. She wanted to believe that she was only mourning the loss of what could have been. Not something more significant.

Sarah remembered the day she'd found Cara crying after she and Kieran had broken up. They had been dating for awhile by that point. Given how much Sarah hurt over recognizing the futility of what she felt for Beau, how had Cara survived losing Kieran?

Picking up her mug, Sarah escaped to the kitchen, and once there, she began to clean up the dinner dishes. Leah joined her a couple of minutes later, but she didn't say anything. Just began to work alongside her.

"I think I'm going to go to a class at Cara's in the morning," Sarah said as she loaded the dishwasher. "Are you interested in coming with me?"

Leah laughed. "When have I ever wanted to go with you?"

"Never. But that doesn't mean you can't change your mind. I think you'd enjoy it."

Leah looked over at Sarah and arched a brow. "The only exercise I enjoy is walking on my treadmill while listening to an audiobook."

"I bet you'd feel more relaxed if you stretched. I mean, Mom and Aunt Norma go sometimes, and I'm not sure they would make the effort if it didn't make them feel better."

Leah just hummed and went back to the dishwasher. They made quick work of cleaning up the kitchen, then when the others finished up in the dining room, they cleared the rest of the table.

Beau had apparently taken her at her word about not spending time with him because he disappeared upstairs without saying anything to her. Though she should have been grateful, she was just hurt and angry. If he'd just told her he was recently out of a relationship, she would have viewed him in a completely different way. A way that would have kept her from ever thinking about anything more than a friendship with him.

Although, if she was going to be honest, first and foremost, it should have been his spiritual status rather than his relationship status that made her view him differently. Instead, she'd made assumptions about both things, believing they were only going to be friends, and now she was paying the price.

That night was definitely going to be a painting night. She needed the escape more than ever.

CHAPTER EIGHTEEN

Beau shifted from one foot to the other, his hands in his pockets as he waited for Julianna and Rhett to appear with the other passengers disembarking from their flight. He was still surprised that they had both agreed to come to New Hope.

He spotted Rhett first because he was tall like Beau, and usually stood above most other people. Julianna was at his side, and Beau felt a smile grow on his face. He couldn't remember ever being this happy to see his siblings.

When they reached them, Beau pulled Julianna into a hug. No doubt, it was surprise that made her body go tense for a moment before she wrapped her arms around him and squeezed tight. Rhett didn't even wait for him to finish hugging Julianna before he wrapped his arms around both of them.

"A group hug? I gotta be part of this," he said. "I believe this is a first."

Beau chuckled. "I've had lots of firsts lately. Glad I'm able to share one of them with you two."

When they finished their hug, they made their way to the baggage claim area. Beau noticed that they were garnering more than a few stares. Julianna may have been traveling, but she was still dressed to impress in designer casual wear. Rhett looked like Beau, albeit a more relaxed version. Even though Beau had on jeans, he still wore a button-up shirt and had styled his hair.

Rhett, on the other hand, wore a worn T-shirt with his jeans, and it looked like he was overdue for a haircut—by several months. He walked with an easy gait as opposed to Beau's more purposeful stride. The brothers were a study in contrasts even though at the base of it all, they looked very similar with their dark hair and blue-green eyes.

Julianna was a female version of them but with their mom's height. She had a mix of Beau and Rhett's personalities, which meant she could be more easygoing than Beau, but she also knew when to be focused. Rhett usually struggled with that concept.

"That's my bag," she said, pointing to the Gucci GG Flora suitcase that matched her purse and carry-on. She was nothing if not coordinated.

Rhett's bag wasn't Gucci, but Beau had no doubt it was pricey in its own right. Though Rhett didn't necessarily look like he was rich, Beau knew he forked out money for designer jeans and T-shirts that looked worn.

Once they had their bags, he led them out of the airport to where he'd parked his car.

"It's definitely cooler here than in Houston," Julianna remarked. "I was expecting it to be raining when we got here. I even bought a new umbrella for that likelihood."

"Well, I've discovered that it doesn't rain every single day, but I'm sure you'll experience a drizzle or two while you're here."

He opened the front passenger door for Julianna then went to help Rhett load their bags into the trunk of the car. That done, Rhett slid into the back passenger side seat while Beau climbed behind the wheel.

He followed the GPS's directions as he once again made his way to New Hope Falls. As he drove, Beau couldn't help but wonder what the McNamaras would think of his siblings. More importantly, he wondered what his siblings would think of the McNamaras and the lodge.

Strangely enough, he found himself feeling rather protective of the family who had welcomed him without question. He wasn't sure if they did that with all their guests, but most of the time now, he didn't really even feel like a guest.

From the moments spent sitting in the kitchen with them to the tour of the area he'd taken—with Sarah—Beau knew he'd never forget his time at the lodge. Not just because of the beauty of the place, but also because of the feelings that came when he thought of his time there with people he now counted as friends.

It seemed wrong to label Sarah as just a friend, though he knew he couldn't—didn't dare—label her as anything else.

"So I'm guessing there's no five-star hotel where we're going," Julianna commented as she looked out the window.

"Sorry. You're going to have to do without your luxury hotel this time around," Beau said. "But it's only for three nights, and the lodge is really nice. Rhett, you'll be staying at a cabin on the property. They only had one room available at the lodge itself, and I figured you wouldn't be any keener on sharing a bed than I was."

"You got that right," Rhett scoffed.

As the two of them remarked on the scenery, Beau mulled over whether he should issue a warning to the two. He didn't want them to treat the McNamaras as the hired help.

"Just a couple of things," Beau finally said. "There's no room service here, and we eat in the dining room of the lodge. Also, the family who owns the property has been very good to me, so treat them with respect, please."

"Beau," Julianna said, a sharp edge to her tone. "We're not disrespectful. Or rather, *I'm* not disrespectful, and I think Rhett could probably restrain himself for the time we're here."

"I'll be good," Rhett grumbled from the back seat. "Wouldn't want to besmirch the family name, after all."

Beau let out a bark of laughter as Julianna said, "Since when?"

"Good question," Rhett shot back.

"So, how have things been at home?" Beau asked.

Julianna sighed. "Things between Mom and Dad have never been warm and fuzzy, but now they're downright frigid. I have no idea why Mom's so upset that Dad shipped you off here."

"I know why." Beau debated how much detail he should go into. Finally, he decided that since his grandfather hadn't said to keep the family story secret, he'd fill them in. Plus, he didn't want his grandfather to have to relive those traumatic memories yet again.

"Oh my word," Julianna said when he finished. "I don't know whether to be angry at Mom or to feel sorry for her."

"I think it's probably okay to feel both. Eighteen is young to have to bear the weight of guilt over the death of a younger sibling." Beau thought of the sorrow etched on his grandfather's face as he'd shared about their family's painful past. "But she's an adult now."

"Why do you think Dad's kept in contact with our grandfather?" Rhett asked, his voice holding a serious note that was out of character. "I doubt it was out of the goodness of his heart."

"I'm not sure that it isn't partly that," Beau said. He'd thought about it a lot since he'd found out about the role his father had played in his grandfather's life. There was only one memory that could come close to explaining it, and it was the first thing that had come to mind after his grandfather had told his story. "I was in my teens when I found him drinking in the library late one night. He was already drunk, and when I asked him what was going on, he was surprisingly forthcoming."

"It turned out that day was the anniversary of his father's death. He continued to drink as he told me about his dad, and how close he'd been to him. He said his father had made so many sacrifices in order for Dad to have every opportunity to succeed. When he made his first million, it was Dad's plan to care for his father so that he could enjoy the later years of his life in a way he hadn't been able to enjoy his younger years. Unfortunately, not long after that, his father was diagnosed with cancer and was gone within months."

"You think he's taking care of Mom's dad as a way to make up for that?" Julianna sounded a bit skeptical.

"Yeah, it's kind of hard to imagine that," Rhett said. "Dad has never been, as Juli stated earlier, warm and fuzzy, not just with Mom but with us kids. There are times I've wondered if he even loved any of us."

Beau couldn't argue with him, but recalling that night and the emotions his dad had shown, had lingered in his mind through the years. Whenever he'd been the most angry and frustrated with his dad during the time since, he would call up his memories of that night to remind himself that his dad must have some sort of emotional depth, even if he rarely—if ever—showed it to his family.

Not that that knowledge had helped ease the sting of his current situation. Still, if anyone was to benefit from his father's hidden emotional depth, Beau was glad it was his grandfather. After so much hurt in his life, it was good to know that someone was taking care of him.

Beau said as much then added, "I hope you will both go with me to see him. I know he'd love to meet you."

"I'm definitely on board with that," Rhett stated without hesitation.

"I assumed we would," Julianna added.

"I plan to go tomorrow afternoon to see him, so I figured you could come with me if you wanted, and we'd spend some time with him."

"So have you run into other people who knew our mom?" Julianna asked.

"Nadine, the owner of the lodge, attended high school with her."

"That's kind of cool," Julianna said. "What are the rest of the family at the lodge like?"

"Eli is the oldest. He does woodworking and is engaged to Anna. She has a YouTube channel from what I understand."

"And she lives at the lodge?"

"She stays in one of the cabins. Eli lives on the property in a really nice cabin that he built. Anna will move there after they're married."

"They don't live together?" Rhett asked.

"No, but from what I understand, it's because they're religious, not because, like with Tiffany and me, they prefer their space."

"That's...interesting," Julianna mused. "And the rest of the family?"

"The other two are twins. Sarah and Leah. They're identical in appearance but very different in personality. If you see one of them and she smiles at you, that is most likely to be Sarah. Not sure Leah has smiled at me yet. Leah is reserved and almost suspicious in nature, while Sarah is much friendlier. They appear to be very close, though. I'm not sure what Leah does aside from working at the lodge. Sarah is a painter."

"Is she any good?" Rhett asked.

Beau smiled as he thought of the paintings Nadine had pointed out as ones that Sarah had painted. "I would guess that the art snobs would say her paintings are pedestrian, but I actually find them captivating. She paints a lot of scenes of the area. And as you can see, the area is beautiful."

"And that's it? No father?" Julianna asked, and Beau was glad she hadn't asked more questions about Sarah because he wasn't sure he'd have been able to keep himself from blathering on about her.

"He's not in the picture as far as I can tell. Not sure if that's because of death or divorce. Nadine doesn't wear a ring."

"So we have Nadine, Eli, Anna, Sarah, and Leah. Anyone else of importance we should know about?"

Beau thought of all the people he'd met since arriving in New Hope Falls and wanted to name them all because, in their own way, they'd become important to him. From the people at *Norma's* to Justin at the grocery store and Michael at the landscape business.

He would never forget them, and he hoped that he'd be able to keep in contact with them even after returning to Houston.

For sure, he'd be in contact with Justin since he was taking care of his investment money and maybe Michael if he had more questions regarding the financial side of his landscape business. Helping those two out had been more meaningful for Beau than anything he ever did at his father's company.

"I'll probably introduce you to a few more people as we meet up with them." Beau paused. "And just a head's up...we'll be going to church on Sunday."

"Say what?" Rhett asked from the back seat. "Church?"

"Yes. Grandfather goes to a local church, and I've been going with him. I think it would be nice if you guys came with us."

"I suppose we could do that," Julianna said. "It's just an hour or so, right?"

"Yep, and Rhett, you won't be hungover because I'm pretty sure the bar I saw in town won't be up to your standards."

Julianna laughed. "I wasn't aware that he had standards when it came to bars and clubs."

"Well, now you've just made me curious," Rhett said.

Beau looked into the rear-view mirror and met his gaze. "No going to any bars while you're here."

"You sound like Dad."

"This isn't for Dad's sake, this is for Grandfather. He doesn't need for word to get around that one of his grandsons got drunk while in town. And believe me, word would get back to him. In this town, everyone is interconnected in some way."

"Fun, fun," Rhett drawled. "Okay. I'll behave."

"Thank you."

As they drove through the town, Beau could tell that Julianna was captivated by the quaintness of it. Brightly colored spring flowers were blooming all along Main Street. Michael and his sister had done a lot of that work after having been hired by the town to take care of it.

As he passed the businesses he'd become intimately connected to, Beau filled them in on some of what he'd been doing while in the small town.

"You were a busboy?" Rhett asked with barely disguised laughter. "And bagged groceries?"

"Don't forget that I also laid sod, cut wood, and planted some flowers."

"I'm impressed," Julianna said. "I don't think Mom and Dad would be, but I certainly am."

As they left the town behind them, Beau finally asked the question that had been bugging him since they'd left the airport. "Have you seen Tiffany?"

"Yes," his siblings said in unison.

"How's she doing?"

"She's still upset with you," Julianna said. "And she offered me her sympathies for having such an emotional robot for a brother."

"Basically said the same thing to me," Rhett added. "Not that it's really your fault. I mean, Dad never really showed you how to have emotions. How to connect with people."

"You certainly don't have problems showing emotion or connecting with people," Beau stated.

"I'm a different personality. I think you're kind of like a flower."

"A flower?" Beau glanced up in the mirror. "What on earth?"

"Or maybe your emotions are more like a flower seed. You just need the right person to come along to water that seed and shower it with sunshine, and your emotions will come to life."

"That's rather poetic of you," Julianna observed. "I didn't know you had it in you."

As the two went back and forth about Rhett's sudden turn to insightfulness, Beau considered his words, and as he did, memories of being in Sarah's presence filled his mind. Though he hadn't put words to his emotions the way Rhett had, being around her felt a bit like basking in the sunshine.

Her joy over life, in general, was infectious. It wasn't something he was used to experiencing. Not that the people around him were grumpy, but everything in his world seemed a whole lot more calculated. The people he worked with knew his social status, and because of that, their interactions seemed less genuine. When he socialized, there was no appreciation for the little things in life. If conversation didn't pertain to the latest designer fashions or newest cars or a vacation taken at a popular luxury resort, it wasn't worth having.

And to be honest, he, Juliana, and to some degree, Rhett had been no different.

But being in New Hope Falls had changed him. And while his parents would no doubt say it was for the worse, Beau wasn't so sure.

"This looks very...quaint," Julianna said as Beau pulled his car into a spot in front of the lodge. "Those flower baskets look absolutely beautiful."

"Anna and Sarah made them," Beau said, remembering the day he'd come home from the grocery store to find flower potting supplies spread across the front porch. Before they got out of the car, he added, "Remember, no condescending remarks."

"I'm beginning to feel like you've found yourself a new family," Julianna remarked.

"Nah, he doesn't have a new family," Rhett said. "He never cared about people being condescending to *us.*"

"That's true, but that's mainly because you two can hold your own. You give back as good as you get, but the McNamaras? This is their place of business, so they'd probably not respond if you acted like that toward them. That makes it an unfair advantage for you."

"Okay. I guess that makes sense." Julianna gave a sniff. "I will endeavor to respect your wishes."

"We both agree...blah, blah, blah." Rhett pushed open his car door. "I need to move. Too many cramped spaces today."

Beau got out and went around to the trunk of the car. Julianna stood observing their surroundings as her brothers retrieved her luggage and carried it up to the porch. Beau opened the door then stepped back to allow Julianna to precede them inside.

"We'll just leave your bags here," he said. "I think Nadine is in the kitchen."

He headed in that direction then glanced back to see Julianna and Rhett lingering near the check-in desk. "Come on."

"You want us to come to the kitchen with you?"

"Sure. I'll introduce you."

Beau waited for them to follow him then he led them to the entrance to the kitchen. He could hear voices, so he knew he was headed in the right direction to find someone to check them in.

"Hey there, Beau," Eli said as they walked in. The man was seated on a stool at the counter directly across from Anna. No doubt, he'd picked the seat precisely because of that. "How's it going?"

A quick glance showed him that Leah and Nadine were also in the kitchen, but Sarah wasn't. The disappointment at her absence was more acute than it should have been.

"It's going well. I just picked up my brother and sister from the airport."

"Wow. There's no denying the three of you are related," Eli said as he got to his feet.

"Yes, but since I'm the original, they're just weak copies."

Eli laughed. "Definitely spoken like an older brother."

"Yep." Beau grinned then motioned to where the two stood. "This is my sister, Julianna, and my brother, Rhett."

Eli approached them and held out his hand. "I'm Eli McNamara." After they shook hands, he said, "This is my mother, Nadine, my fiancée, Anna, and my sister, Leah."

Beau kept his fingers crossed that the two of them would behave themselves.

"It's a pleasure to meet you." Julianna shook Nadine's hand, as did Rhett, showing manners even their mother would be proud of.

Anna also shook their hands, greeting them both with a friendly smile. Leah was washing dishes, so rather than stop, she just nodded in their direction.

"Let me get the two of you checked in so you can relax before dinner if you'd like."

"That would be lovely," Julianna said. "Travel can be exhausting."

"Yes, it can be." Nadine led them back to the foyer area and moved behind the check-in desk.

Beau followed them then waited as Nadine got the information that she needed from them. Once that was done, she handed over the keys to the room and the cabin.

"Grab a bag, will you, Rhett?" Beau said once Nadine had left them. "We'll take Julianna up to her room, then we can go check out where you're staying."

Julianna was in the room next to his, and while it wasn't exactly a luxury hotel, it was still a nice room.

She stood looking around. "This is...pretty."

"I think you'll find that the bed is up to even your exacting standards."

"Well, you boys can toddle off. I'm going to explore the room and relax a bit. What time is dinner?"

"Six," Beau said. "Did you see the dining room? It was right next to the kitchen. That's where we eat."

"Okay. See you later." She shooed him and Rhett out of the room, then shut the door behind them.

They walked down the stairs together then on out to the car to get Rhett's luggage.

"I'm assuming we don't have far to go," Rhett said as he pulled up the handle on his suitcase.

"Not too far. Just around the bend in the road up there."

They set off along the narrow asphalt road, pulling his suitcase and hand carry.

"This isn't quite what I had anticipated," Rhett said. "But it seems nice. The people we met seem nice."

"They are," Beau agreed.

"You seem different. More relaxed," Rhett stated. "I just assumed you were born with an uptight personality. It seemed like you inherited that from both Mom and Dad, while I got none of it. I'm glad to see that you can rise above your genetic disposition. I just hope the new personality sticks around when you get back to Houston."

The mention of returning to Houston made his stomach knot, but Beau knew it was inevitable. His whole life was there.

"I think Dad thought you'd be back way before now," Rhett said as they approached the cabin Nadine had assigned to him.

"I'm sure he thought that cutting off my access to the company server and handing off my clients would bring me running home, willing to make up with Tiffany in order to get it all back."

"I'm surprised it didn't, actually." Rhett climbed the stairs to the porch and used the key to open the door. Inside, he stopped to look around. "This looks suitable."

"Glad it passes muster with you," Beau drawled.

"Whatever that means," Rhett shot back at him.

"Sometimes I forget how young and under-read you are."

"I've got better things to do than read. Especially a dictionary."

Beau settled down on the couch, watching as Rhett prowled around the cabin. He'd always had a restlessness about him, and it appeared that hadn't disappeared in the nearly three weeks Beau had been gone.

Although it really felt much longer than three weeks. How was that possible?

On the flight there, he'd assumed that the month in New Hope Falls would drag, but now he only had a week left, and considering how the three weeks had flown by, he could only assume the final days would as well.

And he really didn't want that.

CHAPTER NINETEEN

"What's on your mind, bro?" Rhett asked, thumping Beau on his shoulder as he made his way over to one of the other chairs. "You seem lost in thought. Thinking about work?"

"Nope."

"Well, that's a first." Rhett stretched his legs out and leaned his head against the back of the chair. "Usually, all you talk about is work."

Rhett wasn't wrong. But Beau felt like a totally different person than he'd been when he'd left Houston. The experiences he'd had in New Hope had added depth to his life. Color to his world. In the same way that Sarah had brought his emotions to life, meeting people from completely different walks of life had broadened his horizons.

"I wasn't sure what to expect when Julianna said you wanted us to come here," Rhett said. "But hey, I'm always up for an adventure. What I didn't expect was to find my brother a changed man. Did you find religion while you were at it? Since you've been going to church?"

Beau didn't give an immediate denial. It wasn't that he'd found religion, so to speak, but he wasn't as apathetic about church as he'd once been. And maybe he was a bit more curious about it now, having seen faith in action that he'd never witnessed before. It was an everyday thing for people like Nadine, Eli, Sarah, and his grandfather. He wasn't used to that.

When he was a kid, they'd only gone to church at Christmas and Easter and for weddings or funerals. As an adult, he'd made the decision to stop going altogether...until he'd met his grandfather. And just like everything else since he'd come to New Hope Falls, his perspective on church and Christians had changed.

"Come on Sunday and see for yourself," Beau said.

"I didn't think I had a choice."

"You're an adult, Rhett. I'm not going to force you to do anything. Would I like you to come? Sure, but I'm not going to insist on it."

"Well, when you put it like that..." Rhett lifted his head to stare at him. "I suppose I could tag along."

Beau grinned. "We'll see if Julianna feels the same way."

"You're giving her a whole new audience to impress. I'm sure she'll go."

He couldn't hold back his chuckle at that. It was true that their sister did like to be the center of attention at times.

"Do you want me to leave so you can rest up a bit?"

Rhett sighed. "I wouldn't mind a bit of downtime. Got in late last night and then I was up early this morning to catch the flight."

"Were you out partying last night?" Beau asked.

Rhett shrugged as he pulled his legs in and sat forward before getting to his feet. "Figured I was out of commission for the weekend, so I'd make up for it before we left."

Beau got up as well. "The life you lead."

"It's charmed, isn't it?"

"I wouldn't say that, but to each their own."

"Should I just head over to the lodge at six for dinner?"

"Preferably a little before, so you're not late."

"I'll be there."

Beau left the cabin and headed back to the lodge. He wondered at the little niggle of worry he had for Rhett. Up until their conversation a few minutes ago, he'd been more frustrated by Rhett and his party lifestyle than worried. Maybe he needed to have a conversation with Julianna about his concern to see if she'd picked up on anything. Unlike him, her emotions had always been more open, and despite her ability to be self-centered at times, she could also be surprisingly perceptive of others.

Back at the lodge, he peeked into the kitchen and saw the same people who'd been there earlier. Where was Sarah? He lectured himself about being so focused on her when she'd made it clear that she needed distance from him. It should be what he wanted too. Who needed complications with just a week left in town?

Him, apparently.

~*~

Sarah stared at the painting, frustration welling up within her. It didn't look right. Normally she didn't have a problem capturing the scenes she wanted, but this time... No matter how she tried to force it, the scene wouldn't come together the way she wanted. It made her want to dip her brush in black and drag it across the work she'd managed to get onto the canvas.

She'd been working on it ever since she'd returned from picking up the flowers from Lani's shop. They'd been as beautiful as she'd promised they'd be, and Sarah had been inspired by them, but as soon as she was in front of her canvas, all that inspiration slipped away.

Finally, she stalked across the room and turned to press her back to the wall. As she stared at the mainly blank canvas, she let the strength go out of her legs and slowly sank down to sit on the floor.

Ever since this...thing with Beau had happened, she'd been struggling to produce the paintings she wanted for her show. She'd tried a couple different scenes now, and neither had stuck. All that her pencils and brushes wanted to capture was Beau's likeness. Not the back of him, like she'd planned. No, she wanted to draw or paint his face.

His dark hair. His rich blue-green eyes. She had just the right colors to paint him. She could imagine mixing them, and what brushes she'd use to apply them to the canvas.

Sarah tipped her head back and closed her eyes. How was she supposed to get past this? She'd been trying to steer clear of him, but each time she did, all she could think about was how the time was slipping away. One more week, and she'd likely never see him again. Sure, his grandfather still lived in New Hope, but that didn't mean that Beau would be making regular trips back to visit him.

Or that he'd stay at the lodge if he did return.

Once he was back to his normal life with his ex-fiancée around, he'd probably forget all about New Hope Falls. He'd had that life in Houston forever, while he'd had only a month in New Hope. It was unrealistic to expect him to remember his time there when he got back home and was busy with his normal life.

She needed to remind herself of that regularly, even though it hurt to think that way. The sooner she accepted that, the better. But while her mind might be well on its way to that acceptance, her heart...not at all.

Sarah still wasn't sure how she'd gotten to this point. She really thought she'd taken Leah's words to heart. It hadn't been her intention to allow anything to happen, but here she was...

"Sare?"

Sarah tilted her head to the side and opened her eyes to see Leah coming into the studio. "Hey."

"What's up with you?" Leah sat down beside her.

"Struggling with the painting." She pointed her brush at the canvas sitting on the easel.

"It doesn't look bad," Leah said. "What you've done so far."

"It doesn't look good either."

"Yeah, but your bad is still better than most people's good."

"Not hardly..." Sarah sighed. "It's just frustrating when it doesn't come together."

"You got time, though, right?"

"Yep. I've got time."

They both fell quiet for a few minutes before Leah said, "The fancies have arrived."

"Yeah?" The term almost made Sarah smile. Almost.

It was something they'd started saying when they were little kids, and rich people would show up in fancy cars wearing fancy jewelry and clothes and toting fancy luggage. She had no doubt that Beau's siblings fit that description since Beau certainly had when he'd arrived.

"They kinda look like triplets," Leah said with a laugh.

"Triplets? Really?" Sarah didn't want to be curious, but she was.

"Yep. The guy looks like a more relaxed, easygoing version of Beau, and the sister looks like a female version of them both."

"Do they seem nice?"

"We only saw them for a few minutes, so it was kind of hard to tell. They were polite, at least."

"That's good."

Leah seemed to be waiting for her to say something more, but Sarah had nothing more to say on the subject. "So, are you coming upstairs for dinner?"

"We're pretty full tonight, aren't we?" she said.

"Yeah. Mom will eat at the table, but we won't."

"I'll come up to help out in the kitchen then," Sarah told her.

"Are you sure?" Leah asked. "Because I'm certain we could manage without you if need be. Anna and Eli both said they'd help out."

"I'm sure. I could use a break from this painting anyway."

"Well, in that case, you have about an hour until we'll need you." Leah pushed up to her feet. "So you have time to scrub the paint off your face. Although maybe if you left it, it would distract from the dark circles under your eyes."

"Love you too," Sarah muttered as she watched Leah disappear out the door.

She sat for a few more minutes, trying not to think about the little bits of information Leah had dropped about Beau and his siblings. Finally, she cleaned up her brushes and went to take a quick shower.

Once out, she applied a bit of makeup to the circles Leah had so lovingly pointed out. She pulled on a pair of jeans and a plain light pink T-shirt before undoing her hair then brushing it up into a high ponytail, which she braided. After putting on her favorite necklace and earrings, she headed upstairs to the kitchen.

"How are you, sweetheart?" her mom asked when she spotted her. "Leah said you were struggling with your painting."

Sarah took the head of lettuce that her mom held out to her and moved to the cutting board that was already laid out. "Yeah. It's just not taking shape as easily as it usually does."

Her mom gave her a one-arm hug and kissed her temple before saying, "I know you'll figure it out. You always do."

Maybe she could eventually figure out her paintings, but her slide down into e heartache was a different and more concerning issue. She was on a slippery slope, descending rapidly, and there seemed to be nothing to stop her.

She was also being far more dramatic about the whole situation than was usual for her. Unfortunately, even acknowledging that couldn't pull her back to normal.

With her gaze on the vegetables she was cutting up for the salad, Sarah tried to pull up images in her mind that had previously served to inspire her.

The snow-topped peaks of the Cascade Mountains in the distance. Even though she'd witnessed them up close, she preferred the picture they made from afar.

A field of sunflowers she'd seen in a picture once. Yellow was her favorite color, so sunflowers appealed to her. There was just no shade of the color that could be anything but joyful.

A forest of evergreens like the ones that surrounded the lodge, their rich deep color filling her with feelings of warmth.

She'd found videos on YouTube of the lagoon surrounding Bora Bora and had fallen in love with the gorgeous blue green hues of the water. Aaaand...she was thinking about Beau's eyes again. And Beau.

With a sigh, she dumped the lettuce into the bowl. How was she supposed to move forward when her thoughts kept veering off onto paths that ended up at something that reminded her of him.

"Sarah?"

And now she was hearing his voice in her head. Was it normal to take leave of one's mind when struggling with unrequited feelings?

Someone jostled her shoulder, and she looked over to see Leah staring at her with concern. "Where are you?"

"What do you mean? I'm right here."

"Well, your body is, but clearly, your mind isn't." She nodded with her head toward the entry to the kitchen. "Beau."

Sarah felt her heart skip a beat or two in the time it took her to turn her head to see Beau standing just a few feet away. His beautiful eyes held a look of concern, along with a healthy dose of wariness. She could hardly blame him for that.

"Hey, Beau," she said, giving him a smile that she hoped looked normal. Maybe she should have practiced in the mirror before she came upstairs. Her heart was thumping wildly in her chest as if trying to break free and go to Beau.

"Hi. How are you?"

Struggling. Missing you. Unable to stop thinking about you. I can't paint what I need to because all I want to paint is you.

"I'm good. How about you? I heard your brother and sister have arrived."

"Uh, yes. I brought them by earlier to introduce them, but you weren't around."

"I'm sorry I missed them. I was working downstairs."

"They'll be here in a few minutes," Beau said, some of the concern on his face fading. "You can meet them then."

"I look forward to it." Sarah gave him another smile that still felt forced.

"Beaumont?" The woman's voice held a soft drawl that was both soothing and intimidating.

Beau turned and motioned to the woman who had spoken. "Hey, Juli. Did you rest okay?"

"I did. Thank you."

A woman, who couldn't be anyone but Beau's sister, stepped to his side. She was a tiny slip of a thing with gorgeous dark hair, styled in loose waves to her shoulders and makeup that accentuated her eyes that were so like Beau's...as if they needed the accent. She had on a pair of dark blue jeans and a fitted green T-shirt. Her jewelry looked simple, but Sarah had a feeling that the studs in her ears and the teardrop pendant on her necklace were real diamonds, not cubic zirconia like the ones Sarah had in her jewelry box.

"By the way, this is Sarah," Beau said, motioning to where Sarah stood. "Sarah, this is my sister, Julianna."

"It's nice to meet you," Sarah said, then held up her hands. "I'd shake your hand, but mine are a bit messy at the moment."

"Don't worry about it. It's a pleasure to meet you." Julianna's gaze met hers then shifted to the side where Sarah knew Leah stood. "You really are quite identical."

Sarah waited for a snarky remark from Leah, and when one didn't come, she turned to look at her. Leah lifted a brow but didn't say anything.

"Yep," Sarah said with a nod. "We don't get mixed up much anymore these days, though."

A smile lifted the corners of Julianna's lips. It was at that moment that Sarah had a realization of what Beau's fiancée—or ex-fiancée—probably looked like. Polished. Poised. Totally put-together even when wearing jeans and a simple T-shirt, which was what Sarah was wearing but with far less style.

"Where's Rhett?" Julianna asked Beau.

"I'm right here, sister dear."

Another figure appeared, and it was uncanny how much he did, and yet didn't, look like Beau. He looked over at them and immediately grinned. "Well, hello. I think I missed meeting one of you earlier."

"Rhett," Beau said, a warning in his voice.

"What? Isn't that a fact? Or am I losing my mind?"

"Can't both be true?" Julianna asked with a lift of her perfectly shaped brows.

"Well, yes. But in this case, one is definitely truer than the other."

Beau sighed. "Sarah, this is my brother, Rhett. Please excuse ninety percent of what comes out of his mouth."

Sarah's smile relaxed a bit at the interaction between the siblings. Unfortunately, seeing Beau in this light only endeared him to her further.

"It's nice to meet you, Rhett," Sarah said.

"The pleasure is *all* mine, believe me." He gave her a broad smile and a wink.

His flirtation kind of set her on edge. Though she had no idea if this was how he always acted, that sort of flirting made her think that he would be that way whether he was single or married, and that didn't sit well with her.

She glanced at Beau and saw him glaring at his brother. Apparently, he didn't like it either.

"Well, we'll get out of your way," Beau said. "I know you're all busy."

"Feel free to tour the lodge, if you haven't already," her mom said.

"Thank you. I think we'll do that."

Once they had left, Sarah focused back on the salad. Leah let out a huff of laughter, drawing Sarah's attention to her.

"What?"

"Just seeing Beau's frustration with Rhett. Kinda reminds me of you and me."

"Excuse me?" Sarah said. "I'm assuming you're casting yourself as Beau in that particular scenario."

"Nah. I'm not saying we have similar personality traits, but more that certain things about each of us drive the other crazy. I thought Beau and Rhett had a similar sort of vibe."

"Oh." Sarah returned to the salad, determined to actually get it done. "Well, yes. I guess I can see that."

The exchange—brief though it had been—had helped draw her out of her thoughts for a short time. But now that the guests were gone, her brain used the new information she'd gained from them to reinforce how stupid she'd been to fall for Beau. Seeing Julianna just showed her—yet again—how different their worlds were.

She could only imagine what Julianna had thought about her standing there in a faded apron, her fingers wet with the juice of the tomato she'd been cutting. Never before had she felt ashamed of what she did at the lodge, but right then, she'd felt like she was nothing but the kitchen help. Which, to be fair, she kind of was.

Well, she'd rock it. She'd make the best salad ever. Not that there were too many ways to screw up a simple garden salad. But in all honesty, if there was a way to mess it up, she'd find it. Hopefully it wouldn't be that day. Because of all the people to mess up in front of, she didn't want it to be Beau and his family.

After the salad was finished, her mom had her place the fresh rolls that Leah had made into a couple of baskets. Sarah was given all the jobs she was least likely to mess up. It had never really bothered her before, but lately, as she'd thought more and more about being in a relationship and wanting to get married, she'd realized that she wanted to be able to cook for her husband and kids.

Since Leah was so good at the cooking and baking, Sarah had never really pushed herself to learn how to do it beyond a couple of dishes that her mom had managed to teach her, before they'd all agreed it was better that Leah and her mom take care of the major food preparation. That was something she needed to change. Leah managed to cook, clean, *and* work on her music. Unlike Sarah, who focused mainly on her painting.

Once the dinner was ready, they set the food out on the table, then retreated to the kitchen while their mom took her seat with their guests. They dished up their own plates from the food still in the kitchen, then sat at the island to eat. Leah and Anna took turns checking to see if the guests needed anything, obviously having discussed that it might make Sarah uncomfortable to have to go into the dining room.

Sarah thought about arguing that she was okay but decided not to. Eli came in partway through the meal and greeted Anna with a kiss then took a seat, at her insistence, while she dished up his plate. Sarah attempted to keep her thoughts from wandering to a scenario like that which included her and Beau. *Never gonna happen...ignore!*

"Did you get Carter all moved?" Anna asked as she set a plate of food in front of Eli, then sat back down next to him.

"Yeah, but I'm not sure what's up with the guy. I would think he could afford a nicer place than what he moved to. He basically went from a small studio to a slightly bigger studio. I'm pretty sure he could have afforded at least a one-bedroom."

"Well, you never know what someone's true financial situation is," Leah said. "Maybe he's paying off debt or something."

"That's true," Eli conceded. "Just would've like to see him living in something a bit more comfortable. The upside was that he didn't have a lot of stuff to move. We just got a late start because he got held up at the station."

Once they were finished with their food, Leah got up and headed into the dining room, returning with some empty dishes. Anna quickly joined her while Sarah began to scrape the plates and put them into the dishwasher. The coffee had already been perking in the coffee maker, and the dessert was set out and ready to be served as soon as the main course was finished.

As Leah and Anna carried the plates of the dessert that Leah had made along with the cups for coffee, Sarah took care of things in the kitchen. Normally, she would have been the one working with Anna to serve the guests, but she was grateful that Leah had stepped in for her that day. She owed her big time.

When the dishes were all dealt with, and their mom and the guests were enjoying their dessert, the rest of the family sat in the kitchen and ate their own. Sarah was happy that it was a rich chocolate cheesecake with a sweet raspberry sauce drizzled over it. Chocolate...yum...

She lingered over the dessert, smothering her feelings with the decadent taste. When Leah finished her piece of cake, she headed back into the dining room. Anna followed her, carrying a fresh pot of coffee for refills.

"You doing okay, sis?" Eli asked when it was just the two of them in the kitchen.

CHAPTER TWENTY

Sarah had no idea how much Eli knew about her current mindset. "Yeah, I'm fine."

"You don't usually hang out here in the kitchen." He tilted his head. "Just wondered if you were feeling alright."

"Sometimes I just need a bit of a break," she said. "But I'm sure I'll be back to normal soon."

"I hope so." He gave her an indulgent smile. "It doesn't feel right when you're not sparkling around."

"No worries. I'm sure I'll be sparkling again soon." How soon, she wasn't sure, but hopefully, once Beau had returned to his regular life, she'd be able to return to hers.

She finished her last bite of cheesecake then began to wash the dishes that wouldn't fit in the dishwasher. Washing dishes wasn't usually her favorite thing to do, but it was a task that didn't require too much of her attention. That was good because if it had been a job demanding her total focus, she would have failed miserably at it.

At that point, she just wanted to be done in the kitchen, so she could escape once again to her studio. And as she washed the last of the pots from dinner, Sarah decided that if her focus was demanding that she paint Beau, then that was what she'd do. Hopefully, if she caved and painted him just once, she'd be able to concentrate on her other paintings afterward.

At least, that was what she hoped would happen.

When Leah and Anna brought the last of the dishes into the kitchen, Sarah finished them up as Eli went into the dining room. After she turned on the dishwasher, she pumped the top of the hand lotion container they kept near the sink, then rubbed the soft cream deep into her hands.

"I think Beau is looking for something to do tonight," Leah muttered as she came to Sarah's side.

"Good luck around here," Sarah said with a laugh.

"Do you have any ideas? In case he asks one of us."

"I don't know." Sarah shrugged. "I mean, Cara and Kieran seem to enjoy going to the escape rooms in Everett. I'm not sure if you have to have a reservation, though. Otherwise, I don't know. A movie?"

"I have no idea, either," Leah said. "It's not like I go out a whole lot."

"Cara says they also go to the ballet, but I'm not sure all three of them would enjoy that."

Leah snickered. "Probably not. Hopefully, Eli or Anna can give them some suggestions."

"I'm going to head downstairs to get some work done. Did you need me to do anything else before I go?"

"Nope. It's all good."

Sarah nodded, then slipped out of the kitchen and headed to the stairs that led to the basement. Once in her studio, she picked up a blank sketch pad and went to the moon chair she kept in the corner of the room.

She'd thought she'd try to do something on canvas, but for some reason, the sketch pad appealed to her more right then. It felt more intimate, moving the charcoal pencil across the paper, then using her finger to smudge or soften parts of his face.

She'd been drawing for a little while, Beau's features slowly coming to life on the paper, when her studio door opened, and Leah rushed in.

"I'm sorry. I know you're working, but you have to come."

Sarah rested her elbows on her knees and stared at her sister. "Come where?"

"It sounds like Beau rented out a whole bowling alley or something in Everett, and now they're rounding up people to go with them. Anna and Eli said they'd go, and they want us to come too. Beau specifically asked if you would be interested in going, and I think Eli was checking to see if Cara and Kieran and a couple of others wanted to go."

With a sigh, she leaned back in her chair, gently clutching her sketchbook to her chest. "I'm not sure that socializing with Beau is the best idea for me right now."

"I know," Leah said, understanding on her face. "But please? For my sake?"

"Why aren't you just saying no?" Sarah asked. "It's not like you usually have a hard time with the word."

"Mom is saying I should go. Anna and Eli are saying I should go. Even I can't hold out against them all when they're this persistent."

It wasn't that Sarah didn't want to go. In fact, there was a huge part of her that absolutely did. That was the part of her that wanted to soak up all the moments she could with Beau before he left.

"I'll stick close to you," Leah said. "I promise."

Sarah could feel her resolve begin to weaken. Maybe she just needed to go and enjoy herself and pay the price later. And there surely would be a price to pay. Having extra memories of Beau would make getting over this period of her life that much more difficult. But right then, she wasn't sure she cared enough to stop herself from going. It kind of felt like she was already so far into her feelings for him that she had nothing to gain by avoiding Beau.

As she accepted that she was going to go, Sarah realized that she had no sense of self-preservation when it came to Beau and her feelings.

"We don't have to stay long, and we can leave as soon as you want to."

Sarah still wasn't sure why Leah hadn't just flat out said no because there were plenty of times when she had. What made this time different?

"Actually, you should just say no," Leah suggested. "And then say you want me to stay here with you. That way, we could both stay home, and they would blame it on you for a change."

"Let's just go, stay for a bit, and then come home." Sarah unfolded her legs. "And maybe we can stop for fries on our way home."

Leah grinned, a rare sight for most people, but one Sarah saw more frequently. "As long as I can get nuggets, it's a go."

"Just let me get changed...again."

"I'll go tell the others we'll be there."

After Leah left, Sarah got up from the chair and wandered into her bedroom. She laid the sketch pad on the bed and changed into a nice pair of dark blue denim capris and a filmy see-through floral blouse over a white tank top with thin straps. Knowing she'd need a pair of socks for the bowling shoes but not wanting to wear them there, she got a pair out of her chest of drawers and put them in her purse. She was just pulling her sandals on when Leah poked her head in the door again.

"Ready to go?" she asked. "The others left already."

Sarah got to her feet and picked up her purse. "I'm ready."

"I got the address from Eli," Leah said as they made their way upstairs. "Want to take your car?"

"Sure."

As they passed by the kitchen, their mom appeared. "I'm glad you're both getting out."

"You guilted me into it, Mom," Leah said. "So don't be too glad."

"Hey. It's my job to make sure you have a well-rounded life," she said with a shrug. "And if that means I've gotta use a little guilt, so be it."

"Well, don't get hurt patting yourself on the back over it," Leah muttered.

"Love you both." Her mom grinned, not at all bothered by Leah's attitude. She probably would have been more concerned if Leah had agreed to the outing without complaining. "Have fun."

"We'll try," Sarah said. "See you later."

It was still light out as they left the lodge, though the sun was already heading toward the horizon. Once they were in the car, Leah put the address of the bowling alley into her phone's map app, though she didn't start the GPS yet since they didn't need the annoying voice prompts until they were closer to the city.

As it turned out, even with the help of the GPS, they managed to make some wrong turns once they got to Everett. By the time they walked into the bowling alley, the people there were already sorting themselves into teams. It didn't look as if Beau had rented out the entire place, but it appeared that they had a few more lanes than they actually needed.

"Thought maybe you'd changed your minds," Eli said when he spotted them. "You two need to get your shoes. You're on a lane with Cara, Anna, and Julianna. It's guys against girls, apparently."

He'd barely gotten the words out when Michael Reed and his sister, Taylor, walked over to where they stood. As they greeted them, Sarah had to wonder what it said about the group gathered there that this many people were available to join an impromptu bowling party on a Friday night.

She knew what it said about her...she had no social life.

They went up to the counter to get their shoes then headed over to where Cara and Anna sat with Julianna. Sarah greeted Cara with a hug before sitting down next to Leah, who was already putting on her socks and shoes.

Julianna, even though she'd been there longer, still hadn't gotten that far. Her bowling shoes sat in front of her, and she was staring down at them like she had no idea what to do with them.

"So let me get this right," Julianna began. "These are shoes that other people have worn?"

"Lots of other people," Leah offered as she bent over to tie her laces.

"Leah," Sarah said in warning. Rather than respond, Leah just shrugged. "Listen, it's not as bad as Leah is making it sound. Yes, the shoes have been worn by other people, but the staff disinfect them. Plus, we bring our own socks, so our feet don't even touch where other people's socked feet have been."

"I know you think that should be reassuring," Julianna told her without any sort of disdain in her voice. "But it's really not. I have never worn shoes that other people have worn before me."

"You've never worn vintage Louboutins?" Anna asked. "Because with few exceptions, I would guess that most have been previously worn. And probably by bare feet or stockings which offer even less protection than socks do."

Julianna still looked like she'd rather face down a pack of rabid dogs than put her feet into a pair of shoes that someone else had worn. Sarah felt a stirring of sympathy for the woman. It was clear that she was far, far outside her element. While Beau had seemed to rise to the challenge of being forced out of his comfort zone, Julianna appeared to struggle a bit more.

Sarah put her own shoes on, watching out of the corner of her eye as Julianna slipped out of her dainty sandals and pulled on her socks. For a few minutes, Sarah wasn't sure the woman would get past that point, but soon she saw Julianna take a deep breath, then slide her feet into the shoes and quickly lace them up.

Smiling at the woman's determined expression, Sarah glanced around at the others who were there. In addition to Michael, Andy had also joined them. When her gaze landed on Beau, she found him watching her.

There was something in his eyes, something that reached into her heart, to the place she was trying to protect, and warmed her.

When a smile curved his lips, she couldn't keep from responding in kind.

Though she knew better—and she absolutely did know better—Sarah allowed herself to bask in his attention. It would only make things worse in the long run, but in the short term, it felt absolutely wonderful to be the focus of that man's attention.

When Rhett leaned close to him and said something, Beau glanced at his brother, and Sarah felt the loss of his attention in a very physical way. Shifting her gaze from Beau to the monitor above the lane, she saw that all their names were now showing there.

Though the lanes closest to them were empty, it appeared that they were only going to use the two lanes with six of them on each team. It would mean the games would take longer, but Sarah suspected that no one was in a hurry.

Soon enough, the games got underway. She had to assume that Eli had handed in the name lists because he and Anna lined up as did Cara and Kieran. After that, it was Leah and Andy. Julianna and Michael. Taylor and Beau. And finally, Sarah and Rhett.

She was happy to see that Leah had relaxed enough to respond to Andy's gentle teasing. Since they'd known each other forever, if there was an unrelated guy that Leah would be comfortable with, it was Andy. He was kind of like another brother. There was some subtle flirting between Julianna and Michael, and it was clear that Beau was comfortable with Taylor as they interacted when their turn came up.

Though she knew that Eli hadn't meant anything with the way he'd paired them up, the jealousy that reared its ugly head when Beau laughed at something Taylor said was fierce and threatened to engulf her mind.

Sarah pulled her phone out and tapped on the screen to open her social media apps. It was so tempting to let her current emotions flood out all over her social media accounts in vague statuses, but she managed to rein the urge in.

Instead, she tapped out an upbeat status about spending time with friends, just so she had something to do other than watch Beau and Taylor banter back and forth when it was their turn. She had never before felt such intense jealousy, so she had no idea how to handle it.

The emotion sat like ugly green sludge on top of a body of water, hiding any beauty that might lie beneath it. It was a horrible feeling, and she didn't like it at all. This wasn't how she lived her life. She'd never thought jealousy was a productive emotion, but at that moment, she felt helpless to its pull, like she was drowning in it.

"Your turn," Leah said, jostling her elbow.

Sarah looked up at the monitor and saw that Beau and Taylor had finished their turn, and now it was hers and Rhett's. Shoving her phone into her pocket, Sarah got to her feet and headed for the ball dispenser.

As she got closer, Rhett motioned to her. Curiosity pushed aside some of the jealousy for a moment. When she reached Rhett's side, he looped an arm around her shoulders and lowered his head to hers as they faced the pins.

"So here's the deal," he said, keeping his voice low. "I've never bowled before."

"I'm shocked to hear that," Sarah said, a bit of the ugly green sludge slipping away in the presence of a bit of humor. "Truly shocked."

"Haha. You're a hoot." Rhett gave her a side-eye. "So if you could cut me a little slack, that would be great. There might even be some money in it for you."

"Isn't there a law about throwing a game for money?"

"Are you really taking the moral high ground over a bowling game?"

"Is your ego really so fragile that you can't handle being beaten by a woman?"

"Yes. Yes, it is," Rhett said, his eyes, so like Beau's, sparkling with humor. "So name your price."

Sarah laughed as she heard people begin to heckle them from behind. "Well, in all honesty, I'm not the best bowler, so you're probably going to win regardless."

"I really would prefer to hedge my bets."

"Leah and I want nuggets and fries after this, so how about thirty bucks?"

"Make it fifty, and we have a deal."

"I'm going to guess you're not much of a businessman," Sarah said. "But hey, I'll take the fifty."

Her turn ended as well as she'd anticipated, and Rhett had a decent result with his, so he was ahead by a couple of points when they both finished. He held up his hand for a high five.

The sludge of jealousy remained, but it wasn't as thick. Realizing that it could thicken again each time Beau took his turn with Taylor, Sarah made sure to shift her attention elsewhere whenever they were up. Rhett helped by keeping things lighthearted. He was a big flirt, but Sarah took none of it seriously.

It was hard not to compare Rhett to Beau. They were completely different, and though Sarah could appreciate Rhett's upbeat and fun personality, Beau's steadiness and focus were definitely more appealing to her.

During each round, she somehow managed—without much effort—to fall short of Rhett's score. The funny thing was that no one called her out on it, especially no one who knew her. After all, they were well aware that she was a terrible bowler.

From the time she'd been a teen, she'd always struggled to excel at the game. In fact, on more than one occasion, teams had flipped a coin to see who was stuck with her. Thankfully, it had all been done in good humor, so early on she'd embraced her role as the worst bowler on any team.

In this case, however, Julianna was faring worse, and she wasn't really taking it as well as Sarah. So, rather than for Rhett's sake, Sarah found herself not even trying just so that Julianna wasn't the absolute worst bowler there.

The benefit to all that was that she could keep her focus off Beau. She wanted to enjoy the evening, and even though there was an undercurrent of jealousy present within her, for the most part, she succeeded.

They ended up playing two games, and though the guys won both, it seemed that everyone had enjoyed themselves. The girls didn't really have much of a chance since they had two of the worst bowlers in Julianna and Sarah. Leah was the best of the bowlers on their team, with Cara being a close second. Anna and Taylor fell in the middle.

"Here you go," Rhett said as he joined her at the counter to turn in their shoes.

Sarah stared at the wad of cash he held out to her. "What on earth is that for?"

"It's payment for our deal."

"Uh...I think I said thirty bucks, and I wasn't even serious about it."

"Well, I was, and this is fifty bucks a turn, so at ten turns a game and two games, that's a thousand bucks."

Sarah gaped at him. "First of all, are you kidding me? Who walks around with that kind of cash on them? And second, there is no way I'm taking a thousand dollars from you."

"You are a rare one," Rhett said, his expression curious. "You seriously don't want a thousand dollars?"

"I wouldn't mind if I'd earned it, but I didn't earn this. I'm a horrible bowler. Ask anyone here that knows me well. It was pretty much a guarantee that you were going to bowl better than me."

"Okay. Fine. You win. Fifty bucks." He peeled off one of the bills and handed it to her.

"I'm still not super comfortable taking it, but I have a feeling Leah will enjoy eating her nuggets on your dime." She took the fifty and shoved it into her pocket. "Did you think you were coming to the wild west or something where we had no ATMs?"

Rhett laughed. "You never know when you're going to need some cash."

"Not many people would consider a thousand bucks as *some* cash."

They were interrupted by others coming up to the counter, so Sarah went to find Leah. That ridiculous interaction with Rhett just reinforced—yet again—how different their worlds were. She'd known Beau was rich, but wow, having that fact shoved in her face the way Rhett had just done, made it hard to ignore.

"Our fries and nuggets are being sponsored by Rhett," she said as they headed for the exit.

Leah gave her a side glance. "How did that happen?"

"He wanted me to let him win our rounds of bowling in order to save his ego, and he was willing to pay me to play badly."

"He clearly didn't know that he didn't have to pay you to do that."

"He knows that now." Sarah laughed as she pushed the door open to let them out of the building. "After he tried to pay me a thousand dollars for letting him win."

Leah grabbed her arm and stared at her. "A thousand dollars? Like, are you kidding me?" She let go of Sarah, then headed for the car. "I'm getting a lot of nuggets. A *lot* of nuggets."

"I didn't take the thousand dollars, Lee." Sarah pushed the button on her fob to unlock the car's doors. "I took fifty dollars, so you can still get a couple orders of nuggets, and I can get my fries."

Once they were in the car, they turned to look at each other, then they burst out laughing. Leah rarely laughed, but when she found something funny, nothing could stop her. And Leah's laughter always made Sarah laugh.

They were doubled over in a fit of giggles when there was a knock on Sarah's window. She held her arm across her stomach as she rolled down the window and looked up at Eli, still trying to stop laughing.

"What is going on with you?" Eli asked.

Anna peeked past him. "Are you two losing your minds? I mean, Leah's laughing. I feel like the world has spun off its axis. Or it's ending."

For some reason, that only made Sarah laugh harder, which made Leah respond in kind.

"They set each other off," Eli said to Anna. "It's some sort of twin contagious laughter thing. When they were little, it always seemed to happen at church. Even Mom's *look* wouldn't settle them down. In fact, it made things worse. It appears something has set them off tonight. I just hope they can get themselves home."

"Should one of us drive them?" Anna asked.

"No!" Leah held out her hand toward them. "Nuggets!"

Not to be outdone, Sarah said, "Fries!"

"You two are crazy." Eli stepped back from the car. "Can I trust you to not drive until you've settled down?"

"Promise!" Sarah said between giggles. "No worries!"

Eli sighed. "Okay. We'll see you at home."

"We're not going to your house, Eli," Leah told him. "We'll see you tomorrow."

Sarah took several deep breaths as Eli and Anna walked away, trying to calm herself down. Finally, the giggles seemed to have subsided, but she knew better than to look at Leah. At least not until they were well and truly free of laughter.

Everyone else had left by the time they finally pulled out of the parking lot of the bowling alley. She had no idea if anyone had noticed their laughter meltdown, but she really didn't care. It had an effect on her similar to crying, leaving her feeling cleansed.

Laughter with Leah was truly a yellow moment. The brightest and prettiest yellow. It overshadowed the last of the darkness and pushed away the lingering green sludge of jealousy. She may have felt like she had been robbed of the opportunity to know love with Beau, but she wasn't without love in her life. As long as she had her mom, Leah, Eli, and Anna, she would always be fine. She'd always have love.

CHAPTER TWENTY-ONE

"What was up with you and Sarah?" Beau asked, even though he'd been trying to keep the question from spilling out.

The unreasonable and totally unexpected wave of jealousy when he'd seen Rhett loop his arm around Sarah's shoulder and hold her in a way that Beau had never even touched her, had taken him by surprise. He'd never felt jealousy like that before. What had started out as a fun evening with some new friends, had taken an ugly turn at that moment.

"Are you jealous, big brother?" Rhett asked, an edge of taunting to his words.

Why he'd suspect that, Beau didn't know. He hadn't spoken about Sarah any more than he had about the other women he'd introduced his siblings to since their arrival. But he *was* jealous, and while he'd been jealous of Rhett in the past, this was the first time his jealousy had been over a woman.

Over the years, Beau had been jealous of Rhett's ability to just cruise through life, never taking anything too seriously. Never worrying about what their parents would say. Never caring what the consequences might be for his actions.

"Curious." And that wasn't a lie. He was curious. Insanely so. "I mean, you've just met the people who were there."

Julianna laughed. "How have you forgotten that Rhett has never met a stranger."

She wasn't wrong about that, but still, Beau wanted to know what that had all been about. Unfortunately, it seemed like he was going to have to ask again.

Before he was forced to do that, however, Rhett put him out of his misery...sort of. Because the real misery, he was coming to recognize, was brought on by the thought of having to leave Sarah behind when he left New Hope in a week's time.

"I offered to pay her if she'd let me win each of our turns."

"What?"

"I told her my ego couldn't take having a woman beat me."

"That's ridiculous," Beau scoffed. "You don't care about stuff like that."

"True," Rhett said. "But it was fun to let her think I did. I didn't find out until afterward that she's a horrible bowler, so it wouldn't have mattered."

"So how much did you pay her?" Beau asked, not feeling as jealous anymore, but he was definitely still curious.

"I offered her a thousand dollars, but she only took fifty. Enough to cover nuggets and fries for her and Leah, apparently."

"You offered her a thousand bucks?" Julianna said. "I can't believe she didn't take it. A lot of women would have grabbed it and ran."

Beau had the same thought, but even as he did, he was fairly confident that none of the women there that evening would have done that.

"Anyway, she took the fifty at my insistence, even though she said she'd never intended to take my money. She said something about Leah enjoying eating nuggets on my dime."

Beau smiled as he turned onto the road leading to New Hope Falls. That sounded like Leah. "Did you have fun tonight, Juli?"

"Sure. Once I got past the ick factor of wearing shoes that had been worn by other people. Lots of other people, as Leah pointed out."

"I'm glad you enjoyed it. I know this isn't your usual scene, but I figured you could do with some new experiences while you're

here. I've had some interesting ones these past few weeks and survived, so I knew you would too."

"If I end up with some sort of foot fungus, you'll be hearing
plenty about it," Julianna warned him. "And if you don't show suf-
ficient sympathy for me, I'll tell Mom."

Well, that was a pretty good threat as he'd never hear the end
of it if she followed through on it. His mom was already pretty upset with him over breaking up with Tiffany which had resulted in
him being banished to New Hope Falls. There was no need to add
fuel to the fire.

"No worries. I will offer you every kind of sympathy I can muster up."

"What are you going to have us do next?" Rhett asked. "Roller
skating? Riding a mechanical bull?"

"What are you going on about?" Beau asked. "You had fun.
You should be excited about what I have planned next."

"Oh, I'm excited," Rhett shot back. "So very excited."

Julianna laughed then said, "Seriously, though, what's next?
Rhett might be excited. I just want to be prepared. Do a little re-
search, maybe."

"Actually, I don't really have anything planned." Beau slowed
to drive through the town. "Tomorrow we'll go see Grandfather
then Sunday is church. Otherwise, we can just do some sightseeing,
if you want."

"Okay. I can handle that," Julianna said. "I don't mind a low-
key weekend."

"I'm not sure I want that," Rhett grumbled. "I'm going to be
bored out of my mind."

"I think you'll be fine." At least Beau hoped he would be. After
all, he knew that a bored Rhett tended to be a troublesome Rhett.

As he drew closer to the lodge, silence fell in the car, but from
the glow emanating to his right, he knew Julianna was entertaining
herself on her phone. He assumed that Rhett was doing the same.

Once he got to the lodge, he pulled into an empty spot. "Do you want me to drop you off at the cabin, Rhett? Or are you okay to walk?"

"Why don't you drive him?" Julianna suggested. "Then I can see what the cabin is like."

Beau backed out of the spot and drove the short distance to the cabin where Rhett was staying. After he came to a stop in front of the cabin, they all got out and went inside.

"This is nice," Julianna said as she looked around the living space. "Quaint."

She wandered over to the bedroom door and disappeared through it. Beau sat down on the couch, his thoughts going back over the evening as Rhett followed Julianna.

Apart from the one moment when his gaze had met Sarah's near the beginning of the game, they hadn't interacted again, and that didn't sit well with Beau. He had a feeling that they hadn't been paired up intentionally. It was likely that Sarah had told her family what she'd told him. That she couldn't allow herself to get closer to him.

He'd actually been surprised to see both of the sisters walk in. Sarah, because of what she'd said to him. Leah, because well...she just didn't strike him as the sort of person who enjoyed that type of socializing. Still, he'd been glad that they'd both come...until that moment when Rhett had draped his arm around Sarah's shoulders and held a whispered conversation with her.

Even after Rhett had explained what the conversation had been about, jealousy lingered. Beau had never been able to have that close, easy interaction with women the way Rhett did. Not even with Tiffany. That was just one of the many ways the two brothers were so different.

"What's on your mind, bro?" Rhett asked as he sat down in a nearby chair. Julianna also sat down on the couch next to Beau.

"Nothing more than usual." He sat back in his seat and turned his attention more fully to the two of them. "Do you guys have any concerns about meeting Grandfather tomorrow?"

When Julianna began to speak, Beau was grateful for the distraction. He'd have plenty of time later to mull over the situation with Sarah, and what, if anything, he would do about it.

The next afternoon, Beau led his siblings into the personal care home. He greeted the nurses at the reception desk, their faces familiar to him now. After introducing Rhett and Julianna, he took them to the room where he'd first met his grandfather.

Julianna kept a tight grip on his arm just above his elbow, the bite of her nails the only indication of her nervousness. Rhett, on the other hand, didn't appear to be nervous at all.

Just like his first visit there, Beau found his grandfather in his wheelchair at one of the tables, his friend Rich seated next to him. When the older man turned in their direction, his excitement was evident in his wide smile.

"Hello, Grandfather," Beau said, bending to brush a kiss to the man's wrinkled cheek. "How are you doing?"

"I'm doing just fine, son. Just fine." He gestured past Beau as his friend left them. "Now, introduce me to your brother and sister."

Grinning, Beau stepped back and made the introductions. As his grandfather held out a shaking hand to each of them, Beau was reminded of the first time he'd met the man. It seemed ages ago. More than just three weeks.

"Sit down," his grandfather said, motioning to the empty chairs at the table.

Rhett settled into a seat to his grandfather's right, while Julianna sat on the other side of him, leaving the seat to their grandfather's left free for Beau.

"I had someone pick up some treats from the bakery. I hope you'll share them with me."

Beau noticed the box sitting in front of his grandfather as well as some plates and forks. He went ahead and set the plates out and then gave his grandfather the first pick of the bakery items.

"Apple fritter," his grandfather stated. "My absolute favorite."

Julianna and Rhett each took a treat from the box as well.

"There's coffee too."

While Rhett spoke with their grandfather, Beau took the initiative to place the mugs in front of each of them then poured the coffee.

He listened as Rhett asked and answered questions. It wasn't a big surprise that Rhett felt comfortable with the older man. It was a rare person that Rhett *didn't* feel at ease with. Julianna, on the other hand, took a bit longer to warm up to people. He suspected that she'd soon begin to interact with the man.

She was lucky. When Beau had come, he hadn't had the option of sitting silently. Or, he supposed, he could have just sat there without saying a word, but his mother had raised him better than that. Though from what he'd heard, maybe she would have made an exception for her father.

Seeing the beaming expression on his grandfather's face and the gentleness that filled his gaze whenever he looked at Julianna, Beau knew he'd made the right decision to ask her and Rhett to come. Whatever the fall-out might be once his mother got wind of the visit, it would be worth it.

"So you'll be at church tomorrow?" his grandfather asked as their visit drew to a close.

Beau had seen the exhaustion on the man's face and had suggested it was time for them to leave. "Yes. We'll be there, and we'll go out for dinner afterward if you're feeling up to it."

"Oh, I'll feel up to it." His grandfather reached out and patted his hand. "Don't you worry about that."

They said their goodbyes then made their way out of the personal care home. The first few minutes of the drive back to the lodge were silent, but then Julianna spoke.

"How could she just leave him behind? Leave him alone knowing he'd already lost his son and his wife?" There was anger in her voice. "I don't understand her at all. I mean, I've never really understood her anyway, but this..."

"I don't get it either," Rhett said, his tone more serious than normal. "He seems like a really cool guy."

"I think Mom has carried a load of guilt for a lot of years. I'm not sure she knew how to deal with it at eighteen, and she certainly doesn't know how to deal with it now."

"We should confront her with this," Julianna announced.

"I'm not sure that's the best course of action," Beau responded. "I don't think anything we say to her would bring her to the point that she'd be willing to come and see him."

"Well, I still think she needs to know that *we* know what she's done to him."

"Maybe I'll talk to Dad about it."

"Do you think he's going to care?" Rhett asked.

Beau had no clue how to answer that. He'd cared enough to make sure the man was looked after in the personal care home, though Beau suspected that had more to do with his own past than with any affection he might hold for his father-in-law.

"Do you want to do some sightseeing?" Beau asked, realizing they weren't going to come to any answers just yet. "Or head back to the lodge?"

"The lodge," Julianna said.

"Yeah. I'm fine with that as well."

That surprised Beau a bit, but he was more than happy to go back to the lodge. He hadn't seen Sarah since the bowling alley, and he hoped that she'd make an appearance later that day.

There were a couple of cars he didn't recognize in the small lot in front of the lodge, but that was no surprise as it was the weekend, which meant that they had people checking in for a day or two. When they walked in, two people were standing at the check-in desk, chatting with Nadine. Beau led Rhett and Julianna into the living room, where they could talk without interrupting the new guests.

"I'm going to go to my room for a bit," Julianna said.

That was what he had suspected would happen once they got back there. After the time they'd had with their grandfather, he knew that Julianna would need time to digest the visit. Rhett...well, he wasn't sure how Rhett would process the information. He seemed to take most things in stride, but what Beau had told them about their mom and then meeting their grandfather might be more than his younger brother could just casually deal with.

"Okay. Just text me if you need something," Beau told her. He turned to Rhett once Julianna had left them. "Did you want to go back to your cabin? Or we could hang out in my room. Watch TV. Talk."

"Yeah. We could do that."

Beau gave Nadine a smile as they moved to the stairs, putting any thoughts of spending time with Sarah out of his mind as best he could. The reality was that the more he distanced himself from her now, the better it would be for both of them when he left. How he wished this had all happened a year later when he already had his trust fund money in hand and could walk away from Houston without looking back.

Timing and circumstances had definitely been against him and Sarah, but maybe that was fate's way of saying that, despite how they both felt, they were not meant to be. Not that he necessarily believed in fate. Maybe it was God's way of saying that.

One thing he did know was that when he compared what he'd felt for Tiffany with what he felt for Sarah, there was not even the remotest similarity.

CHAPTER TWENTY-TWO

Having guests present once again meant that Sarah wouldn't be eating in the dining room, and she was definitely okay with that. After spending another day struggling with her painting, and once again giving up on what she *should* be painting in favor of sketching Beau, she was ready to tear her hair out. And she certainly didn't want to spend an evening trying to appear upbeat and friendly when she felt the exact opposite of those two things.

Of course, serving the table was a special kind of torture as well. Sarah had never had a problem waiting on the table with Leah and Anna when only their mom ate with the guests, but that night, it chafed at her. Mainly because she was already acutely aware of how different her station in life was from Beau's. Serving him and the other guests in that way just felt...wrong.

As soon as she had the thought, she was ashamed of it because there was nothing wrong with a position of servitude. Nothing wrong with providing people, rich or poor, a meal in that way. When they were younger, their mom had often recited a verse to them, reminding them that in God's kingdom, those who were great were those who had a servant's heart. Those who served all.

She was caught off guard by her pride and desire to not be reminded that any woman Beau was associated with would never be caught dead performing such a role. The woman he'd been engaged to had probably never lifted a finger to serve anyone.

Oh yes, she'd spent part of the afternoon doing what she'd sworn she wouldn't. She'd finally googled Beau.

It was her own fault that she now had picture after picture in her head of Beau and a statuesque blonde who looked like she was a model. Only she wasn't a model. She was the daughter of a wealthy politician whose name was being tossed around as a potential candidate for president in the near future.

She'd read the account of their public fight and tacked onto the end of the article had been a quote from a source close to the families. *Sources tell us that Beaumont has left Houston, but it is believed a reunion is in their near future.*

When Sarah had read that, she'd wanted to throw up, and every cell of her body regretted not asking Leah for more details when she'd first warned Sarah about Beau. Either that, or she should have gone right to her computer and googled him for herself. She'd had too much confidence in herself and her ability to just be friends to look for reasons why she should keep her distance from him.

Well, the joke was officially on her.

"You take the right side, I'll take the left," Leah said when it was time for them to check on the table.

Sarah nodded, knowing without looking at the table what that meant. Even though Sarah hadn't asked for that consideration, it was no surprise that Leah gave it to her. Unlike the previous night, she didn't have the option of staying in the kitchen. Anna and Eli had gone to meet with another older couple from their church who were mentoring them in the months leading up to their wedding.

Without looking at Beau or his siblings, Sarah spoke softly with each of the guests on her side of the table, offering them a refill on their water and asking if they needed anything else. Once done, she retreated to the safety of the kitchen to help Leah prepare the dessert. She'd already decided that she wouldn't eat until later. Her stomach was in too much upheaval for her to even contemplate eating right then.

Sarah arranged the plates while Leah dished up the dessert. "This looks yummy, Lee."

Once that was done, she made sure the coffee machine was turned on, then poured cream into a couple of small pitchers and checked the sugar bowls. It was all busy-work because the coffee pot was on a timer so it would automatically switch on, and her mom would never let the sugar bowls run low.

Leah took charge of checking the table from the doorway, and when it appeared people were done eating, she motioned to Sarah, and they made quick work clearing the plates and food away. Sarah had to fight hard to keep her gaze from drifting in Beau's direction. It was like her gaze was a magnet, and Beau was metal. The battle was real.

The serving of dessert went smoothly, then Sarah turned her attention to the dishes. Any other day, she would have protested having to deal with the cleanup two nights in a row, but right then, she was happy to do it.

"Is there anything I can do to help?"

The sound of Beau's voice made Sarah flinch. Before she could turn around, though, Leah rescued her once again.

"Thanks for offering," she said. "But I think we've got everything under control."

"Oh. Okay."

"You're a guest here, Beau," Leah added. "Clean up is not part of the experience we offer guests."

"That's not entirely true though, is it?" Beau said. "I mean, I've heard Anna and Eli's story. You let Anna help."

"Anna's situation is different. She pitched in from the moment she arrived. She has always felt more like a friend than a guest."

Sarah almost laughed at Leah's statement. She certainly hadn't been a fan of Anna's for ages after her arrival at the lodge.

"I had kind of hoped we'd become friends as well." Beau's voice was steady, even in response to Leah's rather pointed remarks regarding how they had viewed Anna.

"Perhaps," Leah said. "But I think we all know that your offer just now would not further that. In fact, I think it would probably hurt any friendship that has been built between you and Sarah."

Sarah gripped the edge of the sink. She was an absolute coward letting Leah fight this particular battle, but she knew she wasn't strong enough to do it on her own. One look into Beau's beautiful eyes, and she'd agree to whatever it was he was offering right then.

Beau sighed. "Sarah, I just wanted to talk to you for a couple of minutes."

Taking a deep breath, Sarah finally turned around, her fingers gripping the dishtowel she grabbed off the counter. Though she faced him, she didn't allow her gaze to meet his.

"I'm really not sure what good that would do. I already told you that it was better—for me, at least—to not spend time together anymore. Especially just the two of us."

Beau lifted a hand and rubbed his forehead. He wore a pair of dark jeans and a green shirt that she was sure brought out that shade in his blue-green eyes. "I know. I know. I just..."

"Beaumont?" Julianna appeared at her brother's side. Sarah saw her look back and forth between her and Beau. "What's going on?"

"I was just talking with Sarah and Leah," he said, lowering his hand. "Have you finished your dessert?"

"Yes. It was lovely once again, Leah. You're very talented."

"Thank you," Leah said.

"You should open a bakery."

Leah shook her head. "I don't think so. Baking is something I enjoy, but it's not my passion. I don't mind doing it for the lodge, but I'm not interested in anything larger scale."

"Definitely everyone else's loss. Well, everyone who doesn't come to stay here, anyway."

Sarah turned back to the sink, plunging her hands into the warm water once again. She was surprised at how chatty Leah was being, but part of her was certain that was because she was trying to divert attention from Sarah. It warmed her to realize the lengths Leah would go to to protect her, but then Sarah would do the same for her.

"Can anyone join this kitchen party?" Rhett's voice was loud and boisterous, and Sarah couldn't help but smile. There were a few beats of silence before he said, "Well, this is awkward. I'm not usually the buzzkill. I bring the party."

"We were just talking about how great Leah's baking is," Julianna said.

"It has all been delicious, I must say," Rhett agreed. "Were there leftovers?"

"There are a few pieces left," Leah said.

"Is there an extra charge for another piece?"

"Tell him yes," Beau said.

"I've heard that Rhett has more money than sense," Leah remarked. "Thank you for the nuggets."

Sarah snickered, and a part of her wished that this would be something they could have with Beau and his siblings all the time. This easy-going banter. But it wasn't to be.

Out of the corner of her eye, she could see Leah opening the container where she'd put the extra dessert. Someone's phone rang, but since it wasn't any ringtone she used, Sarah didn't even look at her phone where she'd set it earlier.

"I'd better take this," Beau said, then she heard his footsteps as he moved out of the kitchen.

"What's going on with you and Beau?"

Julianna's voice at her side made Sarah jump, and the dish she was holding dropped back into the water, causing a bit of a splash.

"Oh. Sorry, I didn't mean to startle you." Julianna rested a hand on her arm.

"It's okay. I wasn't paying attention."

Julianna turned so her back rested against the counter and crossed her arms. "Are you going to answer my question?"

"Sure. I'll answer it. It's been nice getting to know Beau. We're fortunate to be able to meet people from all walks of life here at the lodge. And it was nice to meet Mr. Stevens' grandson. Well, I guess, grandchildren now since we've met you and Rhett as well."

Julianna's dark brows pulled together. "Beau's different here. I could tell it a bit on the phone when we talked, but seeing him now, it's obvious."

Sarah gave her a smile before turning her attention back to the dishes in the sink. "New Hope Falls has a way of changing people."

"Why do you think that is?" Julianna asked.

"I'm not sure. To be honest, it doesn't change everyone for the better."

"True. It doesn't appear to have changed my mom in a positive way."

"I think it's all in the heart of the person. If they're open to change, to adapting to things around them, then New Hope Falls can be a positive place for them."

Julianna laughed. "I never would have pegged Beau as someone open to change, but I'm starting to think I didn't really know my brother."

That comment shifted Sarah's attention from the bowl she was washing to Julianna. "You've noticed that he's different, so you must have known him."

"I knew the person he let us know." Julianna shifted to lean a hip against the counter, facing Sarah more directly. "I think meeting our grandfather changed him, but I think it's something more. There's something in the way he looks at you—"

"Don't." Sarah gripped the dishcloth beneath the water and stared at the soap bubbles. The iridescence mocked her with beautiful colors and shininess. "Just leave it alone, please."

"I guess you know what happened in Houston before he came."

"Yes, but even before I discovered that, I knew that our lives were in two different places. Mine is here, and his is in Houston."

"Long-distance is a thing," Julianna said.

"There are other reasons why a relationship would never work between us."

"That's too bad because I feel like you might be someone good for Beau."

"I'll always consider him a friend," Sarah said, though the words just about choked her. "And you two as well."

"I have a feeling we'll be back in New Hope Falls," Julianna said. "I'm certain Beau will want to visit our grandfather."

That was Sarah's best and worst dream, all wrapped up into one. Would she be able to loosen Beau's hold on her heart when the prospect of seeing him again always loomed on the horizon?

"I'm glad you were able to meet him. Mr. Stevens is a real sweetheart."

"How do you know him?" Julianna asked.

"We've gone to the same church for as long as I can remember. Plus, I've volunteered at the personal care home."

"It seems like a nice place. I mean, if he can't be in his own home, it's the next best thing, right?"

Sarah rinsed the last dish and put it in the drainer, then pulled the plug on the sink and dried her hands. "Yeah. I would think so."

"So, do you still go to the same church as our grandfather?"

"Yes, we do."

"That's good. We'll have some familiar faces when we're there tomorrow."

Sarah looked at her in surprise. "You're going to church?"

"Sure. Beau said we should go with our grandfather. Hopefully, Rhett doesn't get hit by a bolt of lightning when he walks in that takes us all out with him."

She couldn't help but chuckle at that mental picture. "I think you're safe. God wants all people to attend church, not just those who pretend to be perfect."

Julianna's eyes widened. "Pretend to be perfect?"

"Christians aren't perfect, regardless of what some might want you to believe. We have just found forgiveness and grace through Jesus that allows us to appear faultless before God. So, while we try to live our lives without sin, we can only truly come anywhere close to doing that that with God's help."

Before Julianna could respond, Beau came back into the kitchen and said her name. "You need to phone Mom. She's figured out where you and Rhett are, and she's not happy."

Julianna huffed as she moved away from the counter. "She hasn't been happy since Dad sent you here. Could you not have told her I was unavailable?" She turned to Rhett. "How about you call and talk to her? You're her baby. She might not go off on a rant with you."

Rhett shrugged as he handed his empty plate to Leah. "Sure. I can give her a call."

Sarah found it sad that Julianna didn't want to talk to her mom. She could never imagine a time when that would be the case for her. But she knew not everyone had a close relationship with their parents like she, Leah, and Eli had with their mom.

"Thanks for the second round of dessert, Leah." Rhett got up from his stool. "I'll give her a call on my way back to the cabin. Do you two want to come with?"

Sarah glanced at Beau in time to meet his gaze. She had a feeling that he still wanted to talk to her, but it wouldn't do any good. It wouldn't change anything about their situation. He must have read something in her expression because he turned away, a resigned look on his face.

It hurt her heart to see him like that, because she'd been certain he hadn't felt anything for her. It almost seemed worse to think that they were both hurting because they had no other options.

"We'll come with you," Julianna said, walking to Beau's side and hooking her hand through his arm. "We can take turns listening to Mom yell."

Once they'd left, Sarah let out a sigh and turned back to the sink to finish cleaning it up. She had been so convinced that nothing would happen between her and Beau, she'd ignored everything she'd been taught, as well as the warning Leah had given her. She deserved the ache in her chest and the sadness that she couldn't seem to shake.

Leah came to stand next to her, bumping her shoulder. Sarah waited for her to say that everything was going to be okay, but she didn't. Leah wasn't one to offer Sarah platitudes. She never had been, and no doubt she wouldn't start now, particularly when she'd warned Sarah.

She hung the dishcloth over the faucet. "I'm going to go paint for a bit." Or perhaps, *try* to paint would be more accurate. "Did you need me to do anything else before I go?"

"Nope. It's all good."

Back in her studio, determined to at least do what she could to help promote her focus, she put a couple drops of her favorite essential oil in a diffuser then spent some time praying before she loaded up a playlist she'd often painted to in the past. It was her hope that those things would trigger her focus and help her at least get *some* work done on her latest project.

She couldn't let herself spend any more time sketching Beau.

CHAPTER TWENTY-THREE

Beau sat slumped in one of the chairs in Rhett's cabin. Rhett and Julianna had taken turns trying to calm their mom down. Beau hadn't volunteered because he'd already tried to reason with her when she'd first called. Instead, she'd given him an earful, demanding to know why he'd encouraged his siblings to join him in New Hope Falls.

Only she hadn't given him a chance to explain before she'd gone off on his irresponsible behavior that had gotten him sent there in the first place. He'd never really thought much about their intra-family relationships, but this current interaction with their mom was in remarkably sharp contrast to how he'd seen Nadine interact with her children.

He didn't doubt that the McNamaras had their disagreements, but he just couldn't picture Nadine lashing out at Eli, Sarah, or Leah, the way his mom was doing with them. It made him wonder what they'd missed out on as kids because of how their parents related to them. Unfortunately, it was too late to change any of that, but there was a part of him that hoped that somehow, they'd be able to figure out how to have a better relationship with them as adults.

It had only really become apparent to him since coming to New Hope Falls that they were a family in crisis. He hadn't really thought about it until he'd seen how the McNamaras interacted, and then he'd been able to see the huge cracks in the foundation of his own family.

The problem was, he had no idea how to patch up those cracks so that their family could heal. It would have required more than just his effort to fix things. In their current state, he could try to patch things up, but no sooner would he do that, but his mom or dad would take a sledgehammer to it.

They weren't a family. They were five people related by blood who hadn't figure out how to love. Beau was going to try and change that, starting with Julianna and Rhett.

"Mom, I'm done with this conversation," Julianna said, her voice tight. "We'll be home on Monday, and if you still want to talk about this then, we can. But in the meantime, you need to just chill out. We're adults now, and it was our decision to come here."

She fell silent again, only to let out a long sigh a few minutes later. "And if you want to tell Dad to change the terms of the trust funds again, so be it. You two have been using them to try and control us for so long already, I've stopped believing we're ever going to get them."

If Beau hadn't already resigned himself to having to wait for his trust fund, Julianna's words might have given him a heart attack. All they did now was fill him with a sense of futility. Was he holding out for something that would really never be his? Were the dreams he had for a company of his own never going to come to fruition?

Julianna looked down at Rhett's phone and sighed before tossing it onto the couch between her and Rhett. "And here I thought it was kids who hung up on their parents. Not the other way around."

"Given what we now know about her past in this town, I'm not surprised that she's losing her mind." Rhett picked up his phone. "She's probably afraid that this new information will change how we view her."

"Are you saying that it hasn't?" Julianna asked, her tone sharp.

"I don't know that it's changed how I view her necessarily. I mean, she was eighteen when everything happened. It can't have been easy to bear that burden of guilt."

"I don't have a problem giving her a pass for that," Julianna said. "But she's not eighteen anymore. She's an adult. Plus, it's not like her father holds anything against her. I've only spent an hour or so with him, but I can confidently say that the man would welcome her back into his life without hesitation."

Beau knew Rhett couldn't argue with her about that. It hadn't taken Beau that long to recognize that fact either.

"By the way, Beau," Julianna began, shifting her attention from Rhett to him. "I had an interesting little conversation with Sarah."

"Really?" He wished *he* could have had a conversation with Sarah, but she was clearly determined to keep that from happening. In all honesty, he wasn't sure what he was hoping to accomplish by talking to her. He just felt compelled to. He missed her...

"How well have you gotten to know her?"

Beau stared at the empty fireplace as he shrugged. "We've had some good conversations."

"Would you say you know her better than you know Tiffany?"

His gaze shot to Julianna's. "What's that supposed to mean?"

"I don't think it's much of a secret that you spent as little time with Tiffany as possible, and when you *did* spend time with her, it was rarely just the two of you. I doubt you'd say you had many good conversations with her."

"We don't—didn't—have much in common," Beau said.

"And you really have that much more in common with someone outside of our social class living in a small town in Washington? Where a big chunk of her day seems to be playing the role of a maid?"

It didn't make sense, Beau was well aware of that, but Sarah's joy for life and her ability to be friends with everyone was disarming. He hadn't even been aware that he was being drawn to her until he found himself looking forward to seeing her each day, knowing that no matter what kind of mood he was in, being around her would cheer him up.

But what did he have to offer her? It was clear money didn't mean much to her, and that was about all he had. And even with that, he didn't have the amount he would have had if his father hadn't kept pushing back the date for the release of their trust funds. Instead of being a self-sufficient man, he was still working under his dad's thumb, biding his time. Not to mention someone that brought a boatload of familial issues with him.

"For what's it worth," Rhett said. "I think Sarah is nice."

"Me too," Julianna agreed. "Just pointing out a few things for your consideration."

"I'm not ignorant," Beau told her. "I'm aware that I've got some sort of feelings for her, certainly different feelings than what I had for Tiffany."

"Unfortunately, I really don't think there's much hope for the two of you unless you're willing to make some radical changes in your life," Julianna said. "Like seriously radical."

Beau nodded. He couldn't see Sarah ever leaving New Hope Falls, and even if she would be willing to do that, he'd never ask that of her. If he wanted a relationship with Sarah, he would need to give up Houston and the dream he'd once had for his future.

"Who'd have thought your life would have ended up so complicated?" Rhett grinned. "It's like having a front-row seat to a soap opera. And I don't just mean this part. I mean everything starting with the implosion of your engagement to Tiffany."

"Glad you're entertained by it all," Beau muttered. "Can't say I'm all that thrilled with the starring role I've had in it. Particularly the implosion part."

"It's just one more lesson in how not to live my life."

"Is that why you avoid all responsibility? Flirt with anything that moves? And go out of your way to antagonize Dad?"

"Pretty much," Rhett said with a nod.

"Okay, you two. Stop." Julianna held a hand up in each of their directions. "We have to figure out how to deal with this situation with Mom when we get home on Monday. I have doubts she's going to let it go."

They continued to discuss options, and while Beau was glad to have the conversation shift away from Sarah, he had no real insights to offer on how to handle things with their parents. He'd spent the last five years, after his father had shifted the trust fund age requirement from twenty-five to thirty, trying *not* to get into conflict with them. Which is why he'd ended up engaged to someone he wasn't in love with.

He'd been living his life trying not to make waves until the blow-up with Tiffany had sent a tsunami through everything. Now he was dealing with even more waves. Bigger and more deadly, creating even more damage.

He'd tried his best placating efforts with his mom earlier, but she was blaming him for everything, and there was nothing he could do to convince her otherwise. Not that he'd tried too hard since, in reality, she was right.

The next morning as he got ready for church, Beau was feeling beaten down in a way he'd never felt before. Which said a lot given what he'd gone through in the past little while. It just seemed that there was too much going awry in his life at one time. It felt like his life would never recover from the hits it had taken over the past month.

If he knew how to move forward without giving in, he wouldn't be so worried about it. It felt wrong to be almost thirty and facing so much uncertainty in his life. It certainly wasn't what he had planned. Shouldn't a parent try to help their child rather than take actions that threw their lives into disarray?

Of course, if he'd taken a risk and struck out on his own sooner, he wouldn't be in a position where his father could still hold so much sway over his life. That complication was definitely his fault.

After swinging by the personal care home to pick up their grandfather, Beau drove to the church, grateful that neither Julianna nor Rhett had protested his plan to have them join him and their grandfather. They hadn't balked at it when he'd first mentioned it, but he hadn't been sure whether they'd follow through when it actually came time to go.

Once at the church, he helped his grandfather inside and to a row at the back where a chair had been removed to make room for his wheelchair. He knew from the previous weeks that Sarah and her family usually sat near the front. That Sunday was no different as he immediately spotted them already in their seats a couple rows back from the stage.

He let Rhett and Julianna into the row first, then followed them in. His grandfather then maneuvered his wheelchair into position. Beau had discovered in recent weeks that by positioning his wheelchair in that particular spot, his grandfather was able to greet people and talk with them without having to move around.

Beau wasn't sure if it was just old age that had weakened his grandfather or if there was another underlying cause. In the beginning, he hadn't felt it was his place to ask, but now that he felt like he'd gotten closer to the man, he thought maybe he might try to have a conversation with him about it before he left.

"Morning, Mr. Stevens," Michael said. "Hey, Beau."

Beau shook the hand Michael extended before he moved to the row where Taylor was seated. Several more people stopped to greet his grandfather then greeted Beau by name as well. His grandfather introduced a few of the people to Julianna and Rhett before music began to play at the front.

In the past, the only time people usually knew his name and greeted him with any sort of familiarity was when he was with his parents or Tiffany at a fundraiser of some sort. Few of them ever seemed as happy to see him as the people in the church were.

Any of the discomfort he'd felt during the first service had abated. He hadn't thought that would actually happen, but it had, after just a couple weeks.

If Julianna and Rhett were feeling the same way he had that first Sunday, they weren't showing it outwardly. Of course, as children, they'd been trained to behave, regardless of how bored or uncomfortable they were. It might not have been for a church service back then, but the behavior training still applied.

By the time the pastor rose to speak, Beau had a general idea of what to expect from the man. He had an easy way of speaking that felt more like listening to a friend talk than being preached at.

"So today I want to start with a verse that I'm sure a few of you know by heart," the pastor began. "John 3:16."

The verse showed up on the screen at the front. *For God so loved the world that He gave His only begotten Son, that whoever believes in Him should not perish but have everlasting life.*

"That's the verse that's most familiar, but it's just one part of a larger passage that also holds some other important verses." The pastor waited as another verse filled the screen. "*For God did not send His Son into the world to condemn the world, but that the world through Him might be saved.*"

Beau was surprised to find himself considering the words. So often, what he heard about Christians was how judgmental they were, and how everyone who didn't believe like they did were condemned by God to hell. So how did that verse fit?

"Through their disobedient actions in the Garden of Eden, Adam and Eve condemned mankind. They were told by God not to do something, and they did it anyway, thereby condemning all of us. But God, through His Son, provided a way for us to be saved from that condemnation."

A new verse appeared on the screen. *For all have sinned and fall short of the glory of God.*

"It's important that we not forget this. Adam and Eve's actions led to a fallen world. That means that when we're born, we are born sinners. All of us. By our own actions, we can never be saved. We will never be good enough to gain eternal life. It is only through Jesus, God's son, that we have hope.

"We are not qualified to judge whether we are good enough to get into Heaven. For many, as long as there is someone who is sinning worse than them, they figure they're good enough to get to Heaven—if they even believe there is a Heaven. They think they're good enough because they haven't murdered anyone or because they're kind to others. Or perhaps they choose to believe that a loving God wouldn't condemn them to hell, not realizing that, in fact, they were already condemned and that He is offering a way of salvation."

Beau had never really thought much about Heaven, but he was guilty of assuming he was living a basically good life. He didn't cheat, steal, or murder. He tried not to lie. He gave people his best advice and didn't try to swindle anyone out of their life savings. In fact, he tried to help people like Justin when the opportunity presented itself, offering his advice free of charge.

"Some of you may be sitting there thinking, but Pastor Evans, I'm already saved. I have accepted God's gift of salvation. I know I'm going to Heaven. And to that I say, I'm so glad to hear that." Pastor Evans beamed out at them. "Truthfully, nothing makes me happier. So why am I preaching about this today? Because I can almost guarantee that there's at least one person in your life who doesn't have that assurance."

Beau shifted on the pew. He wasn't sure how he felt about what the pastor was saying. Had his mom been taught this? Had she felt condemned beyond saving because of what had happened with her brother?

"When you leave here today, I want you to leave confident that you carry the message of salvation with you. That you are able to share that message with those God brings into your life. And if you're here and don't have that assurance, I pray that your heart will long for the gift God has offered."

He listened as Pastor Evans explained the gift. How Jesus came as a sinless man, to take on the sin of all mankind, and through his death and resurrection, offered them eternal life. A gift of grace and mercy.

Was it really that simple?

Beau had a hard time believing that it really was, because nothing good ever came easy. Surely there was more to it than that.

That pondering continued as the pastor finished his sermon, and the last song was sung. When the service was finally over, Beau pushed his musings aside. He had enough on his mind already without adding to it with this.

"Are you up for lunch at *Norma's?*" Beau asked his grandfather.

"I am, and then, if you'd indulge an old man, I'd love to go for another drive."

"Sure. We can do that. It will give Julianna and Rhett a chance to see the area."

He glanced at his siblings, giving them a chance to object, even if just with a lift of an eyebrow. Neither did anything but nod, so Beau figured those plans were a go.

Glancing over, he saw Sarah walking up the aisle with Leah. When their gazes met, he smiled at her. When she gave him a smile in return—a small one, but a smile nonetheless—his heart lifted. The reminder that he would be without her smiles soon was a thought he didn't want to dwell on.

"We'd better get going," his grandfather said. "Or we'll have to wait forever for a table."

Beau nodded, and together they made their way outside. Julianna and Rhett stayed with their grandfather while Beau went to bring the car to the front of the church. When he returned, the pastor was talking with them, his hand resting on his grandfather's shoulder.

"Hello, Beau," the man said with a warm smile, holding out his hand. "So nice to have you here again this Sunday."

He wanted to say it was a pleasure, but in all honesty, Beau didn't like things that confused him, and that sermon had definitely done just that. But he shook the man's hand and smiled in return. "It's been nice being able to bring my grandfather."

That was about as honest as he could get at that moment.

"Well, I won't hold you up, but if I don't get a chance to see you again before you leave New Hope, I pray God's blessing on each of you. Though I do hope that you will return again soon."

"I'm sure we'll be back," Julianna said with a smile. "You have a very beautiful little town."

"It is lovely, isn't it? You should see it in the autumn and at Christmas. She shows her best colors then."

As Julianna and Rhett said goodbye to the man, Beau helped his grandfather into the car, then shook the pastor's hand before sliding behind the wheel.

As he drove away from the church, he found that despite his confusion about what he'd heard earlier, he was saddened at the idea of not seeing the people of New Hope Falls again after he left. But he had a feeling that Julianna was right. They would be back.

He couldn't imagine never seeing his grandfather again. Never seeing the faces that had become familiar to him over the past three weeks. Never spending time with the people he'd come to consider friends. Never seeing Sarah...

So yes, he would be back. He just didn't know when.

CHAPTER TWENTY-FOUR

Sarah wasn't at all surprised when Beau showed up at Eli's for the hike. Mainly that was because Eli had asked her if it was okay if he invited him. She was a bit more surprised to see Julianna and Rhett with him. After all, Julianna hadn't struck her as a nature-loving woman. And Rhett, well, he also didn't seem like someone who wanted to spend time in the great outdoors. If a party was happening in the forest, his presence would make more sense.

Still, Sarah greeted each of them with a smile. She was glad to see Cara there along with Kieran, and she hoped that Jillian would show since she'd phoned her earlier and invited her. Carter and Andy were both there, but Cece wasn't. Part of her half expected the woman to show up since the hikes were regularly scheduled during the warmer months as long as the weather was nice.

"Hey there," Andy said with a smile as she approached him. "How's life?"

"Life's pretty good." At least as far as she was willing to get into it. "How're you doing?"

He gave a shrug. "Eh. I'm doing okay." He paused, a pained look crossing his face, then said, "It appears Cece has a boyfriend."

Sarah frowned. "Who?"

"Some muscle-bound dude she met on a dating app, apparently." Andy looked miserable about that latest development.

Sarah wasn't sure why Andy was interested in Cece, especially because she'd never given him the time of day. In fact, she barely acknowledged him at all. Why would that make him want to be around her? It made no sense to Sarah at all. But who was she to judge someone over their feelings?

"That must be really new. I didn't even know she was considering trying a dating app." She thought back over their conversations. "Although that's not entirely true. She did mention the idea a couple of months ago, but I encouraged her to not do it without letting someone know so they could keep tabs on her for at least the first meeting. Hopefully, she found someone who did that for her."

"She was just fawning all over Beau, and now she's announcing that she has a boyfriend. Like...I really don't get it," Andy said with a frown.

"I think there's lots we don't understand about Cece," Sarah said, trying to console the man. "She's a unique person, and I think she hides a lot about herself."

"Even from you?" Andy asked.

"Yeah. Even from me."

"I thought about inviting her to come on the hike, but I wasn't sure you'd be happy about that."

Sarah shrugged. "I wouldn't have minded. I'm not mad at her. I just need her to be respectful and kind to people, or I'm going to call her out on it."

"Who's that?" Andy asked as a car pulled up.

Sarah turned to look, smiling when she spotted Jillian behind the wheel. "It's Jillian. Do you remember her?"

"Jillian from school?"

"Yep. She's moved back." Sarah waved at her as she came towards the stairs. "Hey, Jillian."

Jillian looked up and smiled, relief showing on her face. "Hi, Sarah."

As she joined them on the porch, Sarah said, "You remember Andy?"

"Yes. It's good to see you again."

"You too. What brings you back to New Hope? Haven't had too many friends return once they've left."

As they talked, Sarah found her attention drifting to Beau. Kieran and Cara stood talking with the siblings. She wanted to join their conversation, to be a part of their group. But she knew she needed to keep her distance.

Watching Beau smile at something Cara said made her chest tighten with emotion. She hadn't realized how much she enjoyed being the one to make him smile. When they'd first met, his smiles—his real smiles, not the polite ones he sometimes gave— were hard-won. But she had loved knowing that she could bring those smiles to his face. That something about what she said or did brought him some level of genuine happiness.

It was hard to think that in a few days, he'd be gone from New Hope Falls. And once back to his old life, he probably wouldn't look on these past few weeks as anything but a small blip in his life. True, he'd been able to meet his grandfather, but there had been no indication that anything else had changed for him.

"Everyone ready to go?" Eli called out, dragging her thoughts back from where they seemed to always end up these days.

There were several murmurs of assent, then the people gathered quickly fell into step as Eli and Anna led the way around the cabin. Jillian was hanging back, so Sarah waited as well, then the two of them brought up the rear.

The good part of that was that Jillian seemed more at ease not being forced to keep up a pace because of people behind them. The bad part was that it meant Beau was in front of her, and it was hard keeping her gaze off him as they began the walk along the trail.

"Is he your boyfriend?" Jillian asked. "You didn't have to walk with me."

"What?" Sarah glanced over at her friend.

"The dark-haired guy you keep watching."

"No, he's not my boyfriend." She kept her voice low even though they'd fallen back a bit from the others. "He's someone who's been staying at the lodge for the last three weeks. His brother and sister came for the weekend."

"So, they're not from around here?"

"They're from Houston, and he'll be heading back there sometime this next week."

"Oh. You don't seem very happy about that," Jillian observed.

Sarah gave her a smile that felt...weary. "It doesn't really matter how I feel. I know not to get involved with guests at the lodge."

Jillian gave a huff of laughter. "What your head knows and what your heart tells you can be two very different things. Pretty sure you used to tell me that in high school. Weren't you quoting one of those romance books you used to read?"

"Probably," Sarah said, a grin forming at the memory of the books she'd inhaled as a teen.

"Do you still read them?"

"Not as much as I used to, but yeah, I read a book or so a month." Not really wanting to continue talking about Beau, Sarah said, "Do you have a boyfriend?"

Jillian tensed beside her then said, "No. No boyfriend."

"And not interested in anyone?"

"Nope. I'm focusing on my career."

"I get that," Sarah said, wondering what happened to her boy-crazy friend from high school. They all grew up and changed, though, she supposed.

Just because Cece had never gotten past that point didn't mean the rest of them hadn't. It was just a bit of a surprise, since of their group of friends, Jillian and Cece had definitely topped the list when it came to chasing after boys. It was probably one of the reasons the two of them had never gotten along. They'd ended up going after the same guys, more often than not, which had created friction between them.

As a teen, Sarah had thought she'd fall in love, marry her high school sweetheart, and live happily-ever-after in New Hope Falls.

Then her father had left, shaking her faith in love lasting forever and making her wary of the dreams she'd once had.

Now she was smart enough to know that just because her father left, that didn't mean every other man would do the same. It was just unfortunate for her, Beau *was* going to be one that left. And even though she'd known he would go from the moment he arrived, her heart still ached over the thought.

"Sometimes it's just easier to be alone," Jillian remarked quietly, leaving Sarah to wonder if her friend had been hurt by a guy.

"Yeah, I hear ya." She paused for a moment then said, "Have you talked to Cece since the other night?"

"No. And I'll be honest, I've gone out of my way to avoid seeing her. Which makes the fact she works at that bakery unfortunate. I can only imagine the delicious goodies I'm missing out on. Of course, that's probably not a bad thing."

"Yeah, they do have some yummy stuff, but honestly, Leah can make goodies that are just as good. The only things they absolutely do the best are the specialty coffees. So if you're missing those since moving back from Portland, you're out of luck unless you drive into Everett."

"I can make my own drinks at home. I have a fancy coffee machine that I brought with me. So maybe I'll just have to come around to the lodge for my sweet fix."

"Definitely. You're welcome anytime."

Sarah glanced up and saw that they had fallen further behind the rest of the group. She honestly wasn't in the mood to rush, though, so the fact that Jillian was going at a slower pace suited her just fine. And it wasn't like she didn't know the trail. They weren't in any danger of getting lost.

As if reading her mind, Jillian said, "Sorry if I'm holding you up."

"You're not. This isn't a race or a work-out oriented hike. Honestly, I think Eli hosts these to encourage some of us to get out of the house more." Sarah laughed. "Me and Anna being the two main people he's trying to motivate. He's still working on Leah, but she's stubborn. The thing with her is that she usually makes food for after the hike, so he doesn't pressure her too much."

"Smart man."

"Don't say that too loud," Sarah said in a mock whisper. "He's already got a big ego from Anna always loving on him."

The two of them giggled together, and Sarah felt her spirits lift, especially when she saw some of the tension that Jillian seemed to always carry with her ease a bit too. They'd pretty much dropped down to a leisurely stroll at that point, so far behind the others that they couldn't even hear them anymore.

"Were you teaching in Portland?" Sarah asked.

"I was substituting, mainly. But when my grandmother passed away, and I realized I had a chance at a job here, I decided I needed to leave Portland sooner rather than later."

"Well—" Before Sarah could finish her sentence, Beau and Carter appeared on the trail ahead of them.

"You two okay?" Beau asked, concern on his face. "We've been waiting for you at the bench."

"Oh, we're fine," Sarah said, trying not to be touched by his concern. "Just taking our time."

She noticed Carter run a quick look over both of them. Given his first responder training, it was probably instinct that had him checking to make sure they weren't hurt.

"As long as you're okay..." Beau's voice trailed off as he glanced at Carter.

"We'll just head on back and let the others know," Carter finished for him. "No rush."

With that, Carter turned and headed back up the trail. Beau turned a little more slowly, but soon he too was moving back in the direction he'd come from.

"Well, that was cute," Jillian said with a grin. "Methinks that perhaps your interest is reciprocated."

Unfortunately, that didn't make Sarah feel any better, but she didn't feel like rehashing the situation with Jillian. She had a feeling that her friend would try to offer encouragement that maybe things could work out. Sarah didn't want false hope.

While it was true that she and Beau hadn't actually sat down and talked about what might be a mutual interest, Beau had never said anything to indicate that he might be willing to relocate, and the thought of leaving New Hope Falls created a pit in her stomach.

She might have considered moving to Everett or Seattle. Maybe even Portland. But Houston? That was just too far away from her family and her support system, especially if she would end up in a lifestyle that was completely foreign to her.

Where did love factor into things? Would love be enough to overcome all of that? Was it possible that God might want her to leave her home?

Except that Sarah knew that as long as Beau's belief in God didn't line up with hers, everything else was irrelevant. That was what she needed to focus on above everything. Even if Beau was willing to relocate, if nothing changed for him spiritually, there was no hope for a relationship.

When they finally reached the bench, Eli gave Sarah a curious look as he approached her. "You okay?"

"Yep." She smiled. "Jillian and I just got caught up talking, rather than walking. Sorry to hold you up."

"No problem. I just wanted to make sure the two of you were alright." Eli slipped an arm around her shoulders and squeezed. "Did you two just want to sit here at the bench while we keep going on up a bit further?"

"Nah. I think we'll keep going. We'll try to keep you in sight."

Eli nodded then encouraged people to get moving again. Though Sarah and Jillian fell in at the back of the pack again, this time they moved a bit faster. Beau and Julianna walked right in front of them, and periodically, she saw him glancing over his shoulder at them.

They made it up to the point in the trail they usually hiked to and took a bit of a rest before they headed back down. Leah was working in Eli's kitchen when they got back to the cabin, and Eli immediately went to the grill when she handed him a glass dish with a bunch of kabobs in it. Sarah jumped in to help her, though there really wasn't much left to do.

Leah had set out all the dishware and drinks as well as the potato salad, buns, and the other food she'd brought for their meal. Sarah's stomach rumbled in appreciation.

Once the food was ready, Kieran said grace, and they began to eat. Sarah wondered what Beau, Rhett, and Julianna thought about Christianity and what they'd seen of it while they'd been in New Hope. The pastor's message that morning had definitely presented the Gospel clearly, and she had to hope that it had at least made them think about where they might spend eternity.

She couldn't deny that she'd thought about how things might unfold differently if Beau did choose to make a profession of faith. She'd always assumed that if or when she contemplated a serious relationship, it would be with a man who was mature in his faith. Even if Beau did become a Christian, she'd be the one with more spiritual maturity.

The one consolation in that scenario was that Sarah knew that Beau's grandfather would do his best to mentor Beau, even if it was over the phone.

She couldn't allow herself to be caught up in those possibilities. Right then, there was nothing in a future with Beau that was within her control. While she might not be sure of much when it came to Beau, one thing she knew with absolute certainty was that hoping for something to work out between them would only lead to more heartache.

~*~

"It was my intent to have you work this final week at the lodge, but when I spoke to Eli the other day, he wasn't sure it would be a good idea."

Beau stared at his grandfather as they sat at the table in the care home sunroom, enjoying the sunshine that was currently streaming through the large windows. "What do you mean?"

"Apparently, there are some tensions between you and Sarah?"

Beau sighed. "It's not tension, per se. Just an ill-advised interest, I guess you could say."

"Ill-advised?" his grandfather asked.

"Her life is here. Mine is in Houston. And that's just the most obvious thing that makes any interest ill-advised."

His grandfather seemed to be considering his statement, then he nodded. "I had hoped that you could spend the last week working alongside the McNamaras, but I think perhaps Eli was correct that it isn't the best thing at the moment."

Though the idea of helping them out after they'd been so generous with their time and friendship was appealing, Beau couldn't deny that Eli was likely right. His shoulders slumped as he stared down at the table.

"I'd love to have you stay in town through the rest of the week, but if you'd rather return to Houston earlier, I wouldn't blame you."

Beau was torn. On the one hand, he didn't want to leave New Hope any sooner than he had to. His visit there had been life-changing on so many levels, not the least of which was meeting the man seated next to him.

The stress that awaited him in Houston made him want to stay away as long as possible. However, there was also a part of him that wanted to get back to Houston to find out what his dad's plan was for him.

"I don't know what to do," Beau said. He glanced up at his grandfather, surprised that the words he'd been feeling had spilled out so easily. Usually, he would never have admitted something like that to anyone.

His grandfather's expression was sympathetic. "I'm afraid you're the only one who can make that decision. Selfishly, I want you to stay, but I don't know if that's the right thing for you to do. All things considered."

Maybe he just needed to go back to Houston and deal with things there. He knew he'd be coming back to New Hope Falls at some point. If for no other reason than to see his grandfather again.

"I have a couple of things I want to do before I go, but I think maybe it's time to head back and face the music. Staying will only prolong the inevitable."

His grandfather nodded. "I understand, but I do hope you'll be back."

"I definitely will be." If nothing else, Beau knew that with certainty.

"When do you think you'll leave?"

"I'm going to check flights for tomorrow or Wednesday."

"Be sure to come back and see me before you go."

"Once I have a flight arranged, I'll let you know, and maybe we can have lunch or dinner together."

"I'd like that."

Beau smiled at the man. "So would I."

The older man reached out and patted Beau's arm. "Seeing you has made me think more about what my boy might have grown up to be like. I would have been a proud papa if he'd been like you."

The warmth that flooded through Beau at his grandfather's words was foreign. His own father had never said he was proud of who Beau was or of anything he had done. Beau wondered how different their relationship might have been if his dad had taken the time to encourage Beau rather than tear him down and try to manipulate his life.

It seemed he would never know.

CHAPTER TWENTY-FIVE

The next day at breakfast, Beau was glad to see Sarah was there. There was only one other couple present, but they were immersed in their own conversation.

Beau followed Sarah into the kitchen once the meal was over. "Can I talk with you for a couple of minutes?"

Her brows pulled together as she stared at him for a moment before nodding. "Let's go out on the deck."

She glanced over at Leah, and the two of them seemed to hold a whole conversation without words before she led Beau out the back door onto the deck that faced the forest of evergreen and shade trees.

His stomach tightened as he considered the conversation he was about to have with her. Part of him had just wanted to leave without saying goodbye, to spare them that pain, but his heart just couldn't do it.

"I'm leaving this afternoon." He hadn't meant to blurt it out, but it seemed that their ability to communicate with the easy banter they'd had even just a few days ago had gotten lost in a sea of awkwardness.

Her eyes widened, and for a moment, he thought he saw dismay cross her face. But it was gone so quickly, Beau couldn't be sure.

"I thought you were here through Sunday," she said, taking a couple steps away from him, her gaze shifting to the trees beyond him.

"That was the plan, but I think I need to go back to Houston." Beau paused, trying to formulate his next words. "I just wanted to thank you."

"Thank me?" Her gaze darted to his, and the impact of looking into her eyes sank deep into his heart. "For what?"

"Until I met you, I didn't know how to see the joy in life. You helped me realize that a life without joy isn't much of a life. So, for that, I want to thank you."

For a moment, a smile lifted the corners of her lips, but it didn't stay long. She hugged herself, and Beau was filled with an overwhelming need to wrap his own arms around her.

"I'm glad I was able to help you in that way. It was nice meeting you and your family."

His heart hurt at the thought of leaving her, but what else was he supposed to do? They hadn't known each other long enough for him to ask her to consider a move to Houston. And long-distance? He just wasn't sure how that would work when he was heading back into what was probably going to be a hectic schedule.

If previous experience was anything to go by, he was barely going to have time to breathe once he was back in Houston. And he had to know what his father was going to do before he made any sort of plans for his future.

His chest tightened as he fought the unfamiliar emotion rising within him. How was this even possible? How could he be feeling so drawn...so connected...to someone he hadn't even kissed? Wasn't the physical connection supposed to be what drew them together?

Tiffany had resisted a physical relationship with him beyond kissing, insisting that she was going to be able to wear white on their wedding day with a clear conscience. He had been fine with that, hoping that once they had sex, the connection he hadn't felt with her previously would snap into place at least a little bit more.

He'd had one other semi-serious relationship before Tiffany, and in that case, being together physically had happened quickly, and at about that same time, he'd realized the affection he'd had for that woman. Not love, he was fairly certain now, but he'd at least felt something romantic toward her.

That hadn't been the case with Tiffany. And now that he was faced with these feelings for Sarah when they'd never even been physically intimate, he knew they never would have been there with Tiffany. But where did that leave him?

In a mess, that's where.

Beau didn't want to walk away, but he had no choice. He had to figure out his life. Maybe then he could come back, and if Sarah was still single, he could tell her how he felt.

The idea of her not still being single made him feel sick, but given where he was in his life, there was no denying that there was a better man out there for her. Someone who hadn't spent so long kowtowing to his father that he couldn't stand on his own two feet.

Shame flooded him at the thought. He'd thought he was being patient, trying his best to work towards the future he wanted for himself. Instead, all he'd done was build himself a prison and hand his father the key.

"Will you contact me if you ever need anything?" Beau asked, though he wasn't sure why. Maybe it was just the overwhelming desire to be there for her if she should ever need someone.

Sarah tilted her head, regarding him with her beautiful blue eyes, as if trying to figure out the motivation behind his offer. Finally, she nodded, but Beau was pretty sure it would take something pretty drastic to push her to contact him. Her support system would always be stronger than anything he could offer her.

"I'm sorry," Beau said, floundering for what else to say because words had never been his thing. Especially words that adequately conveyed the tangle of emotions within him. "Take care of yourself, okay? You bring sunshine into the lives of so many people, and I'm just glad I was one of the lucky recipients for the time I was here."

Her lips tightened for a moment before she glanced away from him. "Take care of yourself too."

Her voice was soft, and the words barely reached him, making him want to move closer to her. To take her into his arms. But he knew that would be selfish. Though it might make him feel better in the moment, in the long run, it would make leaving that much harder.

Beau shoved his hands into his pockets, his fingers fisting into the fabric. This goodbye sucked. Even though he was sure he'd see her again, it felt like he was saying goodbye to something that wouldn't be there the next time they met. He wanted to make her promises, to ask her to wait for him, but he couldn't do any of that because he had no idea what lay ahead for him.

With one last look at her, Beau turned and headed back inside. He had to get his luggage and check out before heading into Everett to buy his grandfather a cell phone and set up a plan for him. He'd go for a final lunch with the man before he caught a flight out just before four that afternoon.

Then it was back home to face the music.

~*~

Sarah sat cross-legged on the floor, staring out the large windows of her studio. The late afternoon sky was gray and weeping, rivulets of rain streaming down the glass and blurring the forest beyond it. The weather so perfectly suited her mood that she'd felt compelled to sit down and wallow in it. Wallow in her own tears and sadness.

She was beyond frustrated with herself. Over the past week, she'd done everything she could to pull herself out of the emotional abyss she'd fallen into when Beau had left. His sudden departure had shaken her, and it had left her with a level of hurt she hadn't felt since her dad had left. The pain from her dad's departure had eclipsed everything at the time, and now Beau's leaving had managed to hurt her in a way she hadn't thought possible.

In the days since he'd left, she'd alternated between forcing herself to work on her current project and letting herself spend time sketching and painting what she wanted, which, as had been the case even before he'd left, was Beau. She'd gone to every class Cara had offered that week. She'd even worked a couple of shifts at *Norma's.* Trying anything and everything to keep occupied.

When her mom had sent her off to one of the cabins with instructions to clean it from top to bottom, Sarah hadn't even balked. She'd put on her favorite podcasts and scrubbed and scrubbed. In the moment, each of those things had helped to distract her, but they hadn't helped once she had nothing to occupy her thoughts.

So here she was, sitting in her studio, alone with her thoughts yet again.

What was it going to take to get past this sadness and hurt? It made her feel weak, especially when she thought back to how her mom had been in the days and months following her dad's departure. She hadn't wallowed around, crying. No, she'd stayed strong for her children.

A beep from her phone drew Sarah's attention. She made herself count to ten before she picked it up. Too often in the past week, she'd snatched the phone up whenever there was an alert. And not once had it been Beau sending her a message.

...Nine. Ten. She picked her phone up and turned it over to look at the screen. Frowning, she stared at the alert. It took her a moment to figure out what it was for, but then it dawned on her.

In a moment of total weakness right after he'd left, she'd set up an alert for Beau's name, so that if he was mentioned at all online, she would be notified. She knew he had been mentioned online in the past. That was how Leah had discovered the news she had about Beau, and later Sarah had found the same news for herself.

She was fairly certain that nothing she read about him was going to make her feel any better, so she should probably just ignore the alert. But her curiosity prevailed over her common sense, even though ignoring her common sense hadn't resulted in good things lately. Clicking on the email with the alert, she found a link to a blog. It appeared that the blog author liked to report on the lives of the rich and famous of Texas.

Is the engagement back on? The headline took her breath away, but it was nothing like the sucker punch to her gut when she saw the picture underneath it. Beau was walking into a restaurant with a woman Sarah recognized as his ex-fiancée.

Pulling her legs up and wrapping her arms around them, Sarah rested her chin on her knees as she peered down at her phone, unable to keep her gaze from scanning over the rest of the post.

Just moments ago, Beaumont Allerton and Tiffany Newcomb were spotted entering the very restaurant where, in spectacular fashion, Tiffany ended their engagement just a few weeks ago. Does this signal a rekindling of their romance and a possible re-engagement?

Though Tiffany has been seen out and about in the weeks since that night, Beau has been curiously absent from the Houston social scene. His parents and siblings have made appearances at various functions, but he hasn't been around, leading to much speculation as to where he's been.

He certainly chose an interesting way to make his reappearance onto the Houston scene, leaving us to wonder if an announcement will be forthcoming.

Sarah turned the screen of the phone away from her as she gripped it tightly. How was it possible to hurt more over this whole situation? No doubt it was because, while she'd imagined him returning to New Hope Falls, she hadn't ever pictured him doing it with Tiffany in tow. But if they were, in fact, getting re-engaged, it would only be a matter of time before he returned to New Hope Falls to introduce his fiancée to his grandfather.

The very idea made her stomach lurch, and she felt even more helpless against her pain than she had before. Helpless and angry.

The first guy she could have actually imagined herself with—*had* imagined herself with, whether that had been a smart thing to do or not—and it had ended like this.

Why couldn't God have brought her a nice Christian man who was available? Why did her apparent *love-at-first-sight* moment have to be with a man who was spiritually and emotionally unavailable?

And for the millionth time, Sarah wished she'd listened to Leah.

CHAPTER TWENTY-SIX

"What are we doing here?" Beau asked Tiffany as he looked at her across the small table where they'd been seated. It wasn't the same one they'd been at when they'd last been at the restaurant, but just the fact they were there at all didn't sit well with him.

Of course, that shouldn't have surprised him. Nothing had gone as planned since his arrival back in Houston. Not that he'd had much of a plan, if he was honest. It had been more of a hope for how things might go. But it had been a futile hope.

"Mother felt it was important to show the world that I am not a crazy screaming shrew. That we can have a civil conversation even after what happened." She gave him a sly smile. "And maybe I want people to wonder about our relationship status. Give them something to talk about until I release a statement that we're not rekindling our romance but will always remain the best of friends."

Beau didn't want people to speculate about their relationship. He was already speculating too much about his life, and he was weary of it.

And remain the best of friends? He kind of felt like they'd never really even been friends, let alone the best of friends. His friendship with Sarah had felt far more genuine than any part of the relationship he'd had with Tiffany.

"You understood what I said on the phone, though, right?" Beau asked.

"That you aren't interested in continuing our relationship?" Beau nodded. "Oh, I understood that perfectly, and after our conversation, I'm not either."

"You're not?" Beau had hoped that she would be understanding, but he hadn't been certain, since after he'd said what he wanted to say to her, she'd asked to meet him for dinner.

"Honestly, I meant every word I said when we broke up. I realize I could have handled it in a better way, but I was feeling a lot of pressure from my folks to get on with the wedding plans. I figured a spectacular public break-up would be harder to walk back from than if we'd done it in private."

"And yet here we are in public once again, giving everyone fodder for gossip because we're *not* fighting."

"Yeah…" Tiffany dropped her gaze. "I'm just sick of my parents trying to run my life. I want to marry someone I love and can't live without, and I want that someone to feel the same way about me." She looked back up at him. "And I don't think we felt that way about each other."

"No. I don't think we did." In fact, he knew they hadn't. His feelings for Sarah had highlighted that in stark contrast.

"Where have you been for the past month?"

Beau hesitated for a moment before giving her an abbreviated version of the events that had taken place since he'd left Houston for New Hope Falls. He didn't go into a lot of details about meeting his grandfather or any details at all about Sarah because he felt the need to cherish those memories for himself.

"You actually enjoyed hanging out in such a small town? Working at such menial jobs?" Tiffany wrinkled her nose as she spoke.

"You do realize that far more people live that kind of life than one like ours, right?" Beau said. "If it's good enough for them, it's not beneath me. I met some interesting people, learned some new skills, and made some new friends."

"I get that lots of people live like that, but if you don't have to, why would you?"

Beau didn't know how to explain it, especially since he'd have asked the same question just a few weeks ago. Having done it now, though, he had decided that if he ever had kids, he would insist they work at some of those menial jobs, if for no other reason than to meet people from different walks of life.

"It was necessary," Beau said. "And I'm glad I did it."

"Dad said that your folks told them that you were doing some soul-searching and would come to the right decision."

"The right decision being to get back together, I suppose."

Tiffany nodded. "Right for all of them, I'd imagine. Not so right for us."

"You're welcome to blame me for us not getting back together," Beau volunteered. "I doubt it will upset my folks any more than they're already upset, but maybe it will get your folks off your back."

Tiffany sighed. "Until they find another guy from the right kind of family."

"You need to hold out. I spent some time with people in happy, loving relationships, and I realized that by giving in to what our parents wanted for us, we were being robbed of the opportunity to find that for ourselves. If that's the type of relationship you want, Tiffany, hold out for it. Don't settle for less because, in the end, you're the one who has to live with the person, not your parents."

"You would have treated me well, though," Tiffany said. "I believe that."

"I would like to believe that too. But if you wanted some emotional connection from me, from our relationship, that I wasn't able or didn't want to give you, I dare say you would have ended up even more unhappy than you already were with me."

Tiffany sat back in her chair as the waiter returned with their meals. As they ate, their conversation shifted away from their relationship and onto less weighty subjects. Mainly it was Tiffany telling him about all the stuff that had happened with their social peers during his absence. He tried to pay attention, but in reality, he just didn't care all that much about who had bought what expensive car or who had jetted off to Bora Bora.

Too often, Beau found his thoughts drifting to Sarah and wondering what she was up to. On Sunday afternoon, he'd thought about how she was likely getting together with her friends—his friends now, too—to spend time as a group. Meanwhile, he was alone in his apartment because his only other option was his parents' home, which was frostier than the Antarctic whenever he was around.

Tiffany declined dessert, and Beau happily did as well. He was ready to get out of there, even if it meant returning to the loneliness of his apartment.

After he paid for their meal, the two of them left the restaurant. As they walked past a couple of people standing outside, one of them lifted their phone to take their picture.

"Are you two getting back together again?"

Beau scowled at the question, uncertain why anyone besides their family would care about the answer to that question. He kept his mouth shut, and so did Tiffany, though she did grip his arm as they walked out to where the valet had his car waiting.

"Why do they want to know that?" Beau asked as he pulled away from the restaurant a couple of minutes later. "It's not like they'd be invited to the wedding."

"Have you really never googled yourself?" Tiffany asked.

"No, I haven't. Why would I?"

"Are you serious?" Tiffany laughed. "I guess you don't know that there are sites devoted to the lives of the rich and famous. Specifically, the younger age set, like you and me, although they'll also talk about the older people if they do something especially scandalous."

"I had no clue." Beau didn't like the idea that strangers cared enough about his life to document and report on it publicly.

"Well, now you know, but ignorance is bliss, so you're probably better off not putting your name in a Google search."

Beau agreed, and he had no intention of changing that. Except when he got home after dropping Tiffany off, he couldn't seem to keep from checking it out. Within minutes, he wished he'd stuck to his guns and stayed away from the internet.

He shut the lid of his laptop and leaned back in his chair with a sigh. His phone rang as he sat there, drawing his attention from the strangers who thought they knew more about his life than he did.

Father.

Beau's eyebrows rose at the name on his screen. The man had basically ignored him since he'd returned to Houston. He'd told him not to bother coming into work until he was told to, which meant he'd had a lot of hours to fill since coming home.

"Beaumont, you'll be expected in the office tomorrow morning at eight. Report to Hugh Vensel."

Beau had a few questions about those instructions, but he knew better than to ask them. He'd have the answers to them at eight the next morning and not a minute before. "Yes, sir."

And that was the end of that call.

He mulled over all the potential outcomes of his return to work, which ranged from business as usual to being fired by a man who had worked under him in the department. None of them were good...even the business as usual one. He'd really made the decision to move beyond *business as usual* during his time in New Hope Falls.

Pushing back from his desk, he went out to his kitchen and grabbed a drink from the fridge. He wandered over to the floor to ceiling windows in his living room to stare out at the cityscape. Since he lived on the twentieth floor, he had an uninterrupted view of bright twinkling lights that extended as far as he could see.

It was a sharp contrast to the view he'd seen outside his window at the lodge. This view was what had been most familiar, but it had never captured his attention the way the view of the forest and mountains had.

Discontentment and a low level of anxiety settled in his gut, and by the time he went to bed, those feelings had increased in intensity, leading to a restless night.

When he got up the next morning, they were still there, but that didn't surprise him. Until he knew what lay ahead, the uneasiness would be present. He wasn't a fan of the unknown in general, but in particular, he really wasn't a fan of it when it related to his work.

He put on his favorite dark gray suit with a white shirt and blue paisley tie, feeling awkward in the outfit after not having dressed in business attire for several weeks. Looking at his reflection in the mirror, Beau felt like he was seeing a stranger.

The suit fit him as well as it ever had, but it just didn't feel as good as it once had. He had felt powerful in the suit in the past, but now, he realized, he didn't need to feel powerful. He didn't even *want* to feel powerful.

His hair was longer than it had ever been, and he was sure his dad would comment on it when he saw him. Beau didn't care, though. In fact, he was coming to care less and less about the trappings of his job. Maybe it was time to look for other employment.

He stared at himself, wondering where the thoughts were coming from. Changing jobs was something he'd never considered before. In his mind, his options had always been to work for his father or to start his own business. He had always figured he'd do the one until he had his trust fund, and then he'd do the other.

Now there was a third option he was considering, but he didn't know where that particular path might lead. Definitely, there wasn't a place for him in his chosen career in New Hope Falls. High finance jobs and small towns didn't exactly go hand-in-hand.

He'd have to think more about it later. Right then, he had his current job to deal with.

When he walked into the towering office building that housed his father's company a short time later, Beau hoped he looked more confident than he felt.

He nodded at the security guard before swiping his ID to get through the door that led to the elevators that would take him to the upper floors. His father's company owned the building—along with several others in both Houston and Dallas—and they had the top three floors of this one for their offices.

Once he reached the floor where he worked, Beau left the elevator and walked toward his office, planning to put his briefcase away before searching out Hugh. It was a shock—though maybe not a complete one—to find Hugh sitting at his desk, looking entirely too much at home.

"Ah. Beau, c'mon in and have a seat." He gestured to the chair across the desk from him, acting for all the world like this was the norm for them. "Your father said you would be in this morning to meet with me."

Rather than respond, Beau unbuttoned his suit jacket and took the chair offered, setting his briefcase between his feet. Again, he hoped that the unease he felt wasn't reflected outwardly.

"Welcome back," Hugh said, to which Beau gave a nod in response. The other man waved his hand around at the office. "I suppose you're wondering about all of this."

Beau chose to remain quiet—which wasn't that out of character for him—and just arched a brow at the man.

"Yes. Well," Hugh said, shifting in his seat. "While you were gone, your father decided it was in the best interests of the company if I took over your clients, and after much discussion in recent days, it seemed that your father felt my promotion should be permanent." Hugh cleared his throat. "You'll be stepping into my former position for the time being."

And there it was.

No doubt, this was his father's final attempt to get him to fall in line, and rather than use discussion and encouragement, he was going to use humiliation. Beau felt as if his life was falling to pieces at that moment. But as it broke around him, he realized that rather than sadness or sorrow, he felt only relief. Like the building pressure of the past couple of months had finally been released by the shattering.

Mentally, Beau picked up the pieces to deal with later. He got to his feet, buttoned his suit coat again, then picked up his brief-case.

"You'll have my resignation by the end of the day." He held out his hand to Hugh. "Best of luck with your future here."

"Beau." The man looked alarmed as he stood up. "I'm sure you just need time to adjust."

When Hugh didn't take his hand, Beau lowered it and gave him an indulgent smile. "I'm quite sure that I don't need time to adjust to this, because while it may be part of my father's plan, it's not part of mine."

With that, Beau turned and left the office, ignoring the splutter-ings coming from Hugh as he trotted after Beau. People were just getting off the elevator as Beau approached it, so he was able to step in as soon as it was empty. Turning, he saw that Hugh stood there, a slightly panicked look on his face. Beau figured he was imagining how he was going to have to tell Mr. Allerton Sr. that his son had just quit.

"Goodbye, Hugh," Beau said as the doors slid shut.

Relief.

That was the most identifiable emotion he felt right then, but it was edged with a bit of panic of his own. He'd had a plan for the longest time, so now that he didn't have one, he wasn't sure what to do.

His phone rang as he pulled into his parking spot in the under-ground garage at his apartment building.

"Hello, Father."

"Get yourself back to the office," he demanded, his voice tight with anger.

For a moment, Beau tried to reconcile this man with the one who had taken steps to make sure that his father-in-law was taken care of. But try as he might, it just didn't gel.

"No. I'm sorry, but that's not going to happen."

"Then you can kiss your trust fund goodbye. Not just for another few years but forever."

"That's fine," Beau said, even though panic was beginning to edge out the relief. "I'm a grown man, Father, and it's time I made pro-active decisions for my own life, not ones made in response to your manipulations."

"And just how do you suppose you'll support yourself without a job?"

With more confidence than he felt, Beau said, "I'll figure it out. I'm hardly the first person who's quit a job without having another one lined up. It's probably not that uncommon when work conditions are intolerable."

"You are ungrateful," his father spat out.

"No, I'm not. I am trying to be a grown-up and take responsibility for my life like an almost-thirty-year-old man should."

"You'll never get another job in this town."

Beau stared at the wall in front of his car, unwilling to believe that his dad would actively prevent him from getting a job. "Then perhaps it's time to move somewhere else."

His father let out a bark of laughter. "When you need money, you know where to find me."

When the call ended abruptly, Beau let out a sigh.

He got out of the car and grabbed his briefcase, knowing he'd need to at least make a short-term plan if he was going to be able to stick to his decision to walk away from his father's control. He'd never felt more vulnerable and yet strong at the same time.

It was an odd combination, but one Beau knew he needed to embrace because there was no way to escape it for the foreseeable future.

CHAPTER TWENTY-SEVEN

As Sarah drove back to the lodge, she mulled over the conversation she'd just had with Cara over lunch at *Norma's*. It had felt good to be able to moan and groan about how she was feeling, and she hadn't been kidding when she'd said she was going to steer clear of dating for awhile. Although, since it hadn't even taken dating to land her in her present emotional maelstrom, maybe she should avoid men, in general, for the time being.

Sarah had been so certain that she'd reach a clear moment when she'd make a conscious decision that she was interested in a guy as more than a friend. That was obviously her lack of experience talking. She hadn't known that by the time she realized she wanted to be more than just friends, her emotions would be so well-engaged.

She had never wanted to be one of those women who viewed every man as a potential husband, but maybe there was some good reason to approach guys with that mindset. It could only be a good thing to know ahead of time if a man was someone she could see herself in a relationship with and, most importantly, if he was available.

Though she'd learned that lesson a bit too late with Beau, Sarah could only hope it would hold her in good stead in the future. In the meantime, she refused...absolutely refused...to allow herself to feel hurt for longer than the time they'd actually known each other. That meant that she had only a few more days to get her act together and get over her feelings for him.

Every day since he'd left, she had tried to convince herself that she didn't feel anything close to love for Beau. Sure, she'd used to dream of falling in love at first sight—especially as a teen—but she knew that that wasn't a realistic way to approach things as a Christian. How could you truly love someone based only on their physical appearance?

No, she hadn't experienced love at first sight, even though she'd admired Beau's appearance. Love had snuck up on her as they'd spent time together. It had been a gradual thing, until the shocking realization of how she truly felt for him had pushed her off the cliff into freefall.

But how was she supposed to get over it? She'd prayed about it. Tried to keep busy with painting and work around the lodge. Tried to talk it out with Leah, Anna, and Cara. Nothing worked. Absolutely nothing.

I've learned my lesson, God. It wasn't the first time she'd reminded Him of that. She figured that more than anything else, it would be God who helped her move forward. If only He'd get with her program.

Sorry, Lord. She knew that it was best to allow God to work on His timetable, but her impatience kept getting the better of her. Especially in this situation.

"Sare!" Leah came rushing out of the kitchen when Sarah walked into the lodge.

"What's wrong?" Sarah glanced around, looking for her mom.

"Beau called Mom a little while ago to make a reservation for next weekend," she said, her brows pinching together. "With the possibility of extending his stay."

Nope, Lord, that's certainly not gonna help. "Maybe I need to take an extended trip somewhere."

Leah didn't argue with her, which made Sarah consider the idea more seriously. For sure, she wasn't going to get over Beau if she had to see him again so soon. She'd hoped for months, not weeks, to pass before running into him again.

"Let me think about it," she said. "I've got a few days to come up with a plan."

Maybe she'd miraculously get over him and not have to go anywhere. If her plan to be over him before the length of time passed that they'd known each other would just come to fruition, she'd be good to go. Yeah, that would be the dream.

"I'm sorry, sis," Leah said with a frown. "I'd hoped it would be longer before he returned."

"You and me both," Sarah murmured as she looped her arm through Leah's and propelled them back to the kitchen. "Now tell me what you need my help with so I can be distracted."

"If distraction was going to work, it would have already." Leah tugged free then pointed at a laundry basket. "But if you insist, there's stuff to fold."

"That I can do." Sarah set her purse on the counter then tackled the basket of towels as she told Leah about her visit with Cara.

When her mom walked into the kitchen, the first thing she did was come to where Sarah stood, a towel in her hands. She slipped her arm around her shoulders and said, "I can cancel his reservation."

Sarah loved her mom so much in that moment. Turning away business wasn't something she did lightly, but when it came to her kids, she would do almost anything. "There's no need for that. I'll be okay."

Her mom moved to stand in front of her, meeting her gaze full on. "If you change your mind, you let me know."

"I will."

"Good." She leaned forward and pressed a kiss to her cheek. "Now, make sure you fold those towels the way I like them."

"Is there any other way?" Sarah smiled as she finished folding the one she held, grateful to know that even while she struggled with her emotions, her family had her back, doing what they could to support her.

Sarah just hoped it wouldn't take her too much longer to get back to the point where she didn't need to lean on them quite so much.

~*~

The weariness Beau had been fighting for the last few hours of his drive evaporated as he made the final turn and saw the lodge. Had it been just under a month since he'd last been there? It felt like an eternity.

So much had changed in those weeks. After feeling like his world was in pieces following the confrontation with his dad, he'd manage to gather them all up and begin to rearrange them into the shape he wanted for his future, not the one his dad had been fashioning for him.

Beau pulled into a spot in front of the lodge, turned off his car, then let his head drop back against the headrest, closing his eyes as he let out a sigh. Thirty-plus hours on the road with nothing but his own thoughts for company had worn him out. Julianna and Rhett had both told him he was nuts to be driving when he could have flown out and had his car shipped.

About ten hours into the trip, he'd been forced to admit that perhaps they were right. Of course, by that point, it was too late to change his mind, so he'd had no choice but to press on. Sleeping in whatever hotels were closest to the highway, not caring what amenities they provided beyond a clean and comfortable bed.

A rap on his window had Beau straightening, his eyes popping open. Had he fallen asleep?

Turning, he saw Eli peering at him. He hadn't been sure of his welcome at the lodge, but Nadine had taken his reservation without comment, and Eli didn't look as if he was ready to punch him. In fact, the man had a look of concern on his face.

Beau reached for the door handle, slowly opening the door to give Eli time to move. Stepping from the vehicle, he stretched his arms up to work the kinks from his back.

"You doing okay?" Eli asked, his hands on his hips as he regarded Beau with an unreadable gaze.

"I'm fine. Just a bit stiff after spending the last four days behind the wheel."

Eli's gaze went to the car behind him. Though he'd listed his penthouse apartment for sale, Beau just hadn't been able to part with his luxury SUV. But even though it was a comfortable ride, it still hadn't been a great place to spend the last four days.

When Eli looked back at him, his gaze held a curious edge. "Why did you drive?"

He hadn't anticipated having to answer that question quite so soon. "Things are in a bit of an upheaval for me at the moment. I decided the drive might give me some time to think."

"I would imagine that long of a drive would give you plenty of time to think," Eli said. "Or drive you crazy."

Beau couldn't help but smile a bit at that comment. "A couple of days into the trip, I was pretty sure I was crazy for having made that particular decision."

"Well, come on in, and let's get you settled." Eli gestured to the car. "Do you want to bring in your bags?"

"I'll get them later." Beau was anxious to see Sarah...if she was around. Given how they'd left things, it was possible she'd make herself scarce while he was there.

He'd initially only booked in for the weekend, but the previous night, he'd emailed Nadine and requested she extend his reservation for the week, if she had a vacancy. She'd replied that she had space for the week, but the following weekend was fully booked. He had no reason to doubt her since she'd already taken his reservation, but he'd have to find another option pretty quickly if he didn't want to be sleeping in his car in a week's time.

The moment he stepped into the foyer of the lodge, tension he hadn't even been aware of wrapping around his chest suddenly loosened, and he felt like he could take a deep breath for the first time in weeks. The familiar sights and smells greeted him like he imagined a home would...at least for people who didn't live in places that were more showcase than cozy.

"Mom's in town at the moment," Eli said as he rounded the desk. "So I'll take care of checking you in."

It didn't take but a couple of minutes to get all the details taken care of before Eli handed him the key to his room. He didn't know if it was just that that room was the only one vacant or what, but it appeared he was in the same one he'd been in last time. Beau was very much okay with that. Right then, familiarity was a good thing.

Passing on Eli's offer of help, Beau went back to his car and pulled out the overnight bag he'd packed for the trip, leaving his other suitcases in the trunk for the time being. Right then, all he wanted was a shower, a nap in a bed he knew was comfortable, and then a fresh change of clothes. In that order.

When Beau headed downstairs a couple of hours later, he felt at peace. The nap had refreshed him, and the fresh air coming in his window had revitalized him. He wasn't a country boy by any stretch of the imagination, but being so close to nature that he could almost reach out the window of his room and touch it, soothed something within him.

Given that the first time he'd been there, his ultimate plan had been to return to Houston, Beau hadn't dwelt much on how being at the lodge and its surroundings had made him feel. This time, however, he was aware. Aware and so very appreciative.

CHAPTER TWENTY-EIGHT

Though Beau wasn't surprised, he was disappointed that there was no sign of Sarah among the people gathered in the dining room. He would have gone into the kitchen to see if she was there, but he was already running a bit later than he would have liked, and he didn't want to be late for dinner.

Nadine's eyes widened when she spotted him, and then she made her way over to where he stood. "Welcome back, Beau."

"Thank you. It's very good to be back."

The smile she gave him was friendly, if a bit reserved. It was more than he'd expected. While he, Julianna, and Rhett hadn't shared much of the ups and downs of their lives with their parents, he didn't think that was true for Sarah and her siblings. If she'd been upset with him and how things had gone, she would have told her mom.

Beau wanted to ask where Sarah was, but he figured he knew, so he kept his mouth shut. When they began to take seats around the table, he took one next to a man about his age.

The way they ate meals at the lodge had taken a little getting used to when he'd first arrived there. After all, he'd never stayed at a place that had him sharing food with people he'd never met. However, it seemed guests who came to the lodge knew what to expect because they were comfortable interacting with him and the others at the table.

Leah and Anna made trips in and out of the kitchen. Anna dropped her hand on his shoulder and squeezed, smiling at him when he glanced up at her. Leah, however, didn't even look at him.

That didn't bode well for him, but he refused to give up hope just yet. From the time he'd left, not a day—or an hour, honestly—had gone by without him remembering his time with Sarah. And during his drive from Houston to New Hope, she had dominated his every thought and had colored a lot of his decisions—whether or not that had actually been wise.

He had also spent plenty of time on the phone with his grandfather since he'd left New Hope. His grandfather had listened as Beau had spilled about what was going on with his parents and his job. The man had offered words of encouragement and advice, giving Beau plenty to think about.

For the first time in Beau's life, he honestly felt like there was someone he could rely on to give him trustworthy advice. Who truly had his best interests at heart. And when the man hadn't been sure what advice to give him, he'd been honest about that, offering to pray for wisdom for Beau.

They'd even had lots of discussions about God and the faith that had sustained his grandfather through some of the darkest moments of his life. Parts of the sermons he'd heard would come back to him at the oddest times, and his grandfather had answered any questions he'd put to him without hesitation.

However, his explanations didn't always make sense to Beau. But the one thing he'd come to realize after all those conversations with his grandfather was that he wanted to be more like him. More patient. More understanding. More loving.

Though he'd thought about surprising him, Beau wasn't sure surprising someone of his grandfather's age and who had health concerns was necessarily a wise thing. Instead, he had promised him he'd be there by lunch on Saturday to spend some time with him.

"So are you from around here?" the man seated next to him asked as they ate.

"No. I'm from Houston."

"Wow. You are a little ways from home. We're just up from Portland for the weekend." The man glanced at the woman sitting beside him then said, "My wife insists we come here whenever we have something special to celebrate."

"This is my second visit." Beau watched as Leah returned to gather up plates. She'd never really warmed up to him, and he wondered if that would ever change. "I was just here a month ago."

"Business?"

"No. My grandfather lives here."

"It's a nice area."

When he'd arrived in town on his first visit, he wouldn't have agreed with the man. But now? He absolutely did. "It is beautiful here."

"If you can time your visits at all, you should really try and be here for the fall festival or around Christmas. My wife insists we come for at least one of those times each year. Happy wife. Happy life." The man smiled indulgently. "Are you married?"

"No. I'm single." It was a status that Beau was only too happy to claim at that moment. Not forever, but as long as it reinforced that he wasn't back with Tiffany, he would embrace it.

"Well, that's a bit of advice for you for the future. Marry a woman that you want to keep happy, then do everything you can to make that happen."

Beau wasn't sure that was the soundest of marital advice, but he couldn't deny that perhaps his parents might have benefitted from it. "I'll keep that in mind."

He glanced up and found Leah watching him again, looking so much like her sister and yet, so totally different. Her eyes narrowed briefly before returning to the plates she was picking up on the opposite side of the table.

Beau wanted to push back from the table to go in search of Sarah, but he still wasn't sure what to say. For the first time ever, his heart was fully engaged in someone else, and he didn't want to mess things up even more than he already had.

Once dessert was over, Beau left the table then hesitated for a moment in the hallway before turning in the direction of the kitchen.

"She's not there."

He turned to see Leah coming out of the dining room. "She's not?"

"She's out for the evening." Leah had a look that seemed slightly challenging, as if she was waiting for him to ask who she was with and where.

Beau wanted to—oh yes, he really wanted to—but he kept his mouth shut. Hopefully, she'd be around at some point in the next day or so. "Thanks for letting me know."

Leah gave a single nod before turning on her heel and heading for the kitchen. She was so much the opposite of Sarah that Beau had to wonder if, despite their identical looks, they'd ever been able to switch places. He'd stake his life on the fact that he would never get them mixed up.

Upstairs in his room, he settled onto the loveseat and phoned Julianna.

"Everything okay there?" Beau asked when she answered her phone.

Julianna sighed deeply. "What do you think? Even Rhett is walking around with a scowl these days after having to deal with Mom and Dad's sour mood."

"I'm sorry."

"You're not really, and you shouldn't be. It's all on Mom and Dad." She heaved an audible sigh. "I still can't believe you've just walked away from everything here."

"That makes two of us," Beau muttered. "But honestly, now that I'm back here, I know it was the right decision."

"Have you had a chance to talk to Sarah?"

"Not yet. Hopefully tomorrow."

"I wish you much luck, big brother. I have a feeling you're going to need it."

"I have that same feeling." Leaning forward, he rubbed his forehead. "I'm going to see Grandfather tomorrow."

"Oh, that's good. I'm sure he'll be glad to see you."

"He'd be glad to see you and Rhett too if you ever decide to come back." He smiled as he thought of his grandfather. "It's a bit strange to have someone actually feel that way about us."

"Oh, I think right about now that Mom and Dad would be very glad to see you if it meant you were back in Houston."

Beau let out a huff of laughter. "True, but only so long as I agreed to their plans for me."

"I'm proud of you, Beaumont." There was a ring of honesty in Julianna's voice that had Beau swallowing hard. "You're going after what you want."

"Oh, don't be too proud of me. It's taken me almost thirty years to get up the nerve to make my own decisions. I hope you and Rhett can figure your lives out sooner than that."

"I've been thinking more about it all lately," Julianna said then sighed. "I do need more purpose in life than just helping Mom plan fundraisers and charity events while living off an allowance Dad gives me."

"I'm hoping that even though Dad took away my trust fund, he'll let you and Rhett have yours soon."

"I'm not holding my breath for that. It's his way of keeping control of our lives. I've been saving money, though, so I won't be completely destitute if he decides to cut me off."

Beau wanted to reassure her that their father would never do that, but he didn't have that confidence anymore. "If that happens, I want you to come to me. I'm not sure where I'm going to end up, but I'll make sure I have room for both you and Rhett."

"I hope it doesn't come to that, but your offer does help me feel better." Julianna paused. "I think all of this has hit Rhett hard. His eyes—well, mine too, if I'm going to be honest—have really been opened by what's happened with Mom and Dad. It's a bit...unnerving."

He couldn't argue with her about that. The strange thing was that he felt a peace about where he'd now ended up.

Taking control of his life had been kind of scary, but the feeling of being liberated had quickly eclipsed any fear he had about what was to come. He had a plan, and he would be working on it starting on Monday. Hopefully by that point, he'd have had a chance to talk to Sarah.

~*~

Sarah leaned forward to dip the banana on the end of her fork into the chocolate fondue. She needed to stop soon, but she was eating her feelings, so...whatever.

"This is just what I needed," Cara said.

Sarah nodded. "Me too."

"Me three." Jillian took a bite of a chocolate-dipped strawberry.

"So, are you planning your wedding yet?" Sarah asked Cara.

She and Kieran had gotten engaged while her brother was in town not long ago, so now there were two weddings in the works.

Cara dunked a piece of the pound cake into the chocolate then set it on her plate. "You bet. Kieran doesn't want a long engagement, and neither do I. Plus, we're not wanting a big wedding, so it shouldn't be too difficult to plan. Frankly, I wouldn't mind just eloping."

"Nope," Sarah said with a shake of her head, waving her fondue fork at Cara. "You're not allowed to do that. We want to be able to celebrate you and Kieran getting hitched."

Cara chuckled. "Yeah. I think Rose would be kind of upset if we did that. She's looking forward to a wedding."

"Well, so am I." And she was, even though it did make her wonder when her time would come.

"Is Beau back?" Jillian asked softly.

Over the past month, Sarah had shared with both Jillian and Cara how she was struggling with her feelings for Beau. They had both been wonderfully sympathetic and supportive.

"Yeah. He arrived early this afternoon." She jabbed another piece of banana. "And Leah said he was there for supper."

"How are you feeling about things?" Cara asked.

Sarah shrugged with a sigh. "I wish he'd taken longer to come back. I might feel stronger. Right now, I just kind of want to hide out, you know?"

"You're welcome to stay here with me," Jillian offered. "You know I have the space."

Though the house her grandmother had left her wasn't big, Sarah knew it had three bedrooms and at least two bathrooms. She and Cara had come over for supper with her, enjoying a tasty lasagna with breadsticks and a salad, followed up by the chocolate fondue they were currently enjoying.

"It's tempting, but I think I need to just suck it up and deal with him being around."

"I know it's difficult," Cara said as she gave Sarah a sympathetic look. "When Kieran and I broke up, I hardly went anywhere in town for fear that I'd bump into him. I mean, I was making plans to leave New Hope because I didn't think I could stay around and watch Kieran move on with his life."

"I'm so glad you didn't leave," Sarah said. "I would have missed you greatly."

"Yeah. I'm glad none of my moving away plans worked out."

Sarah didn't have the option to leave, even if she wanted to. Her family was there. The gallery was there. She might want to avoid Beau, but that was going to be impossible.

She just needed to get their first meeting out of the way.

It was almost ten when she left Jillian's and headed home. The knot in her stomach tightened the closer she got to the lodge.

The SUV with the Texas license plate was still parked in the same spot as when she'd left earlier. She was surprised that he'd driven all the way from Houston, and it made her wonder how long he planned to stay. Her mom had said that his reservation was for just over a week, but that seemed like a long way to drive for only a week's stay.

Once she'd parked, Sarah sat for a minute before getting out. The lodge was quiet and dimly lit, with only lamps on in the living room and the foyer. She went into the kitchen to fill her water bottle, then headed downstairs to her room.

She avoided going into her studio as she didn't want to have a late night. After fighting for so long to get going on her paintings, she'd finally managed to get another two done. She was finally feeling confident about where she was with regards to what she wanted to have ready for the showing at the gallery.

Instead, she proceeded to her bedroom to get ready for bed, trying not to think about the fact that for the first time in what felt like forever, Beau was back under the same roof as her. Even though she told herself not to let that fact affect her emotions, happiness swirled through her as she curled up under her blanket.

CHAPTER TWENTY-NINE

Beau was disappointed that he still hadn't seen Sarah by the time he left to visit his grandfather on Saturday afternoon. He felt bad for a couple of reasons. First, he really wanted to see her, but more than that, he didn't like the idea that his presence might be making her feel like she had to hide.

As he walked into the home, he smiled at the nurses then headed for the sunroom where his grandfather had texted he'd be waiting. Beau found it funny that the older man had picked up texting and video chatting so quickly on the phone Beau had bought him. But he was also glad that he had, as it had become a convenient way for them to communicate.

The man's face lit up when he saw Beau. "Welcome back!"

"Thank you." Beau bent to brush a kiss on the man's cheek. "It's so good to be back."

"How was the drive?" his grandfather asked as Beau settled into the chair next to him.

"Long. Don't tell Juli or Rhett, but I probably should have done as they suggested and had the car shipped so I could have flown out."

"Oh well. It's done now."

They talked a bit about the situation in Houston before Beau said, "I wasn't sure how I'd feel about being back, but honestly, it's felt a lot like coming home."

"That makes me feel so good," the older man said. "I know you've had a lot of upheaval in your life recently. I've been praying that God would guide you as you search for a new direction for your future."

Beau smiled at him. "I've been thinking a lot about what you've shared with me in regards to the role you feel God plays in your life."

His grandfather tilted his head, a small smile on his face. "What have you been thinking?"

"Do you really believe that God cares about the decisions we make in our lives?"

"I do," he said with a nod. "He wants us to seek His will for our lives. He wants us to trust that His plan for us is better than anything we could want for ourselves."

"Even if I haven't done what the pastor said we should do? Accepting the gift of eternal life?"

"That would be His ultimate plan for your life," his grandfather said. "If it wasn't important to God, He wouldn't have sent His Son to die in order to save us from our sins."

Beau clasped his hands, letting them hang loosely between his knees as he stared down at the table. His long drive had given him plenty of time to think about what his grandfather and the pastor had said about God.

"I want that," Beau said, the words bursting out of him in a way he hadn't expected. It felt like they'd been drawn from the very depths of his soul. "I want the assurance of heaven. I want to live the life God has for me. Everything about my life seems to be so messed up and out of control. I don't want that anymore."

When his grandfather grasped his shoulder, Beau looked up. Tears shimmered in the older man's eyes. "You don't know how happy that makes me. I have prayed for a long time for you and your brother and sister. From the moment that I first read your names, I have prayed that you all would find salvation."

Beau thought of his siblings, wondering if they'd ever get to the point where he was now. Maybe his grandfather would teach him how to pray for them. Beau wanted to be a man of faith the way he was.

"Pray with me, son," his grandfather said, laying his hand palm up on the table.

Beau reached out and grasped the open hand. His heart was pounding as his grandfather guided him through a prayer, asking God's forgiveness for his sins and committing his life to Him. It seemed so easy—too easy—but he trusted that his grandfather would not lead him astray.

"Things won't be perfect now," his grandfather cautioned when the prayer was over. "But when the tough times come, you can be confident that you're not alone. God is with you, and if you ask Him to, He will guide you."

Beau let out a long breath. He wanted that. He wanted to not have to rely strictly on his own wisdom to make decisions. Did it make him weak to essentially be going from having his father control his life to giving God control of his future? Some might see it that way, but frankly, Beau didn't really care what others thought.

"It would be an honor to help you learn more about what it means to trust in God, and I know Pastor Evans feels that way too." His grandfather paused. "And I'm certain that Eli and Kieran would also be happy to answer any questions you might have."

At his grandfather's words, Beau felt his connection to the town and the people in it tighten. He had a sense of belonging in New Hope Falls that he'd never felt in Houston. As he thought of Houston and the people there, he felt a deep longing for his family to find the joy and peace he finally had.

They talked a bit more with his grandfather promising to get him a Bible. Beau was sure he could get a Bible app, but he wasn't going to turn down his grandfather's offer.

"I'll pick you up tomorrow for church," Beau said as their visit wound down.

"I look forward to it."

As Beau headed out of the building a few minutes later, he stepped into a light drizzle as the gray skies that had been threatening rain earlier had finally opened up. He jogged to the car and quickly slid behind the wheel. The rain might have dampened his clothes, but it couldn't touch his mood.

Back at the lodge, he climbed out of the SUV, smiling when he saw Eli working on something on the wide porch. He hurried through the rain to the steps and took them two at a time.

"Hey there," Eli said. "How's it going?"

Beau couldn't help but smile. "It's going great."

Eli stared at him for a moment then said, "I'm not sure I've seen you this happy before. I mean, I haven't known you that long, but last time you were here, you didn't seem this happy."

He wanted to tell Eli about what had happened with his grandfather, but he wasn't sure how to form the words. "I just came from seeing my grandfather, and we had a really good talk about his faith in God."

Again, Eli didn't respond right away. "That's wonderful. Mom told us a bit about what happened with your family. Your grandfather has a real testimony."

Beau nodded. "He prayed with me too."

"Prayed with you?" Eli paused for a moment. "Like...you've become a Christian?"

He wasn't sure of all the terminology, but he knew what Eli said was correct. "Yes. Seeing the peace and joy my grandfather had, despite all the terrible things that had happened to him, made me want that too. I also wanted to know that I would go to heaven when I die, just like Pastor Evans said in his sermon."

"That is wonderful." Eli approached him and took Beau by surprise when he pulled him into a quick hug. When the hug ended, Eli took hold of Beau's shoulders. "This makes me so happy."

Beau could see the sincerity on Eli's face. It was still a mystery to him why someone who hadn't even known him two months ago could be so invested in his life. But it made him feel even more connected.

Eli stepped back from him, a smile still on his face. "Listen. I'm part of a men's group that meets a couple of times a month. We get together to study the Bible and encourage each other to become the men God would have us be. You already know several of the men in the group, and I'm confident they'd be happy to have you join us whenever you're in town."

"I think I'd like that."

"Wonderful. I'll let you know when we're meeting next."

Beau glanced around, noting that one of the swings was sitting on the floor of the porch. "Did something break?"

"Nah. I found some new hooks that I think might be stronger, so I decided to swap them out."

"Do you need some help?"

"That would be great. I had Anna and Leah help me get the swing down, but they don't really enjoy trying to lift heavy stuff."

Beau worked with Eli for a little while, then when both swings were back in place, he headed up to his room. Once there, his thoughts turned to Sarah again. He really wanted to talk to her, to tell her what had happened in Houston and since his return to New Hope.

He was worried that she would continue to avoid him, so he sank down on the loveseat and pulled out his phone. They hadn't exchanged any texts since he'd left, but he had a feeling that a text was the best way to start this particular conversation.

Hi Sarah. Hope you're doing well.

Was that a dumb statement? Probably. Oh well.

I was hoping that we could talk.

~*~

When her phone chirped an alert, Sarah picked it up from where it rested on her leg. She was currently curled up on the couch in the open area in the basement between her room and Leah's. After spending the morning and early afternoon trying to paint, she was ready for a break, so she'd grabbed one of the muffins Leah had baked that morning and settled down to watch some reality television.

She glanced at the phone, expecting there to be a text from Jillian, Cara, or Anna. Her eyes widened when she saw it was from Beau.

Blowing out a long breath, Sarah gripped her phone more tightly. She tried to think of a suitable response. What did they really have to talk about? If he was only back for another short visit, she didn't want to have to rehash all the reasons why they shouldn't spend time together.

That was her logical side, however. Her heart had a different desire. It didn't matter whether or not they had anything to talk about, she just really wanted to see him after so many weeks apart.

Would it set her back emotionally? Probably.

Did she care about that right then? Not so much.

The only problem was that she needed to be careful to not become hopeful for a future with him, regardless of how her heart felt. Even if a miracle had happened, and Beau truly felt about her the way she felt about him, she knew that at the end of the day, as long as their hearts weren't aligned in faith, there was no future together for them. And that wasn't even taking into consideration that his life was still in Houston.

But she couldn't avoid him forever.

Okay. When were you thinking?

Beau: *I'm here at the lodge. So whenever it is convenient for you.*

Sarah glanced down at herself and realized she didn't really want to show up in her paint-splattered clothes. *I can meet you in about 30 mins.*

Beau: *Wonderful. Do you want to meet at the porch swings?*

Sure. I'll see you there.

Nerves immediately flared to life, and Sarah sat for a moment staring at their text exchange. She was going to be seeing him in just minutes. She wasn't ready. She didn't think she'd ever be ready.

Please, God, help me to be strong. To say and do the right thing that will be honoring to You. I failed in that before, so help me to do better this time.

Steeling herself for what was to come, Sarah got up off the couch and went into her room to change. Part of her balked at that. It wasn't as if he hadn't seen her in her messed-up painting clothes. She shouldn't be trying to look nice for him.

In the end, she compromised. She changed into a pair of jeans and a clean T-shirt but then didn't bother to put on any make-up. It took everything within her not to, but she needed to stick to her guns for her own sake. To remind herself of what was at stake.

Stay strong.

As Sarah stepped out onto the porch just before the time she'd told Beau she'd be there, she shivered at the slight chill in the air. The sun hadn't made an appearance all day, and now it was raining. It wasn't that it was super cold, but the temperature was mild enough that when combined with the dampness in the air, it felt chilly.

A glance told her that Beau wasn't there yet, so she went back down to her room to grab a hoodie. She didn't mind sitting on the porch swings when it was raining since the porch was wide enough that the rain wouldn't reach them, but she'd be more comfortable if she wasn't cold.

When she came back out of the front door, she immediately spotted Beau. He stood with his back to the door, his hands in his pockets, staring out at the rain. With her heart thudding at her first sight of him in a month, Sarah stepped onto the porch and closed the door behind her. He swung around, a smile breaking out on his face when their gazes met.

Her heart skipped a beat as she got a real-life glimpse of the face she'd drawn so often during the time he'd been gone. She'd usually sketched him using her charcoal pencils, using grayscale shades to capture his likeness. But now...now he was right there in full color. His dark hair. His lightly tanned skin. His beautiful eyes.

The happiness on his face struck a double chord within her. While she didn't want him to be unhappy, it was hard to see that look on his face and know it was caused by whatever had transpired in his life over the past month.

Sarah stood there for a moment, drinking in the sight of him in his jeans and white long-sleeved Henley, uncertain of what to say or how to act. What she wanted to do was wrap her arms around him and tell him how glad she was to see him again.

What she did, instead, was to just say, "Hi."

"Hey." His gaze softened as he took a step closer to her. "It's so good to see you again."

Sarah wanted to say the same, but she bit her lip to keep the words from slipping free. She was afraid that if she started to say anything like that, she wouldn't be able to stop.

"Can we sit?" Beau asked with a gesture toward one of the swings.

"Sure." Sarah settled on the end of the swing closest to the living room windows.

"How have you been doing?" he asked, his expression sincere.

"Good. Keeping busy."

"With the lodge or your painting?"

"Both." Sarah darted a quick glance at Beau. "It's one of the busiest times of the year here, and right in the middle of it, I'm trying to get paintings done for my show."

"How's that going?"

Sarah rubbed her thigh. "Slowly at times, but I've managed to get a couple done."

"I'd love to see them, but I suppose you'll make me wait until the showing."

The humor in Beau's voice had her looking back at him, shifting a bit so she could face him more directly. "Do you plan to be here in October?"

"I sure hope so, since I'm moving here."

"You're...what?" Sarah was sure she hadn't heard him right. "Why would you move here?"

Beau rested his arm on the back of the swing as he angled toward her, his expression sobering. "Well, there's really nothing holding me in Houston anymore. I quit my job after my dad decided to demote me. Even if he hadn't done that, I think I'd still have quit because I had no desire to work for him anymore."

"Isn't it a family company?" Sarah asked, remembering what she'd read from her google searches of Beau.

He nodded. "But it's not operated at all like your family business is. When I was here before, I could see how your mom valued the effort each of you put into the running of the lodge. She listens to you, even though I assume she is ultimately in charge."

"Yeah, she is, but you're right. She'll listen to us if we have suggestions."

"My dad's not like that. He used the job and some other things to manipulate me. To get me to do what he wanted. I allowed it to happen because I thought the end result would be worth it, and I didn't have any reason to balk at what he was doing."

"But now you do?"

"I saw a different way of life while I was here. I met people who valued each other more than money. It made me realize I wanted more out of life than what I had in Houston."

Sarah wasn't sure how she felt about his news. Part of her was thrilled at the idea that he was going to be around more, but she also knew it would make things more difficult for her.

"Do you have a job or a place to live here yet?"

"Not yet, but I've been looking at properties for sale. I want something big enough for Julianna and Rhett to stay with me when they come to visit."

"And a job?"

"Haven't quite decided that yet, but I have some money set aside that will give me some time to figure that out. It had been my ultimate plan to start my own financial investment business, but I'm not sure if that's feasible right now." Beau shrugged. "I'll figure something out. The good thing is that I'm knowledgeable about finances, so I know how to plan things out."

"That's good. I struggle with that kind of thing, to be honest. Math was a horrible class for me. I used to spend it doodling. Barely passed most of my math-oriented classes."

"Well, I struggled in art class, so I guess we're even. My teacher kept telling me to follow my heart when I'd struggle with the assignments. I could never draw anything but stick figures."

Sarah couldn't help but give a little laugh. "According to my mom, I never drew stick figures."

"That wouldn't surprise me at all. I think your talent and passion for art is like my passion for numbers."

"I still can't believe you're willing to uproot your life like that, though."

"I just want to be where I feel like I have a better chance of finding fulfillment in my life. I already have more friends here than I did in Houston, plus my grandfather's here."

"But your parents are in Houston."

Sadness crept over Beau's face. "I think it's best for all of us to have some distance between us. I definitely don't have the same kind of relationship with my parents that you have with yours."

"Well, with my mom, anyway. I haven't talked to my dad in quite a few years."

"What happened?" Beau asked.

Sarah couldn't remember the last time she'd had to actually tell someone about what her dad had done. Most everyone in New Hope that she was close to already knew. Even Cara knew the story by the time they started to get closer over the past year.

"He left. Decided that New Hope wasn't where he wanted to live."

"He just left all of you?"

"Yep. He paid child support and sent cards at Christmas and our birthdays, but we haven't seen him since he left."

"That's so unbelievable," Beau said with a shake of his head. "There are people who would love a family like yours."

"I really don't know if there was more beyond him just not wanting to live here. Mom never said, but I've often wondered if he left us for another woman. He travelled a lot."

"I'm sorry you had to deal with that." Beau gave her a sympathetic look that tugged at her heart.

"Leah took it the hardest. Well, probably not as hard as Mom, but of us kids, Leah was closest to him. She was definitely Daddy's girl."

"Knowing this just makes me admire all of you that much more. It can't have been easy to do what you have had to do here at the lodge without him."

"He never really did that much here, to be honest." Sarah looked over at the building, thinking of how much it had changed. "A lot of what you see now is the result of Mom's decorating skills and Eli's woodworking. My dad had a job selling medical equipment, so he was gone a lot of the time."

"Still, you guys have done a great job here."

"So, where are you looking at living?" Now that she'd gotten over the shock of his news, she was curious about his plans.

"I'd like to live outside the town. Maybe get a nice piece of land with a house. I've always lived in the city, but after spending time here at the lodge and at Eli's place, I think I'd like to live rurally."

"There's a couple of real estate agents in the church, I think. You could ask Mom for their information."

"That would be helpful. I'd like to have someone I could trust. I would assume that anyone your mom recommended would be trustworthy."

"I would think so, yes," Sarah said.

When silence fell between them, her thoughts went to the articles she'd seen about him and his fiancée. She wanted to ask about her but couldn't bring herself to.

"I wanted to ask you something."

Sarah turned her attention back to Beau, shifting her thoughts off the beautiful Tiffany. "What's that?"

Beau's blue-green gaze held hers, his expression serious. "Would you consider going out on a date?"

Her heart skipped a beat. "With you?"

He gave a huff of laughter. "Well, I'm certainly not asking on Rhett's behalf."

"Oh." Sarah took a quick breath then let it out, glancing away from Beau's piercing gaze. "I'm not sure."

"Hey," Beau said softly, his fingers touching her hand briefly. "Did I misunderstand something? I kind of thought we were both sort of feeling the same kind of way."

She looked back at him. "I didn't know you really felt any kind of way."

This time it was Beau who looked away. "I guess I didn't show it because it felt kind of hopeless. I thought I was going back to my life in Houston. My family. My job."

"Your fiancée?"

CHAPTER THIRTY

Sarah watched as Beau somehow managed to grimace and wince at the same time.

"No. I wasn't going back to Tiffany. That was over before I came here the first time. My parents wanted me to try to win her back, but that wasn't going to happen. I did meet with her while I was in Houston, but that was just to let her know that if she wanted to be with a man who loved her the way she wanted to be loved, it wasn't going to happen with me. I told her that she needed to hold out for that, though. That I'd seen examples of loving relationships while I'd been here, and as long as she didn't settle for less, maybe she could have that too."

Sarah had kind of expected him to glaze over her question about Tiffany, but he hadn't. "Don't you think it's a little too soon to be dating again after something as serious as an engagement break-up?"

"If Tiffany and I had loved each other, absolutely," Beau said with a nod. "But our relationship was set up by our parents. I wouldn't be surprised if my folks try to get Rhett to take up with Tiffany now. My dad seems very determined to have our families united through marriage."

Sarah frowned. "Do you think Rhett will do it?"

"No. He's never really been one to do what our parents want him to. He's the most rebellious of us kids." Beau paused. "Well, I guess that honor kind of goes to me now."

"I don't understand marrying someone you don't love," Sarah said. "Though I realize that lots of people do it."

"My dad was dangling something I wanted in front of me. I didn't hate Tiffany, so I figured it was worth doing what he wanted in order to get it."

"Did you get what you wanted from him?"

"Nope, but that's when I realized that he was using it to manipulate me, and I needed to take control of my own life instead of waiting for him to give me what I'd been waiting for."

"I suppose that's freeing."

"It has been, but also a bit scary, if I'm going to be perfectly honest. This is the first time I've made any sort of significant decision about my life. That's rather embarrassing considering I'm turning thirty next year." He gave her a rueful smile. "But better late than never, right?"

Sarah nodded. She appreciated Beau's honesty, but with it came the realization that aside from her reservations about his spiritual life, it seemed like he already had a lot on his plate. Perhaps starting to date wasn't the best thing, regardless, considering everything else going on in his life.

"I'm not going to deny that I...might have feelings for you, but I don't think that dating right now is a good idea."

Beau frowned, his brows drawing together. "Why's that?"

"You have so much going on in your life at the moment."

Sarah wanted to explain to him about not dating someone who didn't share her faith. But at the same time, she didn't want to wonder about the sincerity of any declaration of faith he might make. She wanted him to find his way to God because of his own desire to know God better, not because it would be a way to get closer to her.

It was her hope, now that he was back, that the more time he spent around men like Eli, Kieran, and his grandfather, he might come to God because of their influence. She prayed for his salvation each night and would continue to do so, even though it felt somewhat self-serving now.

"That's true." Beau shifted on the swing, clasping his hands together between his knees, his head bent. "This is the first time I've ever felt this way about someone. I don't want to lose out on the opportunity to develop a relationship, but I also don't want to rush you."

Sarah reached out and rested her hand on his arm, squeezing lightly until he lifted his head and looked at her. "I'm not saying no outright. We can still spend time together, just not as if we were dating. Not yet."

A glimmer of expectation sprang to life in Beau's gaze, and Sarah prayed that she wasn't offering him false hope. If push came to shove, she might have to explain to him why she wasn't going to date him yet...or ever. Or maybe Eli or Kieran would tell him.

"I suppose that's something." Beau gave her a quick smile that faded as his brows drew together. "This isn't just your way of letting me down slowly, is it? Because if so, I'd rather you just yank the bandage off now, so to speak."

"No, I'm not just letting you down slowly. I don't date as a way to get to know someone. I prefer to know someone prior to dating them because I won't date anyone that I wouldn't be willing to marry."

Beau's eyebrows rose. "So, are you saying that if you do agree to date, you'd be willing to marry me?"

Sarah shrugged. "It means that at that point, I haven't discovered anything about you that would prevent me from considering marrying you."

"Well, that clarifies things...sort of."

"I just prefer to spend time together in groups and casual settings. It takes the pressure off dating until we're more comfortable with each other."

"But that's the thing I really like about you," Beau said. "We've been comfortable with each other almost right from the start. It's never been like that for me with anyone else."

Sarah couldn't deny that she'd felt the same way, but that didn't change how things between them had to be for the time being. "It will still be like that. I mean, we can still hang out with each other like we're doing now."

"I love being able to talk with you." Beau covered her hand with his, and Sarah relished the warm weight of it. "I've missed this while I've been away, but I needed to get my life sorted out before I could come back here and plead my case with you."

"You don't need to plead your case. Just let me get to know you better."

"I'll try my best. I'm not used to being an open book, to talking a lot about myself. Frankly, I'm not sure that there's that much about me that's interesting. Unlike you." Beau smiled at her. "You absolutely fascinate me."

Sarah felt heat rise in her cheeks. "Well, you fascinate me too."

"So, we can be fascinated together? As long as it's not dating?"

"Exactly." Sarah smiled back at him. "I'm glad we understand each other."

"Me, too."

It seemed that with the subject of dating settled, they were able to move on to other subjects. Lighter topics like how Julianna and Rhett were doing. Sarah also caught him up on the news from people he knew in town. Like Cece dating a guy who, according to Andy, had more muscles than brains and who didn't seem to treat Cece very well.

Their conversation was interrupted by some other guests returning to the lodge a short time later.

"I should probably get back to work," Sarah said when they were alone again. "This has been a nice break, though."

Beau smiled. "For me too. Thank you for talking with me and being honest about us dating."

Sarah tried not to wince as she hadn't been completely honest about one of the main reasons why they couldn't date. Still, she held back, knowing that more important to her than dating was his spiritual state. But she really didn't want Beau to connect his need for salvation to them dating.

She had never really imagined that she'd be in this situation. Loving a man who didn't share her love for God. Maybe she was making a mistake by not sharing exactly why they wouldn't be able to date. She honestly didn't know. All she knew was that she wanted his salvation to be genuine, so that even if things didn't work out between them, his faith wouldn't falter.

But she was playing with fire. Sarah knew that. She shouldn't be spending more time with him. She shouldn't be going off the assumption that he would ever become a Christian. How long was she going to be willing to just hang out as friends? How long was *Beau* going to be willing to do that?

If she was smart, she'd keep her distance from him. But, apparently, when it came to Beau, she was *never* smart. So it seemed that her chances of getting burned were high. Very high. And she'd have no one to blame but herself when the pain came.

"I'll see you later," Sarah said as she got up, tucking her hands into the pockets of her hoodie. "If you're around for dinner, that is."

Beau stood up as well. "Since I've already been to see my grandfather, I plan to be."

Sarah was glad to hear that even though she wouldn't be sitting at the table with him. As she made her way back down to her studio, Sarah waited to feel the way she had when she'd had to serve Beau and his siblings. But those feelings never returned.

Maybe it was knowing that Beau had seen her in that role and still felt something for her. That that incident apparently hadn't changed how he viewed her as much as it had seemed to change how she viewed herself. It had been eye-opening for her, and she'd had to work over the past month to bring her thoughts back in line with how God would want her to think of herself in relation to others.

On Sunday, Sarah spotted Beau at church with his grandfather and then speaking with Pastor Evans following the service. She didn't see him again until he showed up at Eli's for the hike and then the meal afterward. He appeared as at ease with them all as he had been before he left.

They spent time together that evening, but not to the exclusion of others, and Sarah was grateful that he was taking her request to spend time in groups seriously.

Throughout the days that followed, Beau usually spent each lunchtime with his grandfather. He was at the lodge every evening for dinner, so after the cleanup from the meal was done, they'd sit out on the porch swing for an hour or so.

The usually talked about their days, then moved on to other things. Her paintings and the upcoming show. His hopes for a new business and how he hoped to accomplish that.

She didn't understand a lot of what he said, but she doubted he understood much of what she said either when she got into the more detailed aspects of her painting. But it didn't matter to her, and it didn't seem to bother him either.

On Wednesday evening, just as she was heading inside after they'd talked, Beau said, "Hey. Uh, would you be interested in going with me somewhere tomorrow?"

"Somewhere?" Sarah angled a look in his direction. "Like where?"

"I've got several properties lined up to look at tomorrow with a real estate agent, and I was wondering if you would go with me to look at them. Give me a woman's perspective."

"Oh." Sarah wasn't sure how to respond to his request. She wanted to say yes. But would that put them in a position of being more than they were? But...she really wanted to say yes. "I'd love to go with you."

Relief crossed Beau's face, as if he had known there was a good possibility that she might say no. "The real estate agent said he'd meet us at the first address at ten. Is that too early?"

"Not so long as I don't stay up all night."

"Well, I don't want to interfere with your painting," Beau said, his sincerity ringing true in his voice.

"No worries." She gave him a smile as she reached out to give his arm a quick pat. "My painting has been going pretty smoothly the past week or so." Particularly since Beau's return. "I think I can wake up in time."

"Nice. Thank you. When I bought my apartment, I wasn't really looking for a place to be a home. My mom pretty much convinced me that that apartment was the perfect place for me."

"Well. No worries. From what you've said about your mom, she would probably hate anything I would think was great. So, if you're looking for the opposite of what you had in Houston, I'm your girl."

"That's what I'm hoping." He paused. "Well, yeah...uh...I mean, I want the opposite of what my mom chose for me."

Sarah felt warmth creep up in her cheeks as Beau tried to clarify what he'd meant. Rather than dwell on that, she sought to ease the awkwardness. "I'll be up here at quarter to ten to help you out with that."

"Perfect. See you then."

She couldn't keep a smile off her face as she headed downstairs. And she couldn't help but keep praying as she painted that night that God would move in Beau's heart so that there would actually be a future together for them.

It kind of felt like she was playing with fire by spending time with him alone the way she was, despite the agreement they'd kind of arrived at to spend time together in groups.

~*~

Butterflies had taken up residence in Beau's stomach. Butterflies hyped up on caffeine, if the flutterings were anything to go by. He was a bit nervous about looking for a new house, but he was also excited about having Sarah along with him.

"Ready to go?" Sarah's voice had him turning.

She wore a pair of black pants and a deep mauve short sleeve sweater with a v-neck. Her hair was loose for a change, and Beau tried to remember when he'd last seen it that way as she always seemed to wear it up in a braid or ponytail.

"You look nice," he said, then worried maybe he shouldn't have said that.

"Why, thank you, kind sir." She gave a small curtsy. "And you look quite nice yourself."

Beau glanced down at himself. It had taken everything in him not to pull a suit out of the closet. The house price range he was looking at seemed to demand he look as successful as possible. In the end, he'd settled for a pair of dark gray pants with a white button-up shirt and a tie with swirls of greens and blues.

"Where's the first house?" Sarah asked as they walked out of the lodge to the SUV.

Beau gave her the address the realtor had sent to him. "Do you know the place?"

"I have a general idea where it is, but I can't say I know exactly. You're probably better off using the GPS."

Beau quickly tapped the information into the navigation system of the car. After the route was mapped out, he glanced at Sarah. At her nod, he put the car in reverse then headed away from the lodge.

"Do you have any information on this first place?"

"Uh. It has land, and the house is a good size."

When Sarah didn't respond right away, he glanced over at her. "That's it?"

"Isn't that enough?" Beau asked. "I mean, I gave him an idea of what I'm looking for and my price range, so I assumed he'd show me places that fit that criteria. Would he show me properties I wouldn't like?"

"Possibly. He's not a mind reader, so he may interpret what you told him a bit differently. Just be prepared for that."

Beau nodded. "I'll keep that in mind."

It didn't take too long to arrive. When they got there, Beau turned at the elaborate lamp post address sign then drove along a winding driveway framed by trees and wrought iron lampstands that Beau imagined would, in addition to being practical, look lovely at night.

"Oh, wow," Sarah breathed out next to him. "This is amazing. Are you sure you can afford this?"

Beau grinned. "I'm sure."

They got out of the car, and Beau greeted the middle-aged man who climbed out of the vehicle that was already parked there. They shook hands then the man turned to Sarah.

"Miss McNamara," the realtor said with a smile as he held out his hand. "Nice to see you again."

"It's Sarah." She smiled at him. "Nice to see you again too, Roy."

Roy sighed. "One of these days."

It quickly dawned on Beau what the exchange was all about. "You seriously can't tell the difference between Sarah and Leah?"

"Oh, I can tell the difference. I just can't remember who's who."

"Okay. Here's what Leah would tell you," Sarah began. "Sarah smiles."

"Leah does too, though," Roy replied. "Sometimes. Which would confuse me because then I'd be thinking Sarah smiles sometimes."

Beau chuckled. "I can see why you go with the Miss McNamara greeting."

"Exactly! I just want to be safe." He gestured to the house that looked like a spacious rustic two-story log cabin, almost as big as the lodge. "Shall we go have a look?"

Beau was already half in love with the property. The house looked amazing, but it was the trees that surrounded it with the mountains in the distance that really beckoned to him. He was almost ready to make an offer on the spot. He held back, though, because he knew Sarah would tell him he was crazy if he did something like that.

As they stepped into the foyer, his first impression was of a tremendous amount of space. The house had an open floor plan so he could see the windows that lined the front as well as the rear of the house, giving him a magnificent view of the forest around the property.

By the time they made it through the house, Beau was even more in love with it. Sarah, too, seemed to really like it, but she was at least asking intelligent questions. Such as when the house was built and whether any upgrades had been done to it.

When he asked her how she knew to ask stuff like that, she just said that she'd learned a lot when Eli was building his cabin and when they'd done upgrades to the lodge and cabins over the years.

He was definitely impressed with her. Not that he hadn't already been, but her knowledge in this instance was just adding to all the things he already really liked about her. Really, really liked about her.

"Why are the owners selling?" Sarah asked.

"Well, they live in Seattle," Roy said. "And this has been their getaway home. However, they've decided they want a place a little farther away from the city. A bit of geographical diversification, if you will."

Beau nodded. "I get that. My mom said that we couldn't have a vacation home anywhere in Texas."

"What's a vacation home?" Sarah asked, then laughed. "Just kidding. I live in a vacation home all year round."

"That you do," Roy said with a smile. "And a beautiful one, at that."

As they walked out of the house behind the realtor, Sarah leaned close and said, "You need to see the other properties first."

"Did you read my mind?"

She laughed. "More like the look of love for this place on your face."

"I'll see you at the next address," Roy called out as he slid behind the steering wheel of his car. "Feel free to follow me."

As he drove to the next property, they discussed the merits of the house. He could tell that Sarah really liked it too, though she was trying to rein him in. Which made him want to laugh, since it was kind of a change in the roles they usually played.

CHAPTER THIRTY-ONE

The next two properties weren't nearly as impressive as the first one had been, though they were less expensive. The final place they looked at had a lovely house—almost equal to the first—but the property was too close to town for Beau's liking and didn't have the trees and mountain view.

When they left the realtor at the final property, Beau told him that he'd call him in a day or so to let him know what he was thinking about what he'd seen. Roy said he might come up with some more properties to show them if Beau wanted to view more.

"If you're going to put an offer on the first one, make sure you have someone check it over thoroughly," Sarah said as they headed back to the lodge. "That's quite a bit of money to spend on a house."

"It's still a lot less than my apartment in Houston cost me." Even though he hadn't sold the apartment yet, it was paid off, and that would allow him to finance the new property until the apartment sold.

"Seriously? A lot?"

"Yep, and I like that house more than I ever did the apartment."

"Well, since you'll have to live in it, it's important you really like it."

"Yes. I anticipate spending more time in this place than I ever did in my apartment."

"I look forward to hearing what you decide," Sarah said.

"Thank you so much for helping me out today."

"Not sure I helped you out much. Unless you count keeping you from making on offer on the spot as help."

"I definitely count that," Beau assured her. "I needed to see them all in order to make sure that the first one was absolutely the best choice. I might not have done that if you hadn't been there. Now, when I make an offer, I know it's because it's the best for me and what I envision for my future."

"I know you're only at the lodge through tomorrow," Sarah said. "Where are you going to go after that?"

"Well, I'd actually made a reservation at a hotel in Everett, but then Eli invited me to stay with him."

"Really?" Sarah sounded surprised. "That was nice of him."

"I thought so, and I must say, I'm grateful. I didn't really like the idea of going that far away," he said. "Even though Everett really isn't that far from here."

"Well, at least now the rooms that Anna insisted he needed to decorate will be put to good use."

"He didn't decorate all the rooms in his place when he built it?"

"Nope. After he finished building it, he only decorated the main floor, which is where his master bedroom and office are. The upstairs was painted white, but there was no furniture until Anna marched into his life and refused to leave anything undecorated."

"I'm grateful he was willing to open up his home to me." Beau knew that Everett really wasn't that far away, but for some reason, leaving New Hope Falls felt...wrong. Now that he'd come back with the intention of making it his home, he didn't want to have to leave for any reason other than an emergency.

Back at the lodge, Beau dropped Sarah off after thanking her for coming with him, then made his way to the personal care home to spend some time with his grandfather. He wanted to talk to him about the houses he'd seen, and the one he was planning to make an offer on.

It sounded like closing would move quickly if his offer was accepted, especially since the buyers were motivated to sell. Roy had said that the property had been for sale for several months already, which would hopefully work in Beau's favor.

It felt like this was the first step in making New Hope Falls his home, and he couldn't wait.

~*~

Sarah didn't usually hang around behind the check-in desk, but her mom and Leah had gone to do some grocery shopping, which meant someone needed to be around to help any guests that might need assistance. There weren't a lot of check-ins going on since it was late Tuesday morning, but guests already in residence might need some help.

She'd brought her sketchbook and pencils up to the desk, and no surprise, she was once again sketching Beau. When the front door opened, she looked up, expecting to see her mom and Leah, Anna and Eli, or even Beau, but instead, a middle-aged couple dressed very much as fancies stood in front of her.

Getting to her feet, Sarah smiled at them. "Hello. Welcome to the lodge."

The man didn't return her smile but did give a curt nod. The man had steel-gray styled hair, while the woman with him had a shoulder-length bob with blonde highlights. It didn't take but a moment for Sarah to begin to see the similarities. The chin with the slight cleft on the man. The shape of eyes on the woman

Dread wound its way through her stomach. When she looked at this woman, there seemed to be an absence of so many positive emotions. Anger rolled off the woman, which should have made Sarah think of red, but it was so intense that for Sarah, it was a white-hot fury.

Sarah shivered as the woman's gaze narrowed on her. It wasn't that she felt the woman was evil, but she couldn't imagine what it would be like to move through life without the emotions that could bring joy to an individual.

"Is Beaumont Allerton here?" the man asked.

Sarah clasped her hands together to keep them from shaking as she glanced at the woman before looking back at the man. Beau's mother seemed to be holding back her anger, if her tight lips were anything to go by, but only just barely.

"No. I'm sorry he's not."

The man looked around. "Where might he be if not *here*?"

Sarah didn't know what to say. She figured he was probably either at the personal care home or at Eli's. However, she didn't want to reveal that to either of these people who were absolutely radiating disdain, anger, and impatience.

"I'm not sure, as I don't keep track of our guests' schedules, but if you'd like to wait in the living room, I'm sure he'll be back soon."

The two exchanged a glance before the woman looked away, lifting her chin.

"We will wait."

"Would you like some coffee or something else to drink?" Sarah offered, knowing her mother would expect that kind gesture of her.

"No, thank you," the woman said before turning toward the living room.

The rejection of Sarah's offer by the woman apparently covered both of them. As soon as they'd disappeared into the living room, Sarah grabbed her phone and darted into the kitchen. She positioned herself so that she could see them if they approached the check-in desk again but stayed far enough away that they wouldn't hear her.

She quickly tapped on Beau's information and waited for him to answer.

"Sarah?"

"Where are you?" She spoke in a harsh whisper, trying to keep from accidentally being too loud.

"What's wrong?" Beau asked.

"I think your parents are here at the lodge."

There was a beat of dead silence before he said, "What?"

"Two people just walked into the lodge asking for you, and I think they're your parents. You need to come. I'm the only one here. My mom's gone with Leah. I'm not equipped to handle this level of anger."

"Well, that would seem to confirm that my mom's definitely there," Beau said. "I'm on my way."

"Okay. Bye."

Sarah hadn't meant to be so abrupt, but she was afraid that one of them would come looking for her and demand to know who she was talking to. Clutching her phone in her hand, she kept watching the entrance to the living room to see if they stepped back into the foyer.

She wasn't sure why they'd managed to intimidate her so badly. It was doubtful that she needed to impress them in order to make Beau happy. In fact, she didn't think what they thought of her would matter to him at all. But still...she didn't want to upset them in case they decided to take it out on Beau.

It seemed like ages—but was likely closer to minutes—before the front door opened, and she heard Beau say, "Sarah?"

She moved to the entrance of the kitchen in time to see him coming toward her, not even pausing to look in the living room.

When he got to her, he reached out to grip her shoulders, concern on his face. "You okay?"

"I'm fine," she said, though she'd be lying if she said she wasn't relieved to see him.

"Beaumont."

Beau grimaced at the sound of his father's voice. "It'll be fine."

Though he sounded confident, Sarah wasn't so sure he was, but she gave him a nod. He turned around, keeping himself between her and his parents.

"Father. What are you doing here?"

"We've come to take you home," his mother said, her voice tight.

Beau laughed. "I'm hardly a child that you have to come to retrieve me. This is my home now."

"This...place is hardly a home, Beaumont," his mother spat out.

"I'm not necessarily referring to the lodge, though it *has* felt more like a home than anywhere in Houston ever has."

"You can't mean that."

For some reason, Sarah had figured that his father would take the lead on this conversation, but apparently, that job was falling to his mother. Reaching out, Sarah rested her hand in the center of Beau's back, needing to let him know he wasn't alone.

"I do mean that, Mom. I have actually made an offer on a house here. I expect to hear back about it in the next day or so."

"Why would you do that?" his mother demanded.

"It became quite clear to me that if I wanted a chance at happiness in my life, I needed to leave Houston."

"That's ridiculous!"

"Beaumont. Clarissa." Beau's father spoke for the first time since he'd said Beau's name. "Let's go into the living room and hold this conversation without an audience."

Sarah felt the immediate tension in Beau's body beneath her hand.

"The audience you're speaking of is a close friend. She knows how I feel about Houston. But to spare her having to hear your rude comments about me and New Hope Falls, I will do as you have requested. Just know that nothing you can say or do at this point will change my mind."

"We'll see about that."

Beau took a deep breath then turned to look at her. "Everything will be fine."

She gave him a smile, hoping to encourage him because she really didn't want his parents to succeed at convincing—or manipulating—him to return to Houston.

In a surprising move, he wrapped his arms around her and gave her a quick hug before releasing her and following his parents into the living room.

Sarah thought about returning to the check-in desk. But really, Beau's conversation with his parents was his business, despite what he said about talking in front of an audience. She settled for sitting at the island in the kitchen, hearing only the faintest murmur of voices.

Please, Heavenly Father, give him the words to say, Sarah breathed over and over. She knew that Beau didn't want to be disrespectful, so she also prayed that he wouldn't say anything that he'd later regret.

Stay strong, Beau. She wanted to will him her strength, but she knew this was something he had to do on his own. It wasn't until she was confronted with the idea that his parents might hold enough sway over him to make him leave New Hope that Sarah realized she needed him to make this choice.

In the face of whatever his parents were going to try to use to persuade him to go back to Houston with them, Sarah needed him to hold his ground. She couldn't ever allow anything to develop between them...even if he became a Christian...if she didn't have some assurance that he couldn't be persuaded to leave New Hope Falls—and her—behind.

Wishing she had her sketchpad, Sarah debated scooting over to the desk to grab it, but in the end, she got up and began to make herself a cup of coffee. She didn't really *want* a cup of coffee, but she needed to keep busy.

Once she had her mug in hand, she sat back down at the island and picked up her phone to tap out a quick message.

You'll never guess who just showed up.

Leelee: *You're quite right. I will never guess.*

She sent her an emoji with its tongue sticking out. *Beau's parents.*

Leelee: *Wow! Seriously?*

Leelee: *You're right. I'd never have guessed that.*

They are quite unhappy with him.

Leelee: *I don't think that's news to anyone.*

How much longer are you going to be?

Leelee: *We had to make a quick run into Everett as Overmeier's didn't have everything we needed. Will be home in a little bit.*

Okay. Probably just as well. I have no idea what Beau's mom would say to Mom if she saw her. Clearly she's not happy to be in New Hope Falls.

Leelee: *Also not news...*

Shut up...

Leelee: *Want me to bring you an iced coffee since you're not going to the bakery these days?*

Would you? I'd love you forever.

Leelee: *Guess I'd better get the drink then because goodness knows you won't love me forever otherwise... -.-*

Haha. Just bring me my drink. My nerves are shot from dealing with Beau's parents.

Well, that and just not knowing how things were going to pan out with their conversation.

"We will be staying at a hotel in Seattle for one night." Beau's father's voice was suddenly crystal clear, causing Sarah to look up from her phone. "After that, the offer is off the table."

"I won't change my mind," Beau said.

Sarah stayed on the stool even though she really wanted to jump up and peek into the foyer to see Beau and his parents. The front door opened then closed, and for a moment, Sarah thought that Beau had gone out with them. Her heart seemed to stop beating from the time the door closed until he appeared in the doorway to the kitchen.

She let out the breath she hadn't realized she was holding, relief flooding her body at the sight of him. He came over to the counter and sat down on a stool next to her. Swinging around to face him, Sarah immediately noticed the strain on his face. It wasn't an expression she'd seen since his return the previous week.

Resting her hand on his arm, she waited for him to look up at her. "Are you okay?"

CHAPTER THIRTY-TWO

Beau gave her a look that held pain, unlike anything Sarah had seen from him so far. "I'm alright. I never imagined they'd come all the way here to try and convince me to go back to Houston."

She wanted to ask what they had offered him to entice him to return with them, but it wasn't any of her business. "I'm sorry that dealing with them stresses you out so much."

A weary smile crossed his face as he sighed. "Not everyone has a great mom like you do."

His sadness tugged at her heart, making her want to wrap him in her arms and hold him tight. "I wish you did, though."

"I wish I did too, but short of a miracle, I don't think either of my parents are going to change."

"Do you want a cup of coffee?" Sarah offered. "And a muffin?"

"That would be nice. Thank you."

She slid off her stool and set about making Beau a cup of coffee the way he liked it. Being able to do something that might make him feel even the littlest bit better, made her feel better too.

When she slid the coffee across the counter to him, he looked up from where he was tapping on his phone and gave her a smile that felt more genuine. "Thank you."

"What type of muffin did you want?"

"Any blueberry ones?"

She pulled the jar where they put all the baked goods closer and took the lid off to peer inside. "You're in luck."

After fishing one out, she set it on a plate for him.

"In luck with muffins. Out of luck with parents." Beau gave a humorless laugh. "Can't win them all, I guess."

Sarah's heart went out to this man who normally seemed so strong and steady. Though it was apparent he was used to that sort of interaction with his parents, it was also clear that it took a toll on him.

Beau set his phone on the island. "Just letting Juli and Rhett know that the parents are here."

"They didn't know?"

"It doesn't seem so." Beau took a sip of his coffee. "Juli, at least, seemed surprised at the news."

"They don't live with your parents?"

"No. Even though it didn't make my mom happy to have the three of us out of the house, we all did abandon ship as soon as we were able to be on our own. Not that that would surprise anyone who knows our family dynamics."

"I guess it must seem a bit weird that we all stay so close to home here."

Beau looked at her and shook his head. "Not at all. I'd love to be closer to my parents—although probably not live in the same house—if we had a better relationship. Unfortunately, any time we spend together—usually just for a meal—is filled with tension. It never boded well for good digestion."

"I would imagine not."

Beau glanced around. "I just realized that Nadine isn't here. She didn't see my mom, did she?"

Sarah shook her head. "She and Leah were in town."

"Probably for the best."

"That's what I figured." For the first time since he'd arrived to speak with his parents, she took in what he was wearing. "What were you doing when I called you?"

He looked down at his dirty T-shirt. "I was helping Eli stain something he was working on."

"Oh. He roped you into some work, huh? We've all been there."

"Once I got the hang of it, it was surprisingly soothing work."

"I'm surprised he let you help him. He hasn't had much luck with the rest of us."

"What do you mean?"

"Neither Leah nor I were very good at following his directions. Anna is better, I think, but her work still wasn't quite up to his standards, depending on the piece."

"I'm not sure mine is either because I'm not working on anything too important."

The front door opening had them both turning to look at the kitchen entrance. Sarah just remembering that she was supposed to be handling the check-in desk. When Eli appeared, she let out a sigh of relief.

"Everything okay?" he asked, glancing back and forth between the two of them.

Beau sighed. "Well, no one is injured or dead, so I guess okay is an accurate description."

Eli looked around. "Are your parents gone?"

"Yep. Issued their ultimatums and left."

"Sorry to hear that, man," Eli said as he rested his hand on Beau's shoulder.

"I didn't mean to abandon you."

"No worries. I got it all finished up."

As the two guys talked about what they'd been working on, Sarah was glad to see the tension leave Beau's face. He relaxed, his smile making a reappearance. When she'd figured out who had walked through the front door of the lodge earlier, she hadn't wanted his parents' arrival to negatively impact Beau or make him question his decision to stay in New Hope Falls.

She wanted to believe that neither of those things had happened. But she really wasn't sure how someone could deal with a situation like that with his parents and not be negatively impacted. It made her want to go after the pair and tell them how wrong it was for them to treat Beau that way. To treat all of their children that way.

"Kieran called me after you left to confirm we're meeting at his place for the Bible study tonight."

"I'm looking forward to it," Beau said as he finished the last bite of his muffin.

Sarah looked back and forth between them, a bit surprised that Beau was going to the men's group. She knew it existed and that Eli was involved in it with Kieran and a bunch of guys from the church, but she didn't really know what the focus was...aside from God, of course. Still, she was glad that Eli had invited Beau and that he seemed happy to go.

That gave her hope. She was happy for what it might mean for them. But more than that, she was excited about what it would hopefully mean for Beau. He'd been to church each Sunday since his return, but she wasn't sure if that was just because of his grandfather or if he actually wanted to be there himself.

She tried not to let the news of Beau attending the men's group get her hopes up. Even if he did become a Christian, it wasn't an automatic guarantee that things would work out between them. But each day she got to know him a bit better, she hoped even more that they would.

Still, there was a bit of lingering concern that Sarah just couldn't escape regarding Beau's parents. There was just something about the couple that made Sarah think that they weren't going to stay one night, then cut Beau loose and go back to Houston. No. The fact that they—especially Beau's mom—had come to New Hope told Sarah that they were quite desperate about the situation.

And desperate people could do desperate things. Things that could hurt other people. From things Beau had told her, his parents hadn't cared about how their actions hurt their own children, so what would they do to people they didn't know? Sarah didn't want to spend too much time thinking about that.

The front door opened again, and this time, it was her mom who called out, "Everything okay here?"

Eli got up and headed out of the kitchen with Beau on his heels. The next little while was spent carting in groceries and putting them away. It was a bigger task now that they were in their busy months, but as her mom liked to say...many hands made light work, so the chore didn't take too long.

"You doing okay?" her mom asked, a look of concern on her face as she rested her hand on Beau's shoulder.

"Yeah. Once I got over the shock of seeing my parents. I honestly didn't think my mom would ever set foot here again."

"She must have wanted to see you," her mom said.

Beau sighed. "That didn't appear to be what prompted their visit."

"Oh?"

"Yeah. They came to once again dangle the trust fund they've been dangling in front of us for years now."

"You mean that they'll give you your trust fund if you go back to Houston?" she asked.

Sarah was glad her mom was willing to voice the questions she'd been curious about but hadn't felt it was her place to ask.

"Exactly. I was supposed to get it when I got my degree, but then Dad decided I was too young, so he said that when I turned twenty-five, he'd release it to me. I can't even remember what the final reason was when he changed that plan yet again. I was supposed to get it at thirty, but that's a year away, and my dad keeps putting up hoops for me to jump through."

"That's a shame."

"I had been holding out, doing what he asked because I had plans for that money, but with everything that's happened lately, I've come to realize that he's just going to keep using it to force me to do what he wants. Case in point, their proposition today."

"Will you be okay without your job there and without the trust fund?"

Beau smiled. "I'll be fine. My plans may change a bit from what I thought I was going to do with my future, but I think they're actually going to change for the better."

"I'm glad to hear that." Her mom wrapped her arm around Beau's shoulders and gave him a hug. "Sometimes the family you're born into isn't the one who values you the most. Remember that there are plenty of others who do value you."

"Thank you. I appreciate that."

And that was just one of the many reasons Sarah was convinced she had the best mom on the planet.

"So what are you guys up to this afternoon?" her mom asked as she moved to the coffee machine.

"I'm heading into town to go by the gallery," Sarah said. "I need to talk to Irene a bit more about the showing. I took some photos of the paintings I've completed so far, so I want to show them to her as well."

"I'm going to put Beau to work again," Eli said with a grin in his direction. "Unless you have other plans."

"Nope. I'd planned to hang around your place today. Unless you were sick of me."

"Not yet."

Leah didn't volunteer her plans, but that was nothing new. She rarely shared that information, particularly with people outside the family.

"Well, I'm about to start dinner prep," her mom said. "So, if you do not want to be put to work, you'd better get out of here."

With a laugh, they all abandoned the kitchen. Sarah knew that if her mom had really needed help, she would have asked them to hang around.

"Guess I'll see you guys later," Sarah said as she picked up her sketchbook from the check-in desk.

She'd decided that she wanted to show Irene some pencil sketches along with her paintings. She hoped to do some sketches based on a couple of the ballet poses Cara had done for her, and since she had a ton of sketches of Beau, she was debating asking him for permission to use one or two as well.

Although, unless she wanted to explain why she had a bunch of sketches of him, she'd have to do new ones. Which, as far as Sarah was concerned, would absolutely be no hardship.

CHAPTER THIRTY-THREE

As he sat on the swing on the lodge porch, Beau tried his best to ignore the ache in his chest. It had been there ever since his dad had called him to say they were leaving Seattle, and since he hadn't agreed to go home with them, he needn't bother coming home at all. Ever.

Beau would never have imagined in a million years that his parents would disown him. When his father had first said those words, he had almost caved to their demands. Almost told them he'd be on the next flight back.

Thankfully, the knowledge of just *why* his dad was saying stuff like that overrode any temptation to give in. It was just one more manipulation, and in all likelihood, it probably wouldn't be his dad's last. Beau hadn't ever known his father to give up when he wanted something.

Which meant they probably didn't actually plan to cut him loose, but that thought didn't ease the hurt caused by knowing that they didn't care how their words and actions impacted him. As long as they got their way, they didn't care how their irrational behavior negatively affected their children.

He looked up as the door opened, his dark thoughts lifting when he saw Sarah step outside. She clutched a book to her chest and had some pencils in her hand. He wondered if he was finally going to get a chance to watch her draw. It was something that had interested him, but up until now she hadn't offered to let him see her work.

"All done?" Beau asked as she joined him on the swing.

When dinner had finished, he'd offered to help with the clean up yet again, but Nadine had shooed him out of the kitchen since she had plenty of help with Leah, Sarah, and Anna. Personally, Beau figured she didn't want to chance him breaking any dishes since he was still new to the clean up game.

"Yep. All done and ready for tomorrow."

"What've you got there?" Beau gestured to the items she held.

"It's a camera."

Beau stared at her for a moment, then shook his head and laughed. "Crazy girl."

"Crazy question will get you a crazy answer." Sarah grinned at him. "It's my sketchbook."

"Yeah. Okay. I did actually know that. You planning to do some drawing?"

"Maybe?" Sarah tilted her head. "I actually wanted to ask you something."

"About your drawing?" Sarah nodded. "Well, you should know I'm not going to give a very unbiased opinion if you're going to ask me what I think of your work."

"It's not that." She opened the book and flipped through a few pages before stopping. "I talked to Irene at the gallery the other day about including some pencil sketches in my art show, and she agreed that that might be a good idea. I've asked Cara about including a drawing or two of her in ballet poses."

"I bet those would be beautiful."

Sarah nodded then bit her lower lip for a moment. "Yes. I think they would be."

She seemed almost nervous, which Beau was having a hard time figuring out. "So, have you already done some of her?"

"A couple of rough ones. Just to give Cara an idea of what I want."

"Okay. Are you going to show me the sketches you've done?"

"Yes. But not just the ones of Cara." She smiled a bit then gave a nervous laugh. "See, the thing is...when I met you the first time, my initial reaction was that I wanted to paint you."

Beau arched a brow. "Really? Paint me?"

"Um, are you a vampire or something? Like do you have no reflection when you look in a mirror?"

He had to chuckle at that. "No, not a vampire."

"Then you know you're not exactly unattractive, right?"

Beau shrugged. "I suppose. My looks aren't something I focus on."

"Well, as someone who likes to draw or paint portraits, that was something I focused on. At least at first."

"So are you saying you want to sketch me for the show?"

"Or maybe use one of the sketches I've already worked on?"

"You've drawn me?" At her nod, Beau held out his hand.

She hesitated a moment before giving him her sketchbook. "You can...uh...just flip through the pages."

Beau's first look at himself through her eyes took his breath away. Not because he thought he was stunningly handsome or anything like that, but rather that her talent was just *that* good. It didn't really even look like a sketch. More like a gray-scale photograph.

"This is really good," he said. "Very lifelike. And you drew it all from memory? Or were you taking pictures of me when I wasn't looking?"

"No." She paused and gave a huff of laughter as a tinge of pink filled her cheeks. "Okay, well, that's not entirely true, but the pictures I took of you don't show your face. Most people wouldn't be able to identify you as being the person in the picture."

"We'll revisit that because I guess I have a confession to make along those lines too, but for now...just wow. You are so talented."

"I never know how to respond to that comment." Her gaze lowered for a moment, then she said, "It seems wrong to say thank you when I recognize that my talent is God-given."

Beau nodded. "But I'm sure you've put time and effort into honing that craft. You can't tell me that at age five, you were able to draw like this."

"Well...no. That's true. I've taken classes, and I draw all the time."

"Take the compliment to heart because you really are amazing at this."

She didn't respond to his statement, gesturing, instead, to the sketchbook. "There are more."

He turned his attention back to the sketchbook and began to flip through the pages. Sketch after sketch appeared in front of him. All of him in various poses. Some of them, she'd sketched him looking directly at the...well, it wasn't a camera, but looking straight out from the paper. Other sketches featured him in profile, but they were no less incredible.

"Do I...uh...have to worry about you being a stalker?" When she didn't reply right away, Beau looked over at her. Her gaze was on the sketchbook, a sad expression on her face. "Sarah?"

"No. I'm not a stalker." She looked up at him and gave him a small smile, her blue eyes reminding him of the Texas sky in the middle of summer. "I just...I missed you."

Her words made Beau's heart stop then restart at an alarming rate. "I missed you too."

He wanted to say more...so much more. Like how his world was brighter because of her. How she had shown him a joy for life that he'd never experienced prior to meeting her. There was no denying that he'd smiled and laughed more in her presence than in anyone else's. And how he was coming to feel more for her than he'd ever felt for anyone in his life before.

Though he would absolutely respect her request for them to get to know each other without dating, Beau hoped with all his heart that someday soon, he'd be able to let the world know how he really felt about her.

After being anxious to disentangle himself from Tiffany, Beau knew it was ridiculous to want to embrace a relationship with Sarah, and yet, he did. Each night before he fell asleep, he prayed as his grandfather had taught him, asking God to give him wisdom where Sarah was concerned.

He wanted to do things the right way this time because he longed for a relationship with her that brought them both joy and also glory to God. Eli had shared about his relationship with Anna and how their faith played a role in it, and Beau wanted to have that with Sarah.

"I had an awful time trying to get any painting done after you left. All I wanted to do was draw you."

"I feel like I should apologize," Beau said with a frown. "It doesn't make me happy to know you've struggled like that."

Sarah shifted so that she sat sideways, her knees bent as she put her feet on the seat of the swing, the tips of her ballet flat slippers touching his thigh. She wrapped her arms around her knees.

"It wasn't your fault," she said. "I had allowed myself to get too caught up in you. In a situation that was hopeless."

It had felt like a hopeless situation to him too, but he hoped she didn't feel that way now. He actually felt quite hopeful for the first time in a long time. Maybe ever.

"I guess you must be my muse," Sarah said with a bit of a smirk as she looked at him through her lashes. "Because I've been able to paint quite happily since you got back."

That made Beau feel much better. "I'm glad to hear that. I'd rather be a muse than a distraction."

"Well now, I'm not saying you haven't still been a bit of a distraction. You remain one of my favorite things to sketch."

Beau looked back down at the sketch pad, flipping through a few more pages. "Would the sketches be for sale? The ones you would display at the showing?"

"No. Not the easily identifiable ones." She leaned forward and flipped to a page almost near the end of the sketchpad. "Like this one of Cara. You wouldn't know it was her from that pose, so I might sell that one if she gives me permission. But the ones that show your faces? I wouldn't sell those unless it was to a family member, and you were okay with me doing that."

"I suppose it would be okay then."

A smile lit up her face. "You'd still have final say over any sketches I would display."

"I trust you. It's not like you'd be posting any questionable poses."

Sarah laughed. "Definitely not. I'm not that kind of artist."

"How many do you plan to use?"

"I'm not totally sure yet." Sarah's toes wriggled against his leg. "Probably just a couple unless I want to do a whole series and title it something like *A Study of Beau.*"

"Not to be confused with *The Study of a Beau,*" he said with a wink.

She stared at him for a moment, her eyes wide, before bursting into laughter. "Yeah. That might be a tad premature."

Though Beau wanted to pursue the idea, he let it drop. The last thing he wanted to do was pressure her. Having been pressured into a relationship himself, Beau was not interested in doing that. If...no, hopefully, *when*...things worked out between them, it would be because they *both* felt it was the right time.

"I trust you to only paint—or draw—me in the best light," Beau said. "You are super talented, and I'm honored that you want to draw me."

Sarah grinned at him, her cheeks pinking slightly. "You're too kind."

"If I want you to paint a picture for my new home, how would I go about requesting that?"

She straightened up, her eyes going wide. "Did you hear back?"

"Yep. Roy called me just before dinner to let me know that everything is a go."

"That's wonderful," Sarah exclaimed. "I'm sure you'll be so happy there."

Beau was sure he would be too, especially if one day he had a family with whom he could share the house. Well, a family besides Julianna and Rhett.

"So? What do I have to do?"

"Just tell me what sort of scene you'd like, and I'll see what I can do." Sarah's smile lit up her whole face. "Or you can pick from the ones I've already done."

"I like the paintings you've done for Eli. You really captured the beauty of his place."

"Would you want me to do a painting of your new house?"

Beau considered it for a moment. "Maybe. We can discuss it more once you're done the art show. I know that needs to be your focus right now."

"That and the wedding that's approaching quicker than I think any of us realize."

Beau listened as she talked about the ongoing plans, including the dresses that she and Leah had finally agreed on. Weddings weren't exactly something he'd given a lot of thought to. Even when he and Tiffany had gotten engaged, he hadn't foreseen himself being involved in any of the planning. Tiffany and her mother would have been in charge of everything.

So while he wasn't all that interested in the actual details of planning a bridal shower or the wedding, he enjoyed listening to Sarah talk about something that clearly excited her. That alone told him just how much he had fallen for this woman, and he couldn't help but wonder if heartache was in his future.

What did he have to offer a woman like this? A woman who wasn't interested in what his money or social position might have been able to give her back when he had a job and the prestige of his family. Now he had even less to offer since he had no job and his parents had disowned him. And then there was the fact that he was far too serious and reserved when compared to her joyful personality and positive outlook on life.

He didn't want to think about living in New Hope Falls without her as part of his life, but the chances of them being able to maintain a friendship if she should choose to not give them a chance, were slim to none. However, he hadn't moved to New Hope just for her, so he needed to keep that in mind.

"Hey." A poke at his thigh had him focusing back on Sarah. "Sorry if wedding talk upsets you."

"What?"

"You're scowling."

"Ah." He relaxed his face. "No, it's not that. Sorry."

"What's bothering you?" she asked, then frowned. "I mean, if you want to share."

Beau wasn't sure he wanted to because it made him look pathetically weak. Asking her what she saw in him seemed the height of neediness, and that was the last thing he wanted to come across as. Leaving his job in Houston, plus the most recent confrontation with his parents, had left him with a sense of vulnerability and weakness. Neither were a feeling he wanted to acknowledge let alone embrace.

"It was nothing you were talking about," Beau assured her. "I'm afraid my mind wandered a bit to everything that's happened lately. I wasn't ignoring you."

"I know that," Sarah said with an affectionate smile. "Eli gets distracted when we talk about wedding plans even though it's his actual wedding!"

Beau chuckled. "Well, that makes me feel better."

"At least you didn't tell me to shut up."

"I'd never do that," Beau said. "I enjoy listening to you talk."

"Ahhh. I appreciate that. I know I talk too much sometimes."

"You don't have to worry about that. You talking will never be an issue for me."

"Can I ask you something?" Sarah said.

"Sure."

"How did you like the men's Bible study?"

"Oh." Beau thought back to the one study he'd been to so far. "It was really great. The guys were all good about answering my questions. Eli and Kieran's encouragement as I learn more about what it means to be a Christian."

Sarah's eyes widened. "What?"

Beau frowned. For some reason, he'd assumed she knew that he hadn't come from a Christian family the way she had, even though his mom had been raised in the church.

"My parents didn't make church a priority, so I didn't know much about the Christian faith until I was introduced to it here by my grandfather and Pastor Evans."

Sarah didn't say anything right away, clearly working through something that he wasn't privy to. Her toes wiggled again as her gaze shifted away from him.

Beau was at a loss to figure out what he'd said that had triggered this reaction from her. And he was at an even bigger loss to understand what her reaction actually was.

When she pulled her feet back, Beau felt the loss of that small contact acutely. And how ridiculous was that? Maybe it was because he didn't understand what had prompted her to pull back from him. She didn't get up and leave the conversation, though, so he counted that as a win.

She had pulled her legs closer to her, resting her arms on top of her knees. Her gaze was assessing as she looked at him. "So, what do you think about what you've discovered since coming to New Hope Falls?"

Beau considered everything he'd learned, feeling the peace he'd come to expect each time he did. Over the time since he'd returned from Houston, every time he thought about his newfound faith, he was filled with a sense of peace. There might be upheaval in most areas of his life but underlying it all was a sense of peace that he'd never known in his life before.

"I think that I wish my mom had kept true to her faith and, in turn, taught it to us kids." He paused, searching for words. "It's given me a whole new focus in my life. One that feels so much more important than trust funds and parental expectations. Where I once felt pressure, I now feel peace."

"So...you've become a Christian?" Sarah asked, an almost hesitant tone to her voice. As if she wasn't sure she believed it was true.

CHAPTER THIRTY-FOUR

"Didn't you know? I told Eli, and I guess I just assumed he'd mention it." Beau hesitated. "I'm still getting used to talking about it in casual conversation, you know?"

He wasn't sure what sort of response he expected from Sarah, but he'd thought it might be something along the lines of how Eli had reacted. Instead, her expression held a bit of sadness.

When she looked at him, her eyes shimmered a bit. "I'm sorry, Beau. I should have talked more about God and His role in my life. I guess I didn't want to scare you off, and that was wrong of me."

Before Beau could react, however, a smile bloomed across her face, making her eyes sparkle with emotion. "But I am so excited and happy to hear this news. It's definitely an answer to prayer."

Surprise robbed Beau of words for a moment. "You prayed for this? For me?"

"Well, sure."

"Why would you do that?"

She gave him a curious look. "Why wouldn't I? You're a friend. A very good friend."

That she thought of him that way warmed Beau. "I think you're probably my best friend."

Sarah's eyes widened as her smile grew. "I am?"

"I think I've talked to you more than to anyone else," Beau revealed. He hesitated then added, "You know me better than most people."

Which was surprising, actually. Since he'd wanted to impress her, one would have thought he'd only try to show her his most positive qualities. That hadn't been the case, however. Instead, she'd made him feel that around her, he was safe to be himself. That she wouldn't judge him for any weakness he might show. That was definitely a novel experience.

"You're my best guy friend," Sarah said. "You're the only person I talk to on a daily basis besides my family and Anna. So that ranks you up there pretty high."

Beau liked the idea that he was important to her—even if it was just as a friend. Maybe someday, it would be as something more. He knew she wanted a friendship before anything else developed between them, so he didn't count the time they spent together as wasted.

If nothing else, their nightly conversations had made him realize just how much she meant to him. When she was sitting with him like this, he tried hard not to focus on anything more than how much he liked her. It was only when he was on his own that he let himself admit that his feelings were much more than just *like*.

At first, he hadn't been sure about how he felt, particularly because he wasn't sure—given his history—that he really knew what love was. But his grandfather had happily talked to him about it, sharing passages from the Bible about love. He'd also shared about his own experiences with love. Then he'd reassured Beau that he was capable of loving and being loved, regardless of the examples he'd had growing up.

Beau thought about how he felt about the older man and knew that he loved him. He loved Rhett and Juliana, and while he wasn't sure how he felt about his parents, he would never say he hated them. Love, however, might be a bit too strong of a word for his feelings for them at the moment.

He was certain, however, that he loved Sarah. She brought out the best in him and made him want to be a better man. One worthy of her and her love.

Would she ever love him? *Could* she ever love him?

There were moments when he thought the answer to both of those questions was no. But he really, really hoped that one day she'd prove those moments wrong. But could that happen if they never went out on a date?

He knew that people from his old life—Rhett and Julianna included—would think he was nuts for saying he loved someone he'd never even dated, let alone slept with. And before meeting Sarah and spending time with her, he absolutely would have agreed with them.

"Are you excited to be moving into your new house?" Sarah asked, her toes poking him in the thigh again.

There wasn't a quick and easy answer to that. He was excited to start his life in New Hope, and having a home was definitely a step in that direction. But he found the idea of moving away from the lodge a little less exciting. His new home was huge, and he was probably going to end up rattling around in it, at least for the first little while.

"I am, but it might take me a little while to get used to living there. Especially since it's so rural. My apartment in Houston was the penthouse of a twenty-story building. I could stand at my living room window and see the city laid out below me."

"Are you going to be okay living so rurally?" Sarah asked, her brow furrowing.

"I'll be fine," Beau assured her. "The view of the mountains will more than make up for the loss of the cityscape."

"Will you be lonely?"

Beau didn't want to admit that he just might be. "I lived alone in Houston, so being on my own isn't anything new."

"Will Rhett and Julianna be able to come to visit you soon?"

"I'm hoping that once I take possession of the house, I can convince Juli to come and help me buy stuff to furnish it. My mom took care of decorating my apartment in Houston, so I'm not really very confident when it comes to buying furniture and décor."

"If you're going to want high-end stuff, you might need to go to Seattle or order online."

"I don't really care about high-end. I just want comfortable and durable."

"Still might want to go to Seattle. I think that's where Mom shopped when she updated the lodge and cabins. She could probably give you the names of good places to check out."

"I'd appreciate that. The decorating part of homeownership is all new to me, to be honest."

"Don't worry, there are lots of people around to help you. I bet Anna would love to give you a hand with that."

Beau found that the help he really wanted was hers. Maybe by the time he had possession of the house and was ready to furnish it, he would feel more comfortable asking her to help him out too.

"I could show you some nice Instagram accounts that I follow that specialize in home décor. Might give you some ideas."

"I'll have to see if I remember my password." Beau considered what he'd last posted on that account. Or rather, what Tiffany had last posted on his account. Some lovey-dovey couple picture that she'd insisted they take. "Or maybe I'll just set up a new one. New life. New Insta. Isn't that how it should go?"

Sarah laughed. "I would say that's as good a reason as any to set up a new account."

"Not that I'm all that active on Instagram or on any of the other social media platforms."

"You might find that different now. It seems like you enjoy taking pictures. You might like having a place to share them."

"Do you have an account?"

She arched a brow at him. "Do *I* have an account?"

"Right." Beau chuckled. "You did just say that you could show me Instagram accounts, so I guess you do."

"Once you've got your new account, look me up."

"I look forward to seeing what you've posted." He wondered if her feed was full of selfies the way Tiffany, Julianna, and Rhett's were. Unsurprisingly, the thought of looking at picture after picture of Sarah held a certain appeal.

It was only when the lights lining the porch came on automatically that Beau realized how long they'd been talking. It amazed him that in spite of how much they talked, they still found more to talk about. He didn't want to end their time together, but he knew that Sarah liked to work at night, and he didn't want to keep her from getting her paintings done. Though it seemed that maybe he'd was guilty of that already.

"I guess I should head back to Eli's."

"Is he treating you well?" Sarah asked, apparently willing to prolong their conversation a few minutes longer.

"Very well. Considering he hasn't known me all that long, he's been very generous in sharing his home with me."

"Eli is a generous man, despite what's happened to him," Sarah said. "Has he told you about that?"

"About his former girlfriend going missing?"

Sarah nodded. "I pray every day that we find out what happened to her, if for no other reason than getting closure for Eli and Sheila's family. But day after day...nothing changes. And the one time we thought it had changed, we were all traumatized because it involved a dead body. And while it would have put an end to the mystery of what happened to Sheila, I don't think any of us want it to end that way."

"It can't be easy living with something like that hanging over your head." Beau hadn't been able to believe the story when Eli had told him. "I'll pray about that too."

Sarah beamed at him like he'd just said he'd buy her a diamond and take her on a trip to Paris. Only she was pleased with so much less than that. It wasn't like he could promise her that he'd make everything right, just that he'd pray for God to do that. And he hoped that God would understand him, since he was still new to praying.

When his phone rang a few minutes later, Beau was loath to answer it, but seeing Rhett's name on the screen, he knew he couldn't ignore him. "I've got to take this. It's Rhett."

Sarah gave him an understanding smile and swung around to put her feet on the floor. She reached out and squeezed his hand as he answered the call, then whispered, "See you tomorrow."

"Beau?" Rhett's voice sounded in his ear as Beau watched Sarah disappear inside the house.

"Yeah. Sorry." Beau got to his feet and headed for the stairs that would take him to the road that led to Eli's. "What's up?"

"You got your house yet?"

"No. Not yet. Why?"

"Think I need to get out of Dodge."

"What's wrong?"

"Mom and Dad have both been unbearable since they got back." Rhett let out a long sigh. "Dad's telling me I need to go back to college to get my degree so I can work for the company. And if I don't, I'll lose my trust fund."

Beau was torn on how to respond. He'd always felt that Rhett should have finished college, but the area of finance would never have been something he enjoyed the way Beau had. But the last thing he wanted was to watch another of his siblings being manipulated by their father.

"I've discovered that there are worse things in life than losing a trust fund." Like the prospect of losing Sarah.

"Yeah. That would be losing a trust fund, not having a job, and being broke."

Beau sighed as he walked down the road, passing through beams of light cast by the lamp posts overhead. "You're not broke."

"Close enough," Rhett said with a petulant tone.

"Not even. You forget that I know how much money you have. I've been investing part of your allowance for years. You'll be just fine until you figure out what you're going to do with your life. As long as you focus on that sooner rather than later and are wise with your money."

"So, can I come do that at your house?"

"Once I've got it, sure. Bring Juli with you. I'd tell you to come sooner, but the lodge is full up most days now."

"I think I can do that without much argument. She's about as fed up as I am. Mom has ramped up her efforts to get Juli to seriously consider one of the eligible men she's got lined up."

Beau could only imagine how livid his parents would be if all three of them ended up in New Hope. But frankly, if that happened, they had no one but themselves to blame. It was either going to permanently drive a wedge between them, or it would make them reconsider their actions.

"Just hang in there for a couple more weeks, then as soon as I've got the house, you two can come. Hopefully, you can deal with Mom and Dad for that long. Just avoid them if you have to."

While he wasn't happy about the circumstances that would likely bringing his sister and brother to New Hope, Beau found he was excited for them to come. Now that he'd had a chance to learn about God and accepted what faith in Him meant for his life, he wanted the same for the two of them.

When he'd voiced his doubts about the likelihood of them wanting to embrace faith the way he had, his grandfather had given him the names of a couple of people to google. He found testimonies of people who, from outward appearances, would never have wanted to give up their way of life for God, but they had. Reading them had given him hope.

"If you do need to leave sooner," Beau said. "Just call me. We'll figure something out."

Rhett let out a sigh. "Thanks, Beau."

"It's the least I can do since it's my fault that Mom and Dad are venting on you now."

"No. It's their fault for not loving us like they should have instead of using us as pawns in their game of life."

"You're right." Beau knew he was, but it still felt like they'd focused in on Rhett and Juli when he removed himself from their manipulations. That probably would have happened anyway, but it had happened sooner because of him.

After they said goodbye, Beau picked up his pace to get to Eli's. After not realizing what it felt like to have a home...as opposed to just a place to lay his head when he wasn't at work...he now felt like he had a storehouse of riches when it came to places to call home.

First, the lodge had come to feel like home, and now he felt that same way about Eli's. Soon, he'd have a home that was officially his. He could hardly wait.

~*~

"Eli," Sarah said when she saw him walk into the kitchen.

"Sarah. What's up?"

She glanced around, checking to see if Beau was with him. "Where's Beau?"

"I think he went to see his grandfather." Eli gave her a curious look. "Why?"

After a quick debate with herself, Sarah sighed. "I think I've gotten myself into a bit of a pickle."

Eli chuckled then said, "How exactly did you do that?"

"Well, it's about Beau."

"You don't say." Eli headed to the Keurig.

"What? Why would you say that?"

"Because it's clear something's going on with you two."

"Yeah, about that." Sarah settled on a stool and watched as Eli made himself a cup of coffee.

Eli turned to face her. "Have you changed your mind about him?"

"Yes. No! Wait..." Sarah tilted her head. "What do you mean?"

He sighed as he pulled his mug from the machine and lifted it to take a sip. "How about you tell *me* what *you* mean. That might be easier." He paused. "And start from the beginning, so I'm not getting just half the picture. I'm not Leah, who knows everything there is to know about you without you ever having to actually tell her anything."

"Okay. Fine. But first, I need a cookie."

Eli slid the cookie jar across the counter to her. "Something tells me I'm going to need one too."

Sarah pulled a cookie out, then she pushed the jar back toward Eli. "You're in luck because I helped Leah make some oatmeal chocolate chip ones this morning."

He paused in the act of reaching into the jar. "Exactly how much did you *help* her?"

With a huff, she rolled her eyes. "All I did was put the cookies on the baking pans. And then eat some of the dough."

"In that case, I'll risk it." He took a cookie out of the jar then pulled a stool around the island so he could face her. "Okay. You have your cookie. Talk."

So, Sarah did. Starting back with how she'd felt about Beau even before he'd left—though Eli knew some of it—and following all the way through to her conversation with him about not dating. "I told him the reason was that I'd rather we be friends first, which was true, but I didn't mention the part about him not being a Christian."

"Except that he is," Eli said, a frown on his face.

"Well, yeah. I know that *now*. I figured it out last night when we were talking."

"So isn't that a good thing?"

Sarah smiled, remembering how happy hearing that had made her. "It's a wonderful thing! I'm so glad for him."

"I'm confused. What's the problem?"

"How am I supposed to let him know that I'd be okay with dating now? Since I'd only focused on us being friends, how do I tell him that I'd be okay with us dating?"

Eli regarded her for a moment. "I know how you feel about being friends first. Having spent time with him since he got back, do you feel like he's someone you'd want to be in a serious relationship with?"

"I realize we haven't known each other that long..."

"It's not about the length of time you've known each other," Eli said. "I think that since he's come back from Houston, he's been a pretty open book."

Sarah nodded. "We've talked about all kinds of things. His family. His failed relationship. His siblings. And I've talked to him about a lot of stuff too."

"Apparently, the one thing you haven't talked about is God."

That comment had Sarah lowering her head. Eli wasn't wrong, and she was ashamed of that. "I can't even say why I didn't pursue more conversations about that."

"It's nothing you can't rectify," Eli said. "And I do think it's important that you do, particularly since Beau is just learning about things you and I have known about our whole life. He's eager to learn, though. I saw that during our discussion at the men's group, as well as the conversations we've had at home."

"I didn't want to tell him about us not dating unless he was a Christian because I didn't want that to be his motivation, you know?"

Eli took a sip of his coffee then nodded. "I can see that, but I have to say that I feel that his interest in God and the Bible seem quite genuine. To be honest, I had doubts about the guy when he first came here, but we've had some really good conversations. You could do a whole lot worse."

Sarah couldn't stop the smile that spread across her face. "I know, right?" But then she sobered. "So how do I let him know that we can go out now?"

"You could always just ask him out on a date," Eli said with a shrug.

Sarah considered his suggestion. She'd always sort of figured the guy would be the one asking when things got serious enough for a date, but she had kind of taken that option away. It wasn't really fair of her to expect that he'd just keep asking her, facing repeated rejections, until she decided the time was right. She'd put the restrictions in place, so maybe she needed to be the one taking the risk of being turned down.

When she said as much to Eli, he laughed. "I think it's a pretty safe bet that he's going to say yes."

Sarah scowled at him. "So, how do I ask him?"

"I don't know. Something along the lines of *Hey. Would you like to go out for dinner?* usually works."

She rolled her eyes at him, then laughed. "I guess I have to take your advice. I mean, you got Anna to go out with you."

"That I did," Eli said with a grin. He got up and rinsed his mug before putting it in the dishwasher. "And now I'm off to meet her. We need to make a final decision on a cake, apparently."

"Are you getting it from the bakery in town?"

"Yeah. Against my better judgment since Cece is still working there, but Anna wants to support local businesses."

"Last I heard, Cece has a boyfriend, so you might be okay."

"I hope so." Eli came over and hugged her shoulders. "And ask Beau. I think you'll be fine."

Sarah hoped he was right. Nothing Beau had said or done seemed to indicate he'd changed his mind. But what if he preferred to be the one doing the asking? Some guys were old-fashioned about those sorts of things. Though if he was going to get bent out of shape by her asking him, then maybe they weren't a good match.

She didn't think that was the case with Beau, however. In all their conversations, she'd never gotten the feeling that she would upset him with something like that. In fact, if he hadn't gotten upset when she turned down his request for a date, she didn't imagine he'd get upset if she asked him out.

It wasn't until after dinner that night that she finally had the opportunity. She finished helping clean up from the meal then made her way out to the porch. Sitting together on the porch after dinner was something she begun to really look forward to. Ending off the day talking with Beau felt right, and she loved every minute of their time together.

"Hey!" Beau greeted her with a smile when she joined him on the front porch.

"Hi." She settled onto the swing next to him. It swayed gently as she situated herself, angling her body to face him more fully with her feet up on the seat.

Wrapping her arms around her knees, she gazed at him, her heart swelling with emotion. Love. Her heart swelled with love. She was allowing herself to name that emotion now. Hoping and praying that it would be something Beau would one day feel for her too.

Her heart was filled with all her favorite colors as she smiled at him. Lovely shades of pale yellow, soft pink, lavender, and light mint green. She was used to feeling in colors, but it was usually one or two at a time, and they weren't always positive.

Beau, though... Beau brought all her happiest colors to life in her heart.

CHAPTER THIRTY-FIVE

"How was your day?" Sarah asked, anxious to be a part of what had gone on with him while they'd been apart.

Beau stared at her for a moment, his gaze soft. "It was good. I had some phone calls this morning about the house, then I went to the care home to have lunch with Grandfather."

"How's he doing?"

"Really well." His gaze drifted away for a moment and when he looked back at her, his beautiful eyes had a sheen to them. "I don't think I can ever express how grateful I am for his presence in my life. The circumstances that brought me here might have been less than ideal, but I don't regret them at all. Just by being himself, Grandfather showed me all the important things I was missing in my life."

"I think we all have that one person who has had a significant impact on our lives. If we're fortunate, they have a positive impact. I'm sure it's no surprise that for me, that person is my mom."

"Yeah. No surprise there. Your mom's amazing." Sarah nodded in agreement, then Beau said, "Tell me about your day."

So she did. Butterflies flared to life in her stomach when the discussion about their days drew to a close, and silence fell between them. "So, uh, do you want to have lunch tomorrow?"

Though she would have preferred a dinner date, now that they were busy at the lodge, a lunch date worked better. One thing she wasn't sure about was where to go. If they went to *Norma's*, they'd probably garner some attention. But was that a bad thing? It wasn't that she wanted to hide that they were dating, but she wasn't sure how Beau would feel about the attention.

"Sure," Beau said without hesitation. "*Norma's?*"

Given that she'd already been thinking about *Norma's*, it didn't take much consideration to agree. "Yep. That would be good."

It might be busy since it was the weekend, but if she gave her aunt a call, she'd probably save a table for them. Or... "Would you mind going for a late lunch? Then we could miss the weekend lunch crowd."

"That sounds better actually. I'll go visit my grandfather until it's time for his lunch then I'll meet you at *Norma's.*"

As they discussed their plan, Sarah felt a little nervous. For some reason, she'd assumed that Beau would react a bit differently to the idea of them going on a date. Was it possible he didn't realize that was what she was suggesting?

So much for Eli's advice...

Oh well, if tomorrow's lunch didn't work to get the message across, she'd have to be a bit more upfront. Maybe he'd just assumed that when she was ready, she'd tell him and then he'd arrange their first date. If that was the case...whoops!

Their conversation on the porch that evening was interrupted by several guests coming and going. Some of the people who'd been at the lodge before stopped to chat with her, giving Beau curious looks when she introduced him. She wished she could have claimed him as her boyfriend, especially when a couple of the women eyed him with obvious interest.

Sarah didn't want to feel jealous again like she had over Taylor at the bowling alley. It was important to her that if they were to ever be in a relationship, she was confident enough in herself and in Beau that she wouldn't feel threatened by other women expressing interest in him.

"We might need to find a new spot for our evening chats," Beau said with a laugh. "Unless you don't mind interruptions."

"I do mind interruptions." Sarah glanced over as another car pulled up in front of the lodge. "From now on, it's going to be like this, especially on the weekends."

"Any ideas of where else we can sit and chat in peace and quiet?"

"There's always the back deck," Sarah said. "There's no swing there, but there are chairs."

Beau gave her a look that she couldn't read. "Are you okay to sit there instead of out here?"

"Definitely. I don't mind interacting with people during the day or at dinner, but evenings are for me." She smiled at him. "And you."

Unfortunately, it was already rather late in the evening to move to the deck, so they just talked for a bit more then said goodnight. Sarah wanted to give Beau a hug, but until they agreed together that they were going to change the status of their relationship, those types of goodbyes were going to have to wait.

When she got down to her room, instead of going to her studio to work, she went into her walk-in closet and tried to figure out what to wear to lunch the next day. Though Beau had seen her in all kinds of attire, she wanted to look as nice as possible for their first date.

~*~

"Sorry I can't stay for lunch, Grandpa," Beau said as he prepared to leave the personal care home the next day.

"Don't you apologize for that, son." His grandfather patted his arm. "I am just thankful you come see me as often as you do. Not everyone here has family visiting."

"I enjoy spending time with you. Plus, I feel like I need to make up for lost time."

"You don't know how much I appreciate that."

"Well, I'll be back to pick you up for church tomorrow," Beau told him before they said their goodbyes.

As he walked to the car, Beau wondered if he should have offered to pick Sarah up from the lodge. He wasn't sure if there was a purpose to them meeting for lunch, but he wasn't going to turn down spending more time with Sarah, especially when she was the one initiating the get-together.

He would have invited her to meet him for lunch sooner, except he didn't want her to think he wasn't respecting her request that they not date. If she wanted to initiate them eating a meal together, however, he was definitely on board with that.

Because he'd left the care home just before noon, and he wasn't supposed to meet Sarah until one, Beau decided to make a stop at the gallery. He found a parking spot not far from *Norma's* then headed down the block to the gallery. However, as he passed the bookstore, he detoured inside.

"Hey there, Beau," Andy called out.

Beau turned to see the man standing on a small stepstool next to a tall bookcase. "Hi, Andy. How's it going?"

"Pretty good." He shelved the books in his hand then stepped down. "How about with you?"

"Just trying to kill some time before I meet Sarah for lunch at *Norma's.*"

Andy's brows lifted. "A date?"

"Nah. Just lunch." Beau shifted from one foot to the other. "We've become good friends."

Andy seemed to consider Beau's comment then shrugged. "Sarah's a good friend to have."

For the first time, it dawned on Beau that perhaps Andy might have feelings deeper than just friendship for Sarah. Beau couldn't imagine a man knowing Sarah and not wanting something more than friendship. He wasn't sure if he wanted to know how Andy felt toward Sarah, but something told him he needed to.

"Are you...uh...do you..." Beau stumbled for words.

"Are you trying to ask me if I love Sarah?"

"Sure. We'll go with that."

"My answer to that would be yes, but like a sister, not a girl-friend." When Beau let out a sigh of relief, Andy laughed. "Well, I guess that answers my question. This might not be a date, but not because you don't want it to be."

"That's true," Beau admitted. "We're just taking it slow at the moment."

"I hope it works out for you both. Sarah deserves a guy who'll treat her well, and I think you might just be that guy."

Beau couldn't help but smile at Andy's words. "Thanks. I've never met anyone like her, and she's brought so much light and joy to my life. I just hope I'm worthy of her."

"The only person that can determine that is Sarah, and I think she's probably decided that she wants you in her life."

"I hope you're right."

"Just don't hurt her."

Beau nodded. "I think I did that once already by leaving when I did, but I won't be doing that again."

"Glad to hear it," Andy said. "I'm glad you'll be hanging around. Any chance you like books?"

With a laugh, Beau glanced around. "I've never had much time to read, but I think maybe that might change now."

"Well, if you want books to read or pretty books for gifts or a coffee table, hit me up. I won't steer you wrong."

"I'll definitely keep that in mind." Since he still had some time to kill, Andy showed him around the store, and Beau was impressed with the selection. "Is this your store?"

Andy sighed. "Even though it feels like it is, it's not. I've worked here since I was in high school and was promoted to manager a couple of years ago."

"Who's the owner?"

"Drake Swanson."

"Is he local?"

"I suppose you could say that. He's from New Hope, but he's not always around."

"That's nice he trusts you enough to take care of things."

"Yep. He's a decent guy. I could work for someone a lot worse. He pays me well, for which I'm grateful."

Beau was happy to hear that. Andy seemed like a nice guy, so he was glad that he wasn't being taken advantage of.

"Well, I'd better head over to *Norma's.* Don't want to be late."

"Nope, you don't," Andy agreed with a grin. "See you tomorrow."

Beau nodded then said goodbye and left the building. He jogged across the street and stepped inside *Norma's.*

"Hey there, Beau," Norma greeted him with a wide smile. "Go on through. Sarah's waiting for you."

He thanked her then looked over at the counter, searching for Sarah. When he didn't see her there, he frowned since that was where they'd sat before. Glancing around, he found her sitting in a booth on the other side of the restaurant. She gave a little wave as he made his way over to where she waited.

Sliding into the booth across from her, his confusion increased as he took in her appearance. Her hair was down, forming a silky curtain across her shoulders, and she wore a dark pink shirt that complemented her complexion. Though he'd seen her in makeup before, she seemed to be wearing more than he was used to seeing on her. Not that he was complaining. Whatever she'd put around her eyes was making them appear even bluer than usual.

Beau gave her a smile, wishing he had a better idea of what was going on between them. Maybe it really was just lunch. But if so, why was she dressed up more than normal?

"So what have you been up to this morning?" Beau asked as he picked up the menu in front of him.

Smiling at him, she said, "I did a little work, then got ready for our lunch."

Beau didn't like how unsettled he felt. So much of his life recently had been filled with uncertainty. And though he still didn't know for certain where things were going with the two of them, spending so much time with her had been encouraging. But now faced with this meal that felt like a date and yet...wasn't, he found he didn't like the uncertainty of where they stood.

Maybe this was just a friendly meal. Friends met for lunch, right? And it wasn't out of the norm for a woman to want to dress up a bit for lunch with a friend. It didn't mean anything. That's what he needed to tell himself and stop overthinking the situation or he'd make things awkward between them.

With that resolved in his head, Beau tried to relax. Once they'd given the server their orders, he told her about going by the bookstore, and she told him a bit more about Andy and Drake, the guy who owned the business.

After their food had arrived and they'd said grace, Sarah shifted in her seat as she dragged a French fry through a pile of ketchup, looking a little uncomfortable for the first time since he'd arrived.

"What's going on?" Beau blurted out before he could stop himself.

He thought that she might deny that anything was wrong, but instead she gave him a small smile. "I kinda need to tell you something. Explain something to you."

In the space of a heartbeat, Beau's appetite vanished.

CHAPTER THIRTY-SIX

"It's nothing bad," Sarah said, apparently reading his mood change correctly. Her smile was reassuring, but Beau still didn't allow himself to relax too much. "Seriously."

"Okay?"

"Here's the thing," she began. "As you know, when you were here the first time around, I kind of...sort of...developed some feelings for you." She lowered her gaze, but after a moment, she lifted her head and looked at him once again. "Unfortunately, I knew that things between us wouldn't work, even if you'd chosen to stay in New Hope."

Beau frowned, wondering where that would leave them since nothing had changed that he could think of. "Really?"

"When you left, I figured it was for the best, and I accepted that eventually what I felt for you would fade, until it was all just a fond memory."

Beau couldn't fault her for that because he'd sort of felt the same way. Except he'd kind of felt like his fading feelings for her would also mean a fading of the light she had brought into his life. Which would have been the worst thing ever.

"When you came back, I wasn't sure what to do," Sarah said, a small frown puckering the space between her eyebrows. "It soon became clear that perhaps my feelings weren't one-sided."

"They weren't," Beau assured her. "They aren't."

She nodded and smiled. "The problem was that the Bible cautions Christians against having a relationship with someone who doesn't share our faith. That meant that as long as you weren't a

Christian, I couldn't allow things between us to go beyond friendship."

Beau found himself frowning again. "But you didn't tell me that."

"No, I didn't...for what I thought was a good reason. I wanted to make sure that if—when—you made the decision to become a Christian, it was because you desired to have a personal relationship with God. Not because you wanted a relationship with me." She bit her lip and reached up to shove a strand of hair behind her ear. "I don't know if that makes sense."

"It does," Beau said with a nod, and it did.

Her concern had been valid. Because he'd wanted to be with her so much, he might have done anything to achieve that. Peace flowed through him, though, at the thought that because she hadn't said anything, God had done a genuine work in his heart. And while he'd hoped to share a spiritual connection with Sarah, his decision to trust in God had been solely his.

"When I realized you'd become a Christian, I wasn't sure how to let you know that I was willing to take things beyond the friendship stage." She gave him a smile that looked the tiniest bit shy, which wasn't a description he would have ever given her. "That's why I asked you out on a date."

"This is a date?" Beau asked before he could stop himself. He straightened in his seat and smoothed a hand over his shirt. "I mean, of course, it's a date. It's a lovely date."

Sarah started to laugh, infectious giggles that lifted Beau's spirits even higher than they already were, and he couldn't help but chuckle along with her.

"Well, maybe we should count this as a prequel date," Sarah said when her giggles finally settled. "The date that came before the real date."

"I don't know." Beau tilted his head and gave her an indulgent smile. "I think any date with you is a real date. I'm not sure you realize how much I cherish any time I get to spend with you."

Sarah's expression softened into one that took Beau's breath away. "I think I do realize that because I feel exactly the same way about you. No matter what might have gone on in my day, spending time with you each evening has been exactly what I've needed. Your steadiness calms me and helps me focus, and there are times I really need that."

"And here I thought that steadiness was boring when compared to your enthusiastic approach to life."

"Never," Sarah insisted with a shake of her head. "I appreciate that so much about you. Don't ever think you're anything less than amazing."

Beau stared at Sarah for a moment, waiting for her to start giggling, but he saw only complete honesty and openness in her expression. That she saw him in that light absolutely blew him away. He took in a deep breath to fight the emotions that were tightening his chest.

"You're amazing," he said gruffly. "I thought that almost from the first moment I met you."

"*Almost* from the first moment?" Sarah said, her brows arching above her mirth-filled gaze.

"Well, that first morning in the kitchen, I thought you were Leah, and when I'd initially met her, she hadn't been exactly friendly."

Another laugh. Another smile. Another burst of joy in Beau's heart. He could hardly believe that what was unfolding in front of him was the beginning of a whole new part of his life. It was something he'd barely let himself hope for, but even barely-existent hope was still hope, and to have it realized was amazing. Just like Sarah.

"Just so you know, Leah doesn't dislike you."

"Really?" Beau gave Sarah a skeptical look as he picked up his burger. "Is that the same as saying she likes me?"

"Well, since you asked...not exactly."

Beau chuckled. "I figured as much."

"Give her time." Sarah lifted her glass of water and took a sip. "Ask Anna how Leah was with her when she first came to the lodge. Leah's even more protective of me than she is of Eli. Once she feels confident that you aren't out to hurt me, she'll warm up to you."

Though he wasn't sure that was ever going to happen, Beau had a more pressing concern. "Are you confident that I won't hurt you?"

Her expression turned serious as she regarded him over the rim of her glass. "There are no guarantees in life, but my heart tells me that it's worth taking a risk with you."

"I would never intentionally hurt you," Beau said, keeping his words low as people moved past their booth to sit at a nearby table. Suddenly he wished they were on the porch swing surrounded by nature. "Maybe this isn't the best place to have this conversation."

Sarah glanced around, then nodded. "So, where *are* we going to have it?"

"Are you up for talking on the deck after dinner tonight?" Beau asked. "Or would you rather have the conversation in a nice restaurant on our next date?"

She considered his words for barely a second. "The deck sounds perfect to me."

"Then it's a date." Beau really hoped that it would be just one of many to come.

He didn't have a ton of experience planning dates. Because of his busy schedule, Tiffany had planned most of their dates, and he'd just showed up when and where she told him to.

"It definitely is," she said.

When she beamed at him, Beau decided he would make an effort to plan some real dates. Hopefully, Eli and Kieran would give him a hand since they'd each managed to get to a point in their relationships where they'd become engaged to the women they loved.

He wanted to get there too, and now he was beginning to think that maybe Sarah wanted to as well.

~*~

Sarah washed the last pan, rinsed it, then put it in the drainer. She wrung out the dishcloth and began to wipe down the counters.

"Go on," Leah said as she bumped her shoulder. "I'll finish up here."

Sarah shook her head. "I don't mind."

"I know you don't mind, but there's no reason you have to hang around when I can finish up."

With a sigh, Sarah handed her the dishcloth. "I'll make it up to you. When there's someone you want to spend time with."

Leah rolled her eyes. "Don't hold your breath. I'd hate for you to pass out."

"Just you wait," Sarah said. "Just you wait."

"Go on." Leah made shooing motions. "Have fun."

Sarah pressed a kiss to her cheek. "Thanks, sweetie."

She scooted out of the kitchen before Leah changed her mind. Though they'd decided to meet on the back deck, Beau hadn't come through the kitchen to get there. On a whim, she went out the front door to check the swings.

Sure enough, he was sitting on their usual one, looking down at his phone. She made her way over to him. When he looked up, his eyes widened, then a smile curved his lips.

"I know we were going to sit on the deck, but I wondered if you might prefer to go for a walk? Maybe sit on Eli's porch swing."

"I'd like that." Sarah waited for him to get to his feet, then they headed down the stairs to the road leading to Eli's house.

When Beau held out his hand to her, Sarah took it without hesitation, appreciating the strength in his grip. Though his fingers lacked callouses that might have come from working with his hands, Sarah knew that he worked as hard as Eli did...just in a different way.

"One of these days, your mom's going to let me help clean up, right?" Beau asked. "I mean, technically, I'm not a guest at the lodge anymore."

Sarah laughed and placed her free hand over their joined ones. Pressing her cheek to his shoulder, she said, "Maybe. But honestly, there's nothing all that great about cleaning up dirty dishes."

"I don't know," Beau mused. "I learned quite a lot from my week cleaning tables at *Norma's*."

"You know my mom likes you, right?" Sarah really wanted him to know that the people who were important to her felt like he was right for her. "Even though she won't let you near her dishware."

Beau glanced down at her. "I was hoping she did."

"She does. So do Eli and Anna." She felt him squeeze her hand and didn't know if it was just a reflex or something more. Tugging on his hand, Sarah came to a stop. Beau turned to look at her, a questioning expression on his face. "And I think it goes without saying that I like you the most of all of us."

Beau stared at her for a moment before smiling. "And that's all that matters to me."

Sarah stepped closer to him and leaned against his arm. Beau untangled their fingers and moved his arm, resting it across her shoulders. She allowed herself to be drawn to his side, her cheek pressed against his chest as her arm went around his waist. It felt perfect. As if the spot beneath his arm had been created just for her.

They began to walk again, slower this time, moving as a single unit. This close to Beau, Sarah got a good whiff of his cologne. It was subtle but undeniably masculine. Though her favorite sense was usually her sight, right then, her sense of smell topped even that. The scent of whatever he wore—she wasn't up on male colognes—would always be tied to Beau in her mind.

"Where would you like to go on our next date?" Beau asked. "Though, if you want to be surprised, I could ask Eli or Kieran for help in planning it."

Sarah shrugged. "I'm not sure."

"Would you like to go for dinner at a nice restaurant?"

The one thing Sarah found she wanted from any date was that it allowed them to be themselves. If she was too worried about which fork or spoon to use, it wouldn't be a date she enjoyed. However, if Beau really wanted to go to a fancy restaurant, she wouldn't turn him down. But she needed him to know that for her, fancy wasn't necessary.

"I'm really not fussy about where we go to eat," Sarah said. "There are some nice casual style dining places around."

"You don't want to go to a fancy restaurant?"

"Not unless you want to." Sarah glanced up at him. "I'm not sure if you haven't figured it out yet, but I'm not really a fancy sort of person."

"I had noticed that, and actually it's one of the things I like about you."

"Really?" Sarah found that a bit hard to believe.

"Really. I've eaten at enough high-end restaurants with their two-bite courses to last me a lifetime. Whenever we'd go out to eat as a family, Mom always insisted we go to some fancy French or five-star restaurant. I don't think I ate at a fast food place until I was in university."

That might have surprised Sarah when they first met, but not so much anymore.

"I've only eaten at a restaurant that I'd call fancy once when my dad took us all out to celebrate my mom's birthday. It was a month or so before he left, so maybe that doesn't help me view fancy restaurants in a positive light. I've kind of always felt like my dad was trying to create a positive memory of himself for us, but if that's what he wanted, it didn't work. For me, anyway."

"Well, how about we find somewhere to go that will give us a good-size portion of tasty food without it costing the earth?"

Sarah could heartily agree with that. When they reached Eli's place, they settled on the porch swing. Usually, when they sat on the swing at the lodge, they each took an end. This time, however, Beau drew her over to sit right next to him.

She curled up under his arm, pulling her legs up and letting them rest against his thigh. Rubbing her fingertips against the denim covering her knee, Sarah gazed out at the forest surrounding Eli's home.

"Do you think you will really be happy here in New Hope?" she asked after silence had stretched out between them for a minute or so. She waited for Beau to ask why she was asking him that.

Instead, he said, "Yes, most definitely. I found peace and joy in my life for the first time when I came to New Hope. I have no desire to leave here except for short periods of time. Other than Juli and Rhett, the people I care the most about are all here now."

Sarah reached over and grasped his free hand. "New Hope definitely moves at a slower pace than Houston."

Beau chuckled. "You say that as if it's a bad thing."

"Well, it's not for me, since I like a slower pace. But for someone like you who is used to a faster pace, it might be a bit boring."

"I can't say that I've been bored here," Beau said. "At least not after the first day or two. And I don't know that I was bored those first couple of days because of the slower pace or just because I went from twelve-hour workdays to doing nothing." He rubbed his thumb across the back of her hand. "I know that New Hope Falls is your home, Sarah. That this is where your heart is. I'd never want to take you away from that."

"Thank you," Sarah whispered through vocal cords tight with emotion.

"Darlin', I don't think you understand that I'd do anything I can to keep you happy." The drawling endearment, as much as his words, filled her with incredible warmth.

Sarah shifted so she could see him more clearly in the soft evening light. His gaze held hers, gentle and...loving? Was it possible? She knew what was in her heart, but then she'd fallen in love with him so easily. Beau, however, had been engaged to be married and hadn't loved his fiancée. His heart seemed to be more well-guarded than her own.

"You seem surprised at that," Beau said, a smile tipping up the corners of his mouth. "While we've been busy *not* dating, but still spending time together, my heart's been busy falling in love with you."

Nothing could have stopped the smile that pushed up from her heart onto her face. "Love?"

"Yes. Love." Beau gazed at her, his incredibly beautiful eyes soft with emotion. "Maybe it's too soon for you, but even though I've never felt this way before, I have no doubt that's what I feel for you. I love you, Sarah."

"Oh, Beau." For some reason, Sarah felt perilously close to tears, her emotions a mad scramble within her. Of course, she had hoped that they would get to this point in their relationship sooner rather than later. But now that they were there, she was overwhelmed with incredible happiness and deep joy. "I love you too."

He lifted his hand and ran the backs of his fingers across her cheek. The cooling brush of air against her skin made her realize that he had wiped tears that had spilled from her eyes. His fingers slid along her jaw to touch her chin, gently urging her to tilt her head up.

When she did, he said, "May I kiss you, darlin'?"

Over the previous weeks, they'd connected first on an emotional level, then on a spiritual level, and now Sarah wanted to feel this physical connection with him. Wanted this first kiss with him. She'd already determined that Beau was a man she could marry...that she *wanted* to marry.

Sarah lifted her hand to grasp Beau's wrist as she gave a single nod. When Beau lowered his head to press his lips to hers, she knew with a certainty that if she could make it so, this would be the first of many kisses they would share in the future.

When the kiss ended, Beau rested his forehead against hers. "You've made me so happy."

With her eyes still closed, Sarah smiled at his words. "As you've made me."

After a couple of moments, Beau moved back, and Sarah opened her eyes to look up at him. She could see the love in his eyes, and she hoped he could see the same in hers.

"I never would have imagined finding you, finding love, when I first arrived in New Hope. I came hoping that I could appease my father for the sake of my future. Never realizing that here was where I'd find the best future ever."

Sarah shifted closer to him. "I never imagined that the gorgeous guest who was only at the lodge for a month would capture my attention and my heart."

"I don't know about gorgeous," Beau said, a smile quirking up one corner of his lips. "But I am so glad you saw something that you deemed worthy of giving me a second chance."

"So am I," Sarah whispered. "So am I."

Epilogue

Beau gazed around at the people gathered on the large deck at the back of his house. They'd been putting the space to good use as the days got warmer. The May weather had thankfully been cooperative for their plans that day, and though there were a few clouds in the sky, they didn't seem to be signaling rain anytime soon.

"Happy birthday, Beau," Andy said with a wide grin. "Thanks for inviting me to your party."

Beau returned his friend's smile. "I'm glad you could join us."

"Had to juggle my busy social schedule and disappoint a few people, but I'm here." Andy had delivered that proclamation with a straight face, though Beau knew him well enough now to see the glint of humor in his eyes.

"I do apologize for depriving others of your company," Beau replied, also trying to keep his expression solemn. That lasted for all of about twenty seconds before they both began to laugh.

"I bet you can't guess what my gift is," Andy said with a wave in the direction of a table that was loaded with far too many presents given that Beau had specified *no gifts* on the invitations that had been issued to their friends and family.

"If it's not a book, I'll be quite disappointed."

Before Andy could reveal anything about his gift, Nadine joined them. "Did you two get enough to eat?"

"More than enough," Beau assured her. "Thank you for all the work you did to get this ready for us."

Nadine rested her hand on his arm and gave him a light squeeze. "It was our pleasure."

Leah, Anna, and Nadine had done most of the cooking, though Sarah had also pitched in a bit. She'd done more of the decorating since she said that was more up her alley.

Beau hadn't been sure how he wanted to celebrate his thirtieth birthday, but in the end, it had been taken out of his hands. The result was this large gathering of people who had come to mean so much to him.

Though realistically, he'd known that his parents wouldn't be there, a part of him had hoped they'd show up to celebrate with him. Unfortunately, he wasn't confident that they even remembered what day it was. He tried not to let that thought get him down because he had so much to be grateful for.

His parents might not be there, but thankfully, Julianna and Rhett were, having both made the move to live with him in New Hope Falls. His mother had been livid, but, as of yet, his dad hadn't revoked their trust funds. They both knew that could change in the blink of an eye, so they were trying to find a path forward in their lives that didn't include a reliance on their parents.

Beau knew they were both struggling. Shifting from the hustle and bustle of Houston to the much slower pace of New Hope Falls had initially been a huge adjustment for both of them, albeit for different reasons. Now that they'd been there for awhile, they were starting to settle in a bit better.

Rhett, after quite a few lengthy discussions between the three of them, had finally agreed to look into going back to school. He hadn't decided what he was going to take yet, or if he was going to go to a nearby college or take courses online. Beau felt it was a big win to actually get him to consider going at all, so he wasn't pressuring him to decide on the rest.

Julianna was still trying to figure out what she wanted to do with her life. Though she might have objected to their mom's plans for her future, she hadn't done a whole lot to create her own path forward over the years. That meant she, too, had to find a direction for her life that would bring her happiness and joy in the future.

Beau wished he could make those decisions for them, but he'd had his hands full with the decisions he'd had to make for his own life. It hadn't taken him too long to decide that he didn't want to have to drive to Seattle every day for work, not if he wanted to have a life outside of work. So he'd been left with either New Hope or Everett as a base of operations.

After doing an analysis and a revamping of his original plan, he'd settled on Everett. It was close enough that he didn't have too much of commute, and yet still provided him with a good base of clients. While his new business wasn't what he'd once dreamed it would be, he found that he liked the smaller, slower-paced environment he'd ended up with.

"What's it like being old?" Rhett asked as he slung his arm around Beau's shoulders. "What do I have to look forward to?"

"You're just going to have to wait and find out for yourself. I'm not giving you any advance notice."

"Some big brother you are."

"I try my best."

Though Rhett still wasn't sold on church and only went occasionally, he'd become friends with the people from the church who were important to Beau. He was also really good about visiting their grandfather.

As Rhett chatted with Andy, Beau glanced around. When his gaze landed on Sarah, he smiled and began to make his way to where she stood next to the table where she and Leah were setting up the cake they'd insisted on buying.

"Is it vanilla?" Beau asked as he slipped his arm around Sarah's waist.

"Part of it," Leah replied. "The other part is chocolate for us non-weirdos."

Beau grinned at Leah's jab. As Sarah had predicted, her twin had begun to warm up to him as time passed. He'd discovered that Leah's language of affection was sarcasm and verbal jabs. Once he'd figured that out, their relationship as potential in-laws had grown by leaps and bounds.

Sarah glanced up as she gestured to the cake. "Do you like it?"

"It's lovely, darlin'." The cake had a scene that showed his house set against the trees and the mountains that had most likely been printed on edible paper from a picture Sarah had taken. He pressed a kiss to her hair. "You did a great job picking the design."

"It wasn't easy to decide what to put on it, but Mom suggested using a picture of something you like the most."

"Then why isn't this a picture of you?"

Leah made a gagging sound as Sarah said, "Ahhhh. You're such a sweetie. But I thought you *loved* me the most, not *liked* me the most."

"You should have been a lawyer with the way you pick apart my words."

Sarah gave him a look. "You're not denying it."

"What's to deny? Although to be technically accurate, I love *and* like you the most."

"I gotta get away from you two, or I'm going to end up in a sugar coma." With that muttered pronouncement, Leah headed back into the house.

Sarah laughed and went up on her toes to press a kiss to Beau's lips. "You're nearly her favorite person."

"Never more favorite than you, though."

"That goes without saying."

"Are you ready to blow out thirty candles, old man?" Julianna asked with a laugh. "Leah asked me to bring these out. Something about her not wanting to be around the sugary sweetness. Not sure if she was referring to the cake or you two."

THE COLOR OF LOVE · 373

With a laugh, Julianna and Sarah got to work putting the candles on the cake. Unfortunately, they were doing all thirty, not just a three and a zero like Beau had hoped. He was going to hyperventilate trying to get them all out.

"I've got the fire extinguisher," Rhett announced as Sarah began to light the candles.

Glancing over, Beau saw that he did, in fact, have a fire extinguisher tucked under his arm. Around them, people were beginning to gather, smiling and laughing. Once the candles were all lit, they began to sing *Happy Birthday.*

As his gaze traveled over the group, Beau's heart swelled with love and appreciation for each person there. Most especially, he was grateful that his grandfather had been able to make it. They'd made some adaptations to the house so that it was wheelchair accessible for him. And though Beau wished he could have had him live with them, his medical care was too advanced for them. Plus, he knew the older man enjoyed the social aspect of living in the home.

His life was fuller than he'd ever imagined it could be, and he wanted to be sure that the people there knew what they meant to him...particularly Sarah.

~*~

Grinning, Sarah motioned for Beau to come closer to the table. "Take a deep breath, babe."

He smiled at her then took a big inhale before bending over to blow out every single candle on the cake, except one. As he straightened, he winked at her. "I've got one girlfriend, you know."

Sarah *did* know, and she couldn't be happier about being that person.

Over the months since they'd started dating, she'd discovered that the things that had drawn her to Beau when they'd first met, had remained true. His strength and steadiness were still the things that she found highly attractive about him. However, as he'd spent time studying the Bible, his desire to be a godly man and to have God as a part of their relationship had become his most attractive qualities.

She'd still struggled with some down, dark moments, but he'd never been impatient with her. Instead, he stayed by her side, quiet and steady. But best of all, he'd assured her that he was praying for her and had even made sure they prayed together. Having that sort of support made all the difference for her...for them.

When Beau held out his hand, Sarah took it without hesitation. He drew her close, smiling down at her. Though Beau smiled more now than when he'd first arrived, these loving smiles were reserved just for her.

"I hope you don't mind if I say a few words as I ruminate on my advanced years."

The group around them laughed, then laughed harder when Beau's grandfather said, "Make it quick because of *my* advanced years. I still got some living to do."

"Will do," Beau said with a grin at the older man before his expression sobered once again. "A year ago, on this day, I was turning twenty-nine and hoping to be celebrating my thirtieth birthday by setting out on the path that I'd been working towards for years. Then things went a little haywire, and before I knew it, I was in the small town of New Hope Falls, trying to figure out what had gone wrong. Little did I know that, in fact, everything had gone right.

"Being in New Hope introduced me to a whole new way of life, one that I found myself wanting. Grandfather, you were a wonderful support and encourager during a super confusing time in my life. It if hadn't been for you, I wouldn't be here today." Beau turned a bit, looking over to where her mom stood with Eli, Anna, and Leah. "Then, the McNamaras. You were so generous to allow me to be more than just a guest at the lodge. Eli and Kieran, I owe you so much for all the guidance you've offered me over the past several months.

"Each of you here has played a role in making my life happier and more meaningful. You've stepped in to become family to not just me, but Julianna and Rhett as well, and I just wanted to say thank you from the bottom of my heart."

Beau turned to face Sarah, smiling as their gazes met. Sarah clutched his hand in both of hers as she looked up at him, her heart thumping hard against her ribs.

"And you, my darlin'." He gave her hand a squeeze. "From the very first moment you smiled at me, you made my world a brighter place. You showed me how to view the world in a completely different way, and you stood by me through some of the most difficult times in my life. I don't know why God thought I deserved you, but I'm so glad He did."

Beau paused as he gazed at her for a moment before slowly lowering himself to one knee. Sarah's jaw dropped as she watched him pull a small box from the pocket of his pants while he still held her other hand. She heard gasps and murmurs from around them, but her world had narrowed down to just her and Beau.

"Nothing would make me happier than to spend the rest of my life with you, doing what I can to make you happy. I love you so much. More than I would have ever thought possible. I hope that you'll be willing to take one more chance on me—on us—and agree to be my wife. Will you marry me?"

Sarah gazed down at Beau, seeing his love for her shining in his beautiful eyes. She didn't have to consider her answer to his question. She'd been prepared for this moment for months already, just hoping and praying that Beau would also be ready to take this step.

Reaching out, she cupped his cheek then smiled at him. "I love you so much. There's nothing I want more than to be your wife. So yes, my love. I will marry you."

Beau stood and swept her off her feet, spinning her in a circle before setting her down and kissing her. People around them clapped and cheered.

When their kiss ended, Beau opened the small box and pulled out a ring. He took her hand and slipped the ring on her finger before kissing the back of her hand.

Taking her in his arms again, he held her tight as he whispered. "I love you so much. Thank you for making me the happiest man on earth."

"I'm so excited to get married and spend my forever with you," she told him, closing her eyes as tears of joy pricked at them. Every beautiful color she'd come to associate with her love for Beau pulsed to an even brighter shade in her heart as they embraced.

They'd hugged plenty over the last several months, but right then, it felt like so much more than just a hug. It felt like a promise that he'd always be there for her, just like she'd always be there for him. She couldn't wait for the moment when, in front of the same people who were there at Beau's party, they said their vows to each other.

And then, for as long as God allowed them to be, they would be together.

~*~*~

ABOUT THE AUTHOR

Kimberly Rae Jordan is a USA Today bestselling author of Christian romances. Many years ago, her love of reading Christian romance morphed into a desire to write stories of love, faith, and family, and thus began a journey that would lead her to places Kimberly never imagined she'd go.

In addition to being a writer, she is also a wife and mother, which means Kimberly spends her days straddling the line between real life in a house on the prairies of Canada and the imaginary world her characters live in. Though caring for her husband and four kids and working on her stories takes up a large portion of her day, Kimberly also enjoys reading and looking at craft ideas that she will likely never attempt to make.

As she continues to pen heartwarming stories of love, faith, and family, Kimberly hopes that readers of all ages will enjoy the journeys her characters take in each book. She has no plan to stop writing the stories God places on her heart and looks forward to where her journey will take her in the years to come.

Printed in Great Britain
by Amazon

26480209R00219